Martin J Frankson's

BLACK CHAMPAGNE

a crime novel

Fortune knocks but once, but misfortune has much more patience.
Laurence J. Peter

To Martina for her support and patience.

PROLOGUE

I sit on the wrong side of the desk in a police interview room. Accusation: Murder. It's not for the first time but this time, it's different. The first rap, a set up, was a hook that took me years to wriggle free from, but this time, I'm as guilty as sin but I ain't crowin' about it. An historical crime, a cause celebre. The victim, well, you may have heard of him, some of you could be a little young but that's no matter.

Jimmy Hoffa, ex Teamster boss, union leader, household name, hero to many, pain the ass to some but he crossed the wrong ass-holes.

You heard that right; take a double take if you like. Jimmy Hoffa. He was just another bloated sweaty face under a badly-combed grease-balled haircut from a strange decade in American history. Vietnam had just pistol whipped Uncle Sam and we all ducked for cover under the skirts of Ford and Carter to suck our thumbs until Ronnie arrived on his bucking bronco and beat our soft as shit metal bang into shape.

James Riddle Hoffa to give his headstone the full chisel, except he don't have a headstone as he didn't have a body to bury. I drove the car that day in July 1975. Hoffa was in the trunk. I watched him get cubed in a car wrecker's joint hours later. They say the cube was shipped to Japan and recycled. Sure beats being chow to the critters.

He was a face, a household name in his time. Someone you either loved or hated. Some of the younger cops don't seem to know who he is. The old hands had to tell them. These young shit-for-brains think they're forgiven from knowing anything that happened before 1990.

Perhaps I'm getting old, thinking like an old man, talking like an old man, dying like an old man.

No two ways about it, I'm guilty as sin but it wasn't my grubby little finger on the trigger of the Rugar that turned Hoffa into a block of Swiss cheese but I was there, I could've stopped it but I didn't. I didn't blow his candle out but I stood beside the man who did. My world went dark that day and I've been skulking in dark corners ever since.

I didn't have a choice. Orders were orders. Ok, looking back, I could have skipped town and started a new life in a new state with a new name but life was easy. Looking back I don't think I was that comfortable much, I just grew used to the spike that I sat on, mistaking it for a sofa, just as long as my bosses kept filling my pockets with dirty money.

'No' wasn't an option.

They would have found someone else instead. If I ran, they would have found me sooner or later. Their fingers are long, bony bloodhounds that never stop sniffin' for furry fright balls like me. Like I said, I really had no choice. They made me an accessory. You could say I could have done a Donny Brasco but that takes tungsten balls. The thought of spending my life looking over my shoulder, hiding in a trailer park in some dust-bowl one-Starbucks township didn't exactly cream my coffee. They fished me from warm waters and tossed me on the sands, gasping for air, flapping my heaving gills. They wouldn't throw me back in until I did what I did.

A few years later, when dust settled, I resigned my position. I became a private detective, a private eye, private dick. Take your pick, call me what you will, as long as the cash is green, untraceable and inside an envelope, I didn't give a shit.

I did good work though. Dull work but steady. Being a PI isn't as exciting as you think. It's not all wine bars and bedding bad women but I'd be lying if I told you there weren't some of those cherries on the pie. I even started going to church after I dreamt one night about being in hell. In the dream, Hoffa held a burning spike, white hot tip, jabbing me and jabbing me until I could take no more. I woke up in sheets of sweat and promised myself to Jesus. It was at church when I met Lorna, my wife. She came from what they call a good family.

A rich family.

She came from New England. Her family didn't like me much but she didn't give a shit about them. 'Good family'. There's something about that sentence that makes me want to shit a kitten. It means rich white people.

Well, that was a long time ago and Lorna is just another memory, her face slipping deeper into the waters of time.

Right now, I sit on an uncomfortable plastic chair with one leg shorter than the other three, in a small interview room, thumbing a white plastic cup of lukewarm water. The door opens. In comes one of the new breed of mineral-water-sipping gym bunnies that pass as detectives these days. Neatly combed blond hair, healthy complexion and perfect teeth. Oh those white teeth. I need a pair of shades just to look at 'em. He leafs through a dossier of some kind. He raises his head and looks at me with his square jaw.

"Mr McCambridge, your lawyer will be here any minute. He sends his apologies but he's stuck in traffic. We'll hold off questioning until she arrives. In the meantime, would you like a coffee and something to eat?"

Human rights eh? That's new but I don't feel very human right now. I ask for a coffee and a twelve-inch sub. He asks me what kind. I say sub of the day. He asks me what that is. I tell him it's Subway. Ersatz reformed meat, he snaps back as if I need a diet lesson. I ask if that's reformed as is Dutch Reformed or just sugared shit. He contains a smirk. I tell him I want Spicy Italian with the works. He furrows his brow. He doesn't know what the fuck I'm talking about. I tell him that they'll know what it means. I want it with ranch dressing, salt and pepper, olives, peppered cheese. All toasted. He writes my order down in his notebook.

"I'd ask if you'd like some music brought in while you wait but we don't play B-sides in here."

I hear laughter from behind the two way mirror. He plays to the gallery and I don't blame him. He leaves and returns with a bag of tapes. He puts the tapes on the table.

"McCambridge, just to give you a heads up, we're playing the B-sides tonight. Special request. First-time broadcast too. Shame Casey Kasem isn't here to spin the disc"

"If you were any funnier, I still wouldn't laugh" I say, sitting back, folding my arms.

Another wise guy stops at the door and looks in.

"My my, the man who killed Hoffa" he says with a put-on southern drawl. "My, he looks just like my daddy."

Cue more yuk-yukking.

I'm done.

I'm history. My name will be infamous.

Jack Ruby

Mark Chapman

Sirhan Sirhan

Add Callum McCambridge to that list. Jesus, I wasn't banking on this kind of immortality. I thought I'd write a book, a novel even, from an insider's perspective off being a private eye and an cop and live of the royalties, growing fat and lazy in a Californian vineyard and glide like a honeybee from book launch to book launch, pollinating a few female readers along the way. Some interview spots on Oprah and C-Span but all that just has to stay a little longer on my bucket list.

It's not as if I wiped a Kennedy, Bush or a Clinton, is it? Had they just dumped Hoffa by the side of a road, he's been buried in the love of the Lord and he would've been forgotten by now but everyone loves a missing person. He became folklore, the gift of conspiracy theories that kept on pumping out the same old sausage meat and I'm going to cop it for being the bogeyman in that great American tale.

"I don't need my lawyer, just play the fucking tapes and get it over with."

I close my eyes and think about last night. I can still feel the frosted dew on the sides of the bottle of Dom Perognon, the smile on her face and the chance of getting my life back for the first time in years. While Mr Preppy rewinds the tapes, I rewind my life in my head. It's a long story but there's a long night ahead.

I fear there will be many long nights ahead.

CHAPTER 1

October 4th, 2008. I phoned Lorna three times inside an hour but no answer. I wasn't coming home for another few hours as I'd some loose ends to tie. There was a dead body to attend to.

Isn't there always?

Contrary to popular belief, private detectives don't see that many dead bodies in the line of duty, in fact, hardly any. It's not like the TV shows. Things seldom are but that night was an exception. I was in a disused car-lot between the Dan Ryan and Adlai Stevenson Expressways in Chicago's South Side.

I stood by the side of the man. I tapped his stomach with my feet for signs of life as a matter of form but nothing, just the dead cat bounce of a loud, dead fart from the dead man's ass.

His final verdict on the world.

Romani De Siciliano, a 52-year-old insurance agent. He was my quarry these past weeks. He didn't commit any crime except for hiding his chorizo in another woman's omelet. His wife knew he was fucking around but couldn't quite prove it. She paid me $4000 to find out for sure.

Romani was screwing his 26-year-old secretary. Romani found out that Sylvia found out and decided that taking his own life was preferable to his wife taking his money and reputation, that's if he had any of both left to take. He had called me about an hour before he shot himself, telling me he knew about me and asked if we could talk business. That happens a lot. Wives chicken out sometimes and tearfully blurt to their husbands that they had him tailed. Sometimes wives spill it when spitting viper's venom in the heat of an argument. Either way, the husband calls the dick and says he wants to talk. This can mean either buying back the evidence or having the dick warned off.

Or worse.

I drove to a spot that gives a good view of the car lot where Romani wouldn't see me. I wanted to see if he was alone or not. That bit's important. Even if a guy's alone, he could be packing. One can never be sure, but in this town, best not to take chances. I had watched him through my binoculars. He sat in the silvery hulk of his Lexus, rubbing his fat, bald head with his hands every couple of seconds. His nervous tic. After ten minutes, he got out and walked twenty yards from the car, took out a gun, put the barrel in his mouth and squeezed the trigger. A geyser of grey and red shot from the top of his head.

One less life and one less wearable Brookes Brothers summer suit. He crumpled and hit the tarmac. With the help of the dim street lighting, I saw a pool of blood form an ever-growing, perfect oblong shape around what was left of his head. It was now safe to meet him so I started the engine and drove over.
I pulled up beside the Lexus and dialed 911. I lit a cigarette and waited for sirens. It didn't take long before the squad cars swept into view, screeching like a cavalry of banshees in blue and red neon. A tall black cop got out of the front car and walked over.

"Hey, Cal, don't tell me, you rejected his advances and he couldn't take it"

I sucked in smoke and grinned.

"Well, I guess I'll be getting no more advances from his wife for sure. Case closed and shut," I said. "That's enough about this one, how's it going, partner?"

"Ticking by," said Alfredo. Alfredo was my partner on the South Side for four years until I plea-bargained my way out of a jail term and my contract with the Police Department for shooting a 14-year-old black kid who pointed a paintbrush at me. I thought it was a gun. I didn't join the force to kill innocent kids but the most Reverend Larry Hudson didn't see it like that. He carpet bagged all the way from New York just to whip my white racist ass. Looking back at it, it was the best thing that ever happened to me.

Leaving the force that is, not killing the kid. I thought it was a gun.

We stared at the corpse and waited for the state quack to arrive, pronounce death and tick the box and go home.

"You know, Alfredo, there's more than one death penalty in life."

"Pardon me?"

"Well, this guy couldn't take what was coming to him. Let me paint you a fresco, my friend. Mr. De Siciliano, a horny, middle-aged insurance salesman, decides that the kind of life that lay in wait for him, one without money and a wife, was too much to take, so he sticks a pellet in his head and checks out."

"He didn't have to do that," said Alfred.

"No?"

I looked down at the corpse. The oblong pool of blood under his shattered head conjured up an image of a halo. His mother would have liked that.

We stood in silence and watched the body being covered and taken away. The ambulance departed without sirens.

Alfredo's radio came on. A homicide outside the Rainforest Cafe, downtown.

"Justice calls, brother, gotta go."

"So long"

Within seconds, I stood alone. I lit another Lucky Strike with the stub of the one I was smoking. I walked back to my car and called Gina.

"Honey, it's me."

"Hi there"

I detected a waning on that last syllable.

"Are you OK, baby?"

"I hate it when you ask me that. I'm fine, just a little tired."

"I thought you weren't at work today?"

"I'm tired doing nothing," she said.

"I need to see you," I said.

"It's after midnight, Cal"

"I've spent an hour with a dead guy in an empty car lot. I need a warmer body to keep me right, honey."

I heard her sigh.

"OK but don't take detours. Where are you anyway?"

"In a car-lot by the Dan Ryan"

"See you in twenty,"

I squished the stub of my cigarette under the sole of my shoe, jigging my feet to avoid the sparks hitting my pants. I hopped in the car and drove off to Evanston on the northern shore of Lake Michigan. The lack of reciprocation of 'I love you' squeezed my heart. A course of emptiness and trepidation lined my veins but it kept me awake. Any hurt is a feeling and any feeling is human.

I pulled up outside Gina's apartment block. I got out and before my finger hit the button, the buzzer sounded. I pulled the heavy wrought iron door and went inside and took the elevator to the fourth floor. Gina stood on the threshold, dressed in a blue silk kimono, clutching a large glass of red wine.

"Hey, baby." I leant over to kiss her on the cheek but she cocked her head away. Just as Eskimos have a hundred words for snow; women have a hundred ways of making a man feel like dog shit.

"Cal, we need to talk."

Nothing good ever comes after that sentence.

She turned around and I followed her silently through the hallway and into the dining area. I noticed how her kimono hugged her figure perfectly like shrink-wrap. She sat down at one end of the Danetti dining table. I tried to sit beside her but she pulled the chairs on either side of her in towards the table. The only one that was free was the one that faced her.

We sat on opposite ends, clutching moribund glasses of red Pinot Noir. The burnt out wrecks of dying hopes and what-might-have-beens lay between us. I surveyed the no-man's-land like a defeated General, mourning lost territory.

"Gina," I muttered. I just wanted to say her name. I moved my hand across the table to hers but she withdrew it and folded her arms before putting her hands on her head.

"Gina, I can't leave her, it would destroy her. We've been over this."

"She's destroyed already and she's destroying you and I can't love a man who destroys himself."

"If I leave her, she will kill herself. Do you think I'd want that on my conscience?"

"I'm sorry, Cal, but conscience is not like flypaper. We choose what sticks to it."

"I leave her, she dies, she kills herself. Jeez, I'm not making this up; you know she's tried it twice already."

"No one is making her do this but herself. She doesn't have to kill herself."

"Do you want her to kill herself?"

"In a perfect world, I'd love it if you went home tonight and found her in crimson red bathwater."

"You don't mean that"

"I'm sorry, Cal, that was low of me, I'm sorry."

"Look, Gina, you knew the deal when you met me."

"No, I knew your situation. I saw a good man steering a broken ship. Duty is a poor wind for the sails, Cal, but I saw through that and knew there was a man inside that cold armory of yours, a man who wanted to get out and live a life and love too."

"So you don't think I'm that man anymore?"

"All I can see in front of me is a man who thrives on being chained within his chivalry. It makes you superior, martyred."

"I'm here, am I not?"

"No, you're not here, you're at home. You're always at home, even when you're with me. Well I've had enough because you're drawing me into your own little prison and I don't do prison."

Gina looked at the floor but she didn't have to say another word. She drained the remains of the wine and lit another menthol cigarette. The smoke slinked from her mouth like ectoplasm. I got up, put on my coat and walked past her on the way out. I didn't look back. I stopped at the door, waiting for some kind of reprieve from her that never came. I closed her door behind me and left the building.

I drove away, down Lake Shore Road, the city lights shimmering through the prisms of the rain. To my left, the eerie pitch blackness of Lake Michigan at night. I guess this is what driving along the North and South Korean border must be like. Lights to one side, black void on the other. A million men could get lost forever in that blackness and nobody would even remember them, let alone find them. It's that black and empty. My eyes lost focus and glazed over. I rapidly shut and opened them to refocus on the road ahead.

I opened the windows fully to feel the cold knives of wind lash and lacerate me like every pine needle in the world declared war on my ass, carving my skin dry and clean. The cut and the cleansing. I felt that I had spent the day crawling through a cockroach-infested junkyard of filth. I drove on and on, through the cold, sweet darkness of the city night toward home.

I know some things get much darker than the night itself. I found this out that night.

CHAPTER 2

I pulled up outside my house, turned off the engine and lights and sat in the confessional silence of the night. I looked around the neighbors' houses. Everyone docked in their harbor. All cars look black at night I noticed. I reached down into the side pocket on the door for a soft pack of Lucky Strikes. The pack felt a little thin. Only four soldiers left in the barracks. I lit one and watched the smoke eddy and weave into nothingness in the night air.

The first one of the day.

Well, it had just gone midnight.

The day really ends when you take your shoes off.

It was time to go in. I opened the window, threw the butt out onto the street and locked the car. I checked my cell-phone.

Two new texts.

Neither from Gina.

Both from Lorna.

Shit, how did I miss those? I checked the side of my iPhone, the little red dot on the top left corner was visible. I must have set it to silent. I put the phone back in my pocket and walked up the driveway.

Inside the house, the lights were out and all was silent except for the low rumble of a dishwasher in full flow. Lorna must be in bed. I didn't want to wake her so I took off my shoes and left them at the foot of the stairs. As soon as I climbed the staircase, a clatter of coins fell from my pocket and onto the wooden steps making a shrill clang of metal on wood. I held my breath and silently mouthed the word 'fuck'. I froze like a statue, counted to five but nothing stirred.

I relaxed and stepped back down from the staircase back onto the foyer and crept into the kitchen but I felt something large and heavy at my feet. It was Lorna. I flicked the light switch and light was cast on but the scene was dark as dark could get. A bottle of pills and a half-bottle of Wild Turkey lay on the floor beside her. I bent down and shook her.

"Lorna, wake up. How many have you had?"

I lifted her wrist feeling for a pulse. Nothing but cold skin. My fingers grappled at her arm, moving up and down, feeling for a pulse in many unlikely places but nothing.

Just the cold dead flesh of a cold dead woman.

Lorna was dead. Some final vestiges of warmth remained but they were only dying embers, reminders of a former flame that danced and raged that now merely left cooling, dimming cinders in its wake.

I put her arm down by her side, stood up and dialed 911.

*

I don't remember everything from that night. Whatever teemed through my veins wasn't blood but frost rushing through me like a torrent of crushed ice, numbing me mercifully. I crouched beside Lorna, stroking her still-warm hair, brushing against her now cold forehead. Her eyes vacantly stared at some distant horizon, beyond any horizon any I could see.

I told her about my day. I hadn't talked to her about my day for years. I felt if I started now that she would come back to life. Lorna always told me that I never talked to her. I always told her there was nothing to talk about. But that night I found myself telling her about my breakfast at Einstein's bagel place and the funny woman in the green elasticized pants who keeps skipping the queue and orders hotdogs even though they don't sell hotdogs. I told Lorna about that woman.

She used to work in those premises years back when it was a diner, owned by an old guy I knew called Wally Grace. One day, a lone gunman came in and shot the place up. Wally, his daughter Carry and five diners all died. The lady in green pants who orders hot dogs was there and was shot in head. She recovered in the end but she was never quite the same. Soon after, the diner was shut and let out to a pharmacy, then a 7/11 and finally Einstein's bagel and coffee joint. Every day, this lady visited the same premises and asked for a hotdog. No one knew why, perhaps it was the final order she ever took.

I told Lorna about the coffee I had and I felt the tears well up inside but I was afraid to cry. I was scared the tears would never stop. I cradled her head in my lap and arched myself over her, covering her like a living shroud. I had often wondered what the worst day of my life would be. I knew it wasn't anything that had already happened for nothing I've ever went through destroyed me. I guess that's what the worst day is supposed to feel like. But that night, finding Lorna, fuck. That was Enola Gay dropping its payload on my soul.

The police and ambulance arrived and had to prize me from her. Paramedics, in their luminous jackets, gathered over her like a Venus flytrap. I saw her disappear beneath the petals of yellow and green and the sounds of medical machinery. I was questioned about where I was and about her state of mind. I told them everything was normal, nothing odd had happened to either of us.

Everything was normal.

After the formalities, I walked around the house reliving old memories, racking my mind for happy ones of my time with Lorna. We were happy once, when we moved in as newly-weds ten years earlier. Two years after that, we had a daughter Kimberly but she died in her sleep when she was only four months old. Kimberly took Lorna with her in spirit. Any semblance of happiness after that was only in the hope that some corner would be turned. After Kimberly, the road was long and straight with a low, cruel gradient and not a corner of comfort ever came into view.

*

In the space of an evening, I lost two women. The one I wanted and the one I needed. I sat on the bed and lay down. The sheets and pillow cases reeked off Lorna's scent. In the kitchen, her spit was warm on some spoon. One of her hairs lay on the pillow but her perfume lived on like a ghost. I closed my eyes and took the deepest breath I could muster and held it in until my head felt like bursting. Not even death can pin a person down.

My cell-phone rang. Unknown number.

"Yes?"

"Mr. McCambridge?"

"Uh huh?"

"It's the hospital. You can collect your wife's things whenever you're ready."

"Uh huh"

I ended the call and stared at the phone. I pressed the message button. The two texts from Lorna remained unread. They were logged in the two hours before I got home. I scrolled down to the first one, 9:12pm. My finger hovered over it before moving away. Two little text icons looked like tombstones crushing me with curiosity and fear.

*

I had to make a few calls, tell the necessary people. The police offered to do this for me but I declined. I had to phone Lorna's Uncle Larry. He was her only surviving blood relative, if you don't count relatives who only turn up for funerals and will readings. Her parents were dead. Larry Lonsdale was a retired PR consultant, living it up near Cape Cod, New England. He never married and regarded Lorna as the daughter he never had. This was not going to be easy. I rehearsed the conversation, pacing up and down the bedroom.

"Larry, its Callum. I'm sorry but…"

"Larry, its Callum, pause, I have some bad news."

"Mr. Lonsdale, its Callum. There's no easy way to say this but…"

I had visited many households over the years where I delivered well-rehearsed baritone renditions of professional sympathy but this time it felt too real. All those times were rehearsals. Rehearsals for the real thing. It's easy to play Hamlet in front of a mirror, holding someone else's skull in your hand. It was mighty different when it was the skull of someone I knew, someone I loved.

I went downstairs, poured a stiff whisky and sank it, grimaced and whipped out the cellphone.

"Larry, it's Callum...Larry, I'm sorry to have to do this over the phone but I've some terrible news."

*

One minute later, the call ended. Two men standing alone in different rooms in different cities in different states, screaming inside, empty. I went down to the study and began writing a letter:

> *Sir,*
>
> *I'll come to the point. I'm in no position to hold the funeral. I'll leave that to you. I have my reasons but I won't go into those now. Sir, I hope you understand and forgive me. I hope Lorna forgives me too. Her things are with the hospital. I'll ask them to send them on.*

I folded the paper and stuck it an envelope. I hadn't called Larry 'Sir' since the first time I met him when Lorna dragged me to her family home in Massachusetts one weekend all those years ago. 'Sir' was a person when the light of Lorna shone on him but now darkness had been cast. No one can have a first name in such circumstances, in such a shaded moment, only the weathered remnants of labels.

I ran upstairs and packed a duffel-bag with sweaters, jeans and shirts. I lifted a couple of suits and headed out to the car. A couple of neighbors, Stanley and Bernice Hawke, stood in their driveway in their candy striped nightgowns, shuffling their way towards me, their bright green crocs with socks poking out from the gaps in the rubbery plastic, making a sound on the concreted driveway like a jazz percussionist shying brushing stretched skin, but they were no Ginger Baker.

"Callum, what happened? Was that Lorna, is she alright?" asked Stan. Bernice quivered.

I replied with a wide eyed stony silence that hid the silent scream of the nuclear war-head that was still exploding inside me.

Stan grabbed my left elbow. The soft wind tousled Stan's long and wispy moustache hairs like a breeze through the ragged sails off a lost schooner.

"She's alright now, she's alright now," Stan said in a tone of reassurance, his old-school voice straight from the Walter Cronkite era when men spoke like men.

"Is she in hospital?" Stan asked.

I smiled and squeezed Stan's arm.

"Lorna's better now, believe me."

Yeah, she's alright now, I thought as I trudged back towards my car. I unlocked the trunk, threw the bag in and hopped in the front and sped off into the cold, sunless world that lay ahead.

CHAPTER 3

I decided to go to the funeral in the end. It was weird. I know that's not an accepted word under the circumstances but all those other words like sad and sorrowful are used by people who attend funerals as guests and not as hosts, who leave when the sandwich plates become platters of crumbs. All I know is that while I stood there watching the woman I loved and felt indifferent to equal measure, packed into a small box of five foot by two, I felt anger. It all felt weird like some Tim Burton movie. Everyone around me looked like a monster. I don't know why. How could they do this to her? How could they bury her? Where was alll that life, love and vitality I once knew? It was then I realized that Lorna had been dead for years before she died. At least everyone finally recognized it in the end.

The coffin melted into the ground, ushered in by four thick, quiet black ribbons until it reached its final resting place. The funeral men whisked away the ribbons with a vulgar swiftness. The funeral director walked over to the pregnant mound of displaced earth, snatched a large handful of dirt and then over to where Lorna's uncle and I stood, spilling a tiny thread of soil behind him.

He held out the earth and we took a handful each. I walked over to the edge of the grave and stared down. A well-burnished brass plate looked right up at me. It didn't seem real. I threw some of the dirt down, some larger bits of grit hit the wood that made a sound like workmen filling a hole, ricocheted through me like the voice of Banquo at the feast. I composed myself enough to throw down the final clumps of dirt in my hand before taking backward steps, away from that terrible, unnatural pit. I couldn't bear to see the dirt starting to hide the sheen of the word 'Laura' that was etched on the brass plate. I wanted to remember that little lamina of shine forever.

I just wanted something to last forever. Does anything?

I walked on, ignored by the other mourners and I ignoring them. There weren't many people left at the end. We stood like islands of silence, fearful to reach out in case the waters between us became wider.

The cleft and clump of spade stabbing soil followed by the muffled thud of earth on pine grew weaker and weaker with every footstep I took towards the car. As I fumbled for the keys, I saw another sorry group of mourners gathering for the dispatch of one of their own.

"Callum"

Gina. Her ginger hair fell over her shoulders like rich vermilion streams. She was like a beautiful vampire, resplendent in black with a very pale complexion.

"Gina, I wasn't expecting to see you, least of all here of all days" I said.

"I came to pay my respects, it's the least I could do for Lorna. God knows what she went through living with you."

"So you've come here to have a little dig at me, is that it? Jesus Christ"

She opened her mouth to launch the next volley but something within her decided to stick its finger in that cannon barrel. Her mouth slowly closed, forming those cupid bow lips that once brought out the animal in me. Right then, all my animals had broken free of their enclosures. I was just an empty zoo. Something in the air had changed; the faint aroma of funeral bouquets caressed my nostrils with a bitter sweetness.

"Smell that scent? Hmmm," I said. But she looked away, slightly blushing.

Perhaps it's wrong for sad things to be beautiful things.

"Callum, I've been doing a lot of thinking over the past few days. I'm moving on. Moving to my sister's place in Fresno."

"For good?"

"I've got a transfer to San Francisco and I'm staying a while with Valerie until I get myself sorted."

"Well, good luck."

The silence hung like a swinging man between us. Gina looked away.

She turned and looked at me, swinging her arms by her side, slowly nodding her head.
"Well I guess its goodbye, Callum."
I nodded and looked away into the distance. I never say goodbye as a rule. I just act it out.

Gina walked up to me and kissed me full on the mouth for the briefest of eternities before she turned on her black high heels and walked out of my life.

I took out a cigarette, lit it, watching a woman I loved, become a vanishing point in a silver car that sped off out of my life. I stood there in that spot until my cigarette became a pillar of ash between my yellowed fingers. I threw it down but the column of ash just turned into a dusty and then invisible ghost of grey mist around my knees. I freshened my breath with some chewing gum and walked back towards my car and drove away.

Leaving it all behind.

CHAPTER 3

Lorna was at home that morning when the doorbell rang.

"Just leave it on the porch," she cried out.

Again, the doorbell rang and then once again.

"What's wrong with these people, are they deaf?" she muttered making her way to the front door. Through the wire gauze and glass, she made out a figure of a man dressed in motorbike leathers with a clipboard in one hand and a parcel in another.

Lorna opened the door.

"Good morning, ma'am, I've a package here that needs your signature but I'm under strict orders to inform you that you must open the package and follow my instructions"

"Say that again?"

"Ma'am, I'm under strict instructions to..."

"Yeah I heard you right the first time but who sent this?"

"I'm sorry, ma'am, but no one tells me stuff like that. I just follow instructions."

"The Nuremberg Defence Courier Service is it, huh?" Lorna replied.

"Sorry, ma'am, that's how it is."

Lorna was slightly impressed. He seemed to know what she meant. She took the package and ripped it open. She noticed there was no address on the side or the back.

"How do you know it's meant for me? It could be for my husband."

"That's easy. The package was put in my hand by the depot manager and he told me who and where."

"Who sent it?"

"Sorry, ma'am."

Lorna looked at him. He was well built and looked almost preppy. She thought he might be on a gap year or a failed medical student making ends meet to support some floozy he knocked up at college. She opened the package and looked inside. A cell-phone and a piece of paper. She removed both and read the note.

"Press the green button as soon as it rings. This will be within twenty seconds from now."

A black SUV with darkened windows pulled up outside the house across the street. "Good day, ma'am," said the boy, slightly bowing his head with more than a hint of old-fashioned country courtesy. Lorna couldn't place his accent, somewhere amongst the southern stars of the Confederate flag, she guessed.

The phone rang.

No name came up.

Lorna pressed the green button and held it to her ear.

"Hello?" Lorna asked.

"It's been a very, very ,very long time...Lorna" said a man's voice.

"Who is this?"

"Oh, Lorna," said the man. "It really has been a terribly long time, hasn't it? Don't you recognise my voice at all? I remember you used to love my voice. You told me I could have been a news reader on ABC"

"I'm...I'm sorry, I, I didn't catch your name" Lorna asked, wiping her forehead.

"But, Lorna, you know who this is. Didn't you get my letter last week?"

Lorna froze.

"No"

Lorna's heart frosted over. The voice on the other end lowered in tone several octaves to a coldness of soul she never knew was possible.

"But Lorna, you knew that already, didn't you? Did you think I'd really vanish like that and not ever come back?"

"I guess not," Lorna whispered.

"Don't you remember we loved each other, Lorna? A long time ago perhaps, but love like that never dies, does it?"

"I thought you were...gone"

"Yes, but now I'm back and nothing can stop us being together. We could away where no one knows us and start all over."

"What are you talking about?"

"Come away with me right now, I'm only across the way, in the big car. See me?"

Lorna looked over and saw the black SUV. The rear left passenger window went up and down twice in quick succession by a couple of inches, just enough movement for Lorna to make out from a distance.

"Dammit, I've moved on even if you haven't. I'm ending the call and if you ever loved me, please don't contact me again."

"But you can't just do that to me, don't you at least even want to see me again, see what I look like now?"

"I'm expecting a baby, Callum's baby" Lorna said. She pinned herself against the wall, feeling her legs get hazy from under her.

"I guess there's nothing more to say, is there?" said the man.

Lorna sighed.

"I can't see you again. I just can't". This time, some tears broke through Lorna's defences. She coughed to cover the momentary lapse into vulnerability but the man knew her inside out. She knew that.

"But Callum" he said

"What do you mean 'but Callum'?"

"But Callum, he doesn't know, does he?"

"Of course he doesn't fucking know, what do you think and that's how it's going to stay."

"But Lorna, is that really possible? Callum going through his honest little life, never knowing the real Lorna? Hmm?"

"Don't you fucking dare" Lorna growled, enunciating each word like a polished warning shot.

"Oh, but I know your address, my sweet. And that means I know Callum's address too. You do, after all, live together and that means I can mail lots of our old letters to him. Or even to his workplace. You know how much I hate hearing the word 'no' being said to me, don't you?"

"What do you want, one more fuck? Is that it? Well, you're going to have to stick it up my ass because I'm pregnant with Callum's child, so go fuck yourself and don't you dare come near me or Callum ever again, you hear me?"

"Daddy would have hated hearing you talk like, well, a cop's wife. A cop's wife. My goodness, how low you have become my sweet Lorna."

"Don't you..."

"Dare? Oh, Lorna, lots of dares not to be done but, you know, I'm giving you one last chance. I shall drop by tomorrow in person, around 8pm, and bring all my old letters with me. I believe Callum should be home around then, after he's fucked his lovely mistress. But I guess you don't know about her, do you? Gina McCall, I am sure you must know her"

"You go and fuck yourself and if you come near me I'll kill you."

"8 o'clock pm, tomorrow, Lorna. Make mine a slice of vanilla cheesecake with fresh cream on the side. That was my favorite dessert of all time. It still is actually. No matter how much there is in the entrée, there's always room for just that little bit more. I'm sure you know that too."

"What do you want from me?"

A second's silence.

"You, just you. Only you. It was only really ever you. Well, goodbye for now, Lorna."

The line went dead. A cold breeze caressed the sycamore trees that huddled together like monks, rustling and hiding stolen prayers beneath the dark whispers of bough and wind.

Lorna stared at the black SUV. The car drove forward several feet and stopped. The rear left passenger window opened. A man's arm came into view, black sleeve, white cuffs, black gloves. The hand waved before vanishing inside. The car window shut as the car turned the corner, four houses up, vanishing out of sight. The sound of the car left an invisible vapour of noise in the air, complementing the muffled voices of the trees.

Lorna went back inside, closed the door behind her and locked it. She walked from room to room, drawing the curtains closed. The sun made the place look dusty. Darkness made it clean.

Lorna went to the bathroom and then to the kitchen and poured herself a glass of water. The vegetables lay on the worktops waiting to be chopped and diced for the beef Wellington she intended to make for dinner later in the evening.

Dinner at 8. Just in time for Callum to come home from work.

Things are usually nice around then.

*****

In a penthouse apartment on the top floor of the Hancock Tower, there was a man and a woman.

He stood.

She sat in an expensive black leather armchair. The apartment was painted entirely in white and barely furnished with only the minimum of ornamentation to break the starkness of vertical corners. The lounge window overlooked the blue and boatless expanse of Lake Michigan. The cities of Gary and Michigan City were mere distant specks of rust on the far shore.

The man walked over to the window and gazed at the horizon.

"Funny how height makes what is distant, somehow curiously closer to us, don't you find, my dear?"

She lifted her coffee cup to her lips. She tasted the scalding steam around her mouth and nose and carefully placed the cup back down on the black marble coffee table.

"I've never really thought about it," she replied.

"I can see the town of Gary from here yet I cannot see the colour or shape of the building we're in. I find life is like that."

"Not seeing the wood for the trees?" she replied.

"Yes, just the proverb I was reaching for" he said.

"You mean you didn't get her?" she said, suffixing her statement with a little cough.

"No. It was too much of a shock. She had no tenderness left. She had none left at all. She used to be so tactile and full of warmth. Now... I don't know. She seemed like a fruit with all

the juice removed. Such a hollow heart. The passing of the years can do odd things to us all."

She coughed and sipped a little water. It was warm and cloudy. Let's cut to the chase, she thought.

"I presume you want me to help you" she asked

"Yes, we all need our little cogs at times like these."

She felt disturbed at how disposable people were in his golden little world. He paid well to keep his little court at hand.

There was a knock on the door.

"Who is it"?

"Me," muffled a man from the other side of the door.

"You'd better come in then."

The man entered the room. He was tall, with Italian features. Dark hair and chiselled looks. He cut the stale air with the sharp swish of fashion and the arrogance to match. He wore a dark single-breasted suit and a crisp white shirt with an ultra-high Lagerfeld collar. She locked her gaze on his form moving across the room. He didn't walk but slithered like a newly polished python. She imagined him leaving a slimy trail of broken lives and unburied bodies in his wake.

He stopped just beside the man and leant slightly forward so that he was only a dark whisper from his ear. The younger man looked at her. His eyes were rooms whose windows and doors were long boarded up. She shivered.
"Will I turn out like him" she thought. "How long will it be before I slither like him, a lithe female version of him, worming my way through the long grasses on a long descent to where

*no return is possible. Fuck, I'm beyond return. The attraction outflanks the repulsion. I'm
here and I'm here for the ride of my life.
And death"*

*The younger man switched his attention to the man. She strained her ears to pick up what
was being said, each word dripped from his lips like a drop of blood from a silent wound.
The young man was an adept whisperer. He needed to be for the older man was seldom
alone. There were always acolytes around him, straining at their leashes to be top dog and
gathering enough crumbs from his master's table to start building their own little empires.*

*The older man's mouth opened and closed like a dying fish before finally closing in so that
his lips disappeared inside his mouth. She saw his nostrils bellow like a flameless dragon.
With a nod, he dismissed the younger man. The younger man swooshed across the deep piled
carpet of azure and the left the room, closing the door quietly behind him.*

Deed done.

*Where was he off to next, she wondered. She couldn't imagine him going for something to eat
or drink or taking a piss even. Only people did things like that. Monsters of efficacy like him
just existed, never ingesting, never excreting.*

*The older man turned towards the woman and walked back to his seat, sat down and leant
forward, clasped his hands, rocked back and forth. In the whole time she had known him, she
had never seen him look so vulnerable. He looked blindsided, as though he was dealt five
Aces without a Joker. She wondered what it was that exposed his Achilles heel, but she
wanted him to tell her what it was.*

"We have a game-changing situation. My sweet Lorna is dead."

*"I don't know what to say" She immediately hated herself for uttering such a banality. She
coughed to cleanse the simpering words from the air, hiding her mouth with her diamante
studded gloved right hand.*

"Not only is she dead but they buried too. I do wish I had been there to see it all. The family, what's left of them, carrying her coffin, standing by the graveside, the skulls plainer in their faces. The wearing of dark clothes, oh yes, I can see it now, the theatricals of it all, competing to look the most forlorn, the most strained"

His face came alive

"I bet the men grimaced and the women shed tears. It would be somewhat interesting to see how old money does emotion, wouldn't it? Dead and buried. Well, this does change the complexion of my homecoming."

"What can be done? You came back for her and now she's...gone."

His mouth formed a hate-curved slit, his eyes narrowing to form bleak oblongs.

"Her husband, McCambridge" he rasped "Come back at six tonight. I'll have a plan in place for him then."

"I should know better than to ask this, but are you OK?" she asked.

He looked up at her.

"At the end of the day," he said, "we all have to be OK. How else can we deal with the endless succession of sunrises, hmm?"

"You sound like a vampire". She instantly regretted saying that.

He raised his eyebrows and smiled.

She was relieved

"Well, my dear, it just keeps going on and on and on" He cleared his throat and put his clinched mouth on top of a clinched fist.

She stared at him, waiting for the cue.

"Call me if you need me, Davina" he whispered. His whispers were low but perfectly audible like low flung razor blades that no one sees coming.

"Yes, I'll be here at six."

She closed her purse, stood up and left the room.

CHAPTER 4

I parked in the basement car lot of the last remaining office block on Creswell Street. My office was on the thirteenth floor, one burrow in a warren of makeshift offices and low-rent apartments. It was a building where fly-by-nighters, conmen, escort girls, and other kinds of furtive folks crept around in the shadows like roaches in faded clothing, in the damp broken-neon lit basements of life. I knew some of them better than others. Most of them were the kind of people who didn't have a birthday.

And then there was me.

I don't know why I ever chose this place, but it had an appeal and it made perfect business sense. Most of my clients are well heeled. They have to be. I'm not cheap at the price. To hire me costs $200 an hour plus reasonable expenses such as meals, drinks, gasoline, motel rooms and the occasional hooker and drug fiend. If I rented a swank-pad in the Magnificent Mile, well, it just wouldn't do. These days, husbands, wives, lovers and fuck buddies may work and play in the same streets and buildings. It wouldn't do for them rub shoulders in the elevator. That's why it's best to operate from garbage-cans like this. It's a place where no one holds their head up long enough to recognize anyone who scurries by.

I got out of my car. Two winos were brown-bagging cheap whiskey just feet away. They sat on the front hood of a red Chevrolet. I tossed them a few coins and felt like shit when I saw them fall out over who got the third nickel. I looked on. Moments ago they were friends. Now they were fighting over a single coin that'll buy nothing in its own right. I looked at the guy on the left. His forehead, nose and cheeks were an atlas of red lines of broken capillaries. The rest of his face was a matted moss of beard. Both the men were a mess of rags, beard and blood, writhing on the ground like beetles fighting over a piece of dog shit.

The basement level foyer reeked of stale urine, decades of piss-artist piss layered on top of one another like nasty olfactory acetates. I pressed the elevator button and waited. The distant crush and grind of worn metal ropes moved the elevator car downwards to my level. With a clunk and thud, the car hit the buffers and the metal doors wheezed open. I stepped in, lit a cigarette and pressed nine.

This was as far as it went.

The building had fourteen floors.

I worked on the thirteenth.

Lucky for me.

The car stopped. The doors ground open and I stepped out. I sprinted up the remaining four flights of stairs towards my office. I lifted my arm and wiped the few pearls of sweat that had formed on my forehead with my sleeve.

"Not bad for a man of your age," said a woman's voice.

I looked down the corridor. A well-dressed young woman, a brunette in her early thirties, stood outside my office. She wore a navy blue suit and matching high heels. I always notice a woman's footwear. Her hair was bobbed, the cut as severe as a scythe. She looked like a poster girl for mean business. She came to the right place, the right man.

She had a certain kind of grace but looked out of place in a joint like this but women like that always do. I guess what I'm running here is a bit like a backstreet VD clinic of the heart. Everyone's called Mr. or Mrs. Smith and everyone wears shades. She clutched a dark purse that glistened and sparkled under the flickering strip lighting.

I wiped my mouth and coughed.

"Good morning, ma'am, are you looking for me?"

"That depends who 'me' is. My name is Mrs. Garantovich. I'll get to the point. My husband's fucking other women and I want his balls. I think you're the man to cut them off and bring them to me on a plate, am I wrong?"

A plume of smoke rose from her thin, brown menthol cigarette. She held her cigarette holder in a black gloved hand. I only ever saw gloves like that in old movies. Yet something about her reminded me of a cartoon. I don't know why. She didn't seem totally real but here she was, in front of me. The color of her money would soon tell.

"Well, maybe I can," I said. "Perhaps it's best if we continue this discussion someplace more private." I gestured towards my office.

"Why the privacy, who else is here?"

"Believe me, ma'am, you'd be surprised. Please, follow me"

I walked down the corridor. I led. She followed but she didn't strike me as a lady who followed anyone. I opened the door of my office and ushered her in.

"Please sit down," I said, making my way to the drinks cabinet. Bottles of Old Tennessee and Cork Dry Gin export stood like dumb butlers on the undusted drinks cabinet.

"Can I fix you a drink?"

She looked at her watch. *Elizabeth Duke*. Not *that* expensive, I thought. When people put on an appearance, there are many links in the chain. Things like hairstyle, clothes and shoes are easy to get right but subtleties like watches, earrings, and costume jewelry can make or break the deception. This one, I didn't quite get. Seventy percent the genuine article? Who knows.

"It's a little early but under the circumstances... Gin, neat, on the rocks."
I fixed us both a drink. She stubbed out her cigarette and before I had a chance to offer one of my own, she pinched a fresh one from her cigarette case and tried to light it but no flame. She flicked on the flint a few more times but no flame.

"Fuck" she said "Do you have a light?"

I smiled and searched my pockets but I couldn't find my Zippo. I scanned my desk but the only lighter I saw was an oversized Chicago White Sox ornamental one. I was loathe to use it but needs must. I picked it up and held the behemoth to her face. She looked at it with puzzlement. I felt embarrassed. I flicked the flint and a flame whooshed two inches into the air.

"Woo, that's not a lighter, that's flame thrower. Be careful not to singe me or my husband will come a calling with you wondering why you burnt his honey"

She leant forward and lit her cigarette and laid back on her chair. I wondered about her. She didn't seem totally ladylike, like some work-in-progress Pygmalion.

"I thought you wanted his balls on a plate" I asked.

"Well, he does have his uses" She smiled. "You can call me Karen, Callum."

I fixed us both a drink and handed her a glass. She sipped on the raw gin and winced.

"Mrs. Garantovich, so tell me…."

"Karen, please"

"I'm sorry but I liked to observe the formalities, if you don't mind"

She raised her brows and nodded. "I don't mind..Callum"

I sat on the edge of my desk and folded my arms.

"So, give me the lowdown, what's the story with your husband?"

"I've been married to Ivan for fifteen years and he's cheating on me. I know this for a fact. I have no hard evidence. He's fucking his PA, Candice Moroney. Slut. I have evidence from his credit card statement. I know they shared a hotel room."

She reached into her purse and handed over a few documents. I read through them. It tied in with what she told me. Credit card statement from him dated July 18th, double room at the

Hilton. Drinks bill for champagne on his credit card statement. Photocopy of the guestbook, Ivan and Candice Hope. Full marks for the imagination of not calling themselves 'Smith'. Minus several thousand for using their real first names.

"Have you confronted him with this?"

"Of course I fucking have, but he still won't give me a divorce. Circumstantial evidence, he calls it. I've spoken to my attorney. She told me that unless I have a photo of his dick in her pussy, I'm stuck - which is why I am here. I need watertight evidence. A. S.A.P."

"Well, I can do that, but why won't he give you a divorce? Why's he fighting it?"

"It's all to do with my aunt. My aunt stipulated in her will that I wouldn't inherit her fortune until her death or my 25th wedding anniversary, which ever came second. Can you believe that? How twisted? The 25th anniversary is ten years away and I'm in hurry to start my life... Again. She died three years ago so I have wait to the anniversary. I swear if I don't get this divorce, I will kill myself...or him. My aunt cited both Ivan and I as beneficiaries. He's hanging on though to get his mitts on the money. Pure and simple. It's a race against the clock."

"I see."

"But you don't see. I was led to believe that she had a fortune. A millionaire, I was told."

"Do you mean she wasn't as rich as you thought?"

"Yes, she was a millionaire alright, in Rands, South African Rands. Do you know how much a fucking rand is?"

I shook my head but I knew it was worth as much as that nickel I threw to the bums.

"A rand wouldn't buy the smell of a KFC chicken wing. She had a million Rands but that works out at just over a ten thousand bucks. Ten thousand bucks. Fuck. What does ten thousand bucks buy in this town? Lunches and spa treatments for a month. I've been had and

I want revenge and you Callum, well, you're my gun. There's no money from her, only Ivan's fortune and I want half of everything the bastard's got."

"So you want me to catch him, in bed with this Candice Moroney."

She stood up and paced around, rubbing her hands. She even shivered. She sounded tough but she was brittle as the broken glass inside her heart. I could almost hear the pieces rattle.

"I want you to set him up. Find a whore, get her to meet him and seduce him and be there when he gets his dick out for candid camera. Then and only then will I serve a divorce petition. He's worth millions. And yes, your fee. You get ten percent, straight"

"Ten percent of what?"

"Millions."

I cleared my throat. I tried to be a Fonzy about it and act like the offer didn't matter. However I was already counting my funds and sipping Daiquiris on a Hawaiian beach having my dick licked by grass-skirted nymphs at the same time.

She must have caught me smile.

"Yeah, that brought a smile to your face"

"Just some on-the-spot financial planning, that's all but I don't spend what I ain't got but I do have two questions for you. One, why should I take this on? And secondly, why did you pick me of all people? I'm not easy to find and this place is hardly in the Chicago Reader"

She crossed her legs and leant back in her chair.

"I chose you because you've got a reputation. You get things done. You found that missing Paulson girl last month? The cops were in a flap about it but you cut to the chase. Besides, what a dumb question, don't you want to be rich? I sure as fuck do" She said, replacing the full stops with sucks of menthol cigarette.

I got off the table and paced the room. All was going to plan so far but it was her plan. I wanted to test her and measure her.

"That does sound very generous, ma'am, but it sounds dirty. Real dirty. Your husband is a rich man. Rich men don't get rich by playing nice. Rich men like him are control freaks, they see the world as a chess set and play us like pawns, moving us around the board whenever they want. Don't take this the wrong way lady but I've met dames like you before. You run around town like spoiled Pomeranians on very long leashes but leashes all the same. Any move you make, old Ivan knows about it. You think he doesn't but I know he knows. Men like Ivan don't get rich by not knowing where their pieces are at all times. I bet he even knows you're here and if he catches wind of me, I'm toast."

She stood up, mouth poised to fire 'how dare you' or some other cliché of indignation at me.

"Sit down, Mrs Garantovich, I'm not finished yet. There are some things you need to know. We need to move very fast with this otherwise he'll start smelling dead rats. No matter how well you tie up rats and hide 'em, the stink will always find a way out. If I take this on, you may feel smug in knowing that you'll win in the end. What's wrong with that you say? Well, that could change your behaviour towards Ivan. You could be tempted to become nice to him. That would make him suspicious. No, you've got to keep the spears sharpened. I know you'll pay me well but you need to play ball too. No sudden changes in behaviour, no running away and no big mouth. No loose talk to your girl-friends over gimlets at the country club neither. I'm sorry if my manner is a little direct or even abrasive but it's nothing personal. It's the standard spiel I peddle to all my new clients, especially women in your position"

She sat down and closed her mouth. She looked at me with big, wide eyes. I felt shit again.

"Ok, I can manage all that," she whispered. "I'm glad you accepted the task, McCambridge, you would have made an enemy of me had you refused. No one refuses me. You would have found that out of course...the hard way"

I raised my eyebrows but kept silent. I admit to being a little scared at how she spoke to me. She was a golden knife, she needed careful handling else one wrong move, even slight or unintended, could have me counting fingers and not coins.

"Well, I am depending on you to deliver the goods for me. It means a lot."

She took out a handkerchief and mopped her eyes. They twinkled but, for the life of me, I didn't see any moisture. There were lines there but they were more like the beds of long-dried rivers.

She blew her nose and I looked away. She put her handkerchief back into her bag and took out a thick brown envelope and handed it to me.

"Pending the ten percent payday, I hope you accept this as a down payment for services not yet rendered but expected."

I opened the envelope. It was thick and tight with dollar bills. I prized out a few notes. They were all fifty-spots. I couldn't begin to guess how many were there but it was plenty. Enough to keep me dreaming of Hawaii.

"How much is in here?"

She leant back and smiled. "Twenty big ones. All used and crinkled"

I smiled at her. She smiled back.

"You better give me the address."

"Not now, wait for my call."

"Why not give me the address now?"

"I need to choose the motel."

"I thought you already had one in mind."

"I have several in mind. Expect my call this evening."

"Ok, but you don't know where I'll be or what I'll be doing."

"Then you'd better tell me where you'll be at six pm this evening."

I felt like telling her that I could be in one of five different places but she was the gal with a check-book in one hand and my balls in the others.

"The Redhead Piano Bar, you know it?" she asked

"Sure do, on West Ontario right?

"I should be there at seven, I take it you know the number."

She smiled and extended her hand.

"I think we can do sweet business together, Callum"

She handed me a card. I looked at it but it was blank side up. I palmed the card face down on the table.

"There are easier ways of doing this, ma'am."

She rose from the chair and perched herself on the edge of my desk, hitching her dress up slightly above her knee. I couldn't help but notice the fine contours of her legs and how delectable they looked under her stockings. My eyes stopped at the hem but my imagination crept further up".

She looked straight at me.

"You won't disappoint me, will you now?"

"No, I'll do my best."

She smiled and looked down.

"Sometimes failure cannot be contemplated. Expect my call tomorrow."

"6pm? The Redhead Piano Bar?"

"Yes. Goodbye for now, Mr. McCambridge."

"Call me Callum."

She turned on her heel, walked to the door of the office and closed it behind her. I gazed at her silhouette as it lingered behind the frosted glass of my office before she strode off back under the golden rock from where she crawled out from.

I basked in the afterglow of the what-the-fuck-was-that. I looked at the money and remembered the card she had given me by accident. I flipped it over.

Blank.

Blank on both sides.

I examined the card and held it up to the light to look for watermarks or imprints of any kind but it was just blank. A black white card with nothing on it.

I sipped my whisky, lit another Lucky Strike and threw the card down. I began to wonder what the rest of my hand would look like when the lady saw fit to deal the rest of the cards out.

And boy didn't she deal me the devil's hand.

Davina's Mission

I sit in the Earwax Cafe in Wicker Park, sipping an iced tea at a table for two that's just set for one. I don't like drinking on my own. It makes me feel more lonely. I am surrounded by lovers and hipsters in skinny jeans and scarves, all talking, all loving. They seem to bob up and down like a happy flotilla of pastel painted rowboats. Me, I'm just one of those uninhabited islands that everyone points to from the ferry but never want to drop anchor on. I guess I've no natural harbour. I tap and swipe at my iPad, looking at nothing in particular, just giving the impression that I'm connected to the world in some way.

I'm on a mission to find a man. Not that kind of man but a man to do a job. More specifically, I've been asked to find an actor. My employer demanded an actor. I don't know why but he does. He's good like that, not quite keeping us in the dark, but in the twilight. He doesn't give the ending away. Only he knows the full story from Act 1 to the final credits. Me, I only know the lines and stage directions for one off the scenes.

I finish my iced tea and settle the check with a jaunty waitress whose mouth is in a perpetual smile. I feel like taking off my brooch and sticking the pin in her hennaed arm to see if she cries. I drop a quarter in to the tip-jar and leave. I cross the street to the *Myopic* bookstore, just down from the Four Corners.

Within seconds, someone taps my right shoulder. I turn around. It's a guy with big curly hair and a grin. He points at my purse.

"Sorry lady but you can't bring bags in here but you can leave it behind the counter and I will give you a token and you'll get your bag back when you leave"

"I'm sorry, I completely forgot, how doodlesome of me," I say in my best girlish voice.

He smiles and gives me a laminated bookmark as way of a token and takes my purse around the back of the counter. I've been here a zillion times and always forget the protocol. He always talks to me as if I'm a first-time customer. If he remembers me from before, he never shows it. He treats me like I'm forever making my first ever visit. I never seem to leave much of a footprint anywhere I go. Perhaps I walk where there's too much dust and wind.

I go and hang around the back of the store. The place smells of paper death. The usual suspects are here, crouching and creeping around the dusty old tomes like human cockroaches. I seldom see anyone buy a book from these depths. They look gaze at broken spines and wipe dust from the covers on ragged sleeves or bare arms. Just for the hell of it, I pluck a book at random and flick through it. Walt Whitman's *Leaves of Grass*. Strange it's a famous book right? Well, there's a whole shelf of them. A bookmark falls out while I'm leafing. I pick it up. It's a torn-out folded-up page from The Golden Pages. There's a list of businesses and numbers but the numbers are at least twenty years old. The column heading is 'Milliner'. I had no idea the city needed so many hats back then but then again, everyone wore hats in the old movies.

I put the book back on the shelf. I stuff the bookmark down the back pocket of my jeans. I wander around a little more. A melancholy comes over me like a cloud casting a shadow over a picnic. I don't know what it is about old book stores that makes me cry. I think it's all those forgotten volumes. Someday, back in time, each of those books had an author and a publisher, so full of hope about having a book to sell. All those press releases, book tours, book readings, champagne-fuelled launch parties and the of razzmatazz and smart talk of the city set but look at them now, all forgotten, unloved like they never ever mattered to anyone.

No wonder I feel so at home here. Home is where you cry the most, right?

Out of the corner of my eye, I see a young guy with a black quiff and purple turtleneck, smiling at me. He looks at me rather intently. He's very handsome.

"I agree," he says. He looks at me

"Excuse me?"

"I agree, with what you just said, about books and how old books make you feel. You put it rather beautifully. A lot of people would feel the same."

"Did I actually say all those things out loud?"

His eyes dart from side to side in one of those mannerisms people have picked up from characters in Indy cinema.

"Yeah, you said it out loud."

I blush. Man I'm such a dick.

"It's ok," he says, "but that can be a dangerous habit, especially when our thoughts are of a more... private nature."

"I shall keep my thoughts to myself," I say.

"Oh, that's a shame," he says. "I bet they're like those diary entries that girls keep in Hello Kitty diaries". He smirked a smirk that accentuated his dimples.

"I don't do girly stuff like that. I save my sinful secrets on Facebook"

"Then they are no longer secrets, are they?" he says.

"I don't use my real name"

I smile at him. He's very cute. I glance at his chest. It's obvious he works out. Then I noticed a pink triangle on his lapel. I point at it like a farm-fresh carrot cruncher.

"Say, that badge, isn't that a bit...Harvey Milk? I didn't think queers wore shit like that anymore"

His smile widens, his teeth are perfect little ivories. Then he looks down at his feet, rocking slightly on the balls of his heels. I think I embarrassed the poor boy. Shit.

"Most of us don't but I do. I make a point of it. I guess it's just an actor thing"

"Uh huh, so I see."

What a shame he's a fag. Why are all the nice guys queer? I sometimes wish I could grow a dick just to get laid by a gay guy who knows how to change bed linen one a week.

I cough and gain composure.

"So you're an actor?"

"Yup, I'm an actor but you can throw a rock in this place and it will hit an actor but it's where the work is, what little there is of it. I'm Mark, I'm sorry, I forgot to introduce myself"

He reaches his hand out. I grab it. His hand is big and warm. My hand feels very small. I feel my hand could disappear into his like a bug in a Venus flytrap and I would never see it again. I tell him my name is Davina.

"I know this sounds really crazy but I could have a job for you. A one-off. Good money. It's an offer you may not want to refuse. Two thousand bucks, cash up-front and the same again once done. No catch. Ten minutes work. I've the cash right here. There, I've said it"

I open my money-clip. He peers in and sees the rolls of tightly-wound green.

He folds his arms and stands back, with a look of smug bemusement and then puts his hands on his hips like the Rocky fucking Horror show. This man can throw a vogue in all the right places.

"Is this for real?" he chuckles.

"I'm deadly for real"

"Forgive me, Davina but we've only just met and now you're offering me rolls of cash for what exactly?"

"It's a one-off bit part. Like I said, it would only last ten minutes. I work for this crazy rich guy who likes to play games on his friends. You know the Red Head Piano bar?"

"Sounds like he has too much time and money on his hands. Always an incendiary combination"

"But you are interested, right? I know I would sure as shit be"

He nods. "Ok, you're reeling me in but I haven't bitten yet. I'm intrigued. Let's go and grab a coffee and you can tell me all about it"

We leave the book store together and cross the road back to the Earwax Cafe. Justine is a little surprised to see me back so soon. In fact, she looks a little nervous.

"Honey, I ain't here for the roaches, I'm here to have coffee with my new friend"

There's that Justine smiles, her shoulders relax and she leads us to our booth.

Mark sits down. He seems excited. I want to tell him to run away and have nothing to do with a crazy bitch like me but we're caught in the slipstream of inevitability. I've a fish to catch and here he is. I can't return to the shore with an empty net. I've seen what happens to such hapless fishers of men. I shiver. A fisher of men, that's what I've become. That was what Jesus was. I may get to heaven yet but not without being nailed to a tree first.

I've got to snap out of this and refocus. Mark orders two Americanos. Justine leaves us and vanishes behind the two big black swing doors into the kitchens of cacophony and steam.

"I hope it's quick" I blurt.

"Pardon me" asks Mark

I meant to say 'she'. I don't think he heard me tell him the only truth I'm ever likely to tell him.

Or anyone.

CHAPTER 5

I had been reading some old case files in my office to while away the time until the rain had passed. The rain beat on the window like a never ending river of shivering teeth pinging sharply on the pane. Minutes later, God had run out of piano and the sound has stopped. I got up from my lazy chair, shoved some papers into the filing cabinet and whipped my coat from the hat-stand. A minute later, I stepped out into the street. Talk about stormy weather. The wind cut my face like the whiskey breath of a tramp at breakfast. I shivered, turned up my collar, lit a cigarette, plunged my hands deep into my coat pockets and walked headlong into the crowds. I remember snow starting to fall the flakes beating down like feathers with attitude. I turned the corner at Washington and Michigan to where my car was parked. I hopped in and swam with the swarm down Michigan Avenue swinging right on Ontario. I found a car-lot opposite the Rainforest Café and parked. It's a dull part of town that tries a little hard but it keeps the day trippers happy.

I would even venture to call it fun sometimes.

Just a few yards from where I stood, was a bus, painted completely in black. Its engine was running and a queue of tourists huddled beside it, clutching oversized cartons of Diet Coke and crumpled maps. The bus was a private gig, definitely not one of the CTA's boneshakers. The door of the bus opened and a big guy with a goatee stepped out. He wore baggy khaki pants and a *Greenday* tee. He looked like an overgrown teenager still waiting for his first date. He started hollering for business.

"Chicago Ghost Bus Tour, right here, right now, leaving this mortal coil at 7pm sharp".

The tourists looked up from their maps and formed an orderly queue before boarding. I envied them. Some of us don't need to pay twenty bucks to see ghosts.

Ghosts find me.

I smirked to myself, lit another cigarette from the embered end of the last one and watched the bus drive away into a ghostly land. I can't really mock it. I took the tour myself once. The part that spooked me the most was at the Chicago River at South Clark.

On July 24, 1915, the Western Electric Company held its annual summer excursion for its employees. They were to sail up the river and across Lake Michigan to the City of Michigan for a picnic.

The boat never made it to the lake.

While still in dock, hundreds of its passengers stood on the upper deck causing the ship to tilt and topple on its side, killing 841 of its passengers in only twenty feet of water. Most of the dead were women and children. Entire departments wiped out. I remember my skin frosting over when the tour guide told this story. I remember staring over the bridge and into the calm river at the exact point where it happened. Somewhere, someplace, there are people still screaming inside their drowning heads for help that will never come.

But I remembered them. I had taken a photo and had it developed, hoping to see orbs of light. There were none only the white orbs of Cadillac's and cabs taking people to and from parties, restaurants and theatres. Some say orbs in photographs are lost souls, forever floating around where they cast their coats of skin and bone. I couldn't help thinking how boring that must be, just floating around like a dead dog in a pond, no one ever noticing you.

I remember tearing up the photo and burning it with my Zippo, holding the photo until the flames bit my fingers. I needed to feel pain. I needed to hold it and bathe myself in it. Lorna threw some cola on my finger. She told me I was on fire.

I never noticed.

I continued walking up Ontario, closing my eyes for a second or two, taking in the whoosh of the cars speeding past and the distant mechanical whirr and clack of the trains circling the city's wagons in the Loop, the city's elevated metro system. I took a few steps forward, testing myself to see how far I could walk without bumping into something or falling off the edge of the sidewalk. I managed about ten paces before I felt I'd pushed my luck a little too far for one day.

I did this every day.

I walked a block or two towards the Redhead Piano Bar on West Ontario. I ambled past the Water Tower and the steps of the Contemporary Art Museum. The steps couldn't be seen for the swarming flock of skaters, sitting one minute and jumping up the next, faces contorted to dictats of cool. Each one, a squib of energy, obeying the laws of vivaciousness that I have long myself forgotten.

I found the Redhead and sauntered in for a drink and to bore Yannick the bar manager with my latest tales, tall and small. It was a quiet, unassuming oasis that many people walk swiftly past, leaving it alone for people like me who like to lick our wounds in jazz infused shadows. There was precious little else on that street but that's why I liked it and made it my second home, even though it was by no means close to my office. Its dark glass tables, stained with the fingerprints of long gone patrons, sparkled under the flicker of fluorescent neon like rhinestones under a plastic cigarette lighter. Tobacco smoke hung in the air like dark rumors, fading like dying men's memories before new plumes rose to replace them.

I stood at the bar and looked out towards the open floor and the booths. The other customers were carbon copies of myself I was sorry to say. White, middle-aged businessmen, sitting as individual islands of contemplation or in the company of women of warning. It made for an almost monkish atmosphere of secrecy, discretion and semi-visibility. This was more than just a downtown bar, it was a trading post for secrets and willing ears for confessionals with strangers whose names you never got or needed to know.

"Hey, Yannick, Old Tennessee on the rocks."

"Coming right up."

I perched myself on a barstool and started pecking at the bowl of freeze-dried Safari peanuts. A blizzard of random thoughts flickered in and out of existence as I stared ahead at the optics, catching my own reflection. It took me a second to register that I was looking at myself. I did wonder what that withered looking guy was, the one with the suit that looked like an unmade bed and a five o'clock shadow from the previous day, was doing in a place like this. He did seem to fit in alright.

Yannick threw a placemat down in front of me and slapped a well filled glass of bourbon on it before continuing to polish the glassware. Light jazz drifted through the air. I recognized it. Chet Baker. There was a man who lived fast and died even quicker.

"All is entropy," I said to Yannick before wetting my tongue with bourbon.

Yannick nodded slowly, wiping a glass with a dirty cloth.

"All is entropy, Yannick. No matter what we plant, it all dies in the end."

"You're one gray cloud this evening, Cal. Sure, one thing dies and another thing grows,"

I didn't reply and let the conversation slide. I started to think about what I was and wasn't anymore. Cop, son, husband, father. Now what was I but an ex-cop private eye in a shit suit that needed dry-cleaning. An orphan, a widower and a father to dead children. I had no tears left to shed and no-one there to wipe them.

My heart had hardened like all scar tissue does in the end. I thought about my livelihood, spying on cheating spouses, setting up husbands for blackmail. If people had any wit, they could do all that themselves but business was based on the laziness of people with money to burn.

On turns the world.

The door opened and a draft of cold air rushed in. At the door stood a young man, dressed in a dark suit. He seemed to be looking for someone. He didn't seem comfortable in his suit. In fact, his suit wore him. He looked nervous. I can tell these tells from a mile off. He kept licking his lips and his eyes were wide.

"You know him?" I asked Yannick.

"No, but he's here to fuck your mama."

"Well, he must be done with your own mama as I saw her hobbling with a big grin on her face a few minutes ago"

"Yeah, she told me how quick you are. She fits you in between irons of a shirt"

Yannick picked up an ice cube and threw it at me. I ducked and missed it. A big smile formed a banana-shaped crater on his face.

"Fuck you."

"Love ya Yannick, don't ever change"

The young man walked over towards the bar, stood beside me and lit a cigarette.

"Bottle of Goose Island, in a glass." he asked.

Yannick turned his head.

"You look a little young, sir, do you have ID?"

The young man reached into his back pocket and threw down a state driver's license. Yannick picked it up and looked at it.

"Sorry kid, nice try but you're underage. You're 19 according to this.", stabbing the license with his stubby forefinger. "Does your mama know you jumped kindergarten"?

Beads of sweat formed on the young man's forehead making it all nice and shiny like an ass slicked in baby oil.

"I just want a fucking beer. I don't see your fucking problem. I get served all over the place, no questions asked."

"Then you better suck your momma's tit for no I serve no milk to no babies in this joint. I don't give a shit if the Governor pulled you a pint at The Signature Room last night, I don't break the law and I don't serve kids. There's a McDonald's across the way. Go get yourself a Happy Meal, there's a good kid, now get out"

"Fuck you, fat man. I want a fucking beer". The young man put his hand inside his blazer. The floorshow suddenly seemed a little less funny.

"Listen to the man, kid. You're not welcome here. Beat it while you can still chew solids"

He sneered and snorted and stared right at me. He removed his hand from inside his blazer and stepped right up to me and grabbed my lapels.

"Didn't that used to be a suit?" he sneered.

The young man stood staring at me, defying me with every pore of his snide little face. I grabbed his arm and with my left fist, landed a heavy punch in the middle of the snipe's face. Teeth, blood and arrogance crumpled to the floor like a sick gazelle dressed in Old Navy. I stood up. Chet gave way to Gershwin who was now infusing the charged air. An unlikely soundtrack but anything more anthemic would have fanned the situation. The heap of disheveled blazer, cheap Cologne and badly applied hair gel got to its feet and felt its jaw with its left paw. He looked up at me and backed away.

"Fuck you, wait until my Dad hears about this, cunt" said the young man, his words the final throw a broken spear of spleen. He rubbed his jaw a second time and ran out the door and into the street. He tried to slam the door but the back draft had cushioned the blow of doorframe on jamb.

"What the fuck" Yannick said.

"That's so old fashioned, friend. If you were really hip and with it, you'd have asked WTF"

"WTF? What's the World Title Fight got to do with it?" Yannick exclaimed with his arms outstretched.

"My sentiments exactly" I straightened myself out and returned to the bar and drained my glass dry.

"On the house"

"It's only now I know what it takes to get a free one in this joint"

"Ha fucking ha. Don't push it"

Yannick filled a second glass to the brim and plunked it down in front of me. The spotlight above me diffracted its light through the amber-like resin of my bourbon spreading slivers of bronze over my fingers that gripped the sides of the tumbler.

"You seen him in here before"?

"Never. He seemed too well dressed for caper like that. If he wanted a drink, all he had to do was ask...nicely"

We looked at one another and then creased up in laughter.

"It was like watching a teddy bear in a leather jacket. Matt Damon trying to be Al Pacino"

"I couldn't have put it better myself, Cal"

"He was on his own too. Nobody with him"

""What's so strange about that? You're on your own aren't you?"

"Yeah but kids, you know, they don't drink alone in joints like this, no offence. What I vaguely remember about being a kid is that kids act up to impress someone they wanna fuck. That kid who came in acting like a warrior, who's he trying to impress? He doesn't look the type to hang around bars pickin' fights."

"Maybe it was a dare. There's probably a dozen preppies outside jerking him off right now to make him feel better"

"Yeah" I mumbled, lifting the glass to my mouth and sinking a good measure of its cargo. I closed my eyes and felt the cold fire slide down my throat and form a warm pool of pleasure in the seat of my stomach.

I felt warm.

I felt at home.

Yannick was deep in the Zen off cleaning glasses. He seemed to have more dirty glass-ware than customers. I straightened up and scanned the lounge to soak in a little atmosphere.

There was a full moon that night. I felt the serrated edge of the night chaffing at my nerves. Everyone's eyes seemed a little more eager, alert. Conversations were clandestine and furtive at the best of times but this evening's seemed to be more urgent than usual. I couldn't put my finger on it but it felt like the city was close to a breakdown. It was Friday evening of ordinary time. Christmas was too far away and the summer a distant memory. The city was tucking into its Tramadol and tequila getting shitfaced for the weekend.

I noticed a young woman by herself at a table close to the door. She sipped at gimlet that kept making her wince. She looked sharp, well dressed, unhappy and out of place. The look of ambition in this town.

She caught my eye and she looked away before getting up to leave.

"That girl by the door, know her?" I asked Yannick

"Who?"

"The girl in the black bob drinking a gimlet like it was lemon juice. I never saw her before. Is she new around here?"

"Oh her, dunno, I served her, that's all. I don't ask for biographies"

"Whatever"

I finished my drink in two more elbow lifts and slammed the glass on the counter, throwing Yannick out off his reverie. He lifted the glass and refilled it. I sank it one and he filled it again.

I decided to take my time with this one instead. I needed to talk to someone, even with bar man with mood swings. No point in hurrying it and having to go early. Let me set sail on a slow boat down this golden, bitter river while Yannick walks patiently alongside, down the bank.

"Another shitty day, Cal?" Yannick gave me that 'you're hitting it hard' look of concern. It was a look I was depressingly getting used to lately.

"Just for a change"

"Hey, I forgot to say, you got a call, from a woman, five minutes before you came here."

I checked my watch. 6:30pm. Too early. Why 6 o'clock when 7 was the appointed time?

"Did she leave a message?"

"Short and sweet. She said something about 9pm at the, let me see, yes, the Lonesome Cove Motel, Grayson Street. I swore that hobo-house was shut by the health people a while ago but what do I know"

He took a note out of his pocket where he had written it and dropped it with a smirk beside my drink.

"That part of town, know it well, mister"?

"I passed through it once or twice. I'm not going to write a Lonely Planet article about it any time soon" I said...

I don't know why I lied. I knew that part of town too well. There isn't a sidewalk or alley in this town that doesn't know the shape of my shadow or the ash-fall from my cigarettes. There are some things in this town I'm ashamed of knowing.

At least out loud.

I finished my drink. I felt the magic cloud of mystery lifting and it was time for my assignation. I bid Yannick farewell and threw a twenty spot on the counter. Yannick picked it up and examined it.

"This pays the tab from August 14th. Nice to see some progress mister"

I grinned and gave Yannick a one fingered salute.

"See you around bud"

I got up from my stool and made my way to the exit. I opened the door and stopped to breath in a lungful of cold night-time city air.

***

Lonesome Cove Motel, Grayson Street. It was now 8pm. I walked around the deserted streets around Union Station. A homeless dude sat on the pavement like a ruined castle of crinkled cloth with his bearded face poking from out of his hood. A crumpled Starbucks cup, half full with pennies and dimes, sat by his feet. He stared straight ahead with hollow eyes. I threw some loose change into the cup.

He didn't thank me.

They never do.

I lit a cigarette and paced up and down Washington Avenue until I smoked it down to the butt. I flicked it into the river and hailed a cab, hopped in and was whisked away into the blackness of the night.

Into the blackness of what lay in front me.

Tom Lockie's Blues

I pace up and down the corridors, creeped-out by all the random noises that empty buildings make.

The things I do.

I've been his goon for decades but I'm coming to the end of it. I've stashed enough coin to bail out and start all over. Yeah, a lot of losers like me talk like this and most of its bullshit but for me, I know it's true. I see it now. I'll ride all the way up to the northern part of Wisconsin and buy small farm with just enough land to tide me over and live out the rest of my days in peace. In the meantime however, I've one final job to do. It's the final mile of the marathon and I've just enough jolt in my legs to cross the line and collapse sweetly into the ground and give the dirty earth a great big fucking French kiss for I know that the taste of that dirt will be the very first taste of the peace that's to wash over me.

I'd like to say that I can taste it even as I talk about it but I never tasted peace so I can't say but I'm sure as shit it don't taste like shit.

It's now seven in the evening. I was told to arrive at The Lonesome Cover by four and spend time casing the joint like a hungry worm in a dead cat's gut.

I'm in a disused hotel in a godforsaken patch of stained tarmac in Goose Island. I'm waiting for someone. I don't know who but I'm told he'll check in later. He'll stay a short while and my job is to help him check out if you catch my drift. I don't need to paint a picture.

I can't hear my own footsteps and that freaks me out so sometimes I stop and scrape the soles of my shoes against the frayed edges of the skirting boards just to hear a sound, to make sure I'm not a ghost. The silence is thick and I move slowly through it but nothing is ever truly silent. Creaks of wood beams and whistles of wind eek and echo from all directions. I try to put them into a box in my mind that is labelled 'Ignore these otherwise you'll freak'.

I go into the long abandoned bedrooms that line the corridors like teeth in a dug up skull. I like to see what's left behind. In most rooms, the furniture and bedding are still there, cased in cobwebs and dust. It strikes me as odd that it wasn't picked clean by the dollar-vultures or wrecked by the zombie bums. The lead on the roof, the mahogany staircase, all untouched. It don't seem right. In this part of town, even the forgotten forgets shit. I got to know this part of town very well from my days in the police department. Goose Island is where the bodies of the dead or soon-to-be-dead end up, like some kind of dark departure lounge.

All cities have a Goose Island. All cities need a Goose Island for its cornered rats to leap to otherwise a lotta good throats get ripped out. You get to know every alley and rat-run in the city and after a while, you start to think like a rat. Some even start to act like a rat. I thought and acted like a rat. I could very well be a rat. Goose Island was once a zone for young industry but young industry grew up and left town leaving behind a lot of empty concrete boxes and unmarked graves in their wake...

Sometimes I pore over Rand McNally maps and wonder just how many unconsecrated graves there are in South Dakota. A state the size of France and the population of souls the size of Little Diomede Island. Forest, forest everywhere.

I once buried Sally Maclean there back in 96. We met in a bar up in Andersonville and I had given Sally her very first line of coke. She loved it and couldn't get enough of it but when she found out I worked for Johnny Friends, well, talk about Miss Congeniality. I didn't get it. I gave her every chance to get away but no. She hated dealers yet she loved what they dealt. Made no sense to me. Nice kid from a nice home who slummed it a little too well and got the jitters when she realised the baddies didn't just do what they did for show but were like that for real and for a reason. She threatened to go to the cops and tell them about Johnny's pimping and my role in his business. Her heart was in the right place but this is Chicago, not Walton's Mountain.

She loved the idea of escaping to a forest and living in a cabin, living off the land and fishing from the waters. I doubt she even knew what a chicken looked like but somewhere in her heart, she had a calling to live life at odds to the one she knew in the city. I just had to take her to the South Dakota where over half of it's covered in wood. We talked it over. I took her to South Dakota and rented a log cabin there. I left her there in South Dakota and I returned to Chicago.

I hope she's at peace.

I walk up and down more corridors, conjuring up the ghosts off parties, trysts and tribulations past. Where have all those conversations, all those parties and suicides gone? Have they all melted away like butter in the hotplate of time or do they go on existing somewhere we don't know about. All that chatter, all those passions just can't disappear into nothing. Can they?

The vibration of my cell phone sends me back up to the surface of reality so fast I feel I'm getting the Benz. It's a text from Johnny. He's telling me it's time to turn on the lights and play the music tape to give this mausoleum the vibe of being lived in. I do just that but it creeps me out even more. Part of me thinks that the light and muzak will summon the ghosts of times past back into play. I expect to hear the thin clink of cocktail glasses and faint wisps of cigar smoke to greet me any second now.

I check the time.

It's just gone 8:15pm. If all goes to plan, a young man will arrive and I will show him to Room 12, just down the hall. I will give him a package and ask him to wait alone in the room. I then text Johnny and wait for further instruction. One of the more unusual missions I've had to fulfil but like I said, this is my last job. After this, I'm done with this so I can spend the rest of my life washing the soot from my soul.

I pace around reception until I hear the crescendo of a car engine approaching. I peer out the window. A yellow cab stops in the middle of the vacant car lot. I see a young man getting out. The cab does a U-turn and screeches out the exit, back towards the city where people with futures live. The young man stops and gives the front of the building a once over. His face has a where-the-fuck-am-I look but he also looks excited. He breaks one of those smirks that young people wear these days with their wrist bands. It's one of those smirks that I'd I like to wash from his mug with a well placed southpaw but this evening, that's not on the agenda.

He checks his cell-phone and looks up and down the front of the building again. I have a feeling these young mutt needs a bit of coaxing.

I go outside.

"You're Mark."

"You must be with Suzy, she told me to come here."

"That's right."

"Well, Mark, come right in." I hold the door open for him and he walks right in. He doesn't say thank you. I take him to Room 12, open the door and turn on the light. A package lies on the bed.

"I presume this is for me, right?" Mark asks.

I nod. I take out my cell-phone and I press the fake-caller app. "Oh oh, I'm real sorry Mark but something's just come up. It's the manager's wife. She's so demanding, it's unreal... You never guess what she's just asked me to get."

Mark shook his head

"Well, I'm not sure if I should tell you but I gotta run real fast but I'll be back soon"

"Sure."

I close the app and send the text. Seconds later I get my next instruction.
I walk to the kitchen and put on a pair of latex gloves, make a cup of instant coffee and put it on tray with a small jug of milk, some sugar sachets and a stirrer. I walk back up the corridor. I knock on the door of Room 12, holding the tray with my other hand.

"Come in," says Mark.

I go in and see him, sitting on the bed, counting a lot of money. He looks content. A book lies face down beside him. I can't make out the title. I set the tray down on the bedside cabinet. Mark continues to count the bills. I take out my gun. Mark looks up. He spots my latex gloves holding a gun. I never saw a smile freeze the way his did in his nitrogen soaked moment of fear before. I think he knows what comes next.

They always do.

You think they'd run but they don't. They hope it will all go away.

I shoot him in the face.
I shoot him in the chest.
I shoot him in the balls.
I shoot him in the side of his head. His brains seep onto the carpet. They look like spilt porridge.

Text message received. The timing is cruelly precise. I return to reception and open the drawer.

There's a yellow Jiffy bag inside. I put the gun inside it, seal it the bag and place it on the desk in full view of whoever comes in next.

I get my coat and leave.

Like I said, I don't know what is going on but I make sure it happens.

*

I got home and drowned myself in a bottle of Smirnoff Black Label and fell into a deep moronic coma. It helps me forget I exist.

CHAPTER 6

"Grayson Street, Goose Island."

"What the hell's there this time of evening?"

"A motel."

"You sure?"

"Positive."

I never had a cab driver question me like that before. His accent was upstate, folksy even. He seemed to know where he was going and knew that the motel was in the asshole of nowhere.

The cab weaved its way through Halstead and Division and then turned left into Elston. Industrial nether-territory, an odd place for a motel, an odd place for anything America being America, there is always a place for a strange place. As we sped along, the ramshackle houses became sparser, the gaps of rubble and broken bricks between became more numerous and wider. Derelict buildings stood like the upright ghosts of dead soldiers, waiting for a call to war that will never happen. Missing windows, some boarded up some just gaped like undressed wounds.

Abandoned houses make me sad yet I am attracted to them. There was a time, perhaps not all that long ago when those windows glinted in the sun and the rooms inside heard the warmth of conversation, the jabber of children, the moans of love and the crackle of cooking.

The noises of the living.

No more.

All those walls and all those rooms, empty, cold, dark.

Damp.

I could almost feel the houses crying out for the comfort of a human heartbeat. I wondered how homes became like that, I mean, one day people lived in them and then bang, all gone. Did the landlords not try to find someone to move in? Why didn't they sell up?

Or was there some kind of black rapture the pastors forgot to tell us about?

"Are we near?" I called to the driver.

"Not long"

"Let me out here, buddy, I know where I am"

"You sure?"

"Yup"

I slipped the driver a twenty spot and jumped out. Curiosity got the better of me. I needed to nose around inside one of those houses and see how things were left. I've always been drawn to dereliction. I can't explain it. I lit a cigarette and watched the smoke dance into the crisp night-time air. I walked up the road and had my pick of a dozen empty houses. They seemed to be in good structural order but of course you never can tell. Let's choose one. A classic Frank Lloyd Wright prairie-style house, porch too.

Two storeys.

The windows were boarded up but the door was in place. Even the glass was intact. I walked up the steps and across the porch to the door. I looked around. No sound but the faint echoes of the city and the wind that whistled a mournful lullaby between the buildings on the street like air through missing teeth.

You never know if a building is really derelict until you go in and check every room. I got caught out once upstate about twenty miles outside Farmer City when I went behind a boarded-up farmhouse for a jimmy riddle. As I was in merry mid-flow, I felt a presence, the sound of feet softly breaking twigs and dry grass just feet behind me. I cocked my head and saw old boy standing there, stooped and staring at me, grinning too. He was told me to carry on but that I had to wash my hands first in case I wanted to make a sandwich. I thanked him but told him I didn't plan on home economics that day. He lifted his hand and turned and went around the side of the house, shunted a door to one side before going back. Not a single sweet blessed window frame or door had kissed glass for years.

Some folk just like the dark.

Back in Elston, I knocked on the door real hard a few times and shouted through the letterbox. "Anyone home?" No answer except for a little parcel of stale air that escaped and caught the back of my throat. I rasped. It smelt like a charity store that needed a window open.

I tried the door handle. A film of cold excitement broke out all over me, on my back and my palms. The door was locked but it was made of flimsy wood. I shouldered it but nothing gave at first. I thought it best to give it a helping foot. I stood back, looked around before giving a good old fashioned heave from my right foot.

Like a frost in a furnace, the door melted away.

I stood in front of the gaping hole and went inside.

The fresh air got the upper hand and rushed through the door and into the house. I felt the long shards of cold air rush past me. I almost felt the house sigh and take a deep breath. I walked in. I tried the power switch but nothing. The moon gave some light but my night vision isn't exactly that of a jackrabbit so I took out my key ring torch to cast a beam around. Carpet was still down. In the corner of my eye I caught the creep of creature's shadow, scurrying. A mouse or a rat.

I stomped my foot hard on the floor. Solid as a granite tombstone. It didn't feel damp, just abandoned. I walked up the hall and into the living room. A wooden chair, a coffee table and a sofa minus upholstery like buffalo bones picked clean by carrion. Several thin sheets of brittle newsprint jumped and shuddered like feathers in a breeze. I picked one of them up and shone my torch to it to see the date.

"October 15, 1994."

Fourteen years ago.

It must have been around that time the house was abandoned.

I stepped into the adjoining kitchen. All the cupboard doors and drawers were shut. I opened the first cupboard the worktop by the sink. Unopened tin cans and withered bread roll that petrified to a rock. I then opened all the other cupboard doors but they were bare. Not one rusted can of Heinz spaghetti hoops left. I tried the drawers. All empty except for one. An envelope.

Bingo.

The envelope was slit rather tidily at the top but the letter was still inside. I removed it and read it. It was a credit card statement for a Mr. Vincent Kerry. He owed First National Bank, $5000 in unpaid credit card debt. Bad boy. I folded the letter and stuck it inside my back pocket for some light reading for later. The letter was itemized with a record of his purchases over the previous year. That kind of thing interests me, the mundane details of nobodies who happen to be somebodies.

It struck me as odd that the letter was dated 1997. The newspapers were from 1994 and this was three years later. How did that happen? Were the papers kept for some special reason? I was in no mind for piecing together *pro bono* shit like this in my own time as I'd got Mrs. Garantovich whims that will keep my idle hands busy for a few more weeks to come.

I almost forgot upstairs. The floorboards creaked and groaned as I made my way up. The tingle came over me. Adrenalin pumped through me and fattened every vein with excitement and fear. I arrived at the landing and explored the bedrooms. Three bedrooms and a bathroom. This house was too big for one guy to rattle around in by his self. A family home but no sign of abandoned toys, comics or kiddy stuff. The first bedroom still had a bed with bedclothes. I walked up to the bed and pulled the clothes off in one fell swoop. A plastic bag with something in it lay tucked next to the pillows. I touched the plastic bag and prodded it with my right index finger. I bent down and took a couple of sniffs.

Dead. I needed to know what was in the bag so I took a pen knife to it from my Swiss card. A plume of dust sighed into the air and a few bits of white stick tumbled out. I picked up one of the white sticks. It was thin white bone. I emptied the rest if it onto the duvet. A small skull rolled out.

A cat's skull.

I didn't want to know what happened to this cat as I am an animal lover but I was pissed. I wanted this to be a human. I wanted to find something unexpectedly malignant that night. I wanted that bag to squelch and stink so much to make an elephant lose its lunch. I wanted to find maggots and final screams frozen in the widened jaws of a cobwebbed skull. I needed something nightmares to replace the ones I had over Lauren. I picked up the cat-skull and, I don't what came over me but I lightly licked it to know what it tasted like.

It tasted of cold bone. I flung it against the wall but the fucker bounced back right onto the bed.

Well what do you know?

The wellsprings of curiosity with the house had just about dried up so it was time to stop pissing about and make my way to the motel. I put the bones into the bag, skull and all, and went downstairs and left the house.

Outside, what was once a garden was now like a convention of Gorgons. Giant weeds, their heads bobbing up and down like screaming Medusas swayed like the arms of the drowning mute. I crouched and with my bare hands, scooped out a hollow from of the crumbly dry earth and placed the bag of cat bones in the hole before palming it over with the soil. It wasn't a perfect job but it was a job. I stood up and whispered 'Amen', lit another cigarette and left.

***

Lonesome Cove Motel was only a mile up the road. I checked my watch. 8:30pm. I was cutting things a little fine but fuck it, I knew I'd make it on time. I always do. The wind was an army of switchblades that cut at my face. I walked straight on, head down and collar up, quickening my pace but it just made the blades of whipping wind up their game. I didn't care though, being the stoical sack of shit that I am. I can convince myself that I somehow deserve it and that the pain is good for me. A warm sensation from god knows where, moved through my body giving me a nice whole body shiver that made me feel safe, cocooned. I felt this from when I was a boy when I discovered that self-pity made me feel good and cozy. It was a sick way to be as a child but I learned from the worst.

1959. Nine years old. In bed. Saturday morning. Spring. Kids playing outside. Not me. "Fuck God, fuck Jesus, fuck everything." Chanted like a mantra from the kitchen. The Public Housing authorities had sent Mom a letter. They turned down our application to move to a better house. Again. Dad was doing his rounds at work. I was alone in the house with Mom. She could have set the ozone alight with all the fucking candles she lit at the chapel to get that house in Springmeadow Drive. God must be one fucking purist of a pyromaniac because He ignored her completely. So I listen to Virginia, my sweetheart, outside playing Frisbee with her little sister while my Mom throws plates on the ground shouting 'Fuck Christ, fuck God, fuck everything' again and again and again. I hid under the covers. The covers became the sky and I was a giant with my head in the pillow-clouds and my feet on the blue earth beneath. No one can touch me now. This is my whole, small world. All to myself. I think about Virginia though. No matter how hard I try, the real world makes a lot of noise and intrudes into mine. Mom comes into the room. She asks why I don't take our housing situation seriously. I am nine years old. We live in a small apartment.

Nice neighbors. Four apartments in the block.

Front doors open onto the street and outside landing. The couple across from us are nice but don't fit in round here. John and Linda. Dad calls him Jack even though he isn't called Jack. Jack sits outside and reads the bible and drinks cocktails. His wife is a nice lady but I don't see her that often. Roberta lived downstairs right underneath us. Mom told me she smoked cigarettes instead of having breakfast. One day Roberta stood on a chair to fix curtain hooks when she lost her balance and smashed her skull against the edge of the radiator and lay dead for a week before her sister found her.

Memories are like shrapnel, you never know when they're gonna start making their presence felt. One day they tickle the next they hurt like screwdriver twisting down on your heart. I screamed like a banshee that was being fucked by a hot poker. I had to. So much was raw, uncooked inside me from all those times before. I didn't care who or what heard me. My throat was sore with the serrated emotions that rushed back and forth and my brain hurt like my head had been shaken by an Irish nanny with a temper.

***

Lonesome Cover Motel. The first thing I noticed was just how big the car lot was yet it was empty. The white lines of the parking spaces were broken and faded, a consortium of weeds bursting through the cracks in the tarmac.

I scanned the façade of the building. Every room was lit. There was something about the place that didn't seem right. No cars parked, all lights on, it seemed a little, set up. People don't just take a bus or a cab to a motel. They drive there. The clue's in the name. Odd name too for a motel, *Lonesome Cove*. An apt name in a Hopper painting or a Lynch movie or somewhere in the sticks but not in Chicago. Not in this district. I put my unease on ice and walked closer to the entrance.

Above lobby door shimmered a sign spelt out in the motel's name in broken blinking neon. A vestige of vanished vanity, like a low-rent hooker. All the letter 'E's were blown. I had a feeling that this was the kind of place ghosts went to hang out. I bet there was a ghost in there right now. I bet his name's Butch or Jed some other name that is worn as a patch on a lumberjack shirt. I imagined Butch shot himself over a dame. The dame fucked his buddy and Butch found them. The dame laughed. Butch slinked off but he didn't go home. He lived with his mother. He couldn't do what he had planned in her house. He loved her too much. No, he booked an anonymous room in a nameless motel in a forgettable part of town and put a gun to his head. I can smell Butch's drugstore cologne. I bet he walks up and down the corridors every evening, wearing a dark crumpled suit, clutching a bottle of Old Tennessee, reliving his final evening, hoping someday God would give him a different ending.

I opened the lobby door and went inside. The first thing that hit me was the smell. It was the smell of houses that don't open their windows. The smell was so thick with damp and mustiness you could have cut it up into slabs.

Brown patterned carpets stretched out before me but they didn't reach the edges. Industrial gaffer tape did its unsubtle duty on the joins. Wood-paneled walls and dime-store reproduction paintings lined the foyer. The reception desk didn't even have a computer, just a few pens and a large leather-bound legal pad. This place wasn't retro, it was time warped. I checked the time.

8:45pm.

I kept my ears cocked for noise outside but I heard nothing, just the low distant hum of a low distant city with my heartbeat providing the brushed percussion.

I bellowed, "Hello."

No reply. I thumped the bell on the desk but still no reply. The tinny echoes stretched and thinned before dissolving and becoming one with the silence itself.

My cell-phone vibrated.

A text: "Room 12, 1st floor, just open the door, no need to knock."

There were two corridors that led from the foyer, one from the right and one from the left. The left corridor was labeled Rooms 1-40. As I walked down the corridor, I heard a television set from one of the rooms. Room 5. No human voices. Just the hammed up shrills of soap opera actresses.

Seconds later, I found Room 12. I pressed my ear to the door but the room was silent. No voices, no television, not even the fart of a stray dog. The text did say there was no need to knock but that's one of those things people say but don't mean, like let's have a beer sometime. I rapped the door three times. Rat-a-tat-tat.

"Mrs. Garantovich, are you in there?" No answer.

I figured she was the kind of dame who liked her games and perhaps didn't go in for the niceties and courtesies of ordinary folk. I thought she was inside, stifling sniggers in diamante black gloves held against her pink Rimmel lipstick. I knocked the door once more but no answer. I turned the brass door knob and the door opened.

I stood at the hinge-end off the lintel and scanned the room for surprises. The room was unlit, pitch black in fact. It was at the front of the building and I didn't remember seeing a dark gap in the row of lit windows when I looking from the outside. I raised my hand to feel for the light switch. I found it but it felt a little wet. I pressed it. Three bed-side table lamps shot to life, giving the room the feel of twilight. I looked over towards the bed. There, there was a darkness that no amount of light could banish. Beside the bed lay a man, a man in a pool of blood.

I went in and walked towards the man, locking my eyes on his form. He stared back up at me, eyes wide open. I crouched to take a closer look. Gunshot in the back of the head. What a mess. I bent over his face and put my ear to his mouth, trying to sense any sign of life. You just never know. There's no drama queen quite like blood. It can make a shaving cut turn your sink into a butcher's playpen.

No breath. He had breathed his last. I was glad for his sake he was dead. It would have been too grotesque to survive and look the way he did.

I reached inside his jacket pocket and found a wallet. Two hundred bucks in used twenty-spots and a well-worn library card with a name on it.

Mark Madigan.

I took out my gun, got up and tiptoed over his body and checked the joint out. I entered the bathroom and felt for the light-pull. I found the string and tugged. The flickering bulb twitched its light across the room. Towels lay disheveled on the floor. I looked at the bath tub but the shower curtain was pulled shut all the way across but something hung over the edge of the tub. A woman's leg, in stockings. There was blood on the enamel and the floor tiles. I clutched the curtain and ripped it out taking the rusted shower rail with it. It fell on the tiled floor with a tinny, yapping clang. I looked into the tub.

A woman's figure alright but a fashion mannequin. Some sick joke alright.

I went back into the bedroom, looking for hiding places. I checked under the bed. Nada. I looked at the walk-in closet. Fear gripped my chest. I swear I saw the door move by the width of a flea. I fired two shots into it. The door fell open but there was nothing inside but a few folded sheets and bathroom towels. I took out my phone, tucked my under my belt and left the room. By now, the air was a cacophony of sound. Every room had its television on set to high volume. Moments ago, all was still. Now it was like the echo chamber of a lunatic's recording studio. Someone in one of the rooms had to have heard something.
I knocked on the doors of the adjoining rooms. The televisions were on but no answer. I knocked again.

"Police, please open up, I have a few questions." No answer. Not a stir.

I knocked on a few more doors, but no answer.

I phoned Mrs. Garantovich. No answer, straight to voicemail. I knocked on the door to Room 15. I took a step back and a deep breath. If someone was in, sleeping, I'd apologize and make my excuses and run as fast as a flame on a bed of gasoline. I took my gun in hand and kicked the door in and threw my back against the wall and waited.

Nothing.

There was a lot of fucking nothing in that place. Except in Room 12.

I entered Room 15. The TV was on. An ancient model. Rediffusion, wooden panel effect. Plastic ersatz silver knobs on the side. I checked out the bathroom, under the bed and inside the closet. I glanced at the television. The presidential debate was on, McCain and Obama.

I like Obama but he hasn't a prayer.

Suddenly I heard a click. The television was now silent. A pregnant white dot sat in the middle of the screen. I recognized that sound. The corridor decayed into a descendo off silence. One by one the televisions were turned off until there was total complete quiet.

I looked behind the television set. The plug was slotted into a large rectangular white box which itself was plugged into the power socket. On the side was a dial calibrated from zero to twenty four with a ring of sliding black notches under the numerals. Two notches stuck out from the rest. A timer. The set was timed to go on at 8:55pm and set to switch off at 9:05pm. I ran out and checked out other rooms. The same deal. There I was, in the middle of Hotel Weird full of empty rooms with televisions that turned themselves on and off and a dead body in Room 12. I needed to sink a large scotch double quick but I suspected the bar hadn't been graced with a wet bottle or the shadowfall of a bar man for quite a while. The whole shebang was what I suspected, an elaborate set up. I sprinted to the lobby and was about to run through the front door but froze when I saw what was happening outside.

The swirling dervishes of blue lit-up the car-lot like the unnatural dawn of an electric blue sun...A discordant symphony of sirens worked up to its too familiar crescendo. For the first time in my life, the blue orchestra was striking up its tune for me and me alone.

Thin strobes of torch light jabbed through the windows and peppered my body with their bright, silent eyes. I ran back into the hotel to get away from the window. To the right of the reception was a stairwell. I took it. Instinct took over thought, my mind was pure animal. I reached the landing. The hullaballoo of the cop circus outside was still audible but muffled. It seemed less of a threat. I walked up the corridor but it was dimly lit with scraps of siren light that scattered and refracted through the windows.

Suddenly the sirens stopped their wail. I know cops never retreat. A trap. I was worried. Silence is seldom a friend. Silence is the sound of a gun being held to the back of your head while you pour yourself a drink. I looked over my shoulder. I saw nothing but something stirred. I didn't know what. The air was sullied and dank. History and time stinks a place up. There was a presence. Not ghosts or shit like that but something untouchable. By now I reached the end of the hall. A silhouette of a drinks cabinet came into view just below a painting of an unnamed well-dressed man in a gray moustache.

Right at that moment, I heard the clean, sharp shatter of glass being smashed. The crisp shards of broken window, minced and spliced the tired, rotten atmosphere. It almost felt welcome under any other circumstance. It felt cleansing like a thunder storm breaking the sapping heat of a long humid night. I knew what it meant though. Danger was close. I took a left. Another corridor. I had no plan. I was hoping to make a sly break for it. I wanted to escape, hide with the bums for an hour until the wolves in blue gave up their quarry and scuttled back to base, return to the Redhead for a spot of medicinal amber before catching a cab home and crawl into bed and put the whole thing down to a bad day at work.

Then I felt something hit my head. I tried to walk but I staggered, reeling from wall to wall like a wounded buffalo. Another whack on the head and I fell. I drifted in and out but I was too scared to let go and lose consciousness. It's something I never let go of unless I'm dead.

So far.

I remember the figure of a man crouching over me. I was too dazed to make out his features but the distant robotic voices from his radio handset swirled like sonic dervishes around my head.

As for what happened after that moment, I don't know but I knew I never made it home that night.

CHAPTER 7

"Wake up McCambridge"

I rubbed my eyes and rolled onto my back and looked up. There were three cops standing in line, staring down at me with leaden faces smelted with menace. One was a middle aged detective with a girth off a lifetime of dollar pizza slices and McMeals. The other two were uniformed rookies, so fresh from the academy that you could almost still see the shrink-wrap marks on their faces. I sat up on my elbows and looked around. I spent the night on a concrete bed in a grey four by eight foot cell that whiffed off the shit of ages. My back was stiff and I was sore all over. My throat was dry and mouth felt like the bottom of a bird cage. I scraped my tongue under the edges of my upper teeth to get rid of the thin layer of acrid filth that gathered during the night but it didn't help much.

"Is my lawyer here yet?"

"No, did you call one?" said the fat guy.

"No, I think I misplaced my cell phone. One of your boys borrowed it when I checked in last night and never gave it back" I said.

He shrugged and screwed his mouth in that seen-it-all-before demeanor and left the room. I sat up on the slab that passed for a bed.

"I'd like a lawyer, I know my rights." I said 'and a glass of water too'

"Sure thing, we'll fix you with a lawyer. I'll make sure he brings some water too" he answered from outside.

"No, I want my own lawyer, not one of the duty monkeys"

Two more uniforms appeared by the door.

"I hear you wanna make a call, McCambridge?" one of them said.

I nodded my head.

"You don't mind the new recruits listening in, do you? They need to learn the ropes."

"I'm not in the mood for talking dirty. I'm sorry but your puppies have to get their hard-ons somewhere else, OK?"

The baby faces looked to the fat alpha male to see how they should react. The fat man held a fist to his mouth and coughed up some phlegm. The baby faces became hard baby faces within seconds.

"A wise guy," said one of the baby faces.

"Well, wise guys don't end up being charged with murder one."

"Charged? I ain't been charged with nothin'" I said

"Do you want to take your call or not?"

"Let me think about it...hell yeah, why not" I said. I swung myself around and put my feet on the floor.

"Phone room. You've three minutes," said the fat guy.

***

I phoned a lawyer who I did some business for. Ruben Eichmann. It rang ten times before going to voicemail. I wasn't in the mood for leaving messages on machines. I put the phone down. Alpha male grabbed my arm to usher me away. I wrested my arm from him and stood my ground.

He remained in static pose for a few seconds, for dramatic effect I guessed. His hands were still in the shape of holding my arm. He turned around. His face contorted in rage, a rage I only ever saw in those who were about to lose everything. If anger and frustration could be made into liquid and boiled to reduction, the dark, bleak tar of hatred that would have remained at the bottom of the pot would have been a doppelganger for the countenance I saw before me, cutting me into pieces with every split second of observance. The baby faces stood watching.

"Look and learn boys," I said aloud. "This is the real police academy."

Alpha male tried to hit me but I shoved his arm down and kneed him in the nuts. He forgot I was once a cop and that I know all the He fell to the ground, squealing like a stuck pig. Before I was able to muster another thought, I was festooned within a nest of arms and sweaty torsos. I was thrown to the ground. I thrashed around but my body came under attack, blitzed by blows, thicketed by thumps, crumpled by kicks of heavy black boots.

I remember being dragged into a double cell. More than a dozen cops came in, kicking and punching me. After twenty kicks, you don't mind anymore. I passed out. The thumps and kicks felt like waves washing against the hull of the boat. I floated on that boat, bobbing up and down with each blow, growing ever more detached.

*

You ask for your lawyer.

Mommy can't help you now, son.

Those who've never stepped foot inside a cop shop before, baulk at the look of the cells, the prisoners and the withered, wizened old detectives who've been mugged by reality once too often. It all looks so familiar yet exotic. Until you get thrown into the mix and see the blades of the system come at you as you thrash around in the blender. Your protests are for nothing, they just vanish like piss in the ocean. Your protests meet with derision and the shaking of heads that wear smirking mouths. Nothing stops the blades whizzing towards you. Bad luck has the sharpest teeth. You might as well face it friend, you're ground chuckmeat and the system will make a burger of you yet.

You get your first round of questioning. You think 'this should be OK, these are smart people, it's just a mix up. I'll be home in time for Grey's Anatomy'. A detective sits down on the chair opposite you.

You smile.

He doesn't.

To you, he's a shiny new experience to regale at a future dinner party. To him, you're just another shit-eating worm that wriggles on the end of his rusty hook.

He asks you where you were on a certain time and date. You tell him. He asks you to prove it. You can't. How can you? He asks if you're sure. Of course you're sure. He asks you again. You tell him again. He tells you that he doesn't believe you and that in fact you've been seen near the crime scene around the time of death. You tell him its bullshit. You know where you were and when. You make some wisecrack about having to carry a digital camera everywhere. He looks at his sidekick, smiles a snide smile. He's heard this one before. He raises an eyebrow.

He throws an evidence bag on the table. He holds his chin in his fingers. He doesn't look at you this time. The question is unspoken. You look at it. You recognize it. It's yours. It's a blue handkerchief with green polka dots. There are a few of them around but you haven't seen yours for a while. You didn't think anything of it. It was always in your sock drawer but you use your sleeve these days to wipe your snot. You've let standards slip in recent times and you hadn't even noticed.

Until now.

You tell him it could be yours but you're sure it's not the only one that was made. Blood withdraws from your legs. You know you can't walk or stand. You slip further and deeper down that dark pipe and that big blue tent of freedom starts to look like a postage stamp in the dim, grim distance above you.

He tells you that it's your handkerchief because your DNA is on it. The lab rats proved it. You segue into disbelief, disbelief into indignation, indignation into fear, fear into free fall. You lash out. Your words flail like burning limbs in a gay disco in Tehran but they make no difference. You hurtle head first towards cold, hard marble at a hundred miles per hour. Until now, you've been told you're up to your neck in stoat shit and you didn't believe them but now you taste it and you had better acquire a palate for it because, brother, that could be your breakfast, lunch and supper for the rest of your natural life.

You go down.

You're now in hell. In a world without women. You eat, sleep and shit in a cell no bigger than a john. You slowly rot alive in the stink and evil fog of a thousand sweating, dying men. You wake up and scream and thank the Lord above that it was all a dream but you don't see your bookcases and lilac bedroom walls fall upon your morning gaze. You see the gray walls of your cell. Then it hits you, it ain't no dream. Those bricks don't speak much but they're going to be the only friends you got.

You wish you got the chair.

First-degree murder carries a life-means-life term. The Guns-Babies-Jesus-Hot-Damn brigade saw to that. I remember Eric Radnor, a born-again neighbor of mine telling me that being born is a curse because God's given you a chance to fuck up and go to hell. I remember asking him why God would do that. He told me God loved us. I asked him how come he loved us but risked sending us to Hell. He told me he didn't know the answer to that but he was sure there was a good reason behind it because God is, you know, God. I took a swig of beer after that one. I remember we both stared ahead at the dying embers of a suburban barbeque in the seconds afterwards, never to exchange words again that evening. Yeah, I went to all the best parties in my time.

Eric was a modest man. I bet Eric ain't in a piss stinking hell hole right now like me. I bet he's wearing an outsized Mason and Perry fluffy white sweater and a pair of salmon pink chinos right now. I bet he's having his beard pulled by his grand-kids, stomach full of grilled chicken salad and Goose Island beer. His God is good to him and his nice white boney ass will never know the pleasure of being forked by a devil's heated trident.

95

I wish I knew where my God was.

I wish he knew where I was.

***

I woke up the next day in a room of many beds. I was no longer in my cell but some kind of dorm. My body was a maggot box of pain. Every fiber in every muscle screamed like an orgasmic Quebecois being fucked by the Eiffel tower. My head, my I wished I were dead. I looked up and took in my strange new hostelry. Each bed was host to a human mound of despondency. Hope did not have a home there. It looked like a bum shelter. A man across from me stared blankly into the vacancy of space. He lay under a stained, yellow sheet, his calves bum-tanned from dirt, his feet sticking out a foot from the bottom of the bed. His socks were melded to his feet, I couldn't tell when cloth started and skin ended. I doubt he could have taken them off had he wanted to without an amputation. A roach slowly crawled along the bottom of his left foot. I watched the critter make its way on its odyssey in the land of torpor and grime.

I was conscious of staring at him. I know he didn't notice me but I remembered from somewhere that it was wrong to stare, even at bums. I turned the other way and looked at other bums instead. Someone in the far corner farted loudly. No one laughed. No one flinched. Nobody seemed to give a fuck.

There were a lot of nobodies in the room that day.

Not having the guts to hang myself, all I could do was pray that some second soon something would squish my life. They say the dead can't die twice. I know that's bullshit. I felt dead and alone yet I felt there was more depth of death to plumb and I was so frightened of how deep it would lead. I wished my body would follow suit. I opened my shirt and looked at the bruises. I tried to gather some sense of beauty from what I saw. But ultimately I couldn't. I ached all over. I fainted and a nullifying sleep came over me. Dreams may have come and gone during that time but I can't remember them. But I am sure they were fun.

A stick poked into my side. A cop stood over me. He was holding a stick and poked me in the side. I didn't recognize him. I jumped up and out of bed. It made him start and he jumped back. I stood and looked at him like a wounded animal. But I was a wounded animal. I didn't feel like a man right then. Not sure if he was really one of them though but he wore the same uniform as them. He relaxed. He sensed the fear and fright. His face wasn't hard or evil.

"McCambridge, you're free to go." He gestured.

I opened my mouth a bit and stared to the right of his head. I began to rock from side to side like those sad fucks of Nam vets you see panhandling.

"Mr. McCambridge, you can go now. Your bail's been posted."

"What have I been charged with?"

"Murder. Mark Madigan. Forgotten already?"

I remembered alright.

"Bail? What bail? Who posted it? No-one knows I'm in here."

"They can tell you at the desk, I think it was a man, one of those men who have black hair."

"What do you mean, 'one of those who can black hair'? I don't understand."

He looked puzzled.

"A clever private dick like you surely is aware that some men have black hair, yes?"

"Uh huh?"

"Well, it was one of them, now move it."

I hadn't a fucking clue what he was gabbing about but I wasn't in the mood to untangle cat cradles. I was escorted to the front desk where I collected my effects and signed the papers. I asked to see the bail papers. The signature was scrawled with a thin, spidery hand that was difficult to read. I squinted until I made out the name.

"L. McCambridge."

I'm sure someone found it funny but I sure as fuck didn't.

The desk clerk gave me an envelope.

"The sucker wanted you to get this."

I took the envelope and left the building. The daylight seared my eyes. I took a deep breath but the change of air made me feel sick. I fell on the steps and puked up a lunch I couldn't remember eating. I felt a little better but my mouth tasted like a hobo's socks in a heat wave. I started walking down the street.

Respectable passers-by just passed on by, quickening their step and clutching their kids closer to them as I came closer to them. I felt like an unwelcome shit that hangs around the pan, ignoring every flush. I could tell they thanked the Lord that they weren't me. My one good deed of the day, being someone else's cautionary tale.

"I'm no fucking Aesop's fable, lady," I shouted. That made her walk even quicker. Yeah, I couldn't believe I said that. That was real bum-talk and I wasn't even drunk.

I stopped and remembered the envelope I was given at bail-time. I opened it. Inside was a typewritten note:

> *Go to the phone booth across the road, next to the garbage can.*
> *Under the phone, there is a package taped to the undercarriage. Take*
> *it out and then phone this number. All will be explained.*

98

Taped to the note was a dime. I didn't recognize the number at first. It was a landline. 847 667 3344, a number from the northern suburbs, Prospect Heights or Wheeling or some other sprawl of strip malls and heavy set hockey moms. I didn't know anyone who lived in those necks of the wood there but someone sure as hell knew me.

I made my way to the crosswalk. The sign flashed 'Don't Walk' but this was no time for patience. I took my chances and played chicken with the fast moving traffic spread over two lanes each way. After a chorus off 'fuck off' and 'hey what the fuck you doin'?', I reached the other side of the road and spotted the phone booth. A young woman was inside making a call.

I stood next to the phone booth waiting for the woman to finish her call. I wondered why she wasn't using a cell-phone. She was well dressed in a dark-brown pinstripe business suit with a tall, wide-collared blouse. Her ass was perfectly pert and shapely beneath the fabric. I felt a bit manly again but no party in my pants. I just enjoyed the view but she looked up and caught my eye. I couldn't make out what she said but I could tell from the panic on her face that she was killing the conversation prematurely. I scared her. I felt bad about that. She slammed the mouthpiece down on its cradle but it slipped and fell, dangling like a pendulum. She scurried off in the direction of downtown before I had a chance to apologize. I whispered 'Sorry lady' under my breath. I went into the phone booth, replaced the receiver on the cradle and ran my fingers in the coin drop for change.

Two more dimes. My lucky day.

I was about to make the call and that's when I heard the screams and the bangs. I looked out to the street behind me and I saw people throw themselves on the ground. Men were shouting, women screamed and cried. I heard another bang but it was closer. A glass pane in the booth shattered. I knew what gun attacks sounded like and ran outside and hid behind a parked green jeep. My wits jumpstarted, heart pumping ninety to the second. A man dressed in black, black wrap-around shades and a Cubs baseball cap walked towards me. He pointed a gun at me. His finger on the trigger.

I did some combat rolls, sprang to my feet and ran like crazy.

Once again in the middle of the road, I slalomed and weaved through the gaps in the moving traffic. I think he fired some more shots at me but he didn't pursue past the park. But I carried on running. I think I ran twenty straight blocks until I collapsed in a doorway in a quiet street in Greektown. I felt my lungs flood like doomed soldiers' did in a cloud of mustard gas. I wanted to pass out and sleep but my survival instinct vetoed that. I had to stay awake.

I had to stay alive.
I had to stay vital.
All I had in the world was the blood that moved in my veins.

CHAPTER 8

Reality check: I was in the middle of Division Street, wearing a blood-stained suit, piss-stained pants and a ripped shirt, unwashed. I'd no cell-phone, no money except for the two dimes I had in my pocket. I walked on for a while and sat down on a step beside another hobo. He ignored me. I started to wonder if this was all some sick stunt that gone way too far. I convinced myself that I was live on some NBC candid camera segment. Conan O'Brien was laughing at me, making wry jokes live on air, exercising his finely honed third-generation Irish jaw-line like a wooden puppet dressed in an out of date suit. The audience is chuckling on cue.

The hobo turned and looked at me. The funny thing was that he didn't look like a loony. His eyes were just dead, dark lakes of long stagnant sanity now host to the islets of little madnesses. It's a mistake to think they're all a prick short of a bee sting. A lot of them are just like you and me. Except that they are singularly the most unlucky motherfuckers you'll ever come across. If luck is like baking a cake, then these folks forgot the eggs. Well I had the recipe and I still fucked up. All my life I was warned about ending up like these people. Work harder, work harder, work harder. In America, work is the garlic you hang at the door to keep the bogeyman away. To be homeless, rootless, destitute musters a frown from Uncle Sam..

I'm on the run. That's a phrase from the movies not real life, but I'm on the run.

"You haven't been doing this for long, have you?" he said.

"How do you know?"

"It's all in how you sit. You sit like a man who's about to stand up."

"Doesn't everyone?"

"No, I don't. I sit like I'm never going to get up again"

He then stood up.

"I thought you said you didn't stand up?"

"You didn't hear me right. I said I can't get up again. This is just me *standing* up so I can scratch my ass."

The hobo picked up his bag.

"You know, mister, what you have to realize is that you've the biggest parlor in the world. Grant Park is a bedroom to me and a good few others too. Nice view of Lake Michigan. Sometimes the neighbors take liberties and walk in without asking my permission but I don't mind. I keep my lips tight and my head down. I don't need no pillows no more, the lawns are my mattress. It's all the rage. I bet you're still breaking your heart over that nice house you can't go back to, am I right? Yeah, thought so... Say, how much space did you have in that house? Well now think about how much space you have *now*."

"Yeah but I'd still like to run a fucking bath," I said.

The hobo looked up at the sky and chuckled while shaking his head.

"Then you should hang around people who can smell the right kind of dirt"

"Are you Jesus or something?" I asked. "How come such a wise old bird like you ends up here"

"Mercy, how do you think I ended up here? Same way we all do, by just being ourselves. We all end up where the world finds us easiest to deal with. Every tin of soup finds its right pantry in the end"

Under any other circumstances, I would have happily spent a morning in brisk conversation but I wasn't in the mood. He picked up his bag and lifted his left hand and waved me goodbye and shuffled off back into his al fresco mansion.

No one was hunting the hobo that night though or any night for that matter. He ain't in anyone's cross hairs. Being on the run sounds glam and glitzy.

Like hell it is.

It's about not cleaning your ass properly for days so much your hole feels like it's stuffed with itching powder. You itch all over all the fucking time. You feel things tickle you under the clothes that you haven't changed in days. Your scalp is the worst. You scratch and scratch till you see blood under your finger nails. You look a little closer. You see white spots under your fingernails. Some of those itty bitty white dots even move because they're alive. Then you can't look anymore or even be bothered looking. It all starts to feel normal. Being on the run does wonders for your breath too. My mouth felt like a fat man's gusset in a hot day in Alabama, but worse. In short, I felt like a turd that was cursed with a brain.

Being on the run might be fun for the bearded freedom fighter that can fall back upon the comfort of a jungle full off fruit-trees, camaraderie and rebel songs penned in his honor. Being on the run and knowing that there's a million bucks buried beneath an oak tree in some field in Mississippi is a pleasant thought indeed but it ain't like that. I had no such crock of gold except the truth. It was down to me alone to find it. I'd no choice but to find it and there weren't no fucking rainbows to help me find it..

I got up and walked way up Division. An hour later and I was in the northern district of Evanston. My feet were sore and I shuffled my way to the corner of Dempster outside The Potbelly sandwich joint.

A couple of college girls were sitting on the edge of a water fountain, dangling their cute little feet in the jets of cold, fresh water. Their girlish voice tickled my ears like champagne bubbles. The brunette one glanced over at me and a grey veil of disgust fell over her face. Their girlish chatter and smiles segued into embarrassed whispers and anxious looks.

They then put their shoes back on and got up on their feet.

"I'm sorry, ladies, but I didn't mean any harm, I'm just here to cool my feet."

But the bum spoke. Even if I quoted Shakespeare, my words would still smell if their ears had noses. There's nothing as scary to a WASP as a talking bum. A bum isn't supposed to speak or show any form of articulation. Grunts, moaning and the random thrashing of limbs are the acceptable high-concept signatures of the bum but not deliberately directed speech.

But a bum that can talk intelligently is even more jarring. This ain't supposed to happen. It frightens people even more because you sound too similar to them. It makes them feel that their marbled floors have a trapdoor somewhere waiting for them to fall in. The girls bustled off. I watched them scurrying off and into the asylum of Starbucks several buildings down to cleanse themselves in the holy water of cool. I imagined them sucking up frappacinos through multi-colored straws, updating Facebook on their phones to tell the world that they were in Starbucks sucking at frappacinos and having been frightened by a bum and getting fifty comments within a minute from young men who pretend to be concerned but all what they really want to do is fuck their cute little preppy asses all the way to the Hancock Tower and back.

I walked past a news-stand. I looked at the Sun-Times front page. My name was in the headlines.

I'm a wanted man.

I didn't feel like a wanted man, I just felt like a sack of shit.

Other papers carried my mug shot, others a full body photo. One of them was from my past, my deep past. I'm in my smart police uniform, all blue, shiny and new. I looked dashing, daring, honest. That young man had a future. That's the trouble with futures, they get chewed up by time and get farted as regrets. I wished I could step right into that frame and give that young man a hot blast of sharp warning. The past is a different country, they say, they do things differently there. That man was a different Callum McCambridge. He lived in a different country, one I wished I could visit again and make things different, make things right.

"Probably cooped up with some leggy Missy La-La in the Copacabana by now," said the vendor.

I wasn't sure if he was talking to me

"Yeah, him, the killer ex-cop. I betcha *he* ain't freezing his balls off by the Lake Shore that's for sure."

"For sure," I said, pulling up my hood and shuffling off before I was recognized. A pang of hunger shot through my stomach. I realized I hadn't eaten in days. I'd survived on fountain water that tasted of rust. I was running on empty and the gauge was at zero. The pangs hit hard. The smell of freshly-baked bread from a nearby deli nearly sent me over the edge. Mountains of luscious white loaves were laid out in a shelf outside the store, all lying there like the wide, teasing thighs of nubile women. I sidestepped over and lifted two bread rolls and stuffed them down my pockets.

"Hey you, get the fuck outta here"

I looked around and it was the owner or the baker, I couldn't tell. He wore an apron and his hands were covered in brown dough. He took a look at me and stepped back. I tuned and sprinted down Division and holed myself up an alley way where I stopped to eat the rolls, tearing at them like a dog, enjoying the primitive feeling of ripping at the quarry with my own teeth. I felt like a wolf. It was beautifully brutal.

My mind wandered back to the Lonesome Cove Motel. I felt the need to visit the scene of the crime and visit my grave like all new ghosts do. I walked to the other end of the alley where it met Adams and turned right against the contra-flowing shoals of commuters who were about to jump into whatever Amtrak sardine tin that took them to Glenview, Glendale or whatever burb-box they lived in. I stopped and watched the people like the lone salmon in the leap. I sidestepped the crowded sidewalk and stood by the gates off the main entrance. I noticed two panhandlers, sitting with cardboard Subway coffee cups by their feet. A few dimes or nickels lay at the bottom of the cups like tiny wishing wells.

No one notices the panhandlers. Sure that's no news these days. They're part of the scenery of modern-day urbanity like the pigeons that shit on my ruined suit. I guessed that those sharply dressed men who sailed past us, clutching Samsonite briefcases, may not be on top of the food chain either. The world, like the jungle, belongs to the hunter with the sharpest teeth, fastest legs and the least conscience. I saw these office workers and I didn't see lions but antelopes, nibbled slowly by mortgages, marriages, mistresses, the ever-larger pre-dinner gin and tonics and ever vanishing sex. The antelopes think they're the winners when they take out half-million dollar mortgages from the leonine bankers in exchange for forty years of worker-bee bondage and weekends in Mall of America.

But what I'd have given to change places with any one of them, to go home to a warm house, toss a clump off chicken salad onto a plate, pour a glass of Merlot and fall on a plump sofa watch a HBO box set on a 40 inch flat screen.

I noticed the bigger of the two panhandlers looking up at me. His face made no secret of the fact that he didn't appreciate my presence. He was trying to work me out. I love it when people try to work me out because there's nothing to work out. I'm just a simple guy, a two plus two equation that somehow makes everyone go and seek out their book of logarithms. I just want to live, work, love, fuck and get drunk, do narcotics and be happy and even make someone else happy sometimes. That's all but, hey, I'm asking for too much. The big dude was still snatching furtive glances. The other guy made his way across the street, dodging and pirouetting between the cabs like a ragged ballerina, marking me with his eyes other split second. He got to the kerb and squared up to me.

"You wanting something, mister?"

"I'm waiting for a buddy."

"A buddy? What the fuck are you, a frat-boy? I know what, I think you're a cop."

"Yeah, you're almost right. I used to be a cop but the thing is, I shot a nigger, yeah, one just like you and I got away with it but I quit the force before they fired me. You could say I retired undefeated. She was a teenager. She could have been your sister for all I fucking know. Now fuck off and leave me alone. I'll stand where the fuck I want, cocksucker."

I put my right hand into my pants as though I were packin'. He widened his eyes and slowly side stepped away.

"Fucking honky freak, if I see you around here again, I'll rip your fucking head off," he said.

"I look forward to it."

An honorable draw. I turned my collar up, hunched my shoulders against the sudden freeze of the evening, and added a few inches to my steps to get the fuck out of here as quickly as I could. At the corner of the block, I took a right and hot footed it like a Hasidic Jew in downtown Ramallah.

The faint noise of life from Michigan Avenue found my ears like a lost radio wave from an old-time radio station. Distant garbled voices, the slamming and screech of brakes, women's laughter. Everyone seemed to be happy and laughing. I wonder did they ever think that someday their laughter would suddenly stop and perhaps stop forever. No, but then nor did I.

I used to laugh like that too, just like those happy people. I hope they enjoy their night out, whoever they are. I try to stay positive and wish positive things. My old friend Buck Hartson told me that. I never met a happier man, always smiling, always a big 'Howyadoin' and a slap on the back that would knock the wind from the sails of a battleship. I knew fine rightly that it was only a front. We all did but what the hell. Sometimes a front is all we have to show the world what we've got. One afternoon his lovely wife Diane packed the family saloon with food, blankets and their two sons and set off to Elburn for an afternoon picnic. On the way there, a mile outside Charlestown, the car skidded, hit a tree and burst into a fireball.

They all got done to a crisp.

Buck never really got over that but always smiled and said stuff like it was God's will. I can't say I understood what he meant but I think it helped him to believe that. Later that year Buck was diagnosed with cancer of the neck of all places. "I've had good use of my brass neck all my life and its time God had it back." God did indeed take his neck back in December of that year. I miss Buck and his smiling spirit, no matter how broken it was.

I keep some of his spirit alive by trying to be like Buck. You may think what you will of heaven, God and all that shit but if you want to keep a dead man living, you dig up a memory of him and hold it. That's all I could do. But man, it was hard work being positive with only two dimes in my pockets, soaked to the skin and with nowhere to go. What gets me the most is not the discomfort but the feeling that I could go one step further and simply vanish and no one would notice.

I felt very tired from hard positive projection and sat down in the doorway of some building. It was called Harrison House. Good on you, Harrison, whoever the fuck you were. I sat down on one off the cold marble steps, the kind that numbs your ass after a minute, and fell asleep. Hours later, I had a dream about being caught in the rain. When I woke up, I found a stray dog pissing on my leg. I kicked him off and swore at him. You can't get more bum than that.

Time to make it back to the Lonesome Cove.

I needed to do some digging.

CHAPTER 9

The car lot looked almost as sorry as I was. How quickly the moss and weeds crack their way through their tarmac graves, their stalks and garish, bulbous heads bobbing about like vegetative zombies. Streetlights flickered and made buzzing noises like dying wasps. I thought they were all staring at me, wanting me, planning to move in unison towards me and devour me. The car lot was bathed in an unnatural, washed out, yellowish light. The delineations of the parking lines were fading, barely noticeable.

The motel stood at the other end. Its neon sign was switched off. It stood in total darkness, not a shadow of any other building or street lamp fell upon it as it was just a silhouette of blackness. Not a light lit anywhere inside. It looked like a skull that licked clean of meat. Any life that was in it had long since crawled out.

I made my way towards it. Broken glass twinkled on the ground outside its run-down facade. The sign said 'Open' but when I tried to open the door but it was locked. I knocked it a number of times but nothing. Not a sound came from within. I was conscious that this was a crime scene and, like a walking cliché, here I was walking straight back into it. I looked around, straining my ears as hard as I could for anything that sounded remotely human. Strewn garbage rolled along the ground, brushed by a broom of breeze.

I aimed my foot at the lock and gave it my best roundhouse kick. As soon as my foot made contact, I closed my eyes and covered my head to protect myself from a confetti cloud of flying glass

The door gave way. No dramatics. It surrendered quietly, glass and wood mostly intact. I held my breath, expecting a nest off screaming gun-toters rushing out from the darkness, pointing hollow metal tubes in my face.

I counted to ten before going in. The place was cold, damp and musty like the interior of a coffin. Despite the broken windows, fresh air hadn't kissed a surface or caressed the atmosphere inside for quite a while. It was only a matter of days since I had last been there, yet in some ways, it seemed like weeks, months even. I ran up to the front desk and banged the bell as hard as I could with the side of my fist.

"Ding."

The noise jarred, metal on metal. Its echoes stretched back and forth like feedback from a broken guitar. The echoes became echoes of themselves. Nothing else stirred in the building. As soon as I turned on the foyer lights, I saw those corridors again, snaking off into the distance from the foyer like dark spokes of the devil's wheel.

A red ledger sat on the desk along with a scatter of black biros. I picked the ledger up, blew the dust off and opened it. It was a typical hotel guestbook except that all the names in the book were the same and many entries were just squiggles. A cold stream of blood snaked through my veins. This was never a real motel. No one else stayed here. I flicked through the book and put it down and that's when I heard a noise. Yes, a noise. Something fell and clamored down the corridor.

I held my breath, hoping it was an animal. A soft thud, then the moist crispness of a peeling sound followed by another soft thud. This was no cat. It sounded like footsteps of feet in fancy new leather shoes. I wanted to call out but the words stuck in my throat, I felt them squash up against one another like a smoked-blinded crowd of panicking disco dancers, squeezing up against a locked fire escape that wouldn't open.

I turned and faced the main door. I locked my vision and soul to that door frame.

I ran.

Gunshots fired from behind but I didn't turn around. I ran the length of the car lot, my heart beating bass lines. The tempo was allegro. I found a corner and threw myself around it and ran and ran and ran, ducking down alleys and side streets, not caring where I ended up but I knew I had lost the gunman. They say history never repeats itself exactly but it sure does rhyme.

But this ain't no poetry. I had my misgivings about the motel from the very second I arrived that first night but I was blinded by the payday. I walked up Bryn Mawr and turned a right into an unnamed street and slithered my way down an alley behind all the restaurants. The cling and clang of kitchen pots and pans oozed into the night air like jazz-cymbals. Cooks, waiters and porters stood outside sucking in furtive cigarette smoke in long, cheek-hollowing drags before stepping back into the hot, steamy, noisy clamor within. They didn't seem to enjoy their smokes all that much, it was all against the clock.

I found a couple of dumpsters up the alley, a few buildings away. I climbed into one and hunkered down out of sight and tumbled over, not caring what shit was in there. I fell into a deep, deep sleep, almost hoping God in his mercy would pluck my weary soul from my worn-out body.

Then a voice

"Hey, buddy... you in there... can you hear me?"

The Final Testament of Tom Lockie

I killed a man back in '75 and every second since, he's been killing me. That's a lot off guilty seconds, each one a bear hug squeezing the last drop of breath outta me and I'm not sure if I can take it much more. Right now, I sit on a cracked red plastic chair with my elbows lampooned into at a desk in my motel room. A desk lamp flickers and there's a fly lopping around inside the lampshade. It's landing on and off the bulb and leaping off like a disco diva on a lava flow.

Condemned to never learn.

Condemned to forever burn.

But who the fuck am I to talk? I used to buzz around and make a lot of noise and burn my feet on a lot of hot water but what am I now but a nobody in the middle of nowhere.

Well I wish I was a nobody. A nobody would be hazing his brain on vodka and television and smiling like kid with socialisation issues. No, I wish I was a nobody. The trouble is, I am a someone and I did something unforgivable to another someone.

Someone you have heard off and will about to hear off again. Someone who's been long gone, long dead and long missing will soon be dug up and come to a Fox News Report in a television near you.

I have decided to commit what I know to paper. I used to be a writer once and I even rented a room in Andersonville, Chicago where I holed up every evening with my Olivetti, punching out reams and reams every night but five months later I fucked a girl I wasn't crazy about . Cue gunshot wedding. Her old man was a cop and I press ganged into becoming one too. My writing dream was over. I tried to write in the evenings but it didn't work out but no matter where I went, I took it with me, even though I never typed a word again.

Until tonight.

I opened the casing and there they were, all my old friends, the keys, the ribbon and the carriage return. I slipped a sheet of paper in and banged a few keys but the ink has long dried and the keys have seized but it looks almost brand new. There's nowhere open right now to fix it. I should take it somewhere in the morning to get it fixed up but I suspect I've used up my quota of mornings in this life.

So what shall I write about?

I had many scenarios in mind but not this one but hey, here I am. I have a pad of paper and a black biro. My biro can tap into the black caldrons of my soul and dredge up the dregs so that they dangle like noodles of shit from the nib.

The nib of the biro rips me open and I spill my guts on the pages. It feels good, the best I've felt in a long time. The more I write, the cleaner I become. I write and write and write for hours.

A bright yellow legal pad, a biro and a 75c bottle of Smirnoff Black Label are my final witnesses. I've had worse friends, believe me. I put down my pen and carefully stack the pages on the desk and I wait. I don't care who finds it. They can't touch me where I'm going. Then the room is darkened with shadow. I look up from my desk. A silhouette of man cuts out a shape from the curtain. He turns to face the window. He walks a little further. The night is so fucking still that I even hear the squeak of his shoe leather. Nice to think he bought a new pair of boots for the occasion. My gun is within reach.

I pick up and point it at the door.

The man stands still.

I remember that day way back in '75. I got up that morning an angel and went to bed a demon.

***

July 30, 1975. Jimmy Carter came to town that day, on the national prowl hunting for his nomination. But that's not the reason I remember it. Not many people remember that day, not even the most famous of peanut farmers.

But I do.

I remember it for darker reasons. Back then, the Chicago PD was in the pay of Johnny Friends. You heard of him?

Unless you hang with the wrong kind of people, then there's no earthly reason why your respectable JC Penny shopper would. Johnny Friends is a big noise in town. He runs the vice rings, escorts, call girls, dope, brothels. You name the pie, he has a dirty little finger wiggling in its gravy.

To some, he was a glad-handing businessman. Rotary Club big noise, presenting cheques to Southside neighbourhood community projects, always with a Sun Times and Tribune photographer in hand to capture the clammy handshakes. The big smiles, big ties, big cigars. They said he was Chicago mayor material. With this town's history, they certainly weren't wrong.

To those who knew his flip side, Friends was a pimp, drug pusher, death monger and long-standing friend of the Democratic Party in Cook County. They say he was Al Capone's bum-boy back in the good old days. He paid dollar-bricks to our top-brass who then shared it with more greedy cops in return for open ears and blind eyes. It was prototype trickle-down economics. Reagan would have been proud.

Once a month, Lieutenant Brewster would call us into his office, one by one, and wordlessly put a crisp, cold roll of cash into our top pockets. No eye contact, no idle chat. No one spoke about it.

A conspiracy of unspoken words. The first months of the arrangement were a period of vigilance. I was being slipped cash every week to keep me on side yet I wasn't doing anything but my normal duties. I expected some kind of big favour to be called in any minute. But the weeks turned into months and I lowered my guard and became more relaxed. The greenbacks

114

kept rolling in and I just sewed them into the fabric of my life. I was under no illusion. I wasn't the only horse Friends backed. He was doing this all over town as insurance. I knew one day I'd be picked for a special job for Friends but I prayed it wouldn't be anytime soon.

The Devil's lottery ticket as someone put it.

A cop's made peanuts back then. They still do. The extra $100 I got per month may have been bagel crumbs to him, but to me they were big, fat, glazed donuts with jelly in the middle. Funny how quickly you learn to acquire a sweet tooth, but a sweet tooth can lead a man into dark corners in the hot chase for that extra hit of candy. Some say Johnny Friends was in the pocket of Mayor Tom Daley. Some say Tom Daley was in Johnny's pocket. They were both so dark in heart and deep in pocket that it's hard to tell from a distance.

But I do know this much, to this very day their grubby little fingers are in a million rotten little pies around town. Cross them and you'll French kiss the meat grinder. If you were lucky, you'd be dead by the time your teeth hit the hydraulic iron pestles.

A mercy some didn't enjoy.

I know this for a fact. My turn came one day by accident. I pulled a jeep over for speeding down the Eisenhower Freeway. The jeep pulled over and rolled down the window. For such a shitty jeep, I was surprised to see Friends himself behind the wheel. No words were spoken. I mumbled an apology and told him to be on his way. The next day, Brewster called me in and slipped me $200 with a pat on the shoulder. Friends took note of my number that night. From that day onwards, I was earmarked for special jobs. At first, it was easy stuff that didn't break a sweat. I used to break into apartments and hotel rooms, plan bags of coke and give the Narc boys a tip off. Then things become more grisly.

The meat grinder. I'll never forget the first time. I pushed down on their kicking, thrashing feet. I wish it was possible to close your ears as easily as you can close your eyes. I never thought it possible for a human to make the sounds I heard that afternoon. No matter how hard I try to forget, I fail. I can never be good again, not knowing what I know and doing what I have done. Redemption is not a destination. It's a thin line. Cross it and it disappears forever.

I was called in for meat-grinder duty several times. You just switch off your conscience and get the job done but some switches can never be turned back on. I closed my eyes to pity and over the space of that year, I grew colder, harsher to everything in my life. I stopped laughing, I stopped smiling. The lightness of my youthful heart had evaporated in the heat of horror and formed a dark cloud that rained on me ever since.

You can only kill a man once but you can kill a soul often. A year later, I had a breakdown. Every time I looked up God's skirts I found the Devil there giving him a blow job. I learned that every time I tried to get up and get back into the light, I just slipped and fell ever harder on the ground. Then I gave up getting up and threw in my lot with Friends. I was a failed angel and I was sick of failure. It was then I decided to go over to the other side.

I impressed him. He made me an offer and I took it. The Devil took me to the cliff top and a splendid kingdom lay before me. The Devil told me it could be mine. Money, houses, girls, the lot. I grabbed it all with both hands. I soon learned that things glitter more brightly in the dark. I was a Prince in this newfound kingdom of mayhem, greed and squalor but I soon found out that no sun ever rose over that kingdom. As for the glitter, well, those were tricks of the light.

Each one a rhinestone-studded tombstone.

That morning in '75, I was asked to kill a man. Tomorrow never comes, the song says, but today sure as hell can arrive as quick and as welcome as the hangman's knock on a metal door at sunrise. I knew the victim. He was no nameless, chinless wonder. Jimmy Hoffa, top dog of the Teamsters Union of America. You've heard of him, right? I bet you have and for all the wrong reasons. He was a man from the TV screen, the radio and the papers. My job was to drive him to an out-of-town beauty spot where he would be taken care off.

At the time, my partner Callum McCambridge and I had just been made detectives basked in the delight of losing the uniforms and wearing our own threads. I got to admit that we oozed style.

A lot of style. I bought two, sometimes three suits a month not to mention countless Van Heusen shirt and other designer labels whose names I've forgotten. That kinda habit oozed a lot of cash too. We were working on our first assigned case, a missing person. Fifteen-year-old Lucilita Marriot had left her Evanston home around 5pm on Wednesday July 5th to visit her friend in Andersonville and hadn't been seen since. She was a bright kid, good at school, and never got into trouble. In fact, she was a model daughter and a face in her church and school hockey team.

A nice kid from a respectable home. I love that phrase 'respectable home'. It's code for God-fearing, black-fearing rich white folks.

But all wasn't as it seemed.

It seldom is.

We interviewed all her friends and teachers. One friend stuck out. Gabriella Kingston, Lucilita's best friend, didn't seem all that upset. Sure, she cried in all the right places but there was something missing. By that time, I had many a date with the meat mincer and I knew what a faked conscience looked like. I looked like mine.

"You're really scaring me"

It's to do with them not wanting to talk to you a second time. Her other friends were only too eager to be interviewed and some even came forward with new information, albeit useless. Gabriella was hesitant. She was aggressive when we interviewed her a second time to confirm details of her story about the last time she saw Lucilita.

"I've already gone over this a hundred times, what the hell do you want from me". A common refrain.

Liars don't like to go over old ground. Their tracks are unbeaten and they lose their way a second time. Liars sweat, liars lash out, liars fold their arms. It sounds corny I know but it's true. Those tells are a cop's best friend.

Apart from his gun.

The next day, McCambridge went to visit her again after school and took her for a ride to Skokie. McCambridge told her that he knew that she knew the truth, but unless she told him what she knew, she would be arrested and get a ten-stretch for wasting police time. None of this was true and McCambridge bent the rules sometimes until they formed a u-bend. Strictly speaking, he kidnapped a minor and threatened her in the course of duty but it worked. I doubt cops have those tricks up their sleeves these days.

McCambridge's gamble paid off. His derrick struck a gusher..

Our girl-most-likely-to-succeed-but-who-went-AWOL turned out to be girl-most-likely-to-fuck-her-father's-golf-buddy-in-St Louis. Lucilita was having an affair, or should I say, a fuck-fest with this guy Scott Parker. He had just taken a two-month sabbatical from his job in First Bank of Illinois where he told everyone he was going to Seattle to look after his terminally-ill brother.

Only that there was no brother and no trip to Seattle .

He was holed up in a lousy motel in Libertyville, forty miles north on Milwaukee Avenue, waiting on Lucilita to show. That morning, McCambridge and I planned going to drive there, surprise them both and like a bad movie, make the world right again at the very end.

Ok, we should have told the Libertyville sheriff's office but we wanted this collar ourselves.

Our first one as detectives.

The sweetest scalp.

But life took a different turn for us that morning. I was at my desk around 9am, drinking coffee, typing up a report with two crooked index fingers punching the shit out off my typewriter when Lt Brewster called us in. He opened his office door, stood at the doorway.

"Lockie, McCambridge, this way please"

McCambridge and I looked at one another.

118

"What the fuck's with the 'please'" said McCambridge. Brewster was a man whose idea of courtesy was taking a shit with the door shut. We got up and did what the man asked and stepped into his office.

We stood by his desk. The muted noise of traffic and trains whispered in our ears. Ghostly plumes of cigar smoke hung in the air like rumours.

"Gentlemen," he said, weaving his fingers together into the shape of a church steeple. "A certain acquaintance of ours needs two men to help him get rid of a problem."

We remained silent, waiting for elaboration. Brewster coughed and sat forward.

"But we gave him information already, what else could he want?" I asked, as if I didn't know.

"What do you think he pays us for, uh? So he wants to know who was in the drunk tank last night? Whose hand was caught up whose skirt? You knew that men like Friends keep coming back for more. You both knew that. It's the unspoken arrangement. He fed us a very long big fat worm and now he's yanking on the line and he wants his little fishes to dance on his little dishes. Me included."

He slurped from his chipped mug of black coffee and sucked hard on his cigar.

"Let's just hope its quick." Brewster added

"What does he want?" asked McCambridge.

Brewster reached into his desk drawer, wheezing on a cigar that was down to the stub, ashes crumbling into his coffee mug. He pulled out a brown manila folder, slapped it down on the table and opened it. There was only one thing in that folder, a photograph of a man.

We both looked at who it was.

We recognised him.

We wished we didn't.

Christ.

"I presume you need no introduction," said Brewster.

"Fuck me," said McCambridge, "is that...?"

Brewster lowered his head for a second. "Yes, Cal, the one and only, Mr James Hoffa."

"What the fuck did he do?" Cal asked.

"All we need to know is that he pissed on Johnny's blue suede shoes and Johnny likes his shoes, and when you piss on Johnny's shoes, he cuts your Hubert off, sticks it down your throat and watches it choke you to death before taking it out and using it as a dildo to fuck your mother with. Jimmy Hoffa pissed on Johnny's shoes. End of. That's what usually leads to men's mug shots ending up in brown folders just like this one," he said, stabbing it with his right index finger.

"Sir, where do we come into this?"

"Johnny wants you both to drive to his house, wash his windows and trim his hedgerows. His gardener's sick and he could do with a couple of extra hands. What the fuck do you think he wants? He wants you to collect our friend Mr Hoffa and drive him to a place of peace and solitude. You don't need me to fill in the blanks," Brewster said, chewing the end of his cigar, now little more than a stub of dark ash wearily defying gravity.

We both stood silent, cold as stone. It was a warm summer's day, the heat was in the nineties, the air-con was stuttering and I felt my shirt cling to my back, but a shard of frost drilled right through me, from the top of my skull to the pit of my stomach. I looked over at McCambridge, his face was as white as a Klansman's ass.

"The itinerary," said Brewster. He cleared his throat, lit a fresh cigar with the dying embers of the old one and took another gulp of coffee.

"Firstly, you drive to 3845 South Wallace, on the Southside for 11am. Park outside. Open and close your driver's-side window four times. That's the signal. One of Johnny's people will come out. Whoever is in the front passenger side, make way for Johnny's man and get in the back. No fuss, no chitchat, no questions. That's what you do. Then you drive to The Lodge at 22 West Division."

"That shithole, what for?" I asked.

Brewster put his cup down and stared, not at me but into me.

"Because that's where Mr Hoffa will be eating his eggs and grits. You drive behind the joint, you'll find a private car lot. Park in the far corner next to the red dumpsters. I have it on good authority that it's one of the few parts of the city that cannot be seen from any window in the city view, a blind spot in other words."

"Did Johnny get someone to find this little fact out?" I asked, putting one hand on my hip.

"I do believe he did," Brewster replied. "Stay there. Wait for Johnny's man to return with Hoffa. For instructions thereafter, you listen to Johnny's man."

"Does Johnny's man have a name?"

"Yes, he's called 'Johnny's Man'. His momma named him after his uncle, 'Johnny's Man'. Any other questions?

I think we both caught that particular drift.

Brewster threw a pair of car keys at Cal. Cal just about caught them.

"Those are for the brown Javelin Fastback Coupe that's in the car lot two blocks up from here. You take that. I don't care who drives it but you better go now."

We all looked at the clock.

"What about the missing girl? We know where's she holed up" said McCambridge

"Oh really? Nice work, pass the details to uniform and they'll pick her up"

"But sir, it's my arrest, first one as Detective. I've broken my neck working this case"

"You'll get a second one if you don't hop to it. Go"

We had no choice but to leave and made our way out to the car-lot as instructed. We found the Javelin and tossed a coin for the privilege of driving. I chose heads and won, if winning is the right word for it.

"What kind of coin is this?" I looked at it closely. *" It's got two heads, not one. What the hell"* I said.

"Oh, that's what's known as a twenty-cent piece," said Cal. *"It was given to me by my granddaddy. He worked in a coinage mint in Carson City, Nevada, way back in the 1870s. It's a rarity and my lucky charm. I never lose by it."*

"But if you knew the coin had two heads, why didn't you call heads yourself?"

"There are some games that are just worth losing, my friend," he said.

I smiled at his candour. I didn't know him that well but I warmed to Cal from that moment. We got into the car and drove to the first destination at South Wallace.

*

"It's also called a Liberty Dollar."

"What is?" I asked.

"The coin. There's only a handful around."

"You're shitting me! Fuck, that's valuable. You could sell that and get out of all this."

"Perhaps all this is what I really want."

"What, driving men we don't hate to their heads turned to pulp?

"We're supposed to be cops, protecting people, not this." I replied.

"Don't you know there are two sets of laws at play at any one time?" Cal said. "One for the tipper and one for the coupon clipper. We've always known that. I don't like it anymore than you do, but if it weren't us, it would be some other schmucks. Let's just get there and get this over and done with." He paused. "When we take royalty payments in advance from the Devil, then we shouldn't be surprised when we see the shadow of his horns fall on our porches."

I felt that I had tuned into one of Billy Graham's more elegiac sermons.

"After this," Cal continued, "I'm leaving the force. I've made my 30 pieces of silver. Let's just clear our heads, get on with it, forget it and move on. There's no other way."

We jumped into the car. I remember Cal taking a deep breath before switching on the ignition. Something like that stays with you. You never forget being a horseman to someone else's apocalypse.

Wordlessly, we weaved through the city traffic. Everything was flowing strangely well that morning, no red light. Green all the way. We drove through downtown and it wasn't long until we left the opulence behind, making our way into the badlands of Chicago's South Side. Run-down shack-houses with shoals of kids teeming around the sidewalks, families sitting on steps sharing jokes and telling stories or staring into space. People seemed to smile a lot more back then. Cars quietly rusted in driveways, boarded windows, tracts of demolished streets with only broken bricks remaining, strewn like the aftermath of a cataclysm that had been frozen in time.

South Wallace was one long street. We drove straight past Kevin's Hamburger Heaven and pulled up outside the The Lodge. It was a three-storey red brick tenement that stood out amongst the bungalows. I looked up and saw only one air-con unit stuck inside a window pane on the top floor, upper left corner. I figured that must be where Johnny's man was.

Cal opened and closed the window four times. On the fourth count, the door of the building opened. A well-dressed white man in a light blue suit and open-necked white shirt ran out towards the car. He jumped into the backseat. No greetings. Just cold business.

We turned around and headed back into town towards West Division.

We drove up North Clark then hung a left on Dempster. Minutes later we pulled up outside The Lodge. It was a dive bar with peeling shamrock decals stuck on the inside windows. I remembered cuffing a dude outside here about four years earlier. Illegal alien, Irish and drunk, he had punched the lights out of his equally drunken Puerto Rican girlfriend. I'll never know why they come over here just to cry into their beer about missing the hills of Kerry. I felt sorry for him. So far from home. Imagine that, travelling half a world to pine for something he probably didn't give a shit about in the first place. I guess that's the human condition. Green fields are only ever green when seen from a distance.

The Lodge hadn't changed much. The shop front boasted a yellow canopy emblazoned with the name 'The Lodge'. Leprechauns and shamrocks and other aspects of Paddy-whackery adorned the bird-shit and dust-stained windows. But still, under the circumstances, I would have gladly swapped what we were doing just to spend an afternoon inside shooting pool with dudes with names like Gus, Shauny, Chuck or Butch.

We drove around the corner and into the car lot behind the bar and parked at the dumpsters in the far corner as directed.

"Stop here," Johnny's Man said.

Johnny's Man got out and went to the back door of The Lodge and knocked. A fat sweaty man opened it holding a cigarette. He took a draw and threw it on the ground and squished it with his right foot. Both men then went in, closing the door behind them.

Cal and I waited in the car for a few minutes until the back door of 'The Lodge' opened again. Johnny's Man came out, this time with another guy, a well-dressed, middle-aged man being frogmarched towards our car.

"Holy shit, do you know who that is? It's Jimmy Hoffa."

I shook my head.

"That's what the man said. It's Jimmy Hoffa alright. Too bad my brother paid his union dues last week."

I looked in the rear-view mirror and saw Johnny's man whip out a pistol from inside his jacket and whacked Hoffa's head so hard he dropped like a stone to the ground. Johnny's Man walked around to Cal's side and knocked on the window, his finger-ring clinking the glass.

"Open the trunk."

Cal got out and opened the trunk. Hoffa was bundled into it and Johnny's friend jumped into the back seat.

"Where to now?" I asked. The words broke the thick but brittle silence.

"Fuck, do you guys hate breathing? It's hot as hell in here, open your fucking windows." He lit a cigarette and we opened our windows. I felt a nervous breeze move through the car.

"You know where Des Plaines is?" he added. "North of the city. Good cruisin' ground so the cops tell me".

McCambridge formed fists, I grabbed him arm and gave them a 'calm the fuck down" made eyes. His fists became fingers but he was mad. He couldn't take a joke and that was his biggest problem.

"I go there with my wife" I replied.

"Well good for you Mr Wife. Well that's where we're going, Des Plaines. How about Mr Angry make a move before the shit sack in the trunk wakes up"

Cal bit his lower lip, started the engine and we went on our way.

We peeled our way through downtown Chicago on that clammy July Friday afternoon, towards the Kennedy Expressway where the traffic swept us north to Des Plaines, a popular beauty spot, a nice place for a picnic for people who are able to sleep at night.

For all his wisecracks at the start, Johnny's Man didn't talk much on the way. It suited me just fin,

On the Kennedy Expressway, I heard banging noises, dull thuds from the trunk.

"Hey turn the fucking radio on, I don't wanna hear that fucking corpse rattling around back there."

I flicked the radio on, set the station to Rock FM and upped the volume to max but I still heard Hoffa rolling and a reeling in his motorised morgue.

It was the hottest day, well over a hundred, and even the tarmac broke a sweat but I was cold. I then heard his moans from the trunk. He must have known. What the hell would that feel like? Knowing you're never going to see another sunrise, see your wife, kids or go to sleep in your own bed ever again. Never seeing the Sox lose or score a whore ever again.

I wished I hated him. I wished he was a rapist. That would have helped me hate him and helped me justify my role but I didn't hate him. He didn't do me no wrong and there I was, complicit in the death of a man I didn't hate.

Hoffa.

He was a bit of a wise guy, a little too big for his boots and had a big mouth. He rubbed some sensitive but brutal people up the wrong way. He did some jail time and had just been released. According to some, the spooks in the CIA had bugged his every word and smelt every shit he took. When get out, he was a spent force in the union, younger fitter men sat on his empty throne and liked the feel of it. Hoffa, being the stubborn soul he was, refused to accept the new realities and refused to bow out gracefully. The CIA though he's get the message but a man like that is a broken radio that only transmits and never receives. They had words with him but still no go. The CIA had their own men, new men in place and that's how they wanted it but the clown in chief still wanted to be the big swinging dick of the flying trapeze. He made noise and stomped his feet but what the spooks didn't reckon on was that Hoffa still held sway, not vital sway but enough to throw grit into the engine oil.

They gave him one last chance, even offered him a pay off so he could retire to Orlando or some other sunny graveyard of rich white twitchers. He laughed in their poker faces and told them to suck his dick. Spooks don't like being told to suck dick and to cut a long story short, Hoffa ended up in a trunk of a car driven by cops to his final repose.

I felt every car that we passed knew our secret. I distinctly remember the car in front at one point. It was a red Pontiac saloon. Three kids in the back and Mom and Pops in the front.

I wished I was like them.

Decent, honest, able to sleep at night. We drove on the same road, the same lane, but the two cars couldn't have been going in more different directions. I imagined them laughing, singing, playing spot the yellow car in that Pontiac. No smell of man-shit in that car, only the smell of women and children. In our car, death, men's sweat and a dying man's shit and whimpers. Yes, he had laid a good length of cable in his pants when we took him out.

At another point, I spotted highway patrol in my rear view mirror. I slowed down and cranked the volume down and tried to act ordinary. The patrol man sped up and positioned himself beside us. I looked at him. He pointed a gloved finger to the lay by. My heart nearly stopped. Johnny's Man told us to flash our badges and not give any backchat.. Cal leant across my knee and flashed his badge. The patrol man nodded and saluted us before spiking off to another lane and vanishing into the traffic.

I glanced into my rear view mirror again. I saw Johnny's Man, his hand was on his lap, tapping his fingers on the business end of his Browning P-35. I had no doubt to what Plan B would have been had the badge trick didn't make the road rat disappear.

Several miles ahead, I exited the freeway at 91N and continued north onto Milwaukee Avenue. Twenty minutes later, we reached Des Plaines. I drove through the town and a mile or so northeast, pulled into the forest preserve. A couple of cars were parked in the lay-by near the entrance and a couple of oldsters were walking their pooches. I revved up and snaked my way deeper into the grove and found a until I found a quiet spot.

"You can kill the engine" Johnny's Man grunted.

I eased up to the far corner and came to a stop.

Johnny's Man reached over from the back and dropped a Rugar on my lap.

"That ones yours. Now get out."

We all got out. Cal and I stood by the doors. Johnny's Man went around the back and beckoned me over to the trunk

"Go ahead, Mr Wife, make some holes"

I knew he wasn't talking about a paint job.

"He's staying inside? Aren't we taking him out first?"

Johnny's Man sniggered.

"And why would we do that? To give him a chance to knee us in the nuts and make a break for it? I like it nice and simple"

"What if he survives?" I asked.

Johnny's Man smiled and lit a cigarette.

"He'll wish he hadn't" he replied, smoke billowing through every loop of every vowel that squeezed through the thin of his lips.

I pointed my Rugar at the trunk. It was a hand cannon I was familiar with from my academy firing practice days but I hadn't used one in a while but one hand gun is much like another, same as cars. I heard moans and man rolling around under the hood. I could tell he was trying to bunch himself up in the lower right hand corner of the trunk, hoping I'd empty the chamber into the middle. I could no longer bear the muffled screams and frantic thrashing of limbs. I didn't want to kill him but he'd die one way or another. I knew exactly what would happen if he survived. There would be no grind of tyres outside the Emergency room to dump him at the doors before screeching off. He's be taken to one off Johnny's secret outhouses and be fed into the mincer. He had to die in the trunk. The alternative was too gruesome to contemplate. The sound of bones and blood freezing screams from the grinder teeth is something from hell itself.

I turned to Cal and the goon and told them to keep quiet. I bent down and pressed my ear to the hood. I forgot how fucking hot it was as it nearly seared my skin to the paintwork. I walked around the front and removed a bottle of Evian from the glove box. I walked back to the trunk and poured water over the metal to cool it down. Cal and the goon furrowed their faces. I could tell they were thinking 'what the fuck is he doing'. I then pressed my ear again to the same spot and listened. Hoffa shad stopped moving but I could him moan and I could tell from where it came from. I took a few steps back and aimed my Rugar in the direction of the moans. I slid the silencer on with my free hand and I wrapped my right index finger around the trigger and emptied the barrel. The trunk was now like a giant cheese grater. A trickle of blood seeped from the undercarriage and dribbled onto the ground, forming a growing pool of deep purple. The pool stopped growing and with the heat of the day, it finally seeping into the dusty soil. It was as close to a funeral as Hoffa was ever going to get.

Johnny's Man opened the trunk. Hoffa's head was a pulverised bag of eye, bone, and raw tissue. Johnny's man had another trick up his sleeve, almost literally. He reached into his jacket and fished out a cardboard tube. He popped it open and stuck his fingers inside and scooped out a roll of paper. He flattened it out on the roof. Cal and I craned our necks to see what it was. It was a set of 'I'm Voting Nixon' decals from the last election.

"You didn't think we'd take this to the cruncher with this looking like a salad shaker did you?"

129

He then covered the trunk with all the Dick Nixon decals on the sheets, hiding all the holes. You may think this would have made the car stand out but not in those parts. It was three years since the election but Nixon was the son of Jesus to many in upstate Illinois and his election stickers and decals were the forerunners of furry dice. I threw Cal the keys and we got in. Cal reversed the car so that the trunk faced away from the road in case strangers arrived. We waited in the car till sundown, sweltering in the heat. Twenty minutes after sundown, around 930pm we drove to a Dusty's Scrap Metal yard where we dumped the car and watched it being cubed, Hoffa and all. Another car was waiting for us. Tinted windows, unusual back then but they did exist. That was our ride back into the city.

*

That was a long time ago. A lot of dark, bloody water has flowed under a lot of broken bridges, but the stink of what I did that day still clings to my soul like a stinking shadow that I can't shake. Now, I sit in a room, drapes drawn shut, closing out the light of the moon. Dust lies on table top, booze bottles and cigarette butts kicked to the corners.

This room is me and I am this room.

I don't deserve the light anymore for it's never shone from me, not for a long time. Cal and I met up by chance not that long ago. He told me he's on the run, killed a gut in some motel room out by Elston. Lonesome Cove I think it was. I didn't have the guts to tell him that he was right, he didn't kill no one because it was me, me hiding the shadows that night, handing Madigan a brick of cash to set him on the way down the river Styx. I didn't know Cal was to be fall guy. I'm just a hit man. I'm paid to hit and run. I forgot to introduce myself, Thomas Wilbur Lockie.

There's a knock on the door. I put drink down.

There's a knock on the door.

And a kick of foot on frame.

I lift my Glock. I coil my finger around the trigger.

CHAPTER 10

"Don't I recognize you, mister?"

I opened my eyes and grappled for the mattress but there was no mattress, just a jumble of stinking garbage bags and empty tins. The sun hit my eyes and made me squint. I rubbed them and focused on the pretty blonde.

"Pardon me?" I said

"You're that private eye, aren't you? My, it is you. I always remember a face"

I gripped the side of the dumpster and flung myself over. I didn't land full square on the ground and keeled over, hitting the wall with my left shoulder. A shot of pain whistled through my ankles. The lady held out her hands. I wiped my paws on my shirt tails, just about the least filthy article of clothing to my name. I grabbed her hands and she helped up.

"I guess if you were a cop, I'd be in cuffs right now"

"Mister, I ain't no cop" she said. "You helped my sister Sally a few years ago, that time she was being stalked by her ex husband, the psycho ex marine from Phoenix? I remember you. You did a good job. Sally still talks about you"

"I see," I said. I looked at her but for the life of me I couldn't remember who she was. "Well, all part of the service, just doing my job...you know it's not a smart thing to be seen talking to you. I could land you in a whole lotta trouble if anyone found you talking to me. You're better just turning me in, you know, to keep you right"

"What do you mean '*turn you in*'? Did you do something bad and wild last night?"

"I have to beg your pardon, but as you may have noticed, I've a lot on my mind recently. I remember you too but I'm not as good with names as I used to be. It's been a long life."

"Tammy, Tammy Southworth and yes, I have heard that the police want to question you, over something to do with a dead actor in some hotel? I'm sorry; I didn't want to freak you out"

I fumbled for my rolling papers and dissected a Marlboro Light and scattered some of its dried innards along the full length of the paper. I breathed on it a couple of times to moisten it and rolled it into a little tube. I stuck it between my lips and lit it but the flame shot down the entire length, burning up the tobacco in one shot. I couldn't be bothered to repeat the process so I lit my spare Marlboro and sucked some smoke.

."If you buy me a coffee, a hot dog stuffed with mustard and jalapenos, and a bowlful of French fries, I'll tell you what really happened. Say, this ain't a place for a young lady? Don't you have a nice, warm bed and a rich man to go home to? Are you just slumming it to see how the other half lives"?

"I do voluntary work for a homeless charity and today's my turn. I walk up alleys talking to guys like you, giving out soup and coffee. And I found you, right here. This is on my route"

"Well how about that?" I said. "Let me guess, you do have a warm bed but no man to go home to. If you had, you wouldn't be here. You know, in my experience people who do great evil or great good have one thing in common"

"What's that?" she asked

"They sleep alone"

"Excuse me!"

"Yeah, I'm just an old cynical bum. What you're doing is really cool, yeah, big up for you but there's a lot of dangerous weirdoes in alleyways these days or hasn't your momma told you? I bet she'd freak if she found out"

"I guess we both have a secret"

I swore I heard my skin crack when I smiled at her.

132

"I think I can trust you enough to take you home for a wash, change of clothes and a pizza. What do you say?"

"It sounds a little too good to be true but yeah, I'll go with it. But Tammy, this ain't a game. I'm a wanted man"

"Don't worry, I've figured it out. I'll tell them you held me hostage. They'll believe my side of the story"

I wagged a finger at her. "You're too cute"

We laughed.

Tammy called a cab from her cell-phone.

"Won't your friends wonder where you are?"

"That's my look-out. I'll tell them I met an old friend and had to go home, that's all."

"Will they buy it?"

"It's the only can on the shelf, they have to buy it"

Tammy reached into her knapsack and threw me a bottle of water and some alcohol hand gel.

"Run that through your hair and over your face. I've a black poncho in here too to cover you up. Once you're done, I've a can of Axe to spray on you. You don't want the cab driver kicking us out when your BO hit his nose"

I took the water and hand-gel and washed my hair, face and hands as best I could. I hadn't shaved in days but at least I looked no worse than a drunk who crashed at his buddies overnight. Tammy sprayed Ax all over me but I couldn't help thinking that instead of smelling of shit, I now smelled of shit and perfume. She handed me a black poncho and I hauled it over my head and wriggled it down my sides. It covered my body and finished just above my knees.

A minute later, a cab pulled up and we jumped in.

"Kingston and Dubrovnik."

Nice neighborhood.

I caught the cab drivers face in his rear-view mirror. His look lingered. I noticed his screwed up face, the look of concentration. I tried my best not to let it spook me. He revved up and we sped though the Chicago nightscape back to Tammy's. I looked at her face. It was perfect, smooth like a lake of cream. Her smile wasn't something she forced. It seemed to be her default expression. Such a sun shone from within her heart. I prayed that life wouldn't jade her. I wanted to hold her hand but I didn't think it appropriate.

Police cars whizzed past us several times on the way, making me a little jumpy but I held onto my nerves and stayed calm. Tammy popped some perfume that smelled of citron and rose several times on the way to hide my ripeness as much as possible.

I huddled down, kept quiet, said nothing and waited till we arrived at Tammy's.

CHAPTER 11

I shaved with a lady-shave, showered, took a shit and toweled myself dry before getting into a blue dressing gown. It fitted me just fine but I guessed it must have belonged to some boyfriend as it was way too big for a little thing like Tammy.

Tammy lived in a second-floor two bed condo off Peterson Road, Oak Ridge. She had good taste, if not a little hippyish for my liking. The walls were covered in mock Aztec throws and bead curtains hung where the doors should have been. The pad was dimly lit with side lamps. The scent of patchouli and sage-smoke made me feel a little giddy. In the lounge there was a blue futon and a two lime green chalk-painted step ladders stood on either side of the window, serving as shelving for tidily stacked books and an assorted of cutely knick-knacks, curios and ornaments. I walked to the ladders and browsed the books. It was a mix of second-hand vegetarian cookbooks, poetry and paperback novels. Three Tim O'Brien hardbacks stood on the top rung. The girl was smart. Her intellect had a wide range.

Tammy returned from her bedroom and threw a bathrobe and bag of fresh clothes and a black garbage liner on the futon.

"Sorry, last season's fashion. It's all I got left. Wanna a coffee? I've a fresh pot on the go"

"Sure, I could use a coffee" I said. Tammy disappeared into the kitchen, making the bead curtains chime like a plastic glockenspiel with cats on the keys. I took off my bathrobe and got into my new outfit. An ironed navy blue shirt, two black tees, a pair of dark Levi's, four pairs of black socks and a pair of black trainers with a red stripe running along the soles and a casual brown blouson and a Cubs baseball cap. I got into my new clothes. I felt like a new man having clean freshly ironed threads on my skin. It was almost as good as making love under silk sheets. The clothes fitted me perfectly. She must have had a wardrobe to dress stray dogs of all shapes and sizes in there. She guessed my size on the button as she never asked me the size of my neck, length of leg or width of my waist.

I put my old rags into the trash bag which I put beside the futon. Tammy returned a minute later and handed me a cup of coffee in a giant yellow mug with the word 'Cappuccino' wrapped around the glazing.

"Take a seat" she said, gesturing towards the futon. We down sat together. It was small futon and we took up the entire length. We took silent sips as our knees brushed together which made me brew a boner. I hadn't been this close to a woman for a while.

"I don't know who to trust." I tumbled those words out like badly-thrown dice, not knowing how they'd land on the baize.

"You can trust me. You helped me before, remember?"

"I was only doing my job. You paid me, I hope." I threw a smile at her. She smiled back at me for a second before casting her eyes over at the ladders by the window.

"True but I still want to help you."

"I'm very grateful but I still don't understand"

She looked me intently. "I think you're innocent, that's why"

"How do you know I'm innocent?" I took another sip of coffee.

Her smile vanished from her now pursed lips. Oh oh.

"Do you want me to think you're guilty?" she asked.

That shut me up. I nodded and took a few more sips of coffee to think up a conciliatory reply.

"The truth is, Cal, I really don't give a damn if you killed the boy or not. If you did, you probably had good reason but if you didn't kill him, well, that's one helluva sticky wicket"

"Sticky what?"

"Oh, I'm sorry. It means deep shit. I once lived in England for an Erasmus year during college. I dated a boy who was obsessed with cricket. Sticky wicket, it's a cricketing term I picked up. Sorry"

"I see. Tammy, I'm a bit older than you and I've been around the block so often that I think I know each of the bricks by name. I just don't want you getting into trouble. If anyone finds out I'm here, you'll be in just as much a sticky whats-it as I am. We both need to be careful, you especially"

Tammy grabbed my left hand. "Cal, change the record. I've been around too. I know how the world works and don't think I did think without my two eyes being wide open. No more stupid talk. You're here right now. We get a good night's sleep and tomorrow we put our heads together and think up your next move"

I squeeze her hand. My boner got a little harder. I crossed my legs and starting thinking of Newt Gingrinch. That usually kills the ardor. It worked like it always did.

"Don't mind my asking Tammy but have you done this kind of thing before?"

"What help killers on the run? No, not recently"

I held my hands up, palms outwards.

"Well, I'm all yours honey"

Tammy squeezed my hand and let go and patted my leg before taking a gulp from her mug.

I took out a squished soft pack of Marlboro Lites from my shirt pocket and pinched out a cigarette.

"You don't mind if I…." I asked, waving it apologetically in the air like a sorry wand.

"Usually I do mind but under the circumstances, I'll give you a special dispensation. I'll have to burn some oil to kill the smell"

I thanked Tammy and lit my cigarette. She got up and lit a tea-light candle under the oil burner that sat on a little square coffee table in the middle of the floor. It seemed to draw a line under the conversation. I had to learn to let things go. This dame wanted to help, pure and simple. God knows I'd run a four-minute mile away from myself had I been her. But I wasn't her.

"Well, what can I say, Tammy? I promise not to cause you any trouble"

She smiled. "You all say that."

"All? All of us fugitives?"

She chuckled. "So funny" she said before returning to the futon. She lay back, cradled the back of her head with intertwined fingers. I drew long deep smoke into my lungs and gazed at the side of her face and the outline of her legs under her thin black dressing gown.

"Despite appearances, Tammy, I do have money but I can't do it. I keep a number of cash deposits in vaults all over town. All legit but none in my name. In the morning, I need you to go to one of my boxes and bring me the contents. I'll throw in a finder's fee as a thank you. Just think of me as one of those old Russian dukes who has lost his horse in a strange land and your job is to help me find my way back to the castle. Who knows, I may even make you my lady". Tammy looked at me and I threw her a wink.

"Sure, Cal, I can do that. Just give me the address and pass codes and shit. See? It's starting to work already. I knew we could put you back on your feet, the two of us I just knew it"

She held up her right hand for a high-five. I prefer handshakes myself but young people seem to be into shit like this. I reluctantly lifted my left hand and we slapped palms in mid air.

"First, you have to go to the branch off Chase Manhattan on Weston and Fourth. Ask the nice lady at the desk to take you to the deposit boxes. Once there, she'll leave you alone. You'll get into the box by keying in a pass number which I'll write down for over breakfast. The door opens and you have two seconds to enter. It's a huge iron-wrought monster, as thick as a battle ship. It slams itself shut behind you. Then you'll see a second door. You key in a second pass code then it opens too. You've ten seconds to enter. You now find yourself in pitch darkness but don't freak out. The lights then come on slowly until it's as bright as the sun. You will see a bunch of silver lockers lined all along the walls. Small ones, big ones. My stash is in the big lockers, the small lockers contain keys to the big ones. My small locker is row three, column fourteen. The big locker is row seven, column twenty-two."

"You a math buff or something?"

"Why you ask?"

"Small locker row three, column fourteen. That's 3.14, pi. And row seven, column twenty-two. You get pi by dividing seven into twenty-two. Neat."

"It never occurred to me."

"Come on, sure it did."

She was now playful. I liked the way she sprinkled the air with giggles, the way she flicked her head back and fixed her cowlick curl with her hand.

"So, Cal, tell me what happened, the whole thing, the whole deal, from start to finish"

I finished my smoke and threw the stub in the mug. It hissed when it hit the puddle of lukewarm coffee that swished along the bottom of it.

"This needs something stronger than this" I said, holding my coffee up.

"I kinda got the feeling it would" she said. She went to the kitchen and came back with a bottle of Johnny Walker and two tumblers. She laid the glasses on the coffee table next to the oil burner and filled them to the brim. She handed me mine. I lit another cigarette and took a swig of whiskey. I almost felt it rush up into my head. A livener.

"I have to warn you it's a long story" I said.

She tugged at her ear lobes and widened her eyes.

"Look! Long ears for long stories"

I gave her chapter and verse. Her expression became stonier and stonier as the story progressed, each twist in the tale, a nail in my coffin. She took quicker and longer sips as I regaled her with the details.

***

"And then you found me in a dumpster the rest they say is history"

"Fuck," she said.

"Yeah, that just about sums it up alright," I said.

"So once you get your money tomorrow, when then?"

"The motel. I need to find out who owns or rents and work things out from there."

"It sounds like someone fronted it," she said.

"They probably did but it shouldn't be too hard to find them and get them to talk There's always a paper trail for fronts."

"Finding them is one thing. What if they don't talk?"

I took a long suck at the amber.

"I've my ways and means"

I could tell from her eyes when Tammy looked at me at that moment, she'd stopped seeing a loser and started seeing a fighter, someone whose shadow would cover her with shade from the heat of her boredom.

"You better write down the pass codes before I forget them, mister."

I tore a page from the pad that sat next to the cordless phone on the floor beside my feet and wrote the codes down. I folded the piece of paper and held it out to her. She gently took it, touching my fingers, and held the note close to her chest.

I continued…"The codes are exactly 111111 less in number than the actual codes I've written. If anyone steals or finds that piece of paper, they wouldn't be able make sense of it, anyone who isn't a professional code-breaker anyway. No one would know to add 111111. Are you OK with this?"

Tammy was now staring at her toes that wriggled in her sandals. She rocked slowly back and forth.

"What if I clean you out?" she asked.

"Then you can splash out on the biggest marble headstone money can buy for I'd come looking for you"

She looked at me with wide frightened eyes. Her toes stopped wriggling. I thought she'd have seen the funny side.

"I'm only joking, Tammy, I'm just playing with you. If you clean me out, then you clean me out. I've other boxes in town. Eggs and baskets and all that jazz"

"I don't know Cal. Perhaps 'Daddy' was right about you. Perhaps I should tell you to get the hell out. Perhaps I should call Homicide."

She got up and lifted her cell-phone. I jumped like a cat that had sat on a dildo and grabbed her wrist.

"You don't want to do this, Tammy. I won't harm you I promise. I'd just run out of here. I'm innocent and you said you want to help me. I've got money and some of it's yours, I promise, but you'll get nothing this way."

She gave me a look that would freeze fire and wrested her arm from my grip.

"Whatever," she said. "I could clean you out and leave forever, just what would you do then?"

"You can do that if you want but four grand in used twenty dollar bills, well, that's not the kind of cash that builds a new life in Mexico these days. Stick with me and the rewards will be great in the end. It's up to you."

"Four grand, is that all?"

"No but it's what I need for now. It's the tip of the iceberg and believe me, honey, if you come through for me, you'll be getting a big old chip of that iceberg once I get through this, one that would keep you floating in style for years, believe me"

I looked at my watch. It was 6 in the morning. We had talked all night long and time had slipped like a drunk on an oil spill.

Tammy smiled and walked into the hall and put her sneakers on.

"In that case, wish me luck," she said.

"From my experience, luck has a low evaporation point. It boils away as soon as you think about it but I'm smiling on you."

She took off her robe revealing her naked body except for a pair of black g-strings. She gave me a dirty girl look and I stared at her, breathless. I was now rock hard and I didn't care. She stepped into a pair of jeans and eased them tightly over her smooth young thighs before buttoning up. Her breasts were perfect with nipples like purple ripe cherries. I wanted to jump her bones at that moment and give her the fuck of the century but before I had the wherewithal, she was now fully dressed, in jeans, sneakers and a grey hooded anorak. She put the folded paper with the codes into her purse and, without a word, left. I sat back on the futon and found a remote control tucked between some cushions. I chain-smoked my way through numerous cable channels, extirpating thought from my mind.

It wasn't hard to do.

CHAPTER 12

I felt asleep. Three hours later, Tammy rushed back through the beads and I woke up. I rubbed my eyes and yawned and looked at Tammy standing in the middle of the floor holding a little silver briefcase in the air like a hunter with a moose-head.

"Smart briefcase, Tammy. I don't remember having that in my locker"

"I bought one at Staples before going to the bank. I always wanted to carry lots of money in a neat silver metal Samsonite suitcase, just like in the movies."

"Thank goodness for movies. How would we know how to behave and speak without them?" I said.

"Hey, you're grouchy" she said. "and where's my thank you?"

"You're right, thank you Tammy. You came through for me big time. I'm sorry, I fell asleep and I'm not the most effusive in the mornings first thing. In fact, this is me being cheerful compared to how I am most mornings but I mean it, thank you honey. Anyway, did all go to plan? Any problems?"

"No problems, sir, all went to plan. No hitches."

She laid the case on the futon beside me and opened it. Twenty bundles of two hundred bucks, all used twenty-spots. Just as I expected.

"You've done good, Tammy girl," I said. I lifted five of the bundles and stacked them on the coffee table. "Those are for you. I'm a man of my word."

Her mouth opened slightly. I could tell she was rehearsing the why-I-couldn't-possibly routine in her mind. I thought I'd spare her blushes.

"It's OK, Tammy, it's all yours. I don't need no thank-you notes or anything. You've taken me into your home, clothed me, fed and watered me. Most of all, you trusted me when I needed it most. Take it. There's more off this to come"

She lifted the money and leant over and kissed me full on the lips. She gently pushed me back on the futon and she lay on top of me. We rolled off and onto the floor. We peeled off our clothes and made the dirtiest love imaginable. I kissed her from her neck, down to her breasts, her stomach before delving my tongue into her sweet warm wet little pussy. It was such a tidy little pussy, her pubes were manicured and clipped in a tall little black rectangle. I rolled my tongue over her bulbous wet clit and flicked at it with the tip of my tongue, over and over and over. I shoved my face into her wet brown folds of flesh between her legs and drank it all up. Tammy moaned and panted and screamed until she squirted a gusher of love juice in my face. It trickled down my forehead, over my nose and onto my lips. I licked my lips and tasted the sweetness. Her whole body was in a spasm, her face flushed red, glistening with sweat. I got up and ease my tungsten hard cock deep into her and ease back and forth until I came an ocean of cum deep inside her. I swear it was the best fuck of my life. I felt faint as if all my life force was spent. I lay on top her, dazed and exhausted, feeling the warmth of her breath against my face. We lay entwined for what seemed like hours.

"More" she whispered. I slowly made my down back between her legs. The day was just about done and night-time was cranking up like a dirty old piston.

We fucked like it was the eve of Armageddon.

CHAPTER 13

The sunrise stretched its long yellow fingers through the gaps in the blinds. A few of them hit my eyes. I squinted and shoved my head deeper into the pillow, trying to carry the heavy load of sleep for another while longer. Tammy had gone out about an hour earlier, leaving me alone in the apartment for yet another day, walled up like a pampered hermit. A week had now passed since we first met and we had settled into a domestic routine of sorts. She would get up and go to work. I would lie on and get up around ten thirty, fix breakfast, watch TV and cook for her when she got home. All very nice, all very safe. We didn't discuss my situation after our first night.

I knew it couldn't go on like that forever.

That morning, I jumped out of bed, had a long soak in the shower, got dressed, fixed some breakfast, scrambled eggs with chives, four slices of bacon and a bucket of Ethiopian coffee. I put the lot on a tray and carried it to the balcony. I sat there, listening to the noise from the world below. I felt smug knowing where the world was while the world didn't know shit where I was. It was like winning hide-and-seek, seeing the frantic feet of your predators from the unseen sanctuary of a cubbyhole.

I was hiding but I had no idea just how hot the pursuit was. The papers found new scalps to adorn the front pages. I fell from page one to occasional columns and then nothing. Was I now forgotten? How do you really know when you've won hide-and-seek unless someone finds you to tell you? New blood is delicious but it quickly gets cold. I was a cop once and I know you can't reheat a cold trail.

I leant over the balcony and imagined what it would be like to fall over. How long would it take? Would it take only five seconds before pancaking on sidewalk below? Would I die of shock while in motion? Would I survive to live a life not worth living, eating dinner through a straw? I wasn't contemplating doing it though, just playing with the idea. Cars, trucks, skater kids and ordinary Joes zipped up and down the sidewalk. Little did they know I was up here, watching them. Little did anyone know where I was. Little did they care. But someone out there cared enough to take my life as I knew it away from me.

I finished my breakfast and poured the rest of the coffee down my throat before going back inside. I walked into the bedroom, turned on the light and opened the walk-in closet. I sifted through the stack of mens' polo shirts that Tammy neatly stacked beside her pile of Lycra gym gear. Behind the polo shirts, there was box. I removed the stack of sweaters and put them on the bed. There was a white address label on the front with the word 'Ronnie' written in blue felt-tip. I took the box down and laid it on the bed.

I sat on the edge of the bed but the box was so close to the edge that when I sat down, the box tumbled to the floor, spilling its contents at my feet. Nothing smashed or clinked, just the whisper of papers rustling against each other. I crouched down and sifted through them. Tammy never mentioned a 'Ronnie' to me. I presumed it belonged to an old room mate who forgot to take it with them. I got on my knees and started to sift through the contents; a mixture of Polaroid photographs and news clippings. I picked up a few photos, landscape photos of coastlines, hillsides and motor vehicles. I continued and found some with people in them. I picked one of them up. It was off a young woman with big hair and hoopy ear rings, smiling in a bar. I held it close to my face. It was Tammy but one from a past life. She looked very different from the Tammy I knew. In the photo, she was still pretty but wore frumpy clothes, the kind you dress you in when going to Wal-Mart when the liquor store has run out of your brand of beer. Curiosity forced my hand and I leafed through the rest, one by one.

Some high-school snapshots, sporting an even different look. She looked so preppy, so proper like Debbie Gibson but in big spectacles. She seemed quite happy in many of them, despite what she'd told me about her home life. Some were of Tammy in her early twenties with a young man. He must have been a steady. They were together in several photos in different bars, restaurants, parties and other places. I figured she must have been with him quite some time. Their hairstyles and clothes changed a lot. I'd say they spanned the late '80s and early '90s. She wore a bridesmaid costume in one photo. She looked like a kitten stuck in a meringue.

She told me she was from Idaho and that her parents were drunks and beat her a lot when they got fed up beating each other.. When she was fifteen, Tammy couldn't take anymore and jumped on an Amtrak and arrived in Chicago all by herself. She never told me the name of her hometown. I guessed it didn't matter. All hometowns are Shitsville, population 'Too Many'. I guessed she wanted a clean break and had the balls to make it.

Then I found another Polaroid, one that stopped the clock.

There was Tammy, draped over a different, much older dude. Not just any dude but Tom Daley, ex Chicago Mayor, the man who turned Cook County into Crook County. I examined the photo for every last detail. It seemed to be some kind of society ball and quite recent too if her hairstyle was anything to go by. I turned the photo over to see any writing or note on the back, and there it was:

"Ronnie and Tommy, Cook County Rotary Club Dinner 2006"

So who was Ronnie? It was obviously Tammy but was Ronnie her name or a nickname? I tried to convince myself that it didn't matter. What's in a name, right? I thought maybe she just met him by accident at some charity ball but there were more photos, Tammy and Tommy on yachts, in ski-wear and one at the Grand Canyon. These were no charity ball snapshots. They were an item. It was obvious as a jackhammer rattling on your toes. I checked the back of every single photo, every single one bore their names. Ronnie and Tom, Ronnie and Tommy R & T. All were date stamped.

I rifled through the photos again, this time putting them in chronological order, oldest first, most recent last. It didn't take me long. When I was done, the line of Polaroid's looked like scenes from a time lapse movie. Changing hairstyles, backdrops, clothes, facial expressions but still the same face, the same person, stretched across time and space.

The first photo was marked 2001.

The last, 2008.

I gathered up the photos and put them in a pile and back inside the box before picking up the newspaper clippings. Each was a torn out page. I flicked through the lot, checking the folio, the newspaper name and date at the top of each page. All of them were from the same publication, the *Priest River Times*. One of the sheets was an editorial page with its mailing address:

34 Jefferson Street,

Priest River,

Idaho.

I figured that this was Tammy's hometown. She did talk about her childhood and coming
from Priest River, one anchor of candour in her sea of secrets. Amongst the ads for used cars,
trailer homes, pit-bull puppies, AA meetings and dress alterations were sombre tales of
teenagers who met their high-speed end in mangled car wrecks or drownings in Lionhead
Creek. Tammy kept dozens of such clippings. One clipping wasn't a clipping but an entire
edition. Star date September 20th, 2000. Almost the entire paper was given over to a murder:

> The body of Blake Gore, a thirty-nine year old male, was found by
> police officers and an Emergency Crew after responding to a request
> for a well-being check. Mr Gore was pronounced dead at the scene.
> Mr Gore worked as a janitor in Priest River High School but failed to
> report for duty since Wednesday 16th. Police would like to talk to Mr
> Gore's wife, Ronnie Gore, sometimes known as Veronica. She is
> thirty five years old, petite build and has short brown hair styled in a
> bob. The Bonner County Police Department would urgently like to
> speak with her to eliminate her from the inquiry. If you know her
> whereabouts, please call the Sheriff's office on 555 448 8877.

A grainy photo of Ronnie printed beneath. There were other articles, detailing sorry
fragments of their lives. Both Blake and Ronnie were known for their tempestuous
relationship and were no strangers to the local law enforcement. Blake was fond of the liquor.
He got into bar-fights and assaulting his wife Ronnie all over town. He was a frequent guest
of the jail-house and drunk-tank but charges were rarely pressed, if ever. One article said he
spent spells in drying-out clinics but the wagon of temperance was too bumpy and he kept
falling over the side.

Then there were vox pops of the know-it-alls and the gossips. Their febrile words of titillation
darted around the pages like flies around a warm turd.

I remember being seconded to help out in murder cases in small towns upstate. Boy they get hard and wet for a good old murder, the gorier the better. It's hot titty time for local reporters tired off recounting council meetings, court proceedings for traffic offences and church outings. The local rags cream their pants and the locals get their fifteen minutes.

"I knew Blake, he cleaned my classroom and the last day I saw him, he ignored me when I said 'hi'. I thought that was kinda weird. He always said 'hi'. Then the next thing I know, he's dead.'"

I gathered up the photos and papers and put them back into the box and put the box back inside the closet. I got dressed, made a fresh pot of coffee, laced with Johnny Walker and sat down on the futon inside and chain-smoked my throat to a sand dune. I waited for Tammy.

Or was it Ronnie?

CHAPTER 14

I spent the rest of the day flicking cable channels, not settling on any one programme. Hours seeped through my fingers. Sometime early in the evening, I heard the key in the lock. I turned round. It was Tammy. She whizzed into the room, a whirlwind of scarf and tails of long woollen overcoat.

"Have a nice day, Cal?"

"I'd like to say I was busy but..."

She didn't wait for me to finish my sentence. She smiled at me with cat-like eyes. I sensed she scored some kind of home run today.

"You know that guy who snuffed it in the motel, well, I've made a connection with two of his buddies and we're meeting them tomorrow for breakfast."

"You, you did? You did that? How did you manage that, Tammy?"

"I could say I have my ways but no, it wasn't that hard. Mark was one of the faces in Wicker Park. I went there and asked a few questions of people who looked like they may have some answers."

"Did they know why you were asking about Mark? Didn't they ask questions?"

"Well, at first. It wasn't easy. One of them thought I was a cop. When I grabbed his crotch and squeezed his balls and asked him if he still thought I was a cop, he kinda changed his mind. I told them that we needed to know who else was in Mark's life in the days and weeks before he died. Then he showed me Mark's photo. He kept it in his wallet. I knew then he was the real deal."

The yellow box of secrets was not just in the closet behind my sweaters, it had formed a giant box-shaped block in my throat and it was about to jump out. I tried as hard as I could to find the right moment to spit it out.

"So, when's the meet?"

"You know the Heartland Cafe in Rogers Park? Well it's there at 9am tomorrow morning."

"So all this time there was me thinking you were some bleeding heart charity worker but all this time, you were doing the legwork I should have been doing myself. You done good, Tammy girl."

She smiled and lifted up a bag and handed it over to me. I took it and reached in and counted the used notes, tens and twenties. Another four grand. I counted out one thousand dollars of it and gave it to her.

She raised her hand to mine and slowly peeled my fingers off her mouth, one by one, and we ended up making a cat's cradle with our fingers. My heart pounded like a piston on a freight train, my eyes scanned her neck as though it were prey, succulent, tender and that perfume, hmm, that perfume…rich ginger soaked in velvet and rose.

It smelt of woman.

Hot woman.

She pulled my hand towards her and began to lick each of my fingers in turn, putting each one into her mouth. I couldn't help thinking just how happy I was to be tossed about in her strange orbit. She pulled me towards her, her tongue was coming out of her mouth before mine crashed against hers, plunging both into her mouth. A war of tongue in the theater of warmth and wetness, writhing around inside our heads. I hitched her top up and thrust my head into her breasts. She undid the zip of her dress and I felt it float to the ground. She wrapped her legs around me, my hands frantically devouring the sensation of black stockings, up and down her thighs. We rolled onto the floor and made frantic love. When I was spent, I nestled my head on her left shoulder and we fell against the wall, upright, crawling our ways back from our respective little deaths, towards some great reward. I knew she was mine from that moment.

Whoever she was.

Eventually we peeled ourselves off one another and went to lie down in the bedroom. We held one another other all night. I didn't want the night to end but it always ends. Everything does. There are some dawns you just don't wanna see and I knew if I saw the sun again, some kind of magic would die in the light. We slumbered and soon slumber gave in to sleep.

Several hours later, daylight stung my eyes. Tammy sat up and shoved at my arm to wake me.

"Heartland Cafe, Cal. We have to make a move."

CHAPTER 14

We weaved our way through the early morning traffic with the windows down, taking in the unorthodox symphony of engines and horns. We reached our destination and parked outside the Heartland Cafe in Rogers Park. The red and white awning gently fluttered in the morning breeze that kissed and caressed my face like the whispers of promises.

We went inside. A couple of Goth kids lurked in the far corner. A frozen nest of black hair sat on both their heads, their faces whiter than nature's intent. The girl rubbed her eyes. The boy stirred his coffee.

"Those guys over there; Mark's friends. I told them I'd have company but don't worry, they think you're an assistant. Just talk as little as you can and leave it all to me. I forgot to say, your name is Mike, OK?"

I nodded and we made our way over and sat down opposite them at the same table. I looked at their white, gaunt faces. The girl loudly sucked the last living dreg out of her vanilla milkshake through a pale blue straw. I held my arm out and squeezed the straw.

"I think that milkshake's dead, honey," I said.

She lifted her head and gave me a cold mean look. Tammy looked awkward. She cleared her throat.

"Guys, this is Mike, the dude I told you about?"

They nodded in sullen silence. I could tell social niceties weren't on the menu. Tammy ordered us coffee and a platter off eggs, bacon, hash browns, toasted muffins and a jar of maple syrup. I took the time to gaze around. A collage of posters and bills advertised a colorful set off lefty underground social events, poetry readings, folk nights, benefit nights for Gaza. No sign of a NRA flyer in sight. Diners at other tables were busy on their net-books and tablets, sipping thimbles of espresso between eager mouse-clicks.

"I'm sorry, guys, but I missed your names. I'm Mike."

"I'm Bobby," said the girl.

"I'm Zoran," said the boy.

"Pleased to meet you both"

They seemed like nice kids now the ice was broken. I didn't think Tammy was impressed. She told me to keep quiet but I just can't help myself sometimes. She looked as comfortable as Liberace in a whorehouse.

"Tammy tells me that you say you didn't kill our friend Mark in that hotel" said the girl.

I didn't count on that sucker punch.

"I'm sorry, Bobby, but what?" I laughed a little but no one else was laughing.

"Tammy tells us you say you were framed for his murder." said the boy

I sipped my coffee even though I felt my throat had contracted.

Head on. I'll take this head on.

Tammy stared into her coffee and rocked back and forth. I thought it was one helluva high-wire act she booked me to walk for without my knowing.

"I didn't know you told them who I was, Tammy"

"Sorry, Cal. I had to. The assistant thing didn't wash. Besides, they know what you look like. You're not in disguise or anything but it's cool. You have to trust us"
"Tammy's right. I didn't know Tammy told you both everything but here we are. I'm a private detective and I was lured to the hotel under false pretences. I was in a fist fight with Mark hours earlier that evening at the Redhead Piano Bar. He came in and verbally abused

me and the bartender. I ask him to stop and get out but he just got worse. I punched him. He fell down. He got up and staggered out of the bar and I didn't set eyes on him until I saw his body at the hotel. You have got to understand that I didn't kill him"

"Why should we understand?" said the boy

"Because it's the truth" Tammy said

"How do you know" said the girl

"If you didn't believe it was the truth, why did you come here this morning?" I asked. "I feel bad about it but there you are. I want to clear my name. Only when my evidence is cast iron will go the cops. If I was guilty, I wouldn't be sat right here right now and if you thought I was guilty, you wouldn't be here either, would you?"

I saw from their slack jaws that my tsunami of honesty had devastated the shanty town preconception they had built. I had put myself in their hands, my future in their hands. Most people can't carry such a weight.

The boy clasped his hands and formed a steeple with his fingers.

"Mark wasn't drunk. He never got drunk" he said.

"He was staggering all over the shop, I've witnesses" I said.

"I'm not sure what exactly it was you saw, mister, but Mark wasn't drunk. Mark didn't drink. The toxicology report says so."

The boy reached into his brown-leather satchel and fished out a dog-eared report. He put it on the table, face up. I noticed it had the Great Seal of Illinois on the front so it must have been the real deal. Tammy picked it up and leafed through it. She stopped on page four and put her finger on the second paragraph down.

"Look at this," she said. "No alcohol in his system." I sat up and looked at the boy.

"Then if he wasn't drunk, why was he acting like a juice-hound?"

"Mark was an actor. I met Mark the day before he died. We met for a coffee before his audition." said Tammy

"His audition?" I asked.

"An audition for a minor part in a day-time soap. We're actors too" the boy said. "Mark told me that the previous day, he was outside the audition-room but he met a woman there who wanted him to play a different part in a different movie. Sure, Mark was all ears. Who wouldn't be? We're all minimum-wage kids, working in restaurants, and bars to make ends meet. Whatever spare time we have, it's spent rehearsing and learning lines. Whatever time is left after that, that's when we eat, sleep and shit. Mark was no different. He worked in a bookstore opposite here. See it?"

Mike pointed out the window to the building opposite.

"Myopic Books. It's a used-book store. Mark loved it there. It kept his creative juices alive, talking to all the folks who came in who liked to read"

"So, this woman he met at the audition…." I said

"Mark goes in, performs at audition and when done, goes outside for a smoke. He always went for a smoke after an audition Then this woman comes up to him and tells him that she needs an actor to take part in an elaborate joke she wants to pull on her husband. At first he didn't know if she was real but she was dressed real neat in a business suit and had a real nice haircut and carried herself very well. He thought she was from Australia or somewhere like that."

The boy grabbed the girl's hand.

"What was her name, this woman?" I asked.

"That bit I don't remember, I don't even think Mark told me," the boy said.

"Would he have written it down someplace?" I asked.

"I don't know. I really can't say"

"He had a cell-phone" said the girl

"So, what exactly did this woman want him to do?" I asked.

"This is why we believe you" said the girl "She asked Mark if he could follow a man into a wine bar, pick a fight with him and then get thrown out. That's it, that's all. Mark thought she was taking him for a ride until she took out an envelope containing $500. That was the down payment and that there would be an extra $3000 on completion."

"That's a lot of money for acting drunk"

"Yeah"

"I'm curious," I said. "You seem to know quite a bit of detail there."

"What do you mean?" the boy asked. His voice was now a tremolo. My question made him nervous.

"I mean, did Mark usually go into such detail or do you remember details to that extent? I'm not being funny but most people only remember the broad brushstrokes, not the fine details. It's OK, it's an observation, that's all," I said.

"We're actors," the girl said. "We're trained to observe and retain details. It comes with the territory"

"I see." I said. "I'm sorry, please, carry on"

"Well, he took the money but there's the thing, she wouldn't tell him the where and the when and the who."

"I don't follow," I said.

"I mean, he asked, obviously, what her name was, who her husband was and where the gig was"."

"She wouldn't tell him shit" the girl said.

"No, she wouldn't tell him," the boy said.

"Did Mark get suspicious? I know I would" I said

"Yes he did but she told him it was essential that he didn't know. Mark told me he would have walked away and put the whole thing down to one crazy crank but it was the $3000 bucks that swung it. That's why he went along with it. Who wouldn't?"

I began to think that in reality, I wouldn't, but then again, I wasn't making minimum wage so fuck knows what I'd do for dough.

"Let me get this straight. This mystery woman paid Mark good money to turn up someplace. He must have known where though. He would have asked her, right?"

"That's the thing, he told me that she told him to phone her at 7pm sharp and to make sure he was in the vicinity of the Rainforest Cafe and only then would she give him the details."

"You mean the Rainforest Cafe in the downtown, near those Irish bars and the Rock'n'Roll McDonalds?" I asked.

"Sure, the one and only."

"Why there?"

"It was close to where he had to go. That's what she told him."

"I see. Does anyone have Mark's cell-phone?"

"I dunno. Do you know?" the boy asked the girl

The girl shrugged her shoulders. "No, I guess his family would have it, the police would have given them his stuff."

"I'm sorry but I'd need to talk to his family about that cell-phone."

"Why?"

"Because her number would be stored. I could check his cell-phone records. Which network was he with?" I asked.

"Jeez, I don't know that shit. I think he had a pay as you go. No contract. People like us don't have contracts, man."

I took a long sip of my now cold coffee and hunched myself over the table, scratching my chin.

"Was Mark not worried about any of this, despite the money?" I asked.

"He just saw life as an adventure man. I don't think he worried about anything" said the girl

"Another good story for parties. He loved anecdotes." said the boy.

"Made some up too" smiled the girl.

Would I have done the same at Mark's age? Does shit smell? Hell yeah, I would have. At that age, young men like strange avenues. Strange avenues contain strange women with the promise of strange scents, sensations and sex. Mark chose such an avenue but it was a one-way trip. I bet it glimmered like Vegas but he fell into a black mirage. I can't imagine a guy like Mark keeping all this to himself. Sure he embellished a bit here and there but it was such a crazy story that it barely needed buffing.

"Did you or anyone speak to Mark after he took the call?"

"Yes, after he got the call, he sent me a text saying he was going to Foley's Bar."

"Foley's Bar?"

"Yeah, Foley's Bar, that's where he was supposed to go and pick a fight with the woman's husband"

"No," I said. "It was the Redhead Piano Bar. That's where I was when he came in"

"Sorry, mister, but that's not right. He got a text saying to go to Foley's. No way would he have confused those two."

"But I know he ended up picking a fight at the Redhead," I said. "I was there. It wasn't Foley's."

The boy looked at the girl.

"Perhaps there was a last-minute change to the plan. All I know is that he texted me later on saying that he had to go to a motel someplace. That was the last text I got but the weird thing was, it wasn't from his normal number, it was from a different number."

"A different number? Are you sure? How did you know it was from him?" I asked.

"Positive, he signed his name on the text. That's how I knew it was him" said the boy.

"Did he have a second phone?"

"Not that I knew off, I don't think so" said the boy.

The girl shook her head.

"How do you know it was really from him?"
The boy and girl looked at one another.

"I guess we don't know for sure. He could have lost his first phone and bought a new one from Walgreen's"

It sounded farfetched but sometimes things like that happen but only sometimes.

"Did you reply to it?"

"I tried to but I ran out of credit. And before you ask, I deleted the thread as I needed to free some space up for to download Doodlejump" said the boy.

"That's a platform game" said the girl.

I took their word for it.

A couple of workmen came in and sat down at the booth next to us. I glanced out the window and saw their blue truck parked outside. The back of the truck was laden with To Let and For Sale signs.

I needed to make contact with Mark's next of kin to see if they had his cell-phone. I wracked my brains trying to think of a humane way not only asking for it but why. I thought of all kinds of subterfuge to get my way into the house and to put on the right velvet gloves on my fist into before I socked them with it. "By the way, may I see your son's cell-phone? Gee, where's my manners, didn't I explain? I'm the guy everyone thinks killed him but it wasn't me but I sure as hell need his phone to prove it. I hope you don't mind Mr. and Mrs. Madigan"

Yeah right.

I could imagine Quincy or Ironside getting away with a stunt like that but this was real life and in real life, roads don't always lead to where you want them.

"Excuse me, ma'am, but can you tell me where the Lonesome Cove is? We think it's round here somewhere," one of the workmen asked the waitress.

The clutching of chins and puzzled looks of the staff behind told me that no one round here heard of it let alone know where it was but I knew where it was. Its name still made me shiver. I rose from the table but Tammy grabbed my hand and look up at me, mouthing a silent 'no'. I squeezed her hand and smiled.

"It's ok honey, they're just dudes" I let her go and made my way to their booth.

"I couldn't help overhearing. You say you're looking for the Lonesome Cove Motel?"

"That's her alright. Been trying to find it but we've driving around in circles all morning. " said the smaller of the two.

"It's right here on the map" said the bigger one. "But there's no signage. No nothin'"

"When you get back in your truck, drive straight for one block. You'll see a giant gray building with lots of boarded-up doors and an overgrown, abandoned car lot. That's the one."

"Really? We're that close huh?" the bigger one said.

"Yup, you're nearly at the bull's-eye. Just out of curiosity, why are you going there?" I asked.

"We work for Dupree and Lyndon."

"Realtors," said the smaller one.

"I see."

"The owners put it on the market and we're putting the signage up."

I got excited. A road had just opened into the murk.

"You wouldn't know who the owners are?"

"They don't tell us shit like that" the smaller one said.

163

"They give us the boards, the addresses and a mallet and we do our stuff. That's all I do and that's all I care about" said the bigger one.

The smaller one raised an eyebrow and forced a smile through his beard, one of those big, wet, red-lip smiles. His mouth looked like a skinned worm nestling in a bed of ginger pubic hair.

"Lonesome Cove? Fuck, that's the place the fags used to meet" croaked an old timer, sitting at the end of the counter, stirring his cup slowly. "Until they shot 'em"

"Excuse me, what was that?" Almost every head turned around.

"The motel, down the street, that's where those two queers met up for a bit of fudge-shoving but they fell out over a dress and one shot the other. Fucking cocksuckers should stick to Boystown and leave decent folks like us alone. One of them was a cop"

He smiled leeringly with a face full of hatefulness, sitting on his stool, pot belly hanging over his belt like a Buddha gone wrong. I looked over Tammy and the Goth couple. They heard every word. I could tell from their raised eyebrows that the bore on the barstool's version of events was a possibility they didn't take into account, but being good Democrats from Wicker Park, they couldn't really condemn the theory of how Mike and I could've truly met.

Not out loud anyway. I know what Democrats are like in private, believe me. I've been to fundraisers.

I stood at the counter, holding my tongue.

"Pay no heed to Greg. His mind's gone. Don't worry, he won't head me. He don't heed anyone but himself" said a voice that piped up from down the counter. A small thin man with large, unkempt moustache, red checked shirt and blue baseball cap with a 'Joel's Fertilizers' logo on the front, smiled into the coffee he slurped.

"His daughter Marion was murdered here, right here, in this diner. The story goes that she dumped by her boyfriend so she went and slashed her throat in that very john over there" he said, pointing a nicotine stained boney finger towards the bathrooms. "Her body wasn't found until the next day. We didn't get many lady customers in those days and the lady's john was hardly used. 1995 it was." He took another swig of coffee. "Greg Skilbeck found her, used to be the cleaner here."

"That's enough of that talk, we've got customers here. Don't' go upsetting people," said the waitress. The old man mumbled under his egg-stained moustache and walked over and sat down alone in a booth and took out a cell-phone and began to fiddle with it.

Greg got up, tipped his baseball cap to the waitress, nodded at me and left the diner.

The waitress tapped me on the shoulder.

"I don't know how Greg has the heart to keep coming back here after what happened. He went a little loopy so after, in and out of the mad house ever since like a yo-yo. They stuff him full off pills and send him out but he always does something stupid and the judge just keeps sending him back" said the waitress, drying cups with the same corner of a blue dishcloth.

I nodded, not saying anything. I turned and walked back to my seat and looked at Tammy and the two kids.

"Well, I think it's time for me to make a start"

CHAPTER 15

A woman took the elevator to the top floor of the Hancock Tower. Five seconds and ninety floors later, the doors opened. She stepped out and strode down the Dior-carpeted corridor until she reached apartment 934.

She knocked twice. The door opened and she was silently summonsed in.

The man with slick black hair and a well-cut, dark-brown Armani suit, stood by the window with his back turned. He stared out across the vast expanse of the gloomy, dark autumn waters of Lake Michigan.

"He's an old-style gumshoe, logic and procedure are in his DNA, he's started to make smart moves," the woman said.

"But wasn't this what we expected?" the man said.

"Yes but it's still a concern. What if he short-circuits the logic and goes straight to the heart of the matter?" the woman said.

"Then we will be there waiting for him. What is this first-smart-move that you find so tantalizing?" the man said.

"He knows about the cell-phone Mark used. He also knows that the cell-phone found on his body was returned to his kinfolk. He knows that forensics could splice and dice it and find all kinds of things on it, things we don't want found."

"But surely our man took the cell-phone from Mark's body before the police arrived, yes?" the man asked.

"I don't know. I really don't know," the woman said.

"Didn't you debrief our friend, Lockie?"

"He's gone off radar. We think he's lost the plot. He's spent, burnt up. I hear he's on the streets, lost his job at Wal-Mart too."

The man turned around and narrowed his eyes.

"Poor Lockie. He was once the future but he never really understood. I guess all our futures eventually catch up with us and outpace us in the end but this situation, it's no good. No good at all. We can assume if Lockie took the cell-phone, then he would have sold it on the street and hey presto, it vanishes forever. Factory reset? Even better. Even if someone did read the texts, there was nothing in them that anyone could understand. Nothing incriminatory, no names, no actions, right?"

"Well, just the final one, the instruction to go to the Lonesome Cove Motel but anyone reading that would think nothing of it," the woman said.

"That may be, but if the cell-phone is with Mark's family then it's a Pandora's Box and, from what I hear, Callum's closer to getting the key."

The lady shivered.

"We need to get into Mark's family home and root around it" she said.

The man pondered at first, clutching his chin. His narrow, thin lips slit into a sick smile.

"Yes but we need to burn Pandora's Box and Pandora herself just to make sure. Fire, I find, is the best disinfectant of them all" said the man.

"Can't we just break in, find it and just take it away?"

"I'm sure that's how an ordinary mind would do it"

The woman pursed her lips and folded her arms.

He pulled out a laptop from a black leather pouch and powered it up. The woman walked over. He opened Googlemaps and keyed in an address. Within seconds, the gray-world matrix was filling up with bits of real blue/green world and the little yellow man came into view right at the target address.

"Look, at the corner of Rockefeller Avenue and Arden. Aw, look how close that it is to Brookfield Zoo. I want a torch put to Pandora, any time of day or night would do," the man said.

The woman swallowed.

"I don't care how this sounds but why can't we just take the phone? Break in and take it. This will just make more problems for us. Wiping out an entire family? Don't you think the cops won't stop looking?" the woman asked.

The man grabbed the woman by the arm. She yelped but didn't say a word. The hand was as ice and a frozen fear gripped her.

"You seem to have lost your bite, that serrated edge which I found so delectable" Perhaps something or someone has filed your teeth a little too smooth, no?" the man asked.

"No, of course not, but..."

He put his right index finger on her mouth and closed her lips.

"Some people sharpen their best knives when they go a little blunt. Some people just get new knives and throw the old ones out. I like to run the tip of my finger up and down the thin edge of a blade and watch a little trickle of blood flow down my hand and onto my wrist. I don't feel a thing. I watch it with a feeling of detachment as though it was someone else's but it's mine. I love the sharp, clear reflection on the steel. I am just a junkie for novelty, a slave to the new. If something or someone becomes a little blunt, a little grubby, a little useless, then it goes. Do you understand me?" the man said.

The woman's legs gave way under the sudden weight of the situation. She fell to the floor, sobbing.

The man crouched down and stroked her hair.

"I am not asking you to burn anything. The boys take care of the frogs and snails side of things. I am, however, a little disappointed in you. I feel I don't have your one hundred percent support but a little opposition now and then isn't always a bad thing. Hush, stop crying, you've no need to worry like this, now get up and dry your face"

The sobbing subsided and the woman got her breath back. The man gently squeezed her left shoulder. She never saw this glimmer of humanity in him before except when he tenderly cared for stray dogs he sometimes saved from rescue.

"Fuck you. I'm done with you, done with all this. I'm so outta here." She brushed herself down and stormed out, slamming the door behind her. The man watched her without expression. He picked up his cell-phone and dialled a number longhand.

"Yes, come by within the hour. Just drop what you're doing. I've some urgent jobs for you."

When he finished his call, he slinked over to the drinks trolley and fixed himself a stiff gin and tonic, with a dash of bitters and a splash of ice. He downed it in one and returned to the window, resuming his pose, staring across the dark expanse of Lake Michigan.

The lakeshore town of Gary on the far side of the lake was a pregnant ink splodge, barely visible in the mist.

So distant.

So ghostly.

CHAPTER 16

"So, Tammy, tell me more about yourself." I asked.

"What do you want to know?" I could tell she was cagey. When she didn't want to talk or tell a secret she would flit between kitchen units and open lots of cupboard doors as if she was dodging bullets.

We were listening to Chicago WXRT's Breakfast with the Beatles show, tapping our toes to *Rocky Raccoon.*

"I mean, you never told me about your history, you know, where you came from, how you ended up here, family and stuff. Sometimes it's like you're Moses in a basket."

"There's not a lot to tell, but if you insist, I was born in Idaho and moved around a lot before coming to Chicago. You know what my family were like. I don't wanna go over all that again. Why are you dredging all this up?"

She smothered her toast with peanut butter and took a big luscious bite from it, leaving a glistening stripe of peanut spread on her upper lip. She licked it clean almost immediately.

"But I'm interested, Tammy. Sisters, brothers, cousins. Don't you miss them?"

She slammed her mug on the table splashing coffee on the coaster.

"Why do you want to know, you're short off Twitter followers or something? Just fucking drop it, ok?

Each word a bullet. I was toying with her, playing around with her like a cat with a mouse, teasing it between its paws, letting it go but pulling it back. I had given her a chance to be honest but she ducked it.

We continued our breakfast in silence. The only conversation was between the clinks and scrapes of Dollar World cutlery on plates with cracked glazing.

"I'm going to visit Howie today," I said, breaking the silence as clumsily as a nerd on an ice rink.

"Howie?"

"Yes, Mark's father. I think he has the cell-phone. All Mark's shit was given over to his next of kin."

"What about his mother?"

"She's not on the scene."

Tammy finished her toast, downed the dregs of the orange juice in one go and got up.

"I've gotta go someplace," she said, wrapping her orange and purple striped scarf around her neck. Her swan-like neck carried her head with a delicate poise like a stem to a bud. Sometimes I couldn't help thinking just how easy it would be to snap it or slice it and watch that girl-head float off like a cotton-tail in the wind. I chose not to ask where she was going. In Tammy's world, the map is full of towns named like Somewhere, Someplace, Across Town, Outta Town. I think she inhabited some kind of parallel State whose name was not Illinois but Vague. She grabbed her cell-phone and keys, kissed my forehead and left.

It was still early in the day, 10:30am. I wandered into the lounge and decided to chill for a bit before the daily rodeo of getting my life back. I put on some Billie Holliday on the Bose and melted into the ether starting with *Miss Brown to You*. I let the words and music squeeze my mind free and let it float like a helium balloon.

An hour later, I rose back to the surface and groggily scrambled onto the muddy banks of wakefulness. I went for a shower and got dressed and left.

It's been too long since I last seen Howie. I was about to put that right.

CHAPTER 17

I parked a few blocks from Howie Madigan's house on Wentworth and Hudson and walked the rest of the way. I was dying for a cup of strong black coffee but I was a man on a mission with my mind fixed on target like an Exocet missile. As I got nearer to Howie's block, I heard the familiar strains of police radios and garbled two-way conversations peppered with cop-speak.

I stopped in my tracks and strained my ears to make out the words.

I was a little paranoid. Paranoia had to be my shadow to keep me right. Paranoia is like chemotherapy, it can kill the bad but it kills the good in you too. I turned my heel and decided to have that coffee. I found a little coffee bar, Mascarino's, and ordered an espresso. It was one of those places where the owner worked behind the counter. You can tell. It's an air of effortless competence. Besides, nobody would employ an out of shape barista in his fifties, especially one who didn't operate the coffee machine like Liberace at the piano. He was bald with beads of sweat on his head like tiny glass pebbles. He wore an old apron with a map of northern Italy on it. He poured the beans into the grinder and cleaned the cutlery with a flourish like it was a re-enactment from some old opera.

"Take a seat, sir, and I'll bring it over"

I perched myself on a high chair by the window. The man brought my espresso over just at the moment two cop cars whistled past the window and tore right up the street.

"Bad business, bad business" said the man shaking his head.

"What happened?" I asked.

"Fire, someone set fire to my neighbour's house. Everyone inside, dead. The man, his girlfriend and her boy. Only seven years old. Who would do such a thing? Dreadful business. No one has been killed around here for over four years. Four years!" He ambled back to behind the counter and took orders from new customers who had just walked in.

Four years without a murder is a mighty good innings for any neighbourhood in this town, even the glam ones like Evanston. Poor folk do their killing with passionate recklessness without thought to cover their tracks. The well-heeled on the other hand, like everything else, pay someone else.

I took a sip of my espresso and looked out the window. A large, black truck pulled up outside, blocking out a lot of light. The window became a mirror. I could see the big Italian guy coming back my direction with a cloth in his hand. While he wiped the tables, I asked him the question I was dying to ask.

"What were their names, the people in the fire?"

"I don't know" he exclaimed "But he was ex-police. Bad business. Bad business"

I started putting two and two together. There are a lot of ex-cops but most of them live upstate, in jail or in the bone yard. The Italian put down his cloth and looked straight into my eyes.

"But he is with his son in Heaven." He clasped his hands together as though he was about to shout 'sweet baby Jesus'. He then jagged his steepled hands upward. Heaven is up there they say. If so, it's a long way from where I was. I thanked him for his time and threw a couple of nickels in the counter and was about to leave.

I thought about the house. What if it was Howie's house and how every time you wanna find a place to pray, they go and burn down the mission.

I left the coffee house and continued on my way towards Howie's block but time, taking detours and zigzagging up and down side streets and back-alleys. From what I know of cops, they mostly think in straight lines.

As I got nearer to Howie's block, the air quickly became a canvas of sirens and wails, a sound-scaped menagerie of urgency. Squad cars, radios, loud voices, screeching tyres. A cordon blocked the end of the street. I had to double back and go all the way round. I had the luxury of time, but I like to move fast. I turned my heel, made several detours and made my way to Howie's street from the opposite end, but it too was cordoned off. I gave in to curiosity as I crept up as close as I could to the cordons to see what was going on.

I was within sight of the cops who manned the cordons and if I could see them, they could see me but no-one expects a fugitive to make a star appearance at such a show.

Squad cars zoomed in and out like wasps. A coterie of cops, forensics and fire crews had spread all along the street. A crowd of people watched on from behind the cordon. Many had blank steely faces, others strained with visible anxiety. Grim faced men comforted upset women. I wasn't foolish enough to go up real close but I needed to visit Howie real soon but I knew that a house visit was out of the question. I didn't want to hang around too long, but I could tell that the runes hadn't fallen in my favour that day. I stood and stared, standing about forty yards from the action. One of the cops who manned the cordon turned around and looked at me and held his gaze.

I froze to the spot, trying to keep my reserve of cool. He screwed his eyes up into slits of concentration. I could feel his stare as someone in a movie once said. I knew how to play this thing. To run would be game over. It would scream of guilt and the hounds of hell would be set upon me. Every inch of me wanted to run like a hound with its ass on fire but I had to let fight win over flight this time. I checked my watch and slowly crossed the street. It was all I could do to stop my feet from breaking into a gallop. I walked slowly away from the cop's neon stare, yet every inch of step felt like I was standing still.

"Hey, you!"

Those two words beat my heart like hammers... I could tell it was a cop, the same cop. The bass voice of a cop, marinated in the dark stews of arrogance, cynicism and authority. The more it moulders, the riper and more hateful it becomes.

I pretended not to hear him and walked on, quickening my gait a little.

"Hey, you. Stop"

The game was up. I flew too close to the sun and my wings had melted. I felt myself hurtling to the stony ground at a million miles an hour. My eyes scanned the street for alleys. I needed to bolt and run like a rat but this was one long, long street. Despite the din of the chopper overhead, I heard the clump of cop-boots behind me, gaining on me.

They say that you should stand still when a bear runs at you but when you see its bare teeth and hear the rumble of its unfed belly; you have to take your chances. I bolted like that rat, the thuds of my feet on the sidewalk rattled through my bones with every beat. A minute later, I stopped and peered around the corner to take stock of the situation.

I was right.

It was the cop.

I carried a Guardian 380 acp pistol in my pants but that was a last resort. When a cop goes down, they never stop looking. I filled my lungs and started running again. I hung the next right, pounding my way down the street but I still heard that clump clump clump behind me. My lungs ached; my body was chewing air faster than I could suck it in.

The cop was gaining on me.

I carried on running but now I was running on empty. My sides felt as if they were about to split wide open, spilling my insides out to drain into the gutters. If they get me, I'm good as dead. It was at that moment I decided to take the nuclear option. I was going to take him down. God forgive me but I don't want to go to hell just yet. It was me or him. Simple as. I reached inside my belt for my gun and it was at that point I tumbled onto the cold concrete slabs of the sidewalk beneath me. I remember the taste of blood in my mouth and the feeling that my lungs had been sandblasted. I couldn't move. The cop had tripped me and he pinned me to the floor.

"Didn't you hear me back there?"

CHAPTER 18

"You were only seconds away from being blown away, you know that?" I said.

Peter Lopes, son of an old comrade of mine, Victor Lopes, smiled as he chewed on his pretzel, washing it down with another large glug of *venti* with an extra shot. "I didn't know you were armed and dangerous, if I knew that, I wouldn't have given chase."

"That's some assumption to make on a suspect, young Lopes. You forgot your basic training already? I haven't forgotten everything you know" I said, lifting a diet coke to my face.

"But you're no fucking suspect, Callum, you're Callum McCambridge, the man who saved my daddy's life."

February 14, 1982. Valentine's Day. The Chicago River was frozen over and was thick enough for people to be thick enough to skate on it, despite the public service announcements. Back in the day, I worked in Homicide along with Victor Lopes. We were driving downtown, past the Tribune building and over the bridge on North Michigan Avenue. It was a freezer of a day yet blessed with a blue sky and cold sunshine. As we snailed along in the traffic, we both noticed an enormous shadow cast itself over our hood and the cars in front.

"Holy Joe Smoke," Victor said. We looked to our right and saw a plane make a gentle descent onto the frozen river. Crowds formed along the bridges. People on the ice scrambled as fast as they could but they looked helpless like wounded gazelles, limping from the leopard in vain.

The plane landed, surprisingly without noise. The plane lay half submerged in its impromptu glacial runway for a while before the doors opened and the emergency chutes were lowered onto the ice. We radioed for as much ambulance and fire crew as could be mustered. Victor mounted the sidewalk, parked and jumped out and ran towards the scene. People were sliding merrily down the chutes and at first it looked like a textbook landing. People stood on the ice and hugged one another and cried and laughed and screamed and yelled. The whole spectrum of emotions lit their faces like fireworks. People started to run down from the bridge above to the frozen river below and formed a human chain to help the survivors. Victor and I ran down to help organize things and to do our bit.

The sirens of the fire crews became audible and made their way down to the scene. We needed ladders to lie across the ice. More passengers were still slip-sliding down the chutes. Some had made their way safely onto the banks. All went well until a sound like the thunder crack of Thor bled the air of human noise. At that moment, the ice-sheet cracked. Crevices a foot wide, criss-crossed as far as the eye could see.

The blackness of the water emerged from the murk beneath. People screamed. People fell in. I looked over and saw Victor jump into one of the cracks. The river had taken a young woman into its icy tomb. I heard her screams. Her arms flailed like a banshee on fire. Victor grabbed her and with all his strength dragged her to the edge of the ice where I and some others winched the woman and Victor from the waters. Hell did freeze over that day and it came to town. More cracks appeared. The plane, a Pan Am DC10, started to sink. The ends of the chutes started to submerge. People were still sliding down them. I'll never forget their faces as they hurtled like lemmings down into the dark, callous waters of hell beneath.

Fire crews and specialist naval squads crawled all over the place, doing the best they could. I jumped into the icy water and dragged a man out and onto the banks. I looked over to see Victor. He had gone back into the water to try to rescue someone else but the cold had got him. I saw him try to clutch a child, her head bobbed up and down in the water, screaming whenever her mouth came up for air, but Victor's arms were frozen. He was crying with rage, helpless and limp. They both were in trouble. I raced over to the part of the bank nearest to them both and jumped in. My arms were just about nimble but not quite. I tried to grab them both by the back of the heads but the child had submerged. I couldn't get to her. I heard a woman screaming, howling with an elemental horror that I didn't think a human could make. A lot of humans stopped doing human things that day.

She was the little girl's mother.

I dragged Victor over to where the grasping hands of strangers grabbed him and lifted him to safety.

I looked over and saw several men do all they could to restrain the mother. I looked back to where the child was. She was gone. It was only a matter of seconds earlier and no one can drown in that time but the water that cold can snap a life in two. The woman bit one the men's hands and elbowed one of the others in the balls and got away and jumped into the water. The men who had held her, jumped in after her. I jumped in too. Her head was above water, looking at the men racing and sliding towards her. When they got within scalp grabbing distance, she ducked her head silently under the surface.

That was the last we saw of her and her child and the two men who had jumped in to rescue her. As we scrambled along the banks, covered in blankets and tinfoil, I noticed something like an envelope floating in the slush. I bent down to pick it up. It was a Valentine's card, a large cloth heart on the front. Inside, the writing was smudged but I made out the name Vincent. Later on, I found out that there was no one called Vincent on the plane but later I found out that two women on the plane had boyfriends called Vincent. One survived, one did not. I locked that card in my filing cabinet at home, never mentioning it to a soul.

Some fire crew told me later that it's not the sight of dead bodies that upset them the most but the sight of the little things. A shoe, a pair of spectacles, a toy. Many found it hard to love again after that day.

Some found it even harder to live.

No post-traumatic stress syndrome in those days. You turned to Jesus or drink.

Victor chose Jesus.

"According to Norse lore, hell is a frosty wilderness. Your daddy and I saw hell first-hand that day."

"You guys in Homicide saw hell most days," said Peter.

I nodded.

"So, Peter, what squad are you in?"

He smiled. "Homicide."

"I should've guessed. Victor must be proud of you."

"I guess. He didn't want me to follow his footsteps you know. He kept telling me to get a proper job, you know, like an accountant or a computer expert but nah, sitting at a desk for forty years didn't appeal to me. I loved Daddy's stories. I didn't want to be the kind of man whose only stories he can tell his grand kids is about the day the server crashed"

I lifted my diet coke like a toast and grinned.

"I take your point but I wouldn't want no son of mine seeing what I saw, doing what I did."

" I guess he was worried about my soul more than anything else."

"Your Daddy was right. How is he anyway?"

"He's doing good. He's a Pastor over in Niles now. Lots of Hispanics in his church. Yeah, they all turned Pentecostal. Don't ask why. Perhaps they've got money now and don't like being told not to use rubber Johnnies by Il Papa"

I smiled. Peter cleared his throat and clasped his hands in front of him. I sensed the small talk was over.

"Callum, can we cut to the chase? My daddy couldn't believe what he read and heard about you, killing that man in the motel. He told me it couldn't have been you but just forget I'm a cop and let me ask you one question. Did you do it? Did you kill that boy?"

I drained the rest my coke and leant forward, clasping my hands together too. Peter looked at me. I locked my eyes on his.

"No-one on the force knew me like your Daddy did. He would know not to ask a question like that but you aren't your Daddy so here's my answer. It was a fit-up. I don't know who did it or why but someone out there wants to make me suffer. If they wanted me dead, they would have done so by now. I don't think they want me dead. They want me in the shit. Now that's what I call hatred that's gone the extra mile but I haven't a clue who it could be. I was a private eye. There's a thousand cheatin' ex-husbands out there don't like me much but this is something else. I've had my fair share of broken noses and slashed car tyres in my time. Occupational hazard but it was all upfront stuff. Man to man. I don't know what's going to happen but I'm still working on it. Besides, are you sure you should be seen with me? You maybe Victor's son but you're still a cop"

Peter shook his head.

"Why were you up there today, at the cordon? I saw you twice, I was manning the furthest one and I saw you but you turned back. I was then assigned to the opposite cordon and a while later I saw you again. Why did you do that? You were lucky it was me and not someone else who clocked you"

"You've some beady eyes. How come you clocked me so quick? It's not as you know me from your last birthday party"

"Daddy keeps a scrapbook of the recent press cuttings about you and also from photos in the past. He takes it out every time I visit him. I guess I'm pretty familiar with what you look like. He still talks about how you saved his life. So are we all."

"I guess that's what killed our friendship in the end," I said. "Victor left the squad six months after that but he rarely spoke to me after that. I guess some debts can never be repaid."

Peter lowered his head.

"I was looking for Howie Madigan. That's why I was there today at the cordons. He lives on that street. Howie Madigan is the father of Mark Madigan, the dead guy from the motel, the dead guy who everyone thinks I killed but didn't."
"So why the fuck would you want to visit his father? Jeez man what kind of welcoming party did you think was waiting for you?"

"It wasn't a social call, son. I was going to burgle his house."

Peter swallowed, eyes wide.

"Break into his house? Am I hearing you right?"

I leant forward and rested my arms on the Formica table top and steepled my fingers.

"Let me explain. Mark was an out of work actor who was paid by some woman to provoke a fight with me in a public place so as to make it look like I was his killer. His instructions were given to him by cell-phone. That's why I need that cell-phone. I know some fone-phreak geeks in Little Italy who can take that phone apart and make a list of all the calls and texts sent and received from that phone. My guess is that Mark's phone was given to Howie as he was his only next of kin. Now we both know that it would be mighty impolite and downright weird of me to just knock on Howie's door and say 'Hi, you don't know me but I do have a passing resemblance to the man accused of killing your boy but while you go and fetch your gun, could you be kind enough to give me his phone to get all forensic on its ass?' Excuse my sarcasm, son, but I've had better circumstances."

I could almost see the hairs on Peter's head fall back into place after being swept back by my rant.

"Howard Madigan you say?" Peter asked.

"Sure, Howie to everyone else who knew him. Your Daddy knew him. Why, do you know him?"

"Sort of, he's the man who died in the fire today, along with his lady and kid. We're trying to establish motive but he's an ex-cop, there's probably snake pits of motive out there, cops tread on a lot of toes as you know too well yourself" Peter said.

"Strange he didn't leave the city like all retired cops and live a safe distance from the grudge-bearers. Which reminds me, why didn't your Daddy leave town? He stayed. Niles isn't that far from the freak show"

"But my Daddy walks with the Lord, and God is better than any gun, well that's what Daddy says. I don't go in for that horseshit though but whatever get's him through his night I guess."

Peter finished eating another pretzel and wiped some salt and crumbs from his mouth with a small purple tissue. He scrunched the tissue into a ball and shoved it up his right sleeve.

"Why do you think the phone would have been at Howie's in the first place?" he asked.

"Like I told you, Howie was Mark's only family and so all his effects would have been processed and given to Howie. People like Mark don't make last wills and testaments."

"I'm sorry, I should have said" Peter said with his mouth full. "One of my buddies in Wicker Park told me that Howie refused to take his stuff. Mark, his son was gay. Howie kicked him out when Mark came out a few years ago. He point blank refused to take stuff a fag had touched, his words, not mine. All heart, wasn't he?"

"So the phone and Mark's stuff would still be at the cop shop, right?"

"You're a bit behind in procedure these days. It now goes back to the coroner's office where it will be held for up to twelve months but after that will be destroyed."

"Could it be signed out, even for just half a day?" I felt the boiling waters of excitement rush back into my cold harbours of hope.

"Sure, I can do that. I can do it tomorrow if you like. I can say I need to take forensics for an ongoing inquiry or shit like that. Leave it with me, I'll see what I can do"

"Peter, I don't know what to say"

"Sure. Only glad to help. Hey, wait till I tell Daddy about this."
I grabbed Peter's arm.

"No, you must never tell Victor about this conversation or that you met me. One thing I know about Victor is his sense of integrity. Sure, he thinks I'm innocent but aiding and abetting a wanted man is a crime even if that man's innocent. If you tell him about me, you're putting him in a pot of hot soup that he doesn't deserve to be in. He was never a man of the street, he played things straight but he worked in a system as bent as a sickle. This could finish him off. Believe me."

"Chill, man, to me, meeting you is like meeting Batman or something, OK, lips sealed."

"I'm sorry but I have to be careful. And about the phone?"

"Meet me outta town tomorrow, way outta town. You got wheels?"

"Sure, I got wheels"

Peter winced. "Just don't get caught by Highway Patrol on a licence check though. Just drive like a Mennonite spinster and you'll be ok. Meet me at Libertyville, that's thirty miles up Milwaukee Avenue, in Starbucks at around 4pm. It's the only one in the street."

Peter threw a clatter of coins on the table. We shook hands and split.

CHAPTER 19

Tammy and I sat facing one another across the table. We sipped cheap Californian Zinfandel and dined upon a tub of stilted conversation. The wine was tepid, the nachos limp and lousy. I went to the freezer to get a bag of ice cubes. They were all stuck together like a baby iceberg so I smashed the bag on the floor to loosen them up. I tore a little hole in the side and plucked out a few bits of broken ice and plopped them into my wine. The wine fizzed with alarm before settling back down again.

"Like some ice with your wine?" I asked.

"No thanks, it just waters it down."

"You like warm wine, huh?"

"What's it to you what I like? Just sort yourself out."

"Only trying to make nice, Tammy. Jeez."

I put the bag of ice back in the food freezer and returned to the table for some frozen atmosphere with Tammy.

"So what's the story with Mark's phone, did you get it?" Tammy asked.

"Now there's a story" I said.

"So, tell it."

"I went to Howie's house only to find it had been torched the night before. Howie's dead, his girlfriend's dead and her little boy, dead. The house was gutted. All destroyed. Why his house? I mean it's like I'm being jinxed or jinxing those who can help me."

I sank my wine in one go. Some of the ice hadn't fully melted and I melted it on my tongue.

"That's too fucking bad, the phone was in his house. So much for Plan A. Plan B, we go back to Mark's friends and grill them a little bit more and perhaps not be as nice about it"

"I don't think that would work. I think they've told us all they know or want us to know, don't you?"

"Worth a shot, except that you are running out of options. Well Plan C is simple. We skip town. We could buy a truck and hit the road and head south."

I refilled my glass and shook my head.

"That shit only works in movies and books. We'd only run out of money and then what do we do? Get jobs? The fucking bean-eaters can't get jobs that pay more than a dollar an hour so what are the chances for the likes of us? No, Tammy. I'm staying put. I want to stay and clear my name and go back to living the only way I know. A running man ain't a free man, that much I do know"

"Better to run that end up stewing in your shit in the state pen."

"Honey, it ain't an option"

"Hmm, so next steps are?"

"Well, hold your horses a minute. Let me finish what I was going to tell you. While I watched the cops and fire crews, this cop spotted me. He screwed his eyes up and started staring right over at me. I knew that he knew who I was. Man I filled my shorts"

Tammy jumped to her feet. The look on her face. She could have gone the distance with Mike Tyson on that look alone.

"And before you jump out of your skin Tammy, it's all good, just hear me out. He's the son of an old buddy of mine from my days in Homicide. His son's in the force now. Remember that story I told you about the plane that crashed into the downtown river? Well, Victor was my partner at the time. I dragged Victor's ass from the frozen water that day. Anyway, his son Peter spotted me and to cut a long story short, he wants to help me. He believes I'm innocent"

Tammy sat back down

"Ok, keep talking"

"Like I said, it's all cool but get this, you know the dead guy?"

"Which one, the town's full of dead guys"

"Mark, the dead guy from the motel?"

"Huh huh."

"Well, he was gay. He came out a couple of years ago and his daddy disowned him. Not only that, but he refused to take Mark's possessions back when the cops came around with cardboard boxes. Mark's shit is on a shelf in the coroner's office, but if it lies unclaimed for twelve months, it's dumpster time."

"So Mark's phone is in a box in a public building?" said Tammy. She lit a cigarette and sucked the smoke so hard that her cheekbones looked like they were about to bust through her skin. She poured herself a glass of wine to the very brim and took a large sip.

"So what do we do, break in and get it? That's impossible, you know that."

I poured myself the last of the wine and took a swig.

"Peter will get it for us. He's a cop. He can get it"

"When?"

"Tomorrow afternoon. That quick"

Tammy sat back, her eyes darted in all directions. I could tell from how her tongue poked the insides of her cheeks that she was deep in thought, thinking up a dozen reasons why the plan wouldn't work just because it wasn't her's in the first place.

She got up and walked over towards me, putting her mouth to my ear. I felt the warmth of her breath.

"It's just, well, I don't like the idea of being in hock to a cop. I know you say he's OK but can you trust him to keep his trap shut? I mean he sounded a little star-struck and what if he brags to his buddies or girlfriend or whatever? You could find yourself with an unexpected little welcoming party in Libertyville tomorrow, that's all."

"Why would he tell anyone? He'd be drummed out of the force if anyone found out he helped a bail-jumper. It's watertight, when I meet him, I get the phone, then I go to Little Italy. If those bad boys don't crack it, I don't know who the fuck would and that would be game over and perhaps then I'll take you up on that truck to Acapulco."

Tammy smiled but I could tell her eyes didn't

"Well, if you say so, Cal, if you say so." She lifted our plates and scraped the nachos into the garbage pail and put the dishes into the dishwasher.

"Cal, I'm off for a quick shower now."

"I'll make us some coffee."

Tammy got up and left. I brought down a couple of cups from the cupboard and tore open a fresh packet of Filicori filter coffee with my teeth and poured enough for four cupfuls into the pot.

Then it hit me.

It hit me like a ton of rock straight on my gut, so much so it took my breath away. I never told Tammy that the meet was in Libertyville. I never mentioned the word 'Libertyville' to her at all.

How the hell did she know? I heard Tammy turn the water on from the electric shower and I sat down, going over the conversation again and again my head. Yeah I had more wine that was good for me but my tongue wasn't that loose. I rocked back and forth and lit a cigarette. I sat, waiting for her to come out.

Twenty minutes later, she came back in, wearing nothing but a purple bath towel.

"Tammy, how come you know about Libertyville?"

CHAPTER 20

My throat was as dry as a Mormon wedding reception. My hands shook like a booze hound without a hipflask.

"Excuse me?" Tammy said, her voice a tremolo.

"It was something you said while we were eating. How did you know I was meeting Peter in Libertyville? I never mentioned where we planned to meet. How come you knew?"

"But, but, that's where you're meeting him, isn't it?"

"It sure is but you mentioned Libertyville before I even told you where the meet was, what do you say about that?"

She folded her arms. Her mouth was open, her lips formed a perfect circle. Her lower jaw shunted from left to right, trying to pluck the right answer out of the ether.

"Well, you must have told me where it was otherwise how would I know? What's the big deal anyways?"

I clasped my hands together and bent forward.

"But the thing is, Tammy, I didn't. But then you warned me that I could expect to be greeted by an unwanted welcoming party, at Libertyville of all places. How on earth would you know to say the word 'Libertyville'? I know I didn't even mention the fucking word 'Liberyville', so please, no bullshit, how did you know?"

"You mentioned it in your sleep. You talk in your sleep and it drives me insane. You talk about a whole heap of shit. You mentioned Libertyville early this morning before sunrise. That's how I know"

"When, last night?"

"Uh huh, last night, you came out with a whole pile of stuff in the middle of the night, I had to get up and sleep on the couch for a while."

I stared at Tammy. It was a good answer. A very good answer. I do talk in my sleep and it's something that pisses Tammy, a lot, but I knew this time, it was hokum.

"Try this. I only met Peter Lopes today, shortly after lunchtime, I've only known about the meet in Libertyville for a couple of hours tops so I couldn't have mentioned it last night. Now what do you say?"

She stood there with a face of a medieval peasant in a room full of iPhones.

"Perhaps the town was on your mind, I don't know, how the fuck should I know? Why did you suggest Libertyville to Lopes at all? You must have had that town on your mind otherwise you wouldn't have suggested it as a venue in the first place."

That girl can think fast, I gave her that much. She dodged each bullet of fact as I shot them..

Now for the cannon-ball.

"But honey, I didn't suggest Libertyville, Lopes did."

I stood up and circled around the lounge. Tammy remained silent. She shifted her weight from side to side. Her mouth opened and closed like a dying trout. I knew she was cornered and there was no way of knowing how she would fight her way out. I knew her well but that not that well. She was a woman. She could get nasty and the whole thing could blow up in my face. I decided to throw her a lifeline and let the some air out of the balloon.

"Tammy, Peter texted me today with a reminder of tomorrow's meet, was that how you knew? Did you read my private texts? Was that it?"

Tammy emptied her lungs.

"Cal, why the fuck are you doing this to me? That's exactly how I knew you were meeting tomorrow. Your cell-phone was lying there and I saw the text come though and I wondered who it was from, I mean, I couldn't help it, I wouldn't normally snoop and I didn't want to tell you. I just wondered what it was. The phone wasn't locked. I just read the text and as soon as I read it, I felt bad and put the phone down."

"What did it say?"

"I don't know exactly but it was something about meeting tomorrow in Libertyville."

I got mad. She grabbed that lifeline as I thought she would but I felt it dragging me into the water. I decided to yank it back and confront her.

"There was no text. Lopes doesn't even have my number. I made that bit up to see what you'd say, so Tammy, it's time you told me some truth here. I'm not going to let this go"

Tammy sat down. She brought her knees up to her chest.

"Who the fuck are you working for, Tammy? Or should I say 'Veronica'? I found the shoebox, in the closet."

"Shoebox?"

"Yeah, shoebox. Tell me what you know about the shoebox and don't bullshit me. I ain't in the mood"

I crouched down in front of her.

"Tell me... what you know... about the shoebox," I whispered.

She looked like Nagasaki after the big one. I had dropped thousands of tons of TNT on her and all I saw in front of me was a woman turned to dust. She looked small, crumpled up. My Enola Gay wasn't for turning back to Uncle Sam's air hanger any time yet though. My payload was far from empty.

Tammy shivered. Her eyes were vacant, staring over my shoulder.

"Let me tell you about the shoebox. I found a shoebox in the closet, our closet. I thought it was the box where we store fuses and batteries. I took it down and opened it. Guess what I found instead, old photos and news clippings. There was a whole lotta you in there. Your name ain't Tammy Southworth. It's Veronica Gore, Ronnie Gore, widow of Blake Gore, killer of Blake Gore, am I wrong?"

"I'm not going to harm you, Tammy, or Ronnie or whatever your name is, and I don't give a shit about your past but the thing is, you know everything about me. That puts me at a disadvantage; you would have to agree wouldn't you?"

She nodded so gently that it barely registered.

"You're working for someone. Who are you working for, Tammy?"

Tammy started to hyperventilate. I didn't know what to do. Its one thing destroying someone, or something but if you land in the middle of the ruins, you feel it's up to you to rebuild everything.

"You got me fair and square" Tammy finally whispered. "I'm working for someone but I don't know who he is. That's the God's honest truth."

"Now we're getting somewhere. Come back to the table and let's have a real drink and a real talk."

CHAPTER 21

I poured a dash off absinthe into two tallboys and swished them around and drained away the excess down the sink. I added a fistful of crushed ice into each glass, followed with cane sugar and filled the glasses with equal measures of Scotch and cognac. My favourite cocktail, the Old Fashioned. I brought them over to the table and I pulled over a chair and sat down.

I handed Tammy her drink. Her hands were still shaking but not as bad as before. I never hit a woman in my life but I'd no qualms about shooting one stone dead if I had to. There's a huge difference between taking a life and hurting one.

Tammy raised the tumbler to her thin mouth downed it in one. She winced as if the world's biggest lemon was fucking her without lube.

"Tammy Southworth is the name I gave myself after I ran from the town of Priest River, Idaho. Blake was beating me and raping me and I could take no more. I had to, I just had to."

I squeezed her hand. I felt the cold wetness of the outside of her glass as she was clutching it. I stroked the glass a couple of times.

"I ended up here with no money. I flopped down at a YWCA and that's where I met this chick called Davina. She was more or less in the same boat as me but had just started turning tricks. She got a job at Hooter's in Lincoln Park. She told me she was a week away from having enough money to put down a deposit on a two bedroom condo in Oak Park. Hell she was only working for three weeks and she was able to rent a pad in Oak Park. She told me the money was the best in town. Cal, no-one plans a career in a titty bar. I was broke, so before you know it, I was poking my butt into fat men's faces five nights a week and making more money than I ever made before."

"Who were you working for?"

"That bit was difficult to work out. We had a manager, his name was on the liquor licence as a front but he wasn't the guy in charge. The manager's name was Astana or something but, like I said, he wasn't the main man."

"Go on."

"Anyway, one day, Astana told me that I had to go and meet this man in a downtown hotel suite. I panicked. I thought Astana was trying to pimp me and I freaked out but he told me that it wasn't anything like that. He told me that an influential businessman had taken a certain liking to me and had a job for me. So I went along with it."

"Where did you meet him?"

"I met him at the presidential suite of the Imperial."

"When was this?"

"I'm sorry, I don't remember the exact date but I remember the month though, it was the first week of August this year, that I remember."

"So tell me all you know about him."

"That's the strangest thing, I went into the suite and there were two well dressed young women, sharp suits, sharp faces, not a hair out of place. Behind them sat a man with the back of the chair to them. I could see the back of his head. He sat perfectly still."

"Did you see his face?"

"No. He told me to sit down. The two women stared at me and then the man began to speak."

"What did he sound like?"

"He spoke very slowly. I thought he was English or something at first. He was creepy. He sounded like Vincent Price but he was American. He told me why he chose me. He thought I was smart. He told me he could tell I was a cut above the other girls by just looking into my eyes. I thought it was bullshit, something he tells every wide-eyed bimbo but it turned a bit weird. He told me that he sensed I had done something terrible and that had he knew I cut and run and that I had renewed myself. He told me it was this quality of renewal and total ability to lie which was crucial to the assignment he was putting me on"

"Did you tell anyone about your past as Veronica Gore, even any of the girls, Davina too?"

"No way, I couldn't dare. I even gave up liquor when I came to town. I couldn't risk a loose tongue or a late night drunken confession. I didn't tell a living soul. But he seemed to know me inside out in such a short space of time and that freaked me. It's one thing guessing my star-sign from the colour of my g-string but shit, he seemed to know more about me that I thought possible"

"He flattered you and you met him halfway. He made you feel special and you liked the idea of him knowing your secret, didn't you? All you girls had secrets, dark ones usually"

I took a large sip and swirled the liquid around the glass. Tammy shifted in her seat and looked straight at me.

"Callum, one of the women gave me a photograph and a file. The photo, it was you."

"Me?"

"Yes, you. I didn't know who you were and it meant nothing to me. The file contained some basic info, your address, cell-phone number, favourite bars, work address, stuff like that. Then he spoke again. He told me that the man in the photo was about to embark on some life-changing events where his world would be turned upside down. I asked what he meant but he told me not to interrupt. He then told me my role was to be his rescuer but to pretend to be a past client and pretend to help him clear his name but the whole while, spy on him and report back on everything you did"

"So all this took place before Mark's murder"

"Months before Mark's murder" Tammy said

"Is he the guy in charge of all what is happening to me?"

Tammy nodded.

"I asked some questions but he told me all I needed to know was he just told me and to wait on further instruction."

"He wanted me dead?"

"Actually, no. I asked him that. He just said he wanted to see you suffer. He never told me why or for what"

I had worked that bit out already.

"Did he say why he was doing it, even a hint?"

"I asked him but he wouldn't say. All I know is that has a team of people working for him with a mission to destroy you but each of us doesn't have the full picture. We only get told what we need to know"

She continued "One night I get a call and I am given the jeep and this apartment and told to pick you up and start the role play. I was told to give you a special cell-phone. It was rigged so that every conversation or text would be picked up by his people."

"But most of the time, it's switched off" I said. "I hardly ever talk into it let alone text."

Tammy sighed.

"It's been rigged really well. It also acts as a microphone and records all the sound and noise nearby. So when you think your cell-phone is turned off, it's recording what you are muttering to yourself in the john. And when you turn your phone back on, it secretly emails the sound files to his people."

"Do you have the cell-phone he called you on?"

"No, it was taken off me. If you're asking if we're being heard right now, yes, we probably are but I don't give a shit."

I jumped up.

"You mightn't give a shit but I do. This is my life we're talking about here"

"Listen, Cal, you can take your phone to your fone phreak buddies and sure, they can work out the email address that it's sending your shit to and yes, they can work out where its location from the IP address but if these people are as smart as I think they are, they'd cover those tracks real well, but it's worth a shot."

"Tammy, if they hear this conversation, then it mean they know about Peter and my meet tomorrow."

"The phone's in the bedroom. I don't think it could pick up from another room. I think we're ok"

Tammy got up and ran into the bedroom. I followed her and she got dressed and packed a bag. She picked up my cell-phone and opened the bedroom window and flung it out in the night. I stood only a few feet behind her, watching her silhouette against the light off the full moon. Then I heard a dull thud. Tammy fell to the floor. I threw myself down and crawled over to where she lay.

She was still. I called her name but she didn't reply. I lifted myself on top of her and saw her face. There was a large dark hole in the middle of her forehead. I put my hand to her mouth but she was gone.

I knelt over her, kissed her dead lips and closed her eyes. She was still warm.

I crawled over to the bedside locker, grabbed my keys, wallet and a wad of cash. I commando-rolled over to the closet and pulled down a couple of pairs of hard-wearing Levi's, a couple of flannel shirts, a jersey and a jacket and stuffed them into a holdall. There was only one way in and one way out of the apartment. Whoever killed Tammy could be now in the building, down the corridor even, waiting on me to make my exit in more ways than one.

The corridor outside the apartment was very long. One could run a few yards but if the assassin is forty yards away, you're still a gazelle rushing a leopard. I had to think quick. Then I thought of creating a diversion. No better diversion that a fire. I crawled out the bedroom and into the kitchen. There was a smoke sensor above the sink. I found an old copy of the Chicago Sun-Times and soaked it in cognac and flung it into the sink. I took out my Zippo, lit it and set the flame on permanent and tossed it onto the sink. Whoosh. Itty bitty bits of blackened paper and ash floated around like black snow. Second later, the whole building squealed with high-pitched alarm.

I heard what sounded like a miniature stampede of buffalo outside the apartment, a cacophony of voices, young and old, male and female, rushing down the corridor outside. The flames were contained in the sink and were dying out. I grabbed my bag, ran out the front door and let myself get swept along with the human current, down stairwells and corridors and more stairwells until the blast of the draught of cold night-time wind hit my face.

I ran and I ran and I ran until I tasted the blood of exhaustion on my tongue. I caught a cab and went to Wicker Park where I spent the night sleeping on a doorway.

I dreamt about the plane in the river and how the ice cracked, swallowing everything up.

Everything has a habit of cracking in the end.

CHAPTER 22

In the morning, I rubbed the night from my eyes and remembered the business of the day. 4pm at Libertyville to meet Peter Lopes who, with any hope, would have Mark's cell-phone, but I remembered what Tammy had told me. The Puppet Master, as she called him, had me trailed and tailed all this time and would have definitely known about my meet with Peter. Was there any point in going there? Even if I did, would I just fall into his trap?

I walked around a bit and went into a clothes store and bought new pants, boots, a shirt and a jacket. Walgreens was my next stop to get a shaving kit and shower gel and several pairs of socks. I walked away from Wicker Park and towards some post-industrial zone of rusted gates, metal scrap yards and truck and tow companies staffed by mean-eyed Hispanics with sweat-stained, work-a-day short-sleeved shirts. I walked a good distance until I found a run-down motel called Joey's. A twenty room flea pit joint where rooms are rented by the hour but it was a place to hole up and be forgotten.

Outside, a neon sign of Elvis flickers, sucking a Margarita through a winking green straw. I stepped into the motel office. The young man at the desk was listening to early Aerosmith, way before they found love in elevators. The walls were covered in fake wooden-panels made from lino. A dog-eared girly calendar and a framed picture of Jack Kennedy inside a cheap black plastic frame hung on the wall behind where the young guy sat. I asked for a room for a few nights. He threw a key on the counter. "Room six" he said without taking his eyes from the lesbian porn on his computer screen. I threw a hundred bucks on the counter and grabbed my keys.

I found my room, went in and locked the door from the inside and drew the curtains closed. I got out of my clothes and stepped into the shower. After getting dressed, I lay down on the single bed which was squeezed in the corner. The room was decorated in dark green wallpaper with black swirls. The floor was carpeted in the dark hard-wearing, no-nonsense fabric one finds in libraries. Years of cigarette burns and stamped-in gum, takeout food, booze and body-juices scarred the furniture and flooring like sins on a soul.

I turned on the TV and channel-hopped. I stopped on the CNN Chicago channel. I was back in the headlines.

Fuck.

On the screen, the apartment building I had shared with Tammy. Her body was found by a fire crew. The CCTV cameras had clocked me and my prints were found all over the pad.

Fuck.

"Law enforcement officers from the Cook County Homicide Division want to question Callum McCambridge in connection with the death of Veronica Gore whose body was found in an apartment in Winnetka Drive. Veronica Gore, who also went by the alias of Tammy or Tammy Southworth, was wanted in connection with the murder of her husband Blake Gore off Priest River, Idaho. Callum McCambridge, an ex-police officer, is also wanted in connection with the murder of Mark Madigan and is still at large. The public are advised not to approach him as he is believed to be armed and dangerous"

I pressed the mute button on the remote and sat staring at the soundless pictures with the blank-mind of a grazing animal. Peter and Victor would definitely know about this by now. Would they still believe me, take my side? That would be stretching it. A bridge too far in fact. Then another man's face, appeared on the screen. He looked familiar. I turned the sound up and lit a cigarette and sucked in an unholy amount of smoke in one go.

"Police are appealing for witnesses of the murder of a Chicago Homicide police officer. Officer Peter Vincent Lopes was gunned down while as he was jogging along the northern foreshore in Evanston in an apparently motiveless attack. Robbery has been discounted at this stage as no valuables were taken from the scene. Cook County Homicide Division are appealing to anyone who saw or heard anything suspicious to come forward."

I felt like a cornered king on a chessboard, hearing the word 'check' at every move. I knew it was only a matter of time before 'check' became 'checkmate'. I was running out of road and there was no way back. I ran over to the window and peeped out from behind the curtains and looked out. There was nothing there.

I went back to sit on the bed. I thought about Victor and how he must be going out of his mind. The poor man lost his only son. I had to make contact with him. But first, I had a number of bits of business to attend to. I still had my old police badge. I was supposed to hand it back but I kept it as a memento and for insurance. No better Access all Areas ticket, invaluable for a private eye and getting into concerts at the House of Blues or Soldier Field. I then remembered what Tammy told me about the presidential suite at the Imperial Hotel at the beginning of August. I had to find out who booked it. Also, I had to find out who owned the Lonesome Cove Motel.

A couple of hours later, I left my room and walked back towards Wicker Park. There was a bric-a-brac store opposite from Quimby's bookstore. I went in and bought a tatty black leather briefcase that seen better days but I knew I could buff it up with some shoe polish later on and make it look good as new. I ducked into a bar and bee lined my way to the john. In a cubicle, I set to work on painting out the scuffed white bits that glared out from the peeling black-panelling. When dried, I polished the whole goddamned thing with the shoe polish and with a bit of spit and a sock, gave the briefcase a nice old shine.

Now it was time to do some business and pretend I'm a cop.

CHAPTER 23

Walking tall and straight with a swinging, empty briefcase in hand, my first port of call was the Imperial Hotel on Michigan Avenue. Two curved staircases swept with opulence from the upper decks all the way down to either side of the reception. The reception was made from marble and it stood with commanding elegance in the middle of the floor. Well-heeled tourists milled around the foyer. Some sat in plump expensively upholstered armchairs reading newspapers with strangely stern, expressionless faces.

Blond Scandinavian couples, dressed in his-and-hers identical outfits, pored over travel guides and maps. The ever-patient receptionists smiling painfully behind gritted teeth at the same old dumbass questions that only tourists never tire off. Where's the water fountain? Where's the Contemporary Art Museum? Where's Lincoln Park Zoo, the Aquarium, Grant Park et-cet-a-fuck-era.

I joined the queue at reception and waited my turn. One by one the tourists melted away, clutching maps and still looking as confused.

"Good morning, sir, how may I help you?"

I whipped out my badge.

"Good morning, ma'am, my name is Lt Colby from Homicide and as part of an ongoing investigation. I need to check your booking records for your presidential suite in the first week of August of this year."

"Of course sir"

Her smile had turned into a look of anxiety. Two elderly tourists looked at me as if I just did a turd at their feet. I smiled at them and said "Don't worry, the homicide was elsewhere, not here. I hope you enjoy your vacation." They scurried off like stupid mice. The receptionist regained her composure and raised her left arm loftily in the air and walked around from behind the counter towards where I was standing, ushering me away from the guests.

"Lt Colby, we will only be too glad to help but I must ask you to come this way, we don't want to alarm the guests."

I smiled. "Sure ma'am"

She led me into an office down the corridor. A dark-suited man sat behind an oak desk, typing on a computer.

"Cleo, don't you know to knock first?" he said without looking up. It mustn't have been the first time she barged in. That would certainly drive me crazy if she worked in my office but with the ass she packed in her short little navy skirt, I'd forgive her for spilling hot coffee on my dick.

"I'm sorry, Mr Hunter, but this gentleman is from Homicide and he wants to check our booking records for the presidential suite for the first week of..."

She looked over at me with a beckoning expression.

"The first week of August," I said, finishing her sentence. "My name is Lt Colby from Homicide and we are investigating the death of a Mr Mark Madigan at the Lonesome Cove Motel on the night of October 13, 2008."

"Lonesome Cove Motel, October? I don't see the connection."

"We believe whoever was behind his murder was linked to the people who used your presidential suite at the start of August of this year. I hope you could oblige without needing to obtain a court order from the Attorney's office."

"That won't be necessary. This hotel prides itself in its civic responsibilities."

He got up from his chair and walked over to a filing cabinet.

"By the way, you won't mind me phoning your department just to check that you are who you say you are."

I had to think fast.

"Well, sir, there you have me. I'm not supposed to be here. It's not official if you catch my drift. My informant has fallen out of favour with my superior and they won't authorize any line of inquiry that comes from my informant. It's internal politics but as far as I'm concerned, my informant's word is as good as it ever was. I'd be neglecting my primary duties as a police officer if I ignored him. However, if you really feel I'm operating outside my jurisdiction, I'll be happy to leave right now but believe me, I am on the tail of a killer and if it's not me asking you this, someone else will down the line so you may as well save a little time and trouble and oblige me the best you can."

Hunter looked at me and folded his arms. His equine face exuded a sense that this was a man who never believed anything he was told in his life. I was spinning some major piece of yarn here but he wasn't to know that.

"I see, Lieutenant. Hmm, that's unfortunate, so this is not a legitimate investigation?"

"Mr Hunter, I did see his badge," Cleo chipped in.

"Thank you, Cleo, I am glad I can entrust you with the basic protocols," he said. "You may return to your position."

Cleo nodded and left, leaving the door open behind her. Hunter shook his head and walked across the room and shut the door himself with an exaggerated sigh. I got the impression he was bullied at school and now loved belittling people to get his own back on the world. Nazis didn't need to invade if they were around, I thought. All they need to do is wake up the light sleepers.

"She'll get the hang of it eventually, sir, we once had a housemaid like that," I said. I sometimes come out with folksy shit like that to calm the nerves, not least mine.

"I certainly hope so, Lieutenant, where were we? Ah yes, so remind me, you are working solo without sanction of your bosses? Hmm, I don't know what to think about that." He went to his desk and lifted the receiver of his phone.

"Well, any investigation conducted by an officer of the law for an open case is legitimate in itself. I'm breaking no law here except pissing on my boss's shoes, but that's my headache" I said

"I don't like mavericks much" he said.

"Well, I don't see myself like that, sir."

"You know, these motels and the like, they're a million miles away from a fine five-star establishment like this of course but I do take a very unhealthy, obsessional interest in the affairs that are conducted in our fine city's many hostelries. Murder indeed. That young man was murdered by an ex-cop of all people, a Mr McCambridge I believe his name was, also wanted for killing some girl only yesterday. Shocking stuff. That motel, Lonesome Cove, was closed for years, you know."

"Really? I've reason to believe it was reopened in recent times" I swallowed hard.

"The 'Cove' as it's locally known as, was built in the 1930s by Morley Case and he and his family ran it until the late 1970s when bankruptcy forced it's closure. The grandson, Jack Case, was the final owner. Awful bad luck in that family. Jack's wife, Alice hung herself in Room 76. Her lover, Frank Weekes, was found dead in the next room. Gunshot wounds. Jack couldn't face working there anymore and tried to sell it but you know how it is, who wants to buy a mote with that history? He ended up doing the next best thing, borrowing a lot of cash on the equity and vanished into the night, taking his money with him. The motel closed and the bank took it over and tried to sell it, but they couldn't. The bank put it down as a bad debt and forgot about it and had it boarded up"

"That's an interesting story, sir."

"That's why I was surprised to hear someone bought it and reopened it."

"You wouldn't know who owns, would you?" I said.

205

"I know it was none of my business but I went to County Hall and checked the records. "DD Holdings" based in Atlantic City, purchased the site from First Illinois Bank in April 2008. Its CEO was a woman named Davina Steiger but my sources tell me she was just a front. Apparently she was a hooker. Don't ask me how I know. I just know"

I raised an eyebrow and nodded. I didn't give a shit about who puts his dick into whom.

"DD Holdings" he went on "They closed down soon after the killing. Money to burn, don't you think?"

"Looks like it, sir."

"Presidential suite, first week of August of this year. Hmm" said Hunter. He leant back on his seat and rose from his desk and went back to his filing cabinet. He plucked out a yellow manila folder and looked inside it. "Hmm. That's odd"

"What's that, sir?"

"Well according to our records, we only rented the suite out to two people that month. Once at the start of August for eight days and the other to a regular client of ours. But the first booking...."

I walked over to where he was standing and looked over his shoulder.

"The booking was made under the name of Callum McCambridge, that wouldn't be the same fellow who killed that poor young man in the Lonesome Cove, would it?"

Someone had used my name to book the suite where Tammy was invited to when she met the man of mystery.

"It certainly looks like that, sir, very interesting indeed."

"Would you like a photocopy?"

I swallowed. "That would be a help."

Hunter walked up to the Xerox, put the page on the glass and pressed the green button. A laser of bright light rolled up and down and a copy eased out of the side of the machine. He picked it up and handed it to me. I looked at it. It was the invoice but in my name.

I had to make sure I didn't refer to myself in the first person for the rest of the conversation.

"How did McCambridge pay for the room?"

"According to the sheet, it was paid for by credit card."

I went cold thinking off the next monthly Mastercard bill but I realised I don't pay my bill no more.

"Would you have the card number at all, sir? That would be very useful."

"Of course, it's right there, that sixteen-digit number to the side of the booking entry."

I saw it. I own three credit cards and I memorise the final four digits of each of the long numbers but this was not one of them.

"You have been a great help, Mr Hunter, I appreciate your time"

"Always a pleasure, unless there is anything else?"

"No, that'll be all. I'll be in touch if I need anything else."

Hunter opened the door and we shook hands and I left.

Follow the money, that's what the man says. I wondered if I could link that credit card number to anything else. I needed one helluva legal crowbar to shunt a boulder that size. I had a few friends left in the force, not many though but it was too much of a risk. Most of the cops I once knew are dead, dead drunk or dead gone.

It was time to make a Ouija board and contact the spirits of the living.

CHAPTER 24

I went returned to Joey's Motel later than night with a six-pack of Bud, cans of rum and cola, a carton of smokes and a box of McNuggets and pigged out. I sat on the side of the bed and chain-smoked and drank one beer after another, tossing the dead soldiers into the wastepaper basket beside me. The six-pack wasn't enough so I made head roads into the rum.

I demolished the first can like a cat on a crippled canary. I felt the dark, slow burn of the rum in the back of my throat and in its journey down my throat. I felt warm and soothed like the afterglow of a good fuck or a nice long warm bath. I could be an alcoholic. There's an option. Give it all up and surrender to the bum-hood. Grow a large, shitty red beard, drink cleaning fluids and with mouthwash chasers, break a million veins in my face and loll around the tourist spots chasing Koreans and barking at Brits. That would be a life of sorts. I wouldn't be Callum McCambridge anymore neither. No, I'd just be a drunken fuck head and end up dying under a bridge somewhere and be eaten by dogs or other bums.

I cracked open another can and another until I passed out.

*

I woke up the following morning with a burning hangover. It felt like a buffalo had emptied its bowels into my bloodstream. My throat burned for water. I got up and my legs wobbled and I fell on the floor. Fuck. I rubbed my eyes red and clung to the side of the bed to help myself stand up. I felt my legs were over boiled spaghetti strings without a pick of bone to hold them up. I sat down on the bed and looked out at what passed for morning. Ling thin nails of rain lashed at the windows, the sky as gray as an East German broken toy factory. I sat and watched the drops slide down the pane, melding into one another, forming little rivulets that meandered down to the sill. Was this how rivers are formed I wondered. Was this how lives turned out too for that matter?

I went to the bathroom and held my mouth under the cold water faucet and drank water like I never drank before. I even wrapped my lips around the metal. When I had drunk my fill, I wiped my mouth, got undressed and stood under the shower head and turned the power up to full throttle. I closed my eyes as I felt the bullets of water hit my skin like vengeful shards of hail. No better way to wake my sleepy blood and get it to reclaim the dried beds of my veins. I stood there for fifteen minutes until I felt a little more alive. I stepped out and dried myself on a damp brown towel, shaved and got dressed. I packed my things and threw the key on the bed and I left.

There was a man who lost his son who I had to go and see him.

CHAPTER 25

I bought an all-day ticket for the Loop at Division and spend the entire daytime riding the network. It's the best place for people watching. The morning passengers ebbed away like a biological tide around mid-morning. Then a rainbow of humanity swept back and forth from the platforms and into the carriages. Kids, tourists, people playing truant, snatching a day to visit the museums and galleries. Me, I was killing time, every second spent in the no man's land of the Chicago Transit Authority was a second less of being my hunter's quarry. I waited hours until sunset before I got off at Union Station and got the northbound Fox Lake Amtrak line.

I had someone to see.

Twenty minutes later, I got off at Glenview and walked up its main drag. It was still busy with shoppers, huddling and scurrying from the rain. I took out a little map I had made of the area to get my bearings. '43 Patriot Boulevard' was only a short walk away, just past the Harley Davidson big-box. I walked up the road and down a number of big house streets until I arrived at Victor's street. It didn't long until I found his house. A couple of dozen cars were parked outside and all along the street, on either side of his house. A knot of men and women milled around the doorway. Dark suits, crisp white shirts and blouses, black netted hats, drawn faces. I stood at a respectful distance and didn't come closer. One by one as the hours passed, the cars melted away leaving a hard core of Lopes family cars parked in the driveway.

The front door opened and two couples stepped outside. Hugs, handshakes and 'if there's anything we can do's'

The younger of the two couples jumped into their Buick convertible, reversed and sped off. Their tires screeched as they vanished beyond sight. The older couple lingered on the driveway. The old man idly kicked some gravel with the heels of his black leather shoes before digging his hands into his pockets. His wife went in, leaving him alone at the door. He looked up at the sky as though looking for an answer.

He looked across the road in my direction. He saw me. This wasn't the time or place for reunions. The credit column I may say that I once saved a man's life but the name of his son was written as a debit. I was the coin in both transactions. I made myself small and walked away, back towards Glenview. I bought a coffee and a packet of smokes and went to sit in the shelter of the train station on the Chicago-bound platform. It was quiet at that time of evening. The meandering, lost noises of distant cars and people and music from bars floated through the night air with the brittle beauty of gossamer. I closed my eyes and let myself drift with the soundtrack of the not-so-distant town.

I was all alone in the wet and the dark of the night. The distant rumble of a freight train hounded away the more fragile sounds until both the train and its sound approached with the subtlety of unwanted thunder. An eternity of carriages and containers hurtled past, all delving deep into the heart and soul of an elsewhere America.

When the horns of the freight train subsided into the distance, I looked at the platform opposite. There, stood a man with gray hair wearing a dark suit under a heavy gray overcoat. I was no longer alone. I stood up and lit a cigarette. He did the same. We both smoked in silence, gray plumes bellowing from our mouths like the vapour from long-dormant steam engines. The dark of the stormy November night felt as thick as a vat of cold tar macadam.

"McCambridge," he shouted. He threw his cigarette down and squashed it with his foot, the plume choked out like a dying ghost.

I stood up straight and nodded my head in silent acknowledgement.

"Let's go for a walk."

CHAPTER 26

We walked along our respective platforms in an unlikely parallel line until we both came to the railroad crossing and stopped.

"I guess this conversation is a long time coming," I said.

He didn't reply at first. He looked at the expanse of the night above, the absence of light in totality. No stars, just bleak cloud.

"Imagine a land where it rained like this for a million years. No one in living memory would ever have seen the stars but there are folktales about them. Tales of stars that no one believes anymore because everyone is too smart to believe anything, except money"

I stood and listened, watching him as he faced me, toying with me with his words, waiting for the stab.

"But what people don't understand is that cloud-cover vanishes in the end. It only takes one wind in one direction and bang, the sky comes out, blue as anything" He continued pacing around. I awaited his next soliloquy.

"I'm sorry about Peter, Victor."

Victor stopped and looked at me.

"I dunno, McCambridge, I think I preferred you as a folk memory."

"Are you saying the cloud's lifted?"

"In a manner of speaking" he said. "The cloud's gone but the sky is a navy blue. Go figure that one out. So what the fuck do we do?"

I lowered my head, looking at my shoes, grazing the ground with the soles. I walked over to the railroad crossing and crossed the track, over to Victor's side. I lifted my head and looked at him, his eyes locked on me the whole nine yards.

"I guess we just know too much about one another for comfort, don't we?"

"Fuck sake, McCambridge, I can't look you in the eyes no more. We're like pens that keep fucking writing in each other's diaries. Tell me, what's next, huh? What's friggin' next" he said, hands outstretched.

"Who says anything's next, Victor?

"Did you kill that guy?"

"No, I didn't. You know that."

"I didn't think you did," he said. He shuffled his feet and looked away from me.

"Set up, was it?"

I nodded and looked into the middle distance. The horizon was indistinct, I couldn't tell where the sky met land. It was liked someone spilled ink on the page and blotted out the join.

"I'm glad you believe me. It means a lot" I said.

"I just know you didn't kill that motel boy but my boy is a cold slab of meat six feet under the ground because of you, McCambridge. What do you say to that?"

He stared spears at me. He stood his ground. The old Victor would have come around and knocked seven bells out of me but this man that stood before me was a husk. Life scooped out and replaced it with soft, heavy, wet mounds of mould.

"I didn't ask him to help me, Victor, but I can't say I wasn't grateful. I needed all the help I could get. I still do. I just don't wanna fry or spend my life in the can for something I didn't do. Peter knew what he was doing. I warned him off but he wanted to help."

He pointed at me. "You've darkness in your heart, McCambridge, in fact it's worse than that, you've a void where no light can ever shine and I can tell, I can tell when a man is his own haunted house."

"You talking about Hoffa now, aren't you?"

He went quiet and lit another cigarette and walked over towards me. He crossed the line.

"That's no name to toss to the big, open wind, there's lots of big, open ears around here. A fuck-nut like you should know that," he said.

"Hoffa's ancient history. He's even in school history books now. Up there with Capone and George Washington, just another dead white guy to write an essay about," I said.

 Ancient history, I said. There's no such fucking thing as ancient history. The past is like a graveyard where memories are buried in shallow graves. The coffins have no lids and it stinks the place up. The stink lingers. Boy it lingers. It gets on your clothes, your tongue, your hair. Nothing can wash it away. The past, I'll tell you about the past. It creeps up on you and shouts 'boo' and you jump..

"You pulling me from the water just pushed me over the edge. I thought it bad enough that I took Johnny Friends's money too. Bet you never knew that but I did. We all did. It didn't sit right with me. I wanted to be punished. I lived to be punished. I wanted to be punished real hard but I never had the guts to do it myself. How do you think I won all those medals of honour and bravery down the years, huh? It was fuck all to do with being Mr Braveballs, I walked deliberately into situations that I hoped would burn me up but then you rescued me. I wanted to drown, but no, you even had to take away my punishment. How can I repay that? With a case of Bud Light? A handshake?"

He continued "Callum, did it ever fucking bother you that he was tied up and shitting himself with fear in the trunk of your car?"

"Yes, it bothered the fuck out of me but, Victor, I've said it once and I'll say it fucking again, it wasn't me who tied him up or stuffed him into the trunk or put a slug in his head. It wasn't you either. See, that's how I deal with it." I said as calmly as I could yet my fists were clenched like a middle manager's butt cheeks.

Victor paced up and down, sucking at his cigarette, walking into the plumes of smoke that lingered in the now still air.

I felt I had run out of words. "I'm sorry about Peter" I muttered

"He was coming back from a wild goose chase, wasn't he?" Victor asked.

"Did he tell you much?" I asked.

"Nada, nothing. Peter was always a fuck nut. I tried to talk him out of joining the force but hell no, it was the only thing he wanted to do. The only fucking job he'll ever do as it turned out and I know you're wondering, ha, I know you're wondering. Well the answer is 'no'. A big fucking 'No'. Peter didn't have a cell-phone when they found him, not even his own."

I expected as much.

"They probably took it"

"You don't get it. Peter never had the frickin' phone in the first place. Peter told the Coroner's Office that he was working a case and he needed access to the personal effects of Mark Madigan. They asked him if there was any specific item of interest. He told them the cell-phone but that's when they told him that there was no cell-phone. They took Peter to the box and showed him. I know all this, the Coroner's secretary made a statement. After that, Peter went and got himself shot like a dog. The papers say it was a mugging but I know it wasn't. They didn't take his wallet or shit. It doesn't make sense."

I shrugged my shoulders.

"Someone knows about me, Victor. Someone knows my moves before I make them. I have a lot of fleas to shake off but I would be proud of Peter, he believed in doing the right thing. I didn't ask him to do it. He helped me because he wanted to. I think you and I have just forgotten what it's like to want to do the right thing."

"Forgotten to do the right thing? Shit, we've forgotten what the right thing is, never mind doing it."

"You might have a point," I said. "Victor, there's something else, Tom Lockie, remember him?"

Victor nodded.

"It was Lockie. He plugged Hoffa."

"Stone me. I heard rumours but I paid no attention. Shot him himself? Lockie was one crazy son of a bitch. What happened to him? Is he dead or in the can these days?"

"Lockie left the force a month later," I said. "He went to ground. No one heard from him again. Probably dead by now," I shivered. The night was getting colder.

Victor smiled.

"In 1979, I was in Narcotics. I was a sergeant then and we were working on an undercover operation. The man in our sights was a certain Johnny Friends. Yeah, him. The force was cleaned up by then"

"We planned to raid some of his warehouses on Drexler. Information received. We were in position. I remember the excitement but we were shitting our pants too. This was the culmination of all our work. All angles covered. We were in unmarked SWAT vans, itching for the nod to rush in. Then, half an hour before the raid, a yellow Jaguar slinks its way in and parks outside the warehouse. Smoked black windows. Its engine ran for a while and then it cut out. Man, we watched that car like hawks. We didn't know what the fuck was going on. Then the driver-side door opens. A man got out. Boy was he was dressed to kill. Black Armani suit, black patent leather shoes, the crispest white shirt. I thought it was Lagerfeld himself, but this guy was smaller. Oh, and did I forget, the shades? Wow, those shades..."

"What were you, Narcotic's fashion correspondent?"

Victor closed his eyes and smiled. He continued.

"I recognised the well-dressed man. It was Tom Lockie. It was over the radio, I heard that the license plate was registered to a cab firm owned by Johnny Friends. Then I twigged. Lockie was working for Friends. We had to abort the raid. We didn't know if Lockie had gone native or whether he was deep undercover. A lot of feverish phone calls were made that day. As for the rumours and hearsay, ha, if only water coolers and coffee machines could talk"

Victor coughed. He continued "Turned out Lockie had gone bad. He was one of Friends's men. Had been since after Hoffa. The raid was called off once the mayor got wind of it," Victor said.

"No shit, Mayor Daley. Him and Friends are like that. The whole town knows it" I held up my index finger, twisting my second finger around it.

Victor smiled.

"There's a Pandora 's Box out there and I suspect you want a take peek inside. You'll never change. I don't think you'll thank me if I let you."

"Was Daley in on the scam?"

"Is the Pope a Catholic? You know the Daleys ran this city like their own medieval fiefdom since the fucking dawn of time. They say the mob come to City Hall for refresher courses. No licences get issued without a Daley getting a cut of the action. I ain't just talking about licences for selling pizza slices down by Navy Pier, no, I'm talking about the kinda licences that don't get printed on paper if you catch my drift"

"The mayor lets pushers peddle and taxes it?"

"Major Phillips was in charge of the investigation into Friends and hadn't told Daley. He didn't trust him. Phillips was clean. He was a good man but he was naive. He didn't have a political bone in his body. I mean, even if he did go all the way and put bracelets on Friends, how long would he have held up that trophy in the air someone cut his arms off?"

"Major Phillips, I knew off him. Never worked with him" I chipped

"Sure, Major Phillips, cleaner than an angel's ass. Not long after a kilo of coke was seized from his basement during a dawn raid. He was a Mormon. Didn't even drink coke let alone sniff it or deal it. He did solitary for fifteen long ones. Hung himself when he came out."

Victor whipped out a hipflask and handed it to me.. I sucked a couple of mouthfuls of the whisky, swirled the devil's mouthwash around my teeth a couple of times before swallowing, feeling the finger of flame licking its way down the front of my insides.

"Whatever happened to Lockie? No one knows where he is? That's kinda hard to believe"

Victor shrugged, took the flask, necked back a drink and wiped his lips.

"He's alive, in a semi-detached state from Friends from what I hear, fell out of favour. He's gotten old, like us. You know how people like Friends get tired of their new toys. I'm surprised he held onto the one bagman as long as he did. Lockie works part-time in Wal-Mart when he isn't soaking or snorting."

I pondered on Lockie stacking shelves and telling suburban retards if they were having a nice day.

"Ever think of paying him a visit?" I asked.

"Nah, what could I say? Besides, he's a snake in the grass, going over the way he did. Who knows what other kinds of vipers would be lying in wait if you stick your head in that nest."

Victor then grabbed my arm.

"Don't even think about it. What companionship can the light have with the dark? Leave that shit in the graveyard and let it rot to nothing." Victor said, eyes bulging. He took another swig.

"Johnny ran vice rings, you knew that, didn't you?" Victor said. "He ran vice rings, imported girls from Latvia, Poland and Romania before it became the fashion. He used a number of swanky Gold Coast apartments. Well, get ready for the newsflash of your life, McCambridge. Those swanky fuck pads were owned by Hubert Lonsdale, your father-in-law. Betcha you didn't know that"

My blood ran cold. I felt faint and stood a few steps back and rubbed my numb face.

"I'm giving you a chance and god knows you want to take a poke at me but that's a heap of shit if I ever I heard it"

"Cool your spurs McCambridge. Hubert knew nothing about it, unlike his son, Hector, though. Hector Lonsdale and Johnny Friends were associates. Hector let Friends use the apartments in exchange for a cheap supply of coke. We suspected Hector sold them to college kids in Northwestern for pocket money. He loved playing the gangster, you know that. Hector was your brother-in-law. You know that too. Hector was like a poodle playing at the end off a long leash."

Hector, Lorna's older brother was the original black sheep. He was also a compete asshole. I can't say I ever liked him. A real creep show artist. Hubert held an even lower opinion of him. He actually ran him out of town before Lorna and I were married. I never found out why and that's saying something as I'm a nosy fucker but it must have been bad. Perhaps Hubert opened the lid on that stinking box and didn't like the smell. Hubert kept those cards real close to his chest and took them to the grave"

"I guess there isn't a lotta room left in that Pandora 's Box of yours for anything more," I said.

I grabbed the hipflask off Victor and finished off the rest of the whisky.

Victor's smile turned flat and he looked at me.

"Even I can't tell you what's left inside Pandora 's Box. I suspect you will find out sometime soon but you can point a gun to my head and I still won't tell you."

"That's all very well, Victor, but if there's anything that will get me off this meat hook then I'm going to put all kinds of cannon to all kinds of skulls, yours included. Sorry, you know how it is."

"Well, I've said too much. I talk some shit when I've a drink in me," Victor said. "It's time I walked into town, grab a coffee and chew on some mints before going home. Oops didn't I say, I buried a son today. You wanna come home and say hi to Mai Tang? She's my new wife."

I shook my head. "Thanks but I think I'll pass"

"That's a shame," Victor uttered. "Did I ever tell you I found Jesus?"

"Oh yeah? Where was he hiding?" Victor winced at my tone.

"Yeah, I've heard all those jokes before. You ain't no Jack Benny"

"Ok, ok. Point taken" I said. "Does Jesus do it for you?"

"Not all the time. Sometimes I lose him and I never know where I left him. He's worse than a pair of pants sometimes."

I smiled at that. I forgot what a wag Victor could be. Life can shovel a hundred feet of shit on someone but their light will always find a way through in the end.

Sometimes.

Victor gave me a drunken salute before shuffling off into the darkness. His outline faded until he became a fibre in the fabric of the night. I lit a cigarette and walked up the tracks. I whipped out my cell-phone and called a cab to take me back into the heart of the city. I needed lights, the noise of cars, the chatter and squeals of people as an antidote to the stillness of the evening. As long as I feel and hear shit like that, I know I'm alive, in some way.

CHAPTER 27

"Mr Lockie, we're giving you the chance to tell your side of the story"

Tom Lockie sat in his chair, armed crossed, feigning insolence, stubborn as a pig-shit on a prom queen's tiara. He looked around the room, cocked his head a few times and blew bubblegum.

"Mr Lockie, you give us no option but to terminate your contract."

"What for? He was a cock sucker, I want Friday morning off. I've a card school late on Thursday and it might be a heavy duty one an' I need Friday off, man."

"Mr Lockie..."

"Fucking asshole won't give it me, I asked him for the morning off and he says no cos Marly's off that day an' we're short but that's not my fucking fault that you cocksuckers can't get someone else"

"So that's why you hit her. You hit Miss Laskoski, your supervisor, because she didn't give you time off work?"

"Her? Her? It's hard to fuckin' tell a he from a she with those fucking Polack dykes. She's a fucking freak. She has a dick. I know because I sucked it. Hahahahah. I'm so fucking out of here."

Lockie pointed his finger at a sobbing Miss Laskoski.

"You're fucking lucky I don't get Johnny to finish you, fuck-bitch." He cleared his throat and spat a ball of greeny-brown phlegm in her direction. It landed with a splat just above her head upon the wall. It stayed still for a split second before sliding down the wall, leaving a wet, shiny trail in its wake.

Lockie walked out and strode down the aisles with his chin up. He saw a couple of cops looking busy further on down towards the entrances and exits.

Lockie figured they weren't comparing shopping lists.

Their demeanour had purpose. The cops walked down one of the aisles in the direction of the manager's office. Lockie took off his ID badge, removed his Wal-Mart-apron and stuffed them under a box of plastic ping-pong racquets and weaved his way through the aisles and out of the store. He walked down past the first corner on the left and bolted down Newfield Avenue. Sirens wailed. Squad cars buzzed and wasped up and down the streets. Lockie hid behind a dumpster and crouched. He snatched a view of the street. As the sirens faded, he snuck out and walked around the block, making his way to Fortnum and Fifth. There was nothing there but a whole lotta abandoned houses, whole streets of them. Benweed and wild grass had boneheaded their way through the thinning concrete. Lockie listened to the distant hum of the city and looked around the ghost town that had grown up around.

"It's been a long time coming. How the fuck are you still alive?"

Lockie looked around. I stood across the way, dressed in jeans and a short, brown camel jacket, smoking a cigarette and swigging from a bottle in a brown bag.

"Well fuck me stone dead, Callum McCambridge, what the fuck man, how did you find me? Did you follow me?"

I smiled. "Don't you remember the date?"

Lockie shook his head. "Man, it's all I can do to remember what my name is, never mind quiz-show shit like that."

"OK, man, chill. It's alright. Remember Melanie Wilkes, Lockie?"

Lockie walked over and sat down on the stone wall next to me. He said nothing but grabbed the bottle off me, took a huge mouthful of it and swallowed hard. I grabbed the few seconds I had just to study Lockie. The years hadn't been kind to him but then he hadn't been very kind

224

to the years either. His skin was gray with thin ribbons of broken veins that threaded from his nose like blue cheese. His nose was well on its transformation to a light bulb.

Hard times, bad living.

The good times had taken a chisel and cut youth and warmth from out of his face.

Lockie finished drinking, burped and handed the bottle back.

"I come here every year, you know. I didn't have time to get flowers this time though. Do you think she'll mind?" he asked.

"I don't think she'll mind at all" I said. "So you come here every year?"

"On the same date it happened, every year, no matter what I'm at or feeling. Every year I come here, to this very spot" Lockie said, repeatedly jabbing the air beneath his index finger to make the point. Lockie then got onto his knees and began feeling the paving stones, running his fingers along the cracks. He rubbed his palms along the cold, coarse smoothness of the slabs. "This is the right spot too, look, the stain, the stain is still here, man."

I looked down and saw Lockie trace his right index finger around an irregular shape on the slab. The shape was a different colour from the rest of the slab. The slab was mottled gray, pitted and pockmarked. This shape was the colour of dried blood.

"All these years, all the suns and all the rains and she still won't wash away. She was a stubborn son of a bitch and still is, man. Look, the bullet hole, it's still fucking here, can you believe it? It's still fucking here," Lockie said

I got up, bent down and put my hand on Lockie's shoulder. "You're torturing yourself, man. This isn't doing you any good."

"It's all I have left, Cal. Sometimes pain is all a man has left, you know? Why can't people just let me keep that, just that at least?" he asked.

I nodded silently and squatted beside Lockie. Lockie was still tracing the rusty silhouette with his finger. I looked on, following Lockie's fingers with my eyes.

"It wasn't your fault, blaming yourself all these years. It's no wonder, no wonder...forget I said that."

"No wonder what, man? No wonder I'm fucked up now, was that it? Let me spare you your blushes but yeah."

"You were on hot pursuit at the time and Melanie stepped out in front of you. You'd only a split second. Everyone knows that."

Lockie buried his head in his hands and rocked back and forth.

"Get off me, man, it wasn't like that."

"What do you mean it wasn't like that?"

Lockie lifted his head and looked straight ahead, blankly.

"Her brother was calling me names. I forget what they were but he called me a retard. That pissed me. I took out my gun as a joke to point at him but I dropped my cigarette on my lap. I burnt my lap and panicked. I pulled the trigger. It happened so quick. I still remember her smiling up at me as she lay dead on the sidewalk. I had to make that shit up about seeing Vincent Caribilo taking aim at me. You remember Vincent Caribilo, stick up artist? If I told the truth, I would have been the end of me, and the job. I figured there was no point in destroying two people's lives. It was a choice between hers and mine."

I remembered Caribilo. He held up almost every major jewellers in town for ten years, constantly evaded capture

"He was nicknamed the Ghost cos no one could catch him" Lockie said. "People say they saw him here and say they saw him there. I played on it. That was my cover. You gotta believe me, it was an accident. I killed Melanie though by playing at being a dumb ass."

We both sat in silence, staring down at the ground. The truth is its own ghost. It haunts itself and those who seek it. It may be virtuous but it don't always make you feel good.

"It's still a long time ago. Details don't really matter now."

"A friend of mine had cancer, he died. He knew he had a lump for months but he ignored it. The lump didn't ignore him though. That's the thing with cancer. The bad always eats the good, it's never the other way around," Lockie said.

"You think good can't overcome evil?"

"No such thing as good, Cal. I've never seen any but I've seen a lot of evil. You have too"

"Most folk think it's the other way around."

"Most folk can eat shit." Lockie laughed at his own joke with a ribald chortle as if his vocal chords had been dipped into a treacly mass of liquor and tobacco tar and lit like a candle. "I was born in one of those houses, Mac."

I shivered a little at being called Mac. Lockie was the only one who ever called me that, all the way through police academy and till the end all those years ago. Even now after all this time.

"That one over there, the second from the right, 344 Coburn Way. I remember this street when it heaved and hived with people, families coming and going, sitting on the steps, talking with everyone who crossed the path. Where does all that life go to, Mac? Where does it all go? Surely it can't just go into thin air. Do you think they all come back at night and live like they did in the past, Mac? Do ya?"

"I don't think so," I said. "I broke into a house like that not so long ago all I heard was myself, my own breathing, my own thoughts."

"Perhaps you broke into the wrong house, man. I bet if you broke into mine over there, you'd hear my brother Kevin trying out his guitar and trying to be Tom Petty or some shit. You might even hear my pop throw mom against the stove and my mom throwing plates on the floor. She would even make a mean Moussaka on a Saturday night. Uncle Georgio and his latest flame would come around. It wasn't all bad. I remember laughter. Do you remember laughter? No one ever laughs anymore, except when they're nervous. People used to be happy. Now we have Apple devices instead. I wish I could go back and press rewind and play it all again, just one more time."

I nodded.

"I wish they would tear these tombstones down. Look at them, fucking mausoleums and the people who used to live in them mightn't even be dead. Sick, man, that's what it is."

"How do you mean, 'sick'?" I asked.

"Them houses are like graves, man, it ain't right. People used to live in them. Houses have souls too. People get born and people get dead and it's the same with houses. Them houses are dead. They should be buried like people. Who lives with a corpse in his crib? That's what I was saying to you, it's the evil that eat the good and the city can ignore shit like this but cancer don't like being ignored. It's like a jealous woman, she always gets her way" Lockie said, shaping his hand into a gun and pointing the fleshy barrel to the side of his head.

"I hear you," I said. We spent the next few minutes passing the bottle back and forth, sitting in silence.

"I loved Melanie, man, it's all gone to shit after that," said Lockie.

"How come you went the way you did and Victor and I, well, went the way we did, you know, after Hoffa?"

Lockie looked at me.

"That's easy. We had tickets for our destinations already bought. What's in us is in us. I was that way anyway, the Hoffa thing, that was the straw that broke the thing. I couldn't go back pretending to be good. I didn't have it in me."

228

"Yeah but how did you get into bed with Johnny Friends, I mean, I don't remember me or Victor being head hunted like that? What was it about you?"

Lockie smiled. It was only then that I noticed his teeth. A few missing at the front, a giant black gap between two yellowing ivories. His smile reminded me of a junkyard piano, missing the D and G notes.

"I was bad from the start. I was dealing since graduation. Get me? Dealin'. They paid me to ignore them plus I sold a bit on the side. They had me more than I had them. The Devil don't renegotiate contracts but it's the Devil, not Jesus, who is the real fisher of men. Man he reeled me in and no amount of wriggling could set me free."

"You could have hopped on a plane and not come back"

"I didn't want to, Mac, I was his right-hand man. I descended into hell and sat at the right hand of the Godfather." Lockie chuckled at his own joke until he started coughing. When he stopped, he wiped his mouth on his sleeve. "Excuse me."

"I could have walked. I did want to but the time was never right. I could ask the same question about you, why the fuck are you still doing a tightrope walk over your own grave when you could be on more solid distant ground?" Lockie asked.

"What do you know about me?"

"Well, you're on the run, but you like putting your face about from what I hear. You're skating on thin ice, man, that's all I'm saying."

"I didn't have you down as a news-hound, you seem strangely clued up on things for a guy in your situation."

Lockie cleared his throat. "Can I've some more of that?"

"Why ask for it when you can grab?"
"Sure." Lockie took another mouthful and downed it and cleaned his face on his sleeve.

"I ain't much of a news hound man but I have been known to make the news happen, if you feel me."

"I don't follow you."

"That boy at the motel? Mark whatever-his-name-was. We've both interviewed our fair share of dames, each one making those big doe 'But I am innocent' eyes at us and we say 'I know you didn't kill him, honey' while all the time they wet thinking about fucking us or a bull-dyke in the big house. Well, pity I don't have a pussy cos I'd be the first bitch to look you in the eye and know for a fact I was telling you the truth."

"What the fuck are you talking about, Lockie?"

"The murder they're trying to pin on you? Well that was me, I killed him but I'd no idea that they were trying to fuck you with that one."

I grabbed Lockie and straightened him up.

"So you killed Mark? Who paid you? Johnny Friends? Tell me fuckhead"

Lockie rolled his head, babbling incoherently. With his long unkempt hair, he reminded me of a brain damaged surfer. "Man, I ain't as high in the organization as I used to be, I fell out of favour, got demoted to hit man, got paid per job. Lost my retainer. That's why I'm, well was, workin' in Wal-Mart. I'm no Mister Big no more."

"Get to the point, who paid you to kill Mark and why?"

"Some dude called Lorimar, he's a friend of Johnny's and he's back on the scene. He called me and asked for a meet. He used to be about in the old days. He disappeared but then he came back. He just gave me a photo of Mark and told me to be at the motel at a certain time and whack him when he goes to his room. I know your next question, the 'why' of it. Man, you should know how the game works by now, hit men don't have the word 'why' in their vocab and if they ever learn it, it could well be the very last word they ever say. You know that Mac"

"Where is this Lorimar? What does he look like?" I felt like grabbing his lapels but I noticed he didn't have any, just a white stained tee. "You must give me something, Lockie. This is bullshit."

"OK OK. He met me in a hotel, don't ask which one, I can't fucking remember. I remember shit I had for breakfast when I was seven but anything last week, forget it, but I do know what he looks like. White, in his forties, black hair, well dressed. Good looking, keeps in shape. You can tell a man who has a gym card after a certain age. That's a card your fat ass could do with, ha."

"After all this time, you're still funny as a cancer story at a christening party. Give me fucking something to go on but perhaps I'm making it difficult. It's OK, I'll make it easy for you, first off, is the man American? There, that should be easy. Is he American?"

"Yeah, he's American but that's all I know of him, man. I can try to find out more about him but that's all for now."

"Lockie, I need to know more about it, where he lives, why he's doing this, I need to know. I've been going around in circles thinking of all the spiteful fucks who could be wicked enough to do this to me but in my line of work, that's just about anybody I come into contact with. I'm getting the feeling I'm not getting much mileage out of you right now. I tell you what, can we meet here tomorrow, same time?"

"Man, it'll take time to get that kind of info you know, longer than a day. I just get told to do shit. You know how it is."

I reached into my pocket and pulled out a fifty-spot. I stuffed it down the front of his tee.

"You not short of a coin I see, how come?"

"I keep a secret stash for a rainy day."

"How does that work?" asked Lockie.

I smiled

"It just works and as a matter of curiosity, just how far up the food chain were you anyway?"

"I wasn't that high. I was a well-paid fixer, that's all. No good with money neither. I figured that people in my line don't have a long shelf life so I just lived for the day and spent for the night. I never figured I'd last this long."

"So you blew it all, huh?"

Lockie smiled. "Yeah, I blew it all but I got blown a few times too." Rasping laughter ended with the coughing.

I got up and finished what was left of the bottle. I looked around and focused on a house across the way. I lifted my arm and flung the bottle towards that house. We both stood and watched the arc of the bottle until it landed behind a wall and onto the wild grass of what was a garden.

"Shit, I was looking forward to the sound of broken glass. Don't you just love the echoes it makes in an empty room?"

Lockie shrugged his shoulders.

"I guess luck ain't on your side when you fling a bottle in a concrete jungle and it lands on the only piece of grass in the neighbourhood. Man, if you tried to do that...that's fucked up luck."

I smiled. "Profound"

Lockie nodded.

"So be here tomorrow, at three, yeah? Even if you have nothing for me, just come back here. There's plenty more cash but don't push your luck."

Lockie took out the fifty-buck note and straightened it out. I got the impression that it had been a while since Lockie had seen such a denomination. Lockie stuffed the note into his pocket, smiled and walked off. I turned around and sat down, choosing not to see Lockie vanish from sight.

I stared at the vacant houses. Their boarded-up windows looked like the pennies they put on the eyes of the newly dead. The noise of the distant city continued to gently hum in the background. I remember thinking that must be how the world sounds inside a casket.

CHAPTER 28

The sun had risen but its rays miserably limped through the brown net curtains and onto Lockie's face as he slept on his camp bed with a charity-store suede coat for a blanket. He woke up and surveyed the room around him. The sun was a prism of light but all it did was make the furniture dust more visible. Lockie rubbed his eyes and got up, knocking a few old bottles away with his feet, and made his way into the bathroom and brushed his teeth.

He stepped into the bathtub and turned the shower on but nothing came out except for a few luke-warm dribbles of water from the shower-head and a muffled choking sound like a dog with a bone in its throat. Unwashed and pissed off, Lockie returned to the kitchen, boiled a couple of pans of water and poured them into a mop bucket and mixed it up with shower gel. He rolled up a white hand towel, stained with hair-dye, and sponged himself down, soaping down his armpits, face, torso and crotch. He dried himself as best he could with a tee shirt and stretched the wet towel over a chair so that it could dry in the stale air of the day and be used again.

He opened his closet and took out a package covered in cellophane and ripped it open with his fingers. Inside was a dark suit and a crisp white shirt, black tie and a pair of black brogues. He put them on and combed his hair and looked at himself in the mirror.

"I used to wonder how it would end up," he said to his reflection.

He picked up a bunch of keys that lay inside a dirty, plain white coffee mug that had 'Happy Birthday' written on it and put them in his pocket. He walked across the room towards the shelf next to his broken wooden clock. From the shelf he took two cell-phones. He put one of them in his pants and the other one in the inside left pocket of his jacket. He looked over the edge of the shelf where his black, leather-bound King James Bible sat. He picked it up, blew the dust off it and opened it. The fell open at the Book of Daniel where a Smith and Wesson was encased in a gun-shaped hole. He took the gun out, kissed it and tucked it inside his belt. He fixed his jacket up to hide the gun, straightened his tie and walked out into the day that lay in wait for him, closing the door behind him.

Lockie caught the blue line to Avondale in the north of the city and got off and walked to a smart apartment complex at West Roscoe and North Maple. He took out his cell-phone and dialled a number and waited.

"Why are you phoning at this hour?" said the voice.

"Mr Lorimar, there's been a development. Meet me at the West Ambassador in one hour."

"What is this about? It's me who tells you where to meet, not the other way around"

"I'm sorry but this is big. Will you meet me there in an hour's time?"

"This sounds serious. I hope for your sake it is serious."

"Believe me, it's serious."

Lockie shut the clam-shaped cell-phone and dropped it down a storm drain only a few inches from where he stood. He stood by a wall with a view of the residents' car lot. A few minutes later, Lorimar appeared and hopped into his black Pathfinder and sped away. Lockie waited until Lorimar was out of sight. Lockie took a deep breath and walked over to the keypad at the front and keyed in the combination. The pedestrian gate opened. Lockie walked on through and towards the front door of the building. As he was about to open the main door, a woman and a little girl appeared, about to leave the building. Lockie held the door open for them and smiled and entered the building.

"Hey you," said a voice that echoed from up the hall.

Lockie stood where he was and reached for his gun and turned around. An old man in red dungarees, a shock of unkempt grey hair ambled towards him. He had a stoop. Lockie relaxed his stance.

"I saw that, tailgating ain't allowed here. You never know who's been let in. I never saw your face here before, do you live here?"

"Yes, I am staying with my brother, Mr Lorimar, only for a week or so. I'm here on business from Florida."

"Oh, I see. Mr Lorimar never mentioned that."

"Should he have? Surely he doesn't need permission to have his brother over."

"In here he does. Let me call him." The old man took out his cell-phone.

"Sir, that's not necessary, he's had to go out on an urgent business meeting and I know he wouldn't want to be disturbed."

"No, sir, it's no problem at all, I think he likes getting calls from me, we had some noise problems lately and he was very grateful. Let me see."

The old man was thumbing clumsily through his list of contacts. Lockie felt his mouth dry up, his heart rate racing up the scales.

"Listen, can we make the call in your office? I don't like my business being discussed in the open like this."

"I'm the concierge, I make calls from wherever the fuck I want. If I'm dropping a depth charge in the pan and the need to make a call comes over me, I make a call there and then. I don't care if they hear me fart"

"OK OK, hey, say, what kind of cell-phone is that? It looks like one of those ones my daughter has."

"Is it? It's nothing special."

"No really it is, are you on contract?"

"No, I just top it up at Walgreen's."

"I can help you. I know a way you can get unlimited calls for free but you're going to have to give me the handset to do it. I work for the phone company. Trade secrets and all that."

"Say what? What are you doing me this favour?"

"Well my brother was very grateful as you say and let's call this a thank you gift. Give us it here."

"Well OK, but I need to call Mr Lorimar."

"No need to call him now before I work my magic. Call him after when it's for free, yeah?"

The old man gave Lockie his cell-phone. Lockie found the contacts list and scrolled down, trying to find Lorimar's name but all the names were stored under initials and numbers. Lockie wanted to compare numbers with the number he had just dialled to Lorimar but he remembered throwing it down the storm drain. Shit, he thought, but he remembered that Lorimar's number ended in 4584. He remembered that number.

Truman Orwell.

The year World War Two ended and 1984. 4584. He scrolled down the contacts and found a number that ended in 4584. It was under AL343. Apartment 343.

Lorimar's.

"Just one second, sir, before I key in the magic code."

The old man stared at Lockie, hands on hips. Lockie changed the 4584 to 7634 and exited out of contacts and quickly scrubbed the phone clean of its call record, received and made.

"Voila, there you are, a lifetime of free calls is yours."

"Thanks, son, so is it OK if I call Mr Lorimar now, if that's OK with you?"

Lockie smiled at the old man and put his hand on his shoulder.

"He just loves getting calls from you." Lockie handed the phone back to him.

"Good day, sir," and made his way to the stairwell and walked up. His heart was racing.

"Number not recognised, what the fuck, I dialled it last week," the old man shouted, his voice echoing up the hall.

"Oh, I think he changed it but I don't have it on me. He'll be back in a couple of hours though, can you wait till then."

"I'll guess I'll fucking have to."

Lockie continued up the stairwell and onto the third floor towards Lorimar's apartment. His chest was tight. Cold sweat glued his shirt and skin together. "That old man came close to being popped," Lockie whispered to himself. "Just as well I'm a quick-thinking motherfucker."

He found apartment 343 and knocked.

"Who is it?" asked a woman's voice from behind the door.

"Concierge," said Lockie. "Are you the only person in the apartment right now?"

"My husband is here but he's in bed. Can I help you?"

"I've some mail that needs his signature. No need to wake him, it's a formality."

Lockie took out his gun. The door opened revealing a woman, a brunette still in her dressing gown.

"Are you Mrs Lorimar?"

"Why, yes, I am." She looked at Lockie and then his hands, looking for mail. She saw the gun. Her mouth opened and made that shape girls mouths make when they are about to scream. Lockie lifted the pistol to her head and cocked back the safety catch.

"I don't give two fucks about you, but if you scream, I blow your head off. Now, just let me in if you know what's good for you"

The woman stepped back and Lockie entered the apartment and closed the door behind him.

"What do you want?" She pulled her dressing gown closed and folded her arms.

"Do you know where Lorimar keeps his records, his boxes?"

"N-no, I haven't seen them."

Lockie lifted his pistol and shot her point-blank in the forehead. She fell back, hitting the back of her head heavily on the radiator on the wall behind her. Her eyes stared straight ahead and a pool of dark crimson was growing from under her head. Her blonde hair mixed with blood and brain. She looked like a poodle that chewed a grenade.

Lockie locked the front door of the apartment from the inside and worked his way through every room, ripping out every drawer, flinging their contents on the floor. He worked his way through the lounge, dining room, bedroom until he hit the closet where he found several brown shoe boxes tucked behind a row of men's suits. He picked up the boxes and brought them into out into the middle of the room. He checked the time. Only twenty minutes since phoning Lorimar.

Forty to go.

He should be still stuck in traffic. He opened the first box and found a bunch of letters tied up in string. He plucked one bundle out and removed one letter. It read like a love letter.

"Those are they," Lockie said to himself and took another bundle out. In the corner of the room was a small briefcase. Lockie took it out and opened it.

It was empty.

H reached into his left inside jacket pocket and took out the other cell-phone and dropped it into the briefcase along with the letters and left the building.

As he made his way across the car lot, the old man shouted over to him.

"Hey, what's this horseshit about free phone calls, huh? They tell me I've just run out of credit, how the fuck man?"

Lockie stopped, smiled and turned around.

"Don't you know everything takes 24 hours to kick in these days? I should have told you. You'll have your free calls tomorrow."

"Well that's no matter, I called Mr Lorimar from the landline, I've his number written down. He tells me he has no brother and is on his way back. Who the fuck are you? I'm going to call the cops"

"I'm his brother and this is me, leaving here." Lockie pointed a gun at him.

The old man stared at him, fear cemented into every line of his mouth and behind his bulging eyes. He staggered back. Lockie put his gun down and turned around and pressed the large green button marked 'Exit' by the pedestrian gate and left. He walked down to the corner of the street and stopped and looked up the road to check for any cars coming that way. The road was quiet. He looked through the gaps in the railings. The old man was now lying face down on the tarmac. He was quiet now. Lockie stared at the old man, looking for signs of breathing.

There were none.

Lockie went on his way.

The old man didn't.

CHAPTER 29

Lockie returned to his motel room with a bottle of Wild Turkey and a bag of ice cubes and set them down on the dressing table. He went into the bathroom and fetched a tumbler and rinsed it under the hot water faucet and poured a measure of whisky right up to the brim. He smashed the bag of ice on the side of the tub to loosen the cubes and walked out back into the bedroom. He stuck his hand into the bag and removed a handful of ice and gently placed a number of cubes into the tumbler. He sat down and reached into his wallet. He removed a white card with a telephone number written on it and picked up the phone in his room and dialled it. It rang a few times before cutting into voicemail. It wasn't the default AT&T voice but the self-assured voice of a man who knows that the muffled noise he hears at his front door every morning is the sound of his dividend cheque falling on the welcome mat.

"It's me, Lockie. I'm in room three at the Stevedore Motel up in Hawk Hollow Forest Preserve on Sterns and Country Farm Road. I'm not sure if you know it but you know it now. The door's open but don't arrive until eight in the evening. That's about four hours away. The thing is, I have a letter for you. I didn't quite catch your address the last time we spoke but I reckon you're not giving that out for free considering the circumstances. Hur-de-fucking-hur. Pardon my French. Well, see you later. Sorry for not making the meet today but I promise you won't be disappointed."

He put the phone down and put the letter on top of the bed and sat back down again. He turned on the radio to WXRT. They were playing *The Green Manalishi*. Lockie loved that song. Peter Green played that that guitar like a Ouija board, making every chord sound like it was possessed by a ghost in pain. That was how Lockie described it to girls he brought home, in an act of fake erudition. It usually worked, until they expected a second erudite sentence that never came.

The show broke for messages.

Mood broken. A jaunty jingle *"Save all your money at Maynard's"* was sung by an old-fashioned gaggle of cheerful women who reminded Lockie of the Beverly Sisters. He turned the volume down and downed the whisky slowly without taking the glass from his lips until the bottom of the glass turned clouded white once more. The whisky had formed a pool of warm lava at the pit of his stomach. He closed his eyes and reached for his gun. The radio messages had stopped and it was back to the show.

"If you have any requests, call us on H-I-T-S-C-H-I-C-A-G-O or if you are using funky Bakelite, remember I said Bakelite and not baking soda, phone us on 448 724 42242." Another song faded in. *Ghost Highway* by Mazzy Starr.

"Ghost Highway, I'll love you forever, Ghost Highway, I'll love you forever."

He drank in the mood until he was intoxicated with atmosphere. When the song finished, he picked up the phone and dialled the radio station.

"Yeah, I'd like to make a request if I may....it's by Diamanda Galas...yeah, I think its spelt the way its pronounced...try it..you'll see.. good man...the song is '*Interlude (Time)*'...why?....oh let me see....I think it's the last song I'd ever want to hear and I mean that in the best possible sense...no reason, I'm just in a reflective mood, thinking about stuff, you know...oh, in twenty minutes? That soon? Well thank you, that'll work. ...have a nice day back."

He sat back and waited till his song came on.

Nineteen minutes later, it came on. He waited until it was nearly over.

"This will be the last the song I'll ever want to hear. In fact, it is the last song I'll ever hear."

***

Next door, lived a woman. Her name was Gail and she was twenty-four. Fear was her Siamese twin. She lived within its shadow and threat. She sat on her bed beside her blue suitcase. She looked at it and tried to hold back the tears. There were pictures of dandelions stuck all over it. Abbey had put them there. She was four. It was over a week since she'd seen Abby.

Her husband kept beating her. He told her she wasn't as good a fuck as her sister Kay. He kept telling her how much he would love a piece of her sister's ass because Kay wasn't as fat or as brute ugly as Gail. He hit Gail once too often. He touched Abby once too often too. He came home drunk and brandished a gun at them as she watched television. Gail picked up a clock and smashed it on his head. He didn't die. He collapsed on the floor, pissing himself in the process. Gail checked his pulse. The bastard still breathed.

"Abby, no one will harm you ever again, I promise you."

Abby was crying and shivering in the corner of the room.

"Abby, look at me, I promise you this. No one will ever harm a hair on your head again. Do you hear me?" But Abby couldn't get words through the blubs. Gail held her and kissed her head.

"Abby, there's something I need to show you. Put your coat on and come with me." Gail grabbed Abby's hand and they left, stepping over the body of her husband. His breathing was labored but he was still alive.

Gail took Abby across the field behind their house. Abby asked where they were going. "I'm taking you somewhere safe, Abby."

They got to the river. Gail asked Abby to lie down beside it. "But I'll get dirty, momma, it's all muddy. Why do I have to lie down, momma?"

"Abby dearest, I'll buy you new clothes, just lie down. I promise you that in ten minutes, you'll understand."

Abby always trusted her mother. Gail never told a lie to Abby in her life. Abby always did her bidding. Abby took her shoes off and lay flat on the bank, facing into the cold gargles of water that streamed over the gullies, only inches from her face.

"Stare into the water, Abby, tell me what do you see?"

"I don't see much, momma, rocks and stuff."

"Do you see any fish, Abby?"

"No, I don't see any fish, momma."

Gail knelt beside Abby and caressed the back of her golden head. "Just keep looking, Abby, and remember, momma will always love you. No one will ever, ever harm a hair on that precious head again, Abby, I promise."

"I love..."

Gail grabbed the back of Abby's neck and plunged her head into the cold grabbing waters. Gail closed her eyes and stared at the clouds that gathered on the horizon like dark plans. It only took minutes but it felt like an eternity. Abby lay limp. Gail lifted her up. "Daddy will never touch you again, Abby. See? You're not in pain anymore, Abby. You know momma loves you."

Gail read magazines. Gail watched Montel Williams. Gail listened to talk radio. Gail knew that fucked-up kids just become bigger fuck-ups. Gail knew Abby would be a fuck-up even though she was a sweet kid right then. Gail knew that there are some things that can't be fixed. After that, Gail ran away from home. The only case she could find was blue, with the magazine cut-outs of dandelions that Abby had stuck all over it. She packed it, jumped into her jeep and drove off.

Now, in the motel room, Gail fell to the floor and slid herself under the bed and never came out till morning. Later that evening, there was a knock on her door and a man called out but she couldn't make out what he was saying nor did she dare move from where she hid herself. The man went away and she heard him knock and open the door of the room next to hers, the one the gunshot came from.

Next thing she heard was the sound of a pane of breaking pane of glass and the loud thud of a heavy object hitting the back wall. Gail screamed in terror and ran out from under the bed and into the bathroom where she locked the door and decided she couldn't take anymore.

"Mal, please, please no, I'm sorry" She picked up a tumbler and smashed it into the bathroom mirror. Shards of mirror glass fell away and fell into the sink below. She looked into what was left of the mirror and noticed the black of the background. It was like a giant black starfish lying on a bed on mirrored sand. She saw her reflection in the broken glass, between the legs of the starfish. She picked up a handful of glass and plunged them into her left wrist and fell into the empty bath and waited and waited and waited for Mal to kick down her door.

She thought he was in the living room.

She faded to black where no one could harm her. Far away, in her family home, lay the body off her husband Mal.

The man who broke in now realised he had the wrong room and left. He then went next door.

CHAPTER 30

I hopped on the Amtrak from Union Station, northbound, and got off at Glendale and hailed a cab. The cab took me through the northern suburbs. Arlington Heights, Palatine, Schaumberg, Hanover Park until the wooded glades came into view. The cab rolled past the Apple Orchard Country Club and came to a stop outside the Stevedore Motel. I handed the driver a twenty and got out. I stood outside the Stevedore Motel. It was the right spot and the right address but I remember playing Lockie's voicemail again, to make sure I got it right. I didn't think Lockie would double cross me but I felt uneasy. I couldn't help thinking about how invitations to strange motels had fucked my life up real bad.

The Stevedore was arranged like a strip mall. Fifteen or so identical rooms in a row, bookended by a reception at the left and a laundry-room to the right. I walked along the path that took me past each room. I noticed none had room-numbers. I guessed that room one would be the one next door to reception but I made a mistake. I counted three up and went to what I thought was room four instead. I tried the handle but it wouldn't budge. I tried a few more times but wouldn't give. It was locked.

"Lockie's giving me the run around. Fuck this." I looked around me to find something I could use to break a window. I saw a rock lying beside the post box, picked it up and hurled it through the window in frustration. I walked back and turned around. I realized my mistake when I noticed the broken window belonged to the fourth door up. Fuck, I hope no one's in there, I thought. I had to do the right thing and check in on the room I had broken into by accident. I put my mouth to the glass.

"Hello? Hello? Anyone home?"

No answer. There was enough of a safe gap of broken glass for me to reach in and pull back the yellowed net curtain. I did just that and I peered in. I peered in and darted my eyes all around the room but no one was lying hurt or unconscious. I felt for a key on the inside. I found it and carefully twisted it, unlocking the door. I went in. The bathroom door was shut but there was no sound of splashing or anything. On the bed lay a blue suitcase with stickers of dandelions all over it.

"Hello? Hello? Anyone home?"

No reply came. I breathed easy. I left the room and walked to reception to apologize for the broken window. There was a sign on the desk.

"Back in ten minutes."

I got the impression that it had been there for an hour.

I walked out and back to where I thought room three should have been. I tried the door. It opened.

"Lockie? Lockie? Are you in there?" I cried out but no answer. Motel rooms don't like giving answers.

I opened the door a little wider and went in. Inside I saw a figure on an easy-chair, sitting up against the back wall. His head was no more. Gray slime had oozed down his chest and stomach. Little bits of skull and flesh were scattered like confetti at a ghoul wedding. There wasn't a face I could I look at but I knew it was Lockie. I recognised the smell, the clothes, the attitude. I could just about imagine the dead red stump that was once a head saying 'Fuck you'. If it did, I wouldn't have been the least surprised. I took a few steps towards the body to take a closer look.

In his right hand, a Rugar, his favourite. Brains and blood fused his head to the wallpaper. I had seen enough dead bodies to be immune to the grimness but each dead body is dead in its own unique way.

When you stop being sickened by it, part of you stops being human. Your ability to feel gets covered by emotional scar tissue that never falls off in the shower. You end up with more scab than flesh, more patch than original cloth. All I feel is hunger, thirst and horniness and fear. Just an animal who can speak English, walk on hind legs and knows how to use a cell phone and a type-writer.

I looked around the dark motel room. There was a white envelope on the bed. I reached over and lifted it. It was addressed to *Mr C McC*. I reckoned that was me unless Lockie knew a guy named Chris McCrumble, which I somehow doubted. I opened it. Inside was a folded piece of paper. I took it out and opened it up. It was a letter.

> *Mac,*
>
> *I've left you some parting gifts. You'll find three packages under the bed. If they're not there, then you're screwed. If you do, take them and use them. You're smart enough to work out what needs to be worked out but allow me to jump start proceedings. The smallest package is your Holy Grail. You will get all the numbers you need from that. The biggest package. Well, like I said, it's the biggest package. It contains indiscretions, of people having a good time and planning good times that they should never have planned in the first place. That's all. See you around someplace, sometime, Mac. If I see you in Heaven, then God's as fucking crooked as we are.*
>
> *Lockie*

Funny fucker.

I got down on the floor and looked under the bed and saw three large objects where the light didn't shine. I stretched my right arm out and felt them - parcels wrapped in paper. I scooped them out and put them on the bed and ripped them open.

The smallest one contained a cell-phone, a Nokia 3310. I pressed the power button at the top and the lights came on. There was a small post-it note stuck to the back of it.

PIN 4455.

I punched the numbers in and it opened its kimono. I checked the contact list. There was only one contact. The name was '*AA*'. I removed a biro from my inside jacket pocket and wrote the number down on the back of my hand and compared it to the ones stored on Lockie's phone. The number on Mark's phone was a perfect match with a number I had already stored. I kept my clients' contact details under the same prefix CLIENT followed by their initials and two-digit year. He had this number stored under 'CLIENT MG 10'.

Mrs Garantovich was on both our cell phones.

Mr Garantovich, my last client as a PI. Jesus on a jive stick. I got up and looked under the sink and found a roll of garbage bags. I tore a bag from the roll and put the packages inside it and tied a knot at the head of the bag to secure it. I decided to leave. As I stood at the doorway, I turned around to look back at what was left of Lockie.

"Thanks, buddy"

I closed the door, and left Lockie behind me, forever. Seconds later, a white truck pulled up in the motel car-lot. Its windows were open and music blared from the inside. I couldn't make out who it was but it was hill-billy coon-hunting country music. It reminded me of big droopy pre Village People moustaches, mullets and checked shirts where every girl was called Charlene. The driver of the car opened the door and got out and strode up to the room next to Lockie's. Room number four where the teddy bear suitcase was.

"Gail, I know you're in there, you're coming home with me, tonight, Gail. Gail, do you hear me? Don't make me kick this fucking door down now."

I turned my back and walked a mile or so up the road towards Walgreen's until the sidewalk ended with last house in the row. Ahead of me, only road banked with grassy verges on either side. Sidewalks don't go forever in burbland like they used to. People don't walk on 'em, except for the waddling distance between Landcruiser and porch. The road was sided with a grassy verge. I continued my walk up the grassy verge for another twenty minutes. Car slowed down and people stared at me. I was probably the first white guy to walk the grassy verge in twenty years. These are the paths off drunks, criminals and Mexicans cycling to work on BMX bikes and offshore Indian IT workers whose firms are too mean to give them rental cars.

Well they weren't wrong about me. I decided I was pushing my luck so I called a local cab firm and waited to be picked up before the cops did the honour.

Minutes later, my cab pulled me and I hopped in and he drove me to Walgreen's. There, I got myself the cheapest cell-phone money could buy. Ten bucks. It was little more than a kid's toy but it fulfilled my basic telephony needs. I left the store and found a quiet spot in the car-park, under a knot of saplings. I ripped the phone from its plastic cocoon and switched it on. It was already prepaid for thirty minutes and had enough power to last four hours, just about enough. I took out Mark's phone and navigated to *Menu>Contacts* until I found *AA* aka Garantovich. Her number glowed like an Everton mint, black on green.
443 442 4534.

I dialled her number from the new handset. I held it to my ear and held my breath expecting a dead-tone. The last thing I expected was a live tone. I got what I least expected.

"Hello?" A woman's voice.. I recognized the voice I didn't want to.

"It's been a while, hasn't it?" I said.

"Sorry, I didn't quite catch your name?"

"I'm a ghost who you thought you got rid off but it must be Halloween. Remember me now? Callum McCambridge. You asked me to set up your cheating husband at a cheap motel for a very pretty penny but little did I think. My, it was too good to be true, wasn't it?"

"You took your time phoning me" the woman said. "You must have worked it out long before now, surely"

"That's something we need to talk about, I think we should meet, don't you think, Gina?"

"If you think it would do you any good but why do you think I would help you? Don't tell me you trust me"

I could have said that I smelled a rat but rats are my world and the smell gets everywhere. My life's a bottle off Tijuana tequila and trouble is it's worm. I had to think fast. Gina wasn't Mrs Garantovich, That was obvious as I met Mrs G in the flesh. I would have recognised her. Whoever she was, it didn't really matter. Gina must have been involved in the whole fucking business but to what extent? It was hard to tell from a distance. Was she in it up to her eyeballs or up to her neck? Perhaps this Lorimar character kept each of his minions in the dark from each other. Perhaps Gina was unwittingly involved but wasn't she supposed to have started a brand new shiny life in San Francisco by now?

"How about we meet at Logan Square tomorrow at 6pm?" I said.

"Ok, honey. I'll meet you then."

I pressed the red button and ended the call. A long night lay ahead. Lots of homework to be done, reading all those letters, listening to all those tapes. I gazed down at the garbage bag of secrets, each a landmine.

Little did I know.

CHAPTER 31

I caught a CTA bus back into the city.

The bus stopped at Fullerton, not far from Navy Pier. I jumped out and walked around the block to clear my head. After about half an hour or so, I stumbled on a small electrical store. I went in and bought the cheapest cassette tape player that money could buy and threw it in with the rest of the stuff in the garbage bag. Further up the street, I bought a small backpack from a Dollar America store. I opened the garbage bag and emptied the contents into the backpack, zipped it up and carried it on my back like a college student.

I walked back towards Navy Pier and mingled with the late autumn tourists. The wind was cold and crisp against my bearded face. I felt the bristles stiffly move like reeds. It wasn't warm enough to sit comfortably outside for very long without wearing several layers of overpriced North Face shit so I kept walking up the pier and back towards Millennium Park. I bought an Americano with extra shot from a vendor-van, and poured a hill of white sugar into it and stirred it to death.

I took a sip but it burnt the top of my lip. I poured some of the hot liquid into the litter hold on the counter to make room for more cream. Steam rose from the litter hole like smoke from a gun, giving my little humble misdemeanour away to the staff. The girl who served me looked over and frowned. The taller geek next to her put his hands on his hips and gave me dagger looks and pursed lips. I didn't give a fuck for that cissy but at least it beat that a sour-faced bitch. I put the lid back on and left. I felt as welcome as a cat who keeps dropping half-chewed mice at people's feet all over town.

I needed to go somewhere quiet to get the lowdown on the tapes and letters. I remembered a cheap boarding house, Sammy's, a few streets behind the Rainforest Cafe. On the way there, I picked up a copy of the Chicago Sun-Times.

'Double Suicide at Stevedore Motel' was the headline. 'Ex-Cop and Stripper Found Dead in Adjacent Rooms' was the by line. I read the article on the street.

The bodies of a man and woman were found in adjoining rooms at the Stevedore Motel, Hawk Creek, yesterday afternoon in what appears to be a bizarre double suicide pact. The deceased man was identified as a Thomas Lockie, 45-year-old ex-police officer who was also known to the Chicago Police Department for his involvement in organised crime in recent years. The woman was named as Gail Schmidt, 24, of 183rd Street, Tinsley Park. She worked as a dancer in Bibi's bar. She leaves behind a husband. Her 9-year-old daughter Abigail was found drowned in Hawk Creek that same morning in what is believed to be a tragic accident. Police are investigating the possibility that Lockie and Schmidt were lovers who entered into a suicide pact. The causes of death are unknown but unconfirmed reports from the scene suggest that the man had shot himself to death and the women had cut her wrists. Forensic officers are still working at the scene and investigation is ongoing. Her husband, Mal, is under sedation.

I scrunched the paper into a ball and chucked it into the nearest garbage can, feeling numb. I walked on. At Sammy's motel, I paid my twenty bucks for a night at the fleas. After I was shown my room, I picked up the backpack that lay next to me and dumped the contents out on the bedspread. I looked down to my left beside the bedside cabinet. There was only one socket and it was already spoken for by the clock radio. I unplugged the clock radio and as I did, it made an odd sound, like a buzz of a dying wasp. I looked at the display, the red of the digitized numbers started to fade until there was nothing but the gray of the templates beneath.

I plugged in the cassette recorder and switched it on.. I rummaged through the tapes. I counted ten in total, all C60, all sealed in clear plastic wrapping but I could tell they weren't fresh. Not one of them was fully rewound. The shrink wrapping was a home job, an afterthought. I looked at them for signs of labelling, past or present but there were none. I lifted a tape at random and tore it free from its wrapping. I inserted it into the cassette deck, A-side up and pressed rewind until the tape heads started to jar. I put the heads out of their misery by pressing stop and then play.

At first, there was no sound but the low whisper of the tape passing through the heads and the low hum of white noise. After a minute, the header reel segued into brown tape. The hiss changed into a deeper tone. The first sound jumped out, a clunk, perhaps the sound of the record button being pressed at the time.

Then voices.

I couldn't make them out at first but they grew louder until they were audible and coherent. I recognised them. They were voices from my past, ghosts both living and dead but I knew them. Such was the company I kept. Male voices. One of them was Brewster, my old Lieutenant from the murder squad back in the day.

Brewster - *Well, son, I don't think you've met the man.*

Man A - *Who is this?*

Brewster - *He's one of my own.*

Man A - *You mean your fucking son?*

Brewster - (laughs) *No fucking way would I bring anyone I cared about in here, no offence. He's one of my boys from downtown, no stranger to the ways of good old Chicago town*

Man A - *Is that a fact? How, lonely it must be for you.*
(Brewster and Man A laugh)

Man A - *Does the boy have a name?*

Brewster - *Tell the man your name.*

Lockie - *Lockie, Tom Lockie.*

Man A - *So, Lockie, do you know why you're here?*

Lockie - *No.*

Man A - *Brewie, do I have to fucking go through the same shit that I had go through with you?*

Brewster - *Well I thought it best, you know, for him to hear it straight from you in case I left anything out or added Chinese whispers. You know I'm a stickler for accuracy, you know that.*

Man A - *Alright, Lockie. You ever heard of a man called James Hoffa, Jimmy Hoffa?*

Lockie - *Yeah, kind of.*

Man A - *Do you know who he is, what he does?*
(Silence.)

Brewster - *He's the head of the Teamsters, surely you fucking heard of them.*

Lockie - *Can't say I have.*

Man A - *Mother of Christ, what the fuck do they teach in schools these days? Don't you ever watch the fucking news or read fucking newspapers?.*

Brewster - *I know, it's like the world is a vague and foggy place beyond the straps of a girl's brassiere or a disco for these youngsters these days*

Man A - *Well then, you don't know who Jimmy Hoffa is. Well, your esteemed boss has lots of photographs of Mr Hoffa which he can show you , and well, we have a job for you.*

Lockie - *What kind of job?*

Man A - *We want you and A.N.OTHER to drive him from one place to another. Details to be provided on the day.*

Lockie - *Is that it?*

Brewster - *That's it.*

Lockie - *Why can't you call a fucking cab?*
(Brewster and Man A laugh)

Man A - *I like him, he's fucking funny. A cab, huh? Why didn't we think of that, Brewie? Here's us, wrecking our brains trying to work out how to take Mr Hoffa from this place to that place and all the time, the solution was out there. A cab. Why can't we think of things like that, Brewie?*

Brewster - (still laughing) *I don't know, Johnny. We never went to college I guess.*

Hearty laugher

I pressed pause.

Johnny.

Johnny Friends. It's gotta be. Lockie knew all along, he knew about the job before that dark day when he and I were assigned the task that blackened our souls forever more. I pressed play and listened on.

Friends - *Well, Mr Lockie, I suspect you're trying to be a bit of a wise guy, am I right?*

Lockie - *Listen, I was just foolin' with you, you know.*

Friends - *Just foolin'? You know, Mr Lockie, you know what this is?*

Lockie - *Fuck, no, please* (and other protests all mingling into one elongated whine).

Friends - *This could be the last thing you ever see if you carry on acting like a fuckhead. I'll let that one go for now and put it down to youth, but you're lucky. You are so lucky. Wanna know why you're lucky?*

Lockie - *Why?*

Friends – *Because you're still able to hear me. That's why.*

*Mumbles. (*I swear I could have heard Lockie's pant turn brown)

Brewster - *Lockie, do you know who this man is? The man in front of you? Do you want me to tell him who are you?*

Friends – *He's amongst Friends here.*
(Brewster and Johnny laugh at their little in-joke).

Brewster - *I'm teaming you with McCambridge on this one. As the man said, the details will come tomorrow but on top of this, I want you, including myself, to do some little theatrics. Let me explain, when I call you two into my office tomorrow, I want you to pretend not to know anything about this. In fact, try to act all cut-up about it, you know?*

Lockie - *How do you know McCambridge will come on board?*

Brewster - *I know he will. He's been on retainer for the past year, same as you.*

Lockie - *McCambridge? But he's straight down the line.*

Brewster - *What fucking makes you think he isn't?*

Friends - *I trust this is all settled then.*

Clunk and hiss.

End of Side A.

So Lockie knew about the Hoffa job before I did but that was as far as my surprise went. I couldn't forget that I and others in the office took retainers for well over a year from Brewster. Brewster was in the thick of it alright, but the tape proved nothing new but Brewster was long dead. Lockie was dead. Friends was still alive but the tape could have incriminated me at any time. For all these years, this tape was somewhere, sleeping but alive, ticking down a very, very long countdown. If it ended up in the wrong hands at the right time, it could have blown several lives apart, mine included.

I shivered at hearing those voices from the past, a land no plane or train can take us too. I reached over and rewound- played-rewound-played the tape several times more, just to make sure I didn't miss a word, a turn off phrase. When I satisfied that I had soaked it all in, I turned the cassette over and pressed play.

Voices.

Lockie - *I don't want to play your games anymore. I just want to be a cop and not worry about some good guy politician popping up some day to take a close look at us because you know, it will happen, you that.*

Brewster – *Oh you're getting a pang of conscience now are you? What's the matter, been listening to Jimmy Swaggart on your day off? Dry your eyes and don't get all holy-Joe. You've eaten from the trough for long enough and it's too late and let me remind you piece of shit that you ARE a cop. Didn't you check what you were putting on your back after you dumped last night's fried chicken into the pan this morning? That is a Chicago Police Department uniform. You can't buy these in a store, son. You are a cop and you're my cop.*

Lockie - *You can't buy a cop uniform but you certainly buy the man who's wearing the fucking thing.*

Brewster - *You've got one fucking mouth on you.*
(Sound of a door closing shut.)

Brewster - *May I remind you why you are still a cop?*

Lockie - *Look, it's not that I'm ungrateful but...*

Brewster - *Listen up, fucknuts, look at this, what do you see?*

Lockie - *Sir, please.*

Brewster - *No look, ahhhh, look, what did you see there?*

Lockie - *Your mouth.*

Brewster - *Not any old fucking mouth but my mouth and how would you describe my mouth? Go on, humor me, what do you see*

Lockie - *A wide-open fucking mouth.*

Brewster - *A wide-open fucking mouth. Not exactly the answer that is written on the card but I give you a bonus point for observation. Yes, it's my wide-open mouth and I'm Mr Fucking Gift Horse that gave you your career back when you shot that nigger in cold blood last year and you, you my friend, Officer Lockie, are staring straight into the mouth of Mr Gift Horse and you're talking all humble and nice as pie and wanting to go back to how things were, but let me fucking tell you, Officer Lockie, things can never go back to how they were because things were never like they were. When you shot the nigger kid, you opened Pandora's fucking box and it took me all my might to put all those fucking bad nasty spirits back in and it's all I can still do to sit my fat hairy ass on the lid and keep it shut. Do you hear me?*

Lockie - *Yes, sir.*

Brewster - *You have a lot to learn, Lockie, but I reckon that's why they have teachers. I needed someone close to watch my back and do the Lord's work but it's lonely in the Garden of Eden, and God saw how lonely I was and said 'It is not good for man to be alone' and so he took a cold-blooded, nigger-killing cop and turned him into my bitch and God saw that it was good. Get me? You were in the wrong place at the wrong time as far as your ass was concerned but for me, you landed on my lap like manna from fucking Heaven. There is no greater love than that of the one rescued from the jaws of the wolverines.*

Lockie - *I could take you down with me. I could turn State on you and spill a lot of sorry beans on the whole show.*

Brewster - *Just you remember who the fuck you are talking to here.*

Lockie - *Sure, I know. Ken Grimshaw, Reginald Dawkins. Duke McKendry.*

Brewster - *Shut the fuck up or I swear I'll have you shut the fuck up for good.*

Lockie - *Susan DeNeyer, remember her? She was well pretty and prime until the way you and your friends left her after their own little carvery.*

Brewster - *You do know what happens to bigmouths here, don't you?*

Lockie - *Sure, but I'm the only bigmouth with tape recordings of every conversation we've had and you know something? I'm in touch with my lawyer once a week. No matter where I am or what I do, if a whole week goes by without me phoning his office, he goes to his safe, takes out the tapes and posts them to the papers, the Complaints Investigation Department, the Governor, CNN, the national press, just about every agency who can stick a knife in your back. Keeping me alive is your best insurance policy.*

Brewster - *You're bluffing. You're fucking lying, you.*

Lockie - *Look at this, have this one. Have it for free.*
(Sound of an object thrown on a desk.)

Lockie - *Plenty more of them.*

Brewster -*So what do you want? You want out?*

Lockie - *Not quite. More money, just things on my terms when I deem it fit and ready for my well-being and betterment. You understand what I mean. We're like Nixon and Khrushchev. I don't think either of us is mad or stupid enough to try to destroy the other without* destroying oneself but it's in my interest to have one or two rockets aimed at you,, just like you have at me. Nothing personal. It's good business.*

Brewster – *Ok Lockie, so what is it you want?*

Lockie - *I want out of the force but I want in at a high level with Johnny Friends.*

Brewster - *I can't control who Johnny hires, there's only so much I can influence.*

Lockie - *If you don't want me to forget to phone my lawyer, you will have to have him hire me.*

Brewster - *You think this is all about the money, don't you?*

Lockie - *My God, whatever gave you that idea?*

Brewster - *This is how the fucking city works. Don't you get it? How many fucking police forces all over the world are busting their balls to kill off narcotics and pornography and prostitution but how many make a difference? Tell me? I'll fucking tell you. Not a single police force in any country in past or present dimensions of time or space have claimed a spot at the top of hour on the national bulletins and claimed "Today, citizens, we have ended the evils of heroin and cocaine and prostitution and have claimed all the streets and corners back for Mr Joe and Jolene Taxpayer, forever and ever. Amen." Have you ever heard such a broadcast? Have you? Well if you have, tell me where you fucking heard it and I'll fly there and find out how it's done so I can take it right home and work those miracles myself, but the truth is, there has never been such a fucking broadcast and, you know, there ain't never will be such a broadcast. You can't defeat them. It's a waste of our fucking time and money in trying to chase dealers and pimps. That's why our Mayor and Johnny Friends and myself got together and worked something out.*

Lockie - *What do you mean?*

Brewster - *Think about it. Johnny, you know Johnny, he's a dealer, pimp-in-chief of Cook County. He don't want drug busts or kerb crawlers indicted or runners taken in. No, it's bad* *for business. The mayor doesn't want to spend lots of futile tax dollars paying the police to chase ghosts either when the city itself is fucking falling apart. The mayor wants to spend money where it can do actual good as opposed to pie in the sky good. Also, he wants more money. The Police Department, well, we want to lock up rapists, murderers, housebreakers, you know, real criminals, not busting sad-ass addicts and low rankers in the drug ladder. So, all three of us got together and agreed that Johnny paid the city a hefty annual fee of $40m a year in exchange for peace and monopoly in the city. His side of the bargain is not to turn Michigan Avenue into one long titty bar. He keeps to designated areas away from tourists and kids. The girls get a weekly check up and medication. The police get a 10 percent cut of the $40 million bonanza and allocate efforts elsewhere and turn blind eyes where necessary. However, if anyone starts to mouth off and puts the arrangement in jeopardy, Friends is allowed to deal with it, up to and including using friendly police to assist as and when.*

Lockie - *Fuck me, I thought we lived in a democracy.*

Brewster - *There's no such fucking thing. You can have democracy or you can have government. You can't have fucking both. Democracy is a choice between Santa Claus and Father Christmas, Government is like making five bucks stretch from Tuesday to the weekend. Take your pick.*

Clunk. End of recording, side B.

I removed the tape and put it back in its casing. I opened another tape and put it on.

Friends - *So, there's a political threat on the horizon, Mr Mayor.*

Daley - *Damn right. The fucking back-stabbing bitch, my daddy mentored her, took her up from nothing and she goes and does this.*

Friends - *What's her name again?*

Man - *Jennifer Vogel.*

Friends - *Charlie, I hear you have a suggestion.*

Charlie - *Yes. From what I hear from soundings taken across Cook County Democratic Associations, Ms Vogel is a potent challenger to the Mayor. As we know, Mayor Daley serves our interests and those of the city. I suggest we make her, less potent.*

Daley - *She's popular, even my own father trusted her. Can we use that? How she turned her back on the family that politically raised her as their own?*

Charlie - *That won't wash. She claims to be loyal to your father but not you. No, it has to be something more substantive, something the people won't find hard to understand. Vogel's husband, Theodore, is a property developer down in Joliet.*

Daley - *Sure, doing very well too.*

Charlie – *Not doing that well I hear. He invested heavily in a land speculation close to Lake Renwick Heron Rookery Nature Reserve but it turned out that this land was also used by our feathered friends, the herons to lay eggs. Stupid fuck, the clue's in the name. The environmentalists kicked up a stink about it down in Springfield and hey presto, his land is virtually worthless.*

Daley - *Well boo-fucking-hoo for Theo, but how does that help us?*

Charlie - *Well, what if we created a clean front persona who acted as a major donor to Vogel's campaign only to find days before the election that a company owned by the same person also rescued her husband by buying the worthless land back for say 75 percent of its original value? Miss Vogel would have some explaining to do.*

Daley - *You fucking devious son of a bitch. That's perfect. How much did the land cost?*

Charlie - *It cost $10million.*

Friends - *I say we buy it back for $10million. Cut to the chase. No negotiations.*

Lockie - *Won't he wonder why someone would want to buy it back?*

Charlie - *Yes but once we make it clear to him that the buyer isn't a good conversationalist but is better at handing out fat checks, I can't see him objecting. Especially when his attorney is preparing his Chapter Eleven application.*

Daley - *How the fuck do you know so much?*

Charlie - *Guess who the attorney is.*
(Regales of laughter.)

Friends - *Tom, this is why we pay him so well. Well done Charlie Greyling. That's why Lonsdale recommended you.*

I pressed stop.

Greyling?

Charlie?

Charles Greyling? That name rang one helluva bell. Charlie Greyling. I got up and walked around the room saying the name out loud over and over until it sounded like a mantra. *Charles Greyling, Charlie Greyling* until the penny dropped. He was my father-in-law's lawyer and close friend

Then I remembered the last line. I went back to the machine. I pressed rewind for a few seconds and then the play button.

That's why Lonsdale recommended you.

Lonsdale. All these people were as crooked as the spinal columns of road kill critters.

Lonsdale knows Greyling.

Greyling knew Hubert, Lorna's father. I knew both Lorna and Hubert and Lockie. Lockie knows, well just about everyone. Greyling knows the Mayor and Johnny Friends.

I put the tape back in its box and put both tapes back in the bag.

I checked the time. It had just gone after 5 in the evening. I lifted the bundle of letters and put them in my pocket and made for Kavanagh's Irish bar a few blocks away. It was a dive but I was in a dive kinda mood. I felt dirty. The whole thing made me itchy. I looked at the streets, the people walking on the sidewalk, the cars in the traffic and felt a mixture of pity and contempt. Pity the ones trying to make an honest buck and live an honest life but I despised them for how weak and powerless they allowed themselves to become, just like myself. Everyone of those sorry fucks plants a stars and stripes in the garden in July and for what?

Celebrating the birth of a nation founded by giants but bequeathed to pygmies? I stood waiting for the DONT WALK to change to WALK. When it did, I crossed the road and went into Kavanagh's bar. Smoking indoors was just about legal then for a fog of stale smoke hit my face. The bar was dimly lit by half a dozen bare light bulbs that hung like shaven-headed lynch victims from the ceiling. A row of silent, glowering men sat on stools by the bar, each one with a solitary beer half-drunk from tall glasses. A soccer match was in full silent swing on the wide screen that hung above the optics but the sound was turned down full.

"Soda and lime," I said, wanting to keep a clear head.

"Soda and lime?" piped up one of the men across the way. "What the fuck is this, Boystown?" They cracked with laugher. I walked right into it.

The bartender poured a tall glass of soda and jammed a wedge lime on the rim and stuck an outsized cocktail umbrella in the glass and handed it to me with wink. Sometimes, for a city, its people can be a little backward.

"Yeah, yeah. Good one, didn't see it coming," I said. I lifted my glass and found a quiet spot next to the pool table and sat down. I put the bundle of letters on the table and plucked the umbrella from my drink and threw it on the floor.

I sipped my drink and untied the bundle of letters. There was a good fistful of them, in old style envelopes that seemed to have opened with letter opener and not anger like most people. A sign of refinement or contained frustration. The envelopes were all addressed to a 'L' or a

'H'. No names, just initials and only one and not two. Were they between lovers who lived together or hand delivered their love letters? I went with the latter as the letter weren't franked or stamped. I removed the letters from their envelopes and folded them out, flattening them with the palm of my right hand. They were written in two styles of handwriting, each set was tight and tidy, old-fashioned even. I picked the first letter from the top of the first pile.

"Dear Hector," It was dated April 2, 1979. No address. I read on. It read like a love letter written by people who still have one-in-bed-sex-sessions.

"I've ached for you for years and years and I don't know how much longer I can stand waiting" was the essence of the sentiment, retold in a myriad of variations of the theme. It was signed *"Your love, L"*.

Why would Lockie give me my brother-in-law's teenage love letters? Was this his parting gift? Making me throw up?

I took another drink but it was doing nothing for me. I cocked my head up and caught the eye of the bartender.

"Can you make this a JD, double, on the rocks?"

"The man's grown nuts everyone. A double JD coming right up, on the double," said the bartender.

"Fuck you," I muttered. I plucked a few more letters from the pile. The bartender returned with a tray with the Jack Daniels and a small tub of dry-roasted peanuts and wordlessly put them on the table. I started reading the letter. This one was more intense and physical. The letter was also signed 'L'. The next one was in a different hand.

"My dearest Lorna, it pains me too that our father tore us apart."

I reread this line again.

And again.

And again.

I switched to the end of the letter to double check who wrote it. "*Your darling Hector*". I went back to the top of the letter and read it closely, making sure my eyes didn't deceive me. With every word I felt my heart heave ever so slightly down towards my gut. My legs felt like columns of jellied piss under the table. I couldn't stand up even if I wanted to. It was no mistake.

These were love letters alright.

Lorna and Hector, brother and sister and incest fuck-monkeys.

I checked the date stamp. August 1980. The details were there. They described what they did to each other, how much they loved each other and how they wanted to be seen as normal in the eyes of the world.

I tied the letters up and put them back in the box. I finished my Jack Daniels and beat a hasty retreat from the bar and ran across the road, dodging and weaving cars until I reached the flop-house and ran upstairs to my room where I should have stayed in the first place.

My room was humid with the dead heat of wall-mounted electric heaters that came on at fixed times of day. The dust had finished its daily dance and had resettled on all the surfaces. I tried to open the window but it only gave an inch or so of a gap. I put my mouth to the gap and sucked in the fresh cool air of the night. It had just started to rain.

I lay down on my bed and my thoughts turned to the people I loved, or thought I loved or loved me or thought who loved me. Fuck it, who knows what love is. Did it really matter that Lorna fucked her brother when she was a teenager? He died years ago and she was faithful. Now she's gone. I'd like to think I'd see her again but I don't know. I replay her in my mind like a VHS tape, rewind and play, rewind and play. I worry I'll wear it out or invent storylines that didn't exist just for the hell of it.

I couldn't settle so got up and forced myself to read the rest of the letters, each sentence a Medusa-head of hurt. I systematically read each one with the eyes of a scientist, branding every word, line and sentence to my eyes without skipping a comma. I took notes and gradually constructed a rough timeline, taking care to check if Lorna and Hector fucked each other during our marriage or while we dated

I found that their incestuous affair had lasted months but not into the time me and her dated. The final letter from Lorna had ended things with Hector on account of her having met the man she thought she would marry.

That would be me.

There were several more letters from Hector, begging her to change her mind and to come away with him to start a new life in Mexico but Lorna seemed to have ignored them but she did keep them. I flung myself down on the desk, exhausted, drained of energy. I rubbed my face and felt grease on the tips of my fingers. My skin had gone to pot in recent weeks and began oozing gunk. I got up and went into the bathroom and splashed liquid soup and hot water on my face and neck before returning to my room. I sat on the edge of the bed and turned on the television and there it was, an old rerun of *Hee Haw*. Funny old hillbillies, you could almost see the shadow and smoke of burning crosses behind the cardboard set of Kornfield County.

Shame what happened to old Stringbean and his wife in real life. They arrived home one night and were shot dead by the Brown brothers when Stringbean, real name David Ager, refused to give up his nest egg. He was a child of the Great Depression and knew the value of money and knew what life was like without it. Old guys like him didn't trust banks so he invested his money in a hole behind a loose brick that lay an arm-stretch up his chimney stack.

No-one knows what happened that night or what was said but God mustn't have blessed the Brown Brothers with the powers of persuasion for they didn't get what they came for and left the cabin with only a chainsaw, a couple of unlicensed guns. Their bodies were found the next day by Grandpa Jones.

The Brothers weren't the brightest buttons in the coat and their loose talk put tight bracelets on their wrists. During the trial, Marvin and John Brown tried to blame one another but the court saw through that dog and pony show and jailed them for the rest of their natural lives. Marvin died in 2003. John still rots.

Police found twenty thousand dollars in cash up that chimney but the paper was there for so long that it was rotten and unusable.

I never looked at Hee Haw in the same way again when Lt Brewster told me that story all those years ago. It was like watching a party in Pompeii before the big one erupted.

When done with Memory Lane, I took an exit to the here and then it only crossed my mind that I only played two of the audio tapes that Lockie left me. I emptied the tapes on the bed and played each one in turn.

Woman - *You've done this kind of thing before, right?*

Lockie - *Once or twice.*

Woman - *Ok, It's called the Lonesome Cove Motel, here's the address.*
(Sound of paper shuffling.)

Lockie - *Do I wait in the car lot?*

Woman - *No, you go in and hide in a room near room ten.*

Lockie – *Ok...I know it...it's been closed for years, want me to break in?*

Woman - *No, it's back in business.*

Lockie – *Oh...shall I make a reservation?*

Woman - *That won't be necessary, it's not that kind of hotel.*

Lockie – *I get the picture. So I go to the room. What then?*

Woman - *First, before you go into the hotel, you wait on my call to get the go ahead. Then you go in and sit quietly in your room. You wait until you hear a noise.*

Lockie – *A noise?*

Woman – *A man will go into room 12. Then you wait until he's inside. Then you go into his room and well, you know. When done, you then go to reception. There will be a brown jiffy bag on the desk. You put the gun inside, seal it and leave it where you found it. Then you get out. A car will be two blocks over beside Joe's Diner. There, you get paid.*

Lockie - *This dude, who is he?*

Woman – *He's a man who's in someone's way. That's all you need to know.*

Lockie – *I gotcha Tammy baby. I just love pushing those envelopes, pardon the pun.*

I pressed stop. Tammy. I knew her voice was familiar if not a little deeper and slower than what I remembered. So she was involved in the set up but went cold on the idea after she met me. Nothing like seeing the whites of the eyes to keep a knife in the sheaf, sometimes.

Both Lockie and Tammy were dead, the two missing keys but the lid was still shut tight but I couldn't help think I had slightly loosened it.

A million thoughts and suspicions galloped through my mind like wild buffalo that night but if I could have caught and trapped them all, killed and skinned and boiled their bones down to mash and stuck my hand in the middle of that soup of filth, I bet I would have found the dog-tag of the man behind whole game.

CHAPTER 32

"I don't know where to begin," Gina said, frowning into her frappacino, stirring the frothy, sugary fog with a thin brown wooden stick. I reached over and grabbed her hand.

"I'm sorry, Callum, I thought, you know."

"Let's recap the situation. There was this dead guy in a motel room. Someone shot him and someone's trying to pin it on me. Your number's the only one stored on his cell phone, listed under just the letter 'A'. An explanation would be, well, nice to have if I put it like that"

"I can explain"

"I think it would be quicker if I do. Just up when I get something wrong. I won't go into the details on how I found out but Madigan was murdered by an ex-cop called Tom Lockie. I might have mentioned him once or twice over a lazy supper or two but perhaps you weren't listening at the time but Lockie was a partner of mine when I was in the force. I go and visit him the day after we met but Lockie shot his brains out and left me a number of interesting things in his will. One – he had the dead guy's cell phone with your number on it. That wasn't Madigan's personal phone, it was a special one given to him by the people who set him up. And it gets better. Lockie also leaves a bunch of letters and tapes. My, my, my, I tell you, tapes and paper are better than landmines, honey. A landmine couldn't rip lives apart as good as those bad boys. You'd never guess what I found out."

"But you're about to tell me"

I leant forward and licked my lips.

"Many things were on the tape but I'll start with Lockie being given instructions on the hit on Madigan by Tammy Southworth, aka Ronnie Gore. Lockie had left a force a long time ago and worked for Johnny Friends as his bag man and muscle. In recent times, Lockie fell out of favour and didn't give a fuck anymore. He just took the money and drank it, smoked it, mainlined it and fucked it. The last call Madigan got was 7:05pm on the night in question, from your phone. I get a call from a woman at 7:30pm. I arrive at 9pm and find a body and a posse of cops on my ass. I know it wasn't you who phoned me but it was you who phoned Madigan. Tammy phoned Lockie to tell him to go to the motel, you phoned Mark and I was phoned by person unknown. Over to you, Gina. Any blanks you'd like to colour in?"

"Callum, I had no idea that the whole picture turned out the way it did, I swear to Christ, no one did."

"How the fuck did you end up pulling your skirt over your head for Johnny Friends?"

"Callum, I've nothing fucking to do to Johnny Friends. I'm not that crazy. No, I was doing interior design work for this guy called Lorimar. He hired me to revamp his apartment. I told him I wasn't available for the job at first because I'd plans to move out west. He told me he liked my artwork and had come recommended. I thought about it and thought 'what the hell, go for it'. One last yuppy fuckpad for the road. We met a few times, going over swatches and catalogues, nothing out of the ordinary but one evening, over dinner, he told me he had a fault in his phone and ask me to pass on a message to someone on his behalf, you know, from mine"

"Couldn't he have used a payphone or spoke on the phone himself?"

"It seemed churlish to turn down such a simple request. Also, I knew how he treated people who didn't live up to his expectations. He fired people all the time. I heard he even had his previous secretary blacklisted from working in the Chicago area ever again for refusing to skip her son's birthday party for him. He was both charming and dangerous to cross. I needed the money and I thought it best to comply."

Sometimes the most strangest explanations seem the most plausible.

"Lorimar, the king of divide and rule, keeping his minions in the dark, each one a cog in his machine of malignancy"

"Callum, I swear, I didn't even know I was a fucking minion. Do you know something about Lorimar that I don't know?"

"Not much, no"

"The story doesn't end there. The day after, I got a check in the post paying me for the work done to date plus an extra two thousand on top and an apology for having to end our business relationship due to unforeseen circumstances. I went up to the house in case he was there, just, you know, to say goodbye in person but it was cleaned out and I mean cleaned out. Every fixture and fitting, gone. It was like the house had just been built, you know?"

"What did you do then?"

"I went to the bank and lodged the check."

"What was Lorimar's first name?"

"David."

"What does he look like?"

"He was about your height, moustache, let me see, actually, I know what's better, why don't I show him to you?"

"What do you mean, 'show him to me'?"

"I've a photo of us back in my apartment. We met at a Democratic Party fundraiser. He was in several background photos."

"I'm all eyes, let's go."

CHAPTER 33

Within the hour, I was outside Gina's apartment block. The last time I was there turned out not to be the last time.

"What's up, Cal?" Gina asked, rummaging through a tiny purse for the key.

"You know, I can't honestly remember being here in daylight. I'm sure I must have been but for the life of me, I can't."

"Well, that sums up our relationship, always in the shadows. If you did see any sun around here, it was probably five minutes after sunrise when you jumped out of bed and went home to your wife"

"There's no point going over this old battle ground, is there?" I said. "The battle's done and lost. Let's just put up a monument to it, lay down some wreathes, salute and move on as I've a bigger, more important fight on my hands here."

Gina locked her car, folded her arms and pursed her lips.

"This might sound sick," I continued, "but had you waited twenty-four hours, you and I, we could have been together. Not at first but..."

"Well, Cal, I guess we'll never know, will we? Why are we standing outside freezing our nuts off? Let's go inside, we've a man to meet..."
*

I walked around Gina's thinking about the good bad good times we had together. The wallpaper and carpets were different, brighter but the aroma of cinnamon and lemon candles tripped my mind. I never smelled that anywhere but here, in this special room with that special smell. I closed my eyes and summonsed old memories.

"Cal, are you ok?" Gina's voice cut through and swept up my reverie like a tornado.

"Sorry, I was taking it in, being here again, you know, those candles, you still burn them, right?"

"I sure do"

"They say smell has a way of finding lost memories."

Gina coughed, ignoring my nostalgia trip. "Let me get those photos. Listen, I'd offer you a drink but I have to be someplace in an hour's time."

"You once told me you were going to San Francisco and you didn't. Look at that!" I quipped, holding my arms out like hammy singer from a musical.

"You know what? I lied. There, no bullshit, no crap, I lied. If I was still here, you would have come back in the middle of the night, all drunk and telling me you loved me and how it wasn't the right time to be together. I figured if I told you I was going a few thousand miles west, it would have forced you to wake up to things, handling things on your own and not using me as a walker. There, I said it. Cruel but true."

Gina folded her arms. I could tell she felt better for her outburst of indignant honesty.

"No point in wasting time, is there, Gina? Just let me see those photos of Lorimar and I'll be outta your hair."

I took a little pleasure from taking wind out of her sails. I winked at her as she turned to leave the room. I stood. I didn't sit. I was too nervous to sit. Less than a minute later, she came back.

"Well here are a few. This one was taken at the Ambassador West."

She handed me the photo. There were a lot of well-dressed, well-heeled people in that photo. The photo stank of money.

"I see you, honey, but where's Lorimar?"

"He's right here." She stuck her right index finger on top of the figure of a man in the background.

I squinted. I held the photo up close to my eyes and stared at every pixel.

"Do you have more of him?"

"Do you recognize him?"

"I'm not sure, if I see a few more, perhaps I could mentally build a composite"

Gina handed me a few more photos.

"All these were taken on the same evening, you're lucky I have those because I never get photos taken with clients. There's never any need for a family portrait with one's interior decorator"

I leafed through the photos before stopping at one in particular. I had to before my heart did.

"Are you sure this is Lorimar? I mean, did he show you any ID or anything?"

"No, I just take my clients at their word, he told me his name was David Lorimar"

"And this is that man?" I held the photo up, pointing at Lorimar. My hand was shaking like a freshman at Betty Ford's.

Gina nodded. I dropped the photo and held up another one. "And this is Lorimar here, holding a Scotch, this man. Is he Lorimar too?"

"Sure, that's all Lorimar. Why are you shaking Cal?"

I grabbed Gina's hand and looked straight into her face.

"Gina, this man is not David Lorimar. I know who he is. His name is Hector Lonsdale. Lorna's brother. My brother-in-law. He's supposed to be dead, killed in some accident in the Caribbean. Closed casket funeral. No-one ever saw his face. It's all starting to fit together. By the way, I didn't tell you about the letters, did I?"

CHAPTER 34

"Lorna was fucking her own brother? Man, that's sick. Are you sure?" Gina said, cradling a tumbler, 4 parts rum and one part coke, shaking the ice against the sides..

I swirled my Scotch in mine and downed the half of it. I seldom sip anymore.

"It's all true, all in the letters." I patted the bundle of letters for emphasis. Gina looked at them.

"I thought her brother was dead."

"Hector vanished from the scene pretty quickly as I remember, shortly after I married Lorna. It was all a bit vague and sudden. We were told he had business in Guadeloupe. No one seemed to know shit about what kind of business but I remember everyone was guarded on the subject. Anytime I asked about him, just stone silence, quick changes of conversations, asses shifting on leather seats. I remember Hubert, my father-in-law, sternly telling me he didn't want Hector's name ever mentioned again. I asked why. He didn't speak at first. I remember that conversation. We were hunting in the woodlands behind his house. His face went the colour of a beetroot with high blood pressure, turned his back to me and emptied his magazine round into the nearest tree. He pointed his finger at the tree and said

"If that tree was Hector, I'd take a machine gun to it too. Do you get the picture now?"

I never saw him so angry. He told me that Hector had betrayed the family in such an unspeakable way that it was best if we considered him not just dead but never born. I respected Hubert but I knew him well enough not to fuck him over. I kept my counsel and we never spoke of him again. A year later, we were told that Hector was killed in a car accident in Bermuda. The body was burnt beyond recognition and his remains were flown home. Hubert had them incinerated and flushed them down the john and filled an urn with cigarette and wood ash. Lorna and her mother buried the urn in secret the family plot in Niles. And that was that. I never had the heart to tell them they grieved over dozen of spent packs of Pall Mall's and twigs"

"How did Lorna take the news?"

"She said they weren't close and didn't feel like crying. I put it down to shock but they were all New England people. Emotion wasn't in the cargo of the Mayflower"

Gina flicked her hair, a mane of red chiffon hair danced like a flame from her face to the side of her head. I now saw those blue eyes, wide and urgent, pierce me. Her cheekbones sculpted her fine clear skin like mountain ridges beneath freshly fallen snow. I remembered how often my fingers skied on her every slope.

"You don't think Lorna knew he was still alive?"

I stared into the melt water at the bottom of my glass before reaching over for the decanter. I poured myself another brimful and sank it in one - again. Gina watched me and leant over, running her long fingers through my hair.

"I honestly don't know if she did or not. There were no letters between them in the time Lorna was with me."

Gina screwed her face up into question mark. "Why would he do all this? Do you think he wanted revenge, like some kind of jealous lover?"

"For marrying Lorna? But after all this time? It doesn't make sense. I'm not sure but first things first, I need to find Greyling."

"Greyling?"

"Charles Greyling, Hubert's attorney. He might hold the key to this, I can't think of anyone else who can."

"Charles Greyling?"

"The Lonsdale family lawyer. Hubert and Greyling go all the way back to childhood. Greyling was like Hubert's rabbi, his confessor. If anyone knows the lowdown and dirt on that family and this city, it's him. I don't know. It's my last roll of the dice."

"Can you trust him?"

"I don't have a lot of options, Gina."

We finished our drinks in silence. Outside, the sun started to set and a cabaret of stars came out onto stage but I heard no music. Gina stood up and closed the curtains and fixed herself a gin and tonic and sat down beside me and lit a giant yellow candle. The room was bathed in a dark orange glow and the scent of lemongrass. I took out my cell-phone and walked over to the book shelf. I glanced through the neatly arranged volumes and plucked out a copy of the Golden Pages found Grayling's entry. I dialled the number. I knew it was out of hours but Greyling wasn't exactly a nine to five jockey.

"Oh good evening. Can I make an appointment to see Mr Charles Greyling? Yes, tomorrow? 10am? That suits. My name is..."

Gina looked at me full on. She mouthed the words 'No names for now'. I nodded. "The name is Timothy McGovern. It's a family issue. Thank you." Dead tone.

"Well here's to tomorrow, honey," I said, lifting my whisky.

CHAPTER 35

Gina kept a couple of my old suits and shirts at the back of her closet. Trophies or fossils, I'm not sure but both have their uses when the situation demands it.

"Gina, Gina," I cried out but no answer. On the floor beside me was a piece of paper. I stretched over to pick it up.

> Dear Cal,
>
> I've put out some smart clothes for you. Under the clock on the
> mantelpiece are a spare set of keys for the building and the apartment.
> I'm at work but will be home around 7.
>
> Love,
> Gina
> X

I held the letter to my lips and kissed it. I got up and fixed myself a cup of coffee from the pot Gina had made earlier. It was cold and bitter but sometimes I like it like that. I walked to the bathroom down the hall, had a piss and undressed. After my shower,
I picked the dark gray suit, crisp white shirt and dark brown boots.

Gina remembered my chest and foot sizes after all this time. I was impressed but she was that kind of girl. She never forgets. Women seldom do. I sat down in the chair, waiting for the call back from the cab firm, while dreaming of my exoneration in court. I walk down the court house steps, Greyling thrusting my arm high in victory after having all charges dropped. On my other arm is Gina, standing by her man. We walk down the steps like flies into the cobweb of reporters, flash photography and microphones. A stretch limousine waits – all tinted windows. The driver gets out. He wears shades and a sharp black Italian suit. He opens the passenger side door. Gina and I slip inside the limo. Greyling covers our heads with a protective bony hand as we clamber in, smiles a fatherly smile and closes the door. Driver locks the doors from his command and control dash. Car speeds off into the sunset to a life of Jacuzzis, endless Martini's, book deals and hot sex.

The phone rang.

"Hello?"

"Your cab's outside."

I grabbed the keys from under the clock and left.

CHAPTER 36

"Mr Greyling shouldn't be too much longer," said Grayling's secretary, looking at me over her Pierre Cardin spectacles before returning to her computer. Her severe ponytail reminded me of a military horse. I couldn't tell if she was efficiently polite or politely efficient. She seemed keen like new people.

"You new here?" I asked.

She smiled and blushed. "I'm sorry, is it obvious?"

"No, no, just making conversation."

"I started four weeks ago."

I expected more lobs of small talk but I got the impression neither of us could be bothered. The conversation faded and throats were cleared. She went back to her computer and I went back to staring blankly at the same page of the Chicago Herald and Tribune which I had been pretending to read. I tried to concentrate but not a word sank through my skull. I looked up from my paper to distract myself in other ways.

The reception area was almost steampunkishly decorated. Wood-panelled walls, carpets of deep crimson pile and reproductions of the screaming popes of Francis Bacon on the walls. An aspidistra broke the sharp corner behind the secretary's desk. Muffled voices filtered their way through the heavy oak door further down the hall. Hushed tones, silences, whispers. I imagined a clutch of medieval friars emerging, hooded and scurrying to some dark corner, away from the prying eyes and ears of the lost souls of the moderns. On that dark oak door, a bright, brassy well polished plaque:

'Charles K. Greyling', followed by an alphabet soup of accreditations. The doorknob twitched, the voices grew a little louder. The door opened and a well-dressed silver fox of a gentleman, clean shaven with Grecian face strode out into the foyer. He seemed to float on an invisible self-laid red carpet of confidence, arms swinging by his sides like limbic metronomes all the way out the door.

"Mr McGovern" a voice said. " I'm very sorry to keep you waiting," said Greyling. He stood with his arm outstretched. His poise, aristocratic - his face, equine and distinguished. Life was kind to Greyling. No better anti-wrinkle cream like money. I remembered him from the early days. I met him first at my wedding, along with a thousand other people, and a few times since at family occasions but I doubted if Greyling remembered me at all. I could care less one way or another but he'll sure as hell remember me from now on though.

"Have we met before?" asked Greyling.

"It's possible"

Grayling's smile became more quizzical than welcoming. "Well, please, step into my office, can we get you a coffee or anything stronger?"

"Not for now but thank you"

I walked through the oak door of Grayling's office. A behemoth of a solid oak desk held court in the middle of the room. Leather armchairs flanked the desk on either side. Behind the desk and to the left of it, a breathtaking view of Lake Michigan and the city. Great vistas, great power. If Jesus were alive today, the Devil would take him to the thirtieth floor of a downtown skyscraper. He would then tempt him with Evanston and Lincoln Park. Only a son of God or a liberal who worries what his friends think would refuse that one.

"Please take a seat, Mr McGovern, I am sorry but you do look terribly familiar."

Greyling folded his arms and tongued his lips.

"Let me cut to the chase. I came here under a false name but, under the circumstances, I'd no choice. I need to clear my name so I can use my real name in the open"

Greyling sat down in his leather throne, resting his elbows on the writing pad, criss-crossing his fingers.

"So McGovern's not your real name."

I shook my head. "It's McCambridge."

His smile morphed into an arc of concern.

"Callum McCambridge? Lorna's husband. Suspected of the murder of Mark Madigan? You skipped bail and have been on the run ever since."

"That's right. You must have taken a keen interest, Mr Greyling, there's been one or two murders in this town since to knock me off the top of the Billboard chart."

"Yes but it's not every day the son-in-law of my oldest buddy gets himself into such shit as you have. Personally, I thought you did yourself in but obviously you haven't. So, you seek to exonerate yourself? I'm not cheap but I think you know that. And to save any embarrassment, I don't do *pro bono*"

I sensed he didn't like me and had no room for sentimentality.

"I guessed 'old time's sake's not a sentence in your book, Mr Greyling. I didn't come here to make friends or talk about old times because those weren't my old times. I'm here to help clear my name. I have all the proof I need right here, in this bag, taped conversations, letters, the works. It's all here, my ticket back to my life, Mr Greyling."

Greyling leant back in his chair, his hands behind his head. He looked like a man who had a full house but I knew I had a four of a kind.

"Tell me what you've got."

"First off, there's a man called Lorimar. He's behind my predicament. He employed a number of people to do different jobs all over town. One of them lured Mark Madigan to the

Lonesome Cove Motel and had him murdered. His killer was an ex-cop who worked a pay-as-you-go hit man. Tom Lockie. I was lured me to the scene shortly after"

"That's quite a story, McCambridge, one that needs watertight proof. You've been in court many times, often enough to know that there is evidence and there is evidence. I trust you have the latter?"

"The latter on a platter. A conversation between Tammy Southworth and Tom Lockie. It's all there on tape. They even mention Madigan's name, the location and instructions for Lockie. No gray areas, no interpretations. Hell, they even drop each other's names."

Greyling looked at me with eyes of cold, gray marble.

"How did you find these tapes?" he asked.

"Lockie, we used to work together. He went to work for Johnny Friends. Long story. Worked as his bagman and hit man and whatever-fucking-else kind of man. Our paths crossed recently. He was down on his luck. He carried a lot of guilt for a long time and wanted rid of it. We arranged a meet at the motel where he was holed up. The Stevedore. When I got there, he was dead. Shot himself but he left a bag of letters and tapes for me"

"Technically, you disturbed a crime scene but we'll overlook that for now."

Greyling now grinned. His smile looked bright enough but I still felt a chill.

"Yeah, I took them. Read them, listened to them. It's all there. I'll take a rap for disturbing a potential crime scene for sure but I'm sure the jury would understand my somewhat mitigating circumstances."

"Hmm. It could be argued you killed Lockie after he attempted to blackmail you."

'Lockie left me a letter. They can argue what they like'

Greyling held his hands up.

"Did you touch his gun?"

"Yes, I touched his gun."

"Not good, McCambridge, but at least you're playing straight with me. The waters are little muddied.., a bit thin none the less but if your tapes say what you claim, it's a nail to hang a defence off. OK, what else you got?"

"My friend Gina Webster worked for Lorimar as his interior decorator. He asked her if he could use her phone as his was out of action. Turned out the message was passed to Mark Madigan. Gina was duped. Lorimar knew I'd make that connection to Gina sooner or later, why else would he have used Gina like that if not to spook me"

"So, this Lorimar character. You are saying that he framed you for murder?"

"Gina showed me photos of Lorimar and I recognised him. His name's not Lorimar"

"Really? Who is he then?"

"I'm glad you're sitting down Mr Greyling...Hector Lonsdale. Yup, you heard that right. My dead brother in law"

Greyling 's eyes and mouth narrowed as though the news was too bright to see and too spicy to taste. He rubbed his forehead with his left hand and leant back in his chair, staring up at the ceiling. He got up and walked over to the window.

He stared out the window, out across the lake. Fishing for thoughts and the right thing to say. I found it hard to believe that this man of rhetoric was lost for words. It was like a ho being lost for thongs.

"Hector's body was never formally identified. We just took the Bermudans word for it. He's in the photographs, no doubt about it. It's him alright. I also found that the Lonesome Cove Motel was bought by a company registered in Grand Cayman Island. That's in the Caribbean"

"I know where it is. I spend my weekends there". Greyling opened a drawer and took out a box of cigars and opened it. He took out a fat Cuban and stuck it between his lips and lit it with a monogrammed silver brick of flame thrower. The smoke plumed from his mouth like the God of Vesuvius.

He didn't offer me one. I continued.

"It also happened to be the same company that booked the presidential suites of several downtown hotels where the plans were being laid. The company is owned by Hector Lonsdale aka David Lorimar I know it's crazy but it's the truth"

"It's not crazy at all," Greyling said. "It might be shocking for you to know that I've known Hector to be alive all this time. His death was staged, faked to get him off his Daddy's hook. It was only a matter of time before it came out but I never thought it would be like this."

"You knew all this time?" I asked.

Greyling nodded. "Yes. Until today I was the only one who knew."

"Even when everyone grieved, you knew the body wasn't his?"

"That's correct"

"So whose body was it?"

"Oh, some hobo we picked up. No one anyone would miss. He was dead already. His body was put into the wreckage of Hector's car. Those days, forensics weren't they became"

"Why did he stage his death?"

"Hector felt his life was in danger."

"From who?"
"Hector got it into his head that Hubert had hired a hit man to do him in"

I went over to the drinks cabinet and poured two stiff whiskies. I handed one to Greyling. I wasn't sure if it was his drink but it sure as hell was now. He took a large sip and wiped his lips.

"Mr Greyling..."

"I think we can dispense with formalities, don't you think? Charles, call me Charles."

I took a sip of my whisky. I felt like jumping into the glass and drowning in it"

"Hector disappeared in haste" I said. "I seemed to be the only one who thought it odd but no one told me what happened. I never knew the real story until recently but I'm giving you a chance to tell me in your own words. Charles, I have the letters here. Love letters. Do you need me to spell it out?"

"Callum, this is such a matter of sensitivity that I ask you to put your cards face up on the table. I'll show you my hand but only when you show yours. Not a minute sooner"

"Love letters between Lorna and Hector. They were fucking each other. Hubert found out and banished Hector, didn't he? Isn't that what happened?"

Greyling winced and knocked back the rest of his drink. He walked over to the drinks trolley and stuck a small trowel into the bucket of ice and scooped cubes into his tumbler. He opened the bottle of Bushmills and filled the glass to the brim.

"Hubert came home early. He heard noises. Hubert being Hubert, reached for his pistol, took his shoes off and went upstairs."

"Spare me the details, Charles, I can fill in the blanks"

"Hubert was this close to shooting the pair of them. As I understand it, Hector claimed full responsibility for the whole sorry thing"
"That's nice"

"Knowing them as I knew them, both were probably to blame. Lorna was no one's fool, even then. She might have been only one year Hector's junior but she was at least a decade more mature than him. Lorna pleaded for Hector's life. When I say Hubert came close to shooting them, it's not just a figure of speech. He would have done it. How would you have felt had it been you, coming home to find your son and daughter? Well anyway. Hubert banished Hector, disowned him and cut him out of the will and forbade him to make any contact with the family, least of all Lorna."

"Where did he go?"

"Guadeloupe at first, then Barbados. In fact, he bummed around the Caribbean for a couple of years, working as a crewman on boats. For all I know he could have worked on mine but I have five of them. I never mix with the deckhands. It was in Barbados when he found out that Hubert had put a contract on him."

"How did he find that out?"

"The man Hubert employed for the hit, approached Hector and asked him to top Hubert's offer, which of course, he did. Goes to show, you can't find an honest assassin anymore." Greyling took another long sip. "Hector paid him off but he saw the writing on the wall. He could have gone someplace else but the only thing that would have put Hubert off the scent was being dead. You know, deep down, I never thought Hubert bought the car-crash story. It was too much of a convenient ending but what could he do?"

I went back to my chair and sat down, making myself comfortable.

"Charles, how come you know all this?" I asked. "I mean, why did Hector confide in you? Wasn't he worried you would tell Hubert?"

Greyling held his head back and drank the rest of his whisky and walked over to the drinks trolley for another refill. I detected a slight wobble in his gait.

"I thought Hubert went over the top. Hector was his only son and he cut him off. Not for me to pass judgement but that was cruel and unusual. I liked Hector, he was my Godson.. Hector still had business he just couldn't just walk away from. People disappear everyday to start new lives but they end up repeating the same old life as before, making the same old mistakes, shitting the same old shit but under a different name in a different town. If only changing our luck was as simple as changing our name from Smith to Jones. Besides, not only is he my godson, he is also my client. Confidentiality is paramount. Sinners have priests to talk to. The worst sinners have lawyers. Even this conversation shouldn't be taking place but this is a highly unusual alignment of circumstances."

"You almost make me feel sorry for the asshole. Excuse me for not crying but he had me framed for murder"

Greyling shook his head and looked down into his whisky.

"For that one, I'm at a dead loss. That's something you need to ask him yourself. Perhaps it could have been the will."

"What do you mean?"

Greyling walked up and down by the window. His put his hands together as if in prayer.

"Hubert bequeathed half of his estate to Lorna but held in trust until her fortieth birthday. The other half went to a company"

"Let me guess, DD Holdings, that's the company that bought the Lonesome Cove and paid for those hotel suites I told you about, remember? I found out that the CEO of DD Holding's is one David Lorimar, or should I say Hector. It's him alright."

"You've done your homework and you've done it well. Shame you never stayed in the force. You'd have made detective lieutenant in no time."

"Thanks for the gold star, teacher, but let's get back on track. Why would Hubert leave half his fortune to a firm owned by his son, his son he hated?"
Greyling finished his drink and looked straight at me. His lifted his right hand and pointed, jagging the air with his forefinger.

"So, detective, tell me your theory. You got a theory, there's always a theory."

"OK, let's see, could they have reconciled without your knowledge?"

"Absolutely not," Greyling shouted. "That would never have happened. I knew Hubert better than he knew himself. His son was dead to him. Period."

"Could Hector have wormed his way into DD Holdings under some pseudonym and taken it over from within?"

"Good theory but no, impossible. DD Holdings is not a publicly listed company. It's a limited company. Oh Callum, stretch the fabric of your imagination. Surely a devious, whisky-soaked mind of an ex-Homicide cop could think up of all kinds of likely scenarios. Come on, Callum, you disappoint me."

Greyling was drunk. Drunks are pathetic but there nothing as pathetic as a drunk in his own office at ten-thirty in the morning who realises his Rome is crumbling all around him but stays to pour another drink.

I leant over, grabbed my glass off the table and drained it dry.

"Try this for size, the will, it wasn't the real thing. Hubert would have jumped out of his grave rather than leave that fuck a pot to piss in. Think about it, why would anyone leave money to a shell offshore company that was owned by someone else, someone you hated?"

Greyling stood up, waving his right arm around like a demented conductor.

"Detective, you are right. You have hit the nail on the head."

"And how the hell did that happen, Charles? How?"
Greyling stubbed the end of his Cuban on the crystal brick that slummed it as an ashtray. He reached for his whisky glass but I beat him to it and winched it away.

"You've had enough, Charles. Stop stalling. Tell me."

"Very well then. As you know we live in more enlightened times these days but you also know that it wasn't always the case."

"I don't follow."

"Callum, you know my marital status, don't you?"

"I didn't know you had one"

"Not married. I came close on an occasion or two but no cigar. The fact is, McCambridge, I made a mistake once. A mistake a long, long time ago, one for which I still pay. You see, I shat on my very doorstep, trod on it and the smell is still on my shoe, decades later."

"Go on"

"OK, here goes, I play for both the Sox and the Cubs."

"Excuse me?"

"I bat for both sides, Callum. I'm what they call bisexual these days. I'm a dabbler"

"So what? Who gives a shit"

"In the old days, such things could destroy a man" Greyling said. "One didn't dare tell a soul. It was a crime. People were sent to sanatoriums to recover so to speak but they never came out. These days we have coming-out parties and pride festivals but back then there were only dark corners and underground bars. All my clients were card-carrying Democrats, but they hated queers. Everyone did. I saw what happened to the careers of the less discrete. They ended up spending their lives in Shitsville, Alaska if they were lucky"
"So you were blackmailed, is that it? Who caught you?"

"Hector was my Godson. I never had kids of my own but he turned out to be an evil son of a bitch. He was into all kinds of bad business. I arranged to meet a male escort in a downtown apartment. I did it all the time. Sometimes it was a lady, sometimes it was man. That's how I was. However this one time, the apartment was owned by none other than Hubert. I didn't know. He owned shitloads of apartments, all over town. He let them out for short-term leases to businessmen and tourists. A lot of the time, they were vacant. They were mostly a tax dodge. Hector weaselled his way in and asked Daddy if he could play at being his property portfolio manager. Hubert shrugged his shoulders let him. What Hubert didn't know was that Hector had teamed up with Johnny Friends and ran a Cook County wide escort agency using Hubert's apartments. They kept track of all the johns, well, all the rich ones and blackmailed who they could."

"So Hector caught you with your pants down, is that it?"

Greyling closed his eyes.

"He sure did"

"Let me guess, Hector wanted you to falsify Hubert's will in his favour?"

"They never made financial demands of me though. They only wanted me to fix things for them and their friends. They even paid me for it, which was bizarre come to think of it. I had to take on cases I wouldn't have touched with a very long stick. I won them all too but I lost my moral reputation because of it. I got down with the dogs and got up with the fleas. I bet they reckoned that they struck gold in finding their fallen angel and making him their very own little pet devil. Smart, huh?"

I felt sorry for Greyling. The broken man behind the gilded lair.

"Did Hubert find out about Hector's little sideline?"

"That's the funny part. He found out when he booked himself a pretty little thing from Panama only to find that she was holed up in one of his apartments. He had just bought it the month before"

"I reckon they all were as bad as each other."

"Cal, you have to understand something, Hubert and Hector respected each other's cunning more than they loved each other. It was that kind of family. That's why we have family law." Greyling smiled. He looked down at his sleeves and pulled out his cuffs from under his dark sleeves to fix the links. I noticed the cuff links were silver replicas of the Eiffel Tower, Paris.

"Did Lorna know any of this?"

"Lorna had no interest in business. She knew nothing"

"Charles, I need to find and confront Hector but I need you with me."

Greyling twisted his mouth and looked up at me before sidestepping across to his desk. He sat on the edge of his desk and put his empty glass carefully on a coaster.

"Firstly, I wouldn't advise on that," he said. "Hector is hell-bent on seeing you in the state pen. From what I hear on the grapevine, his grip on reason is not what it was. He sees you coming, Cal. He's probably waiting with one final mantrap to finish you off."

"So you know he's in town? How do you know that?"

"When Hector is in town, certain social gravities are affected. His presence makes certain orbits wobble, if you catch my drift."

"So, what do you advise?"

"OK, I'll take your case on. Give me what you have and we'll go to the State Prosecutor with the evidence. You'll need witnesses to testify. Tammy and Gina, are they both on your side?"

"Tammy's dead. Gina's on my side. I think can count on her."

"OK, let's roll but, firstly, your tapes. We'll present what we have but before we go, I have to tell you you're not the only one in this town with a box of tapes under his arm. I've been dealing with crooked fucks all my life. I've taped every conversation, every meeting. This office, that chair you're sitting on, it's a recording studio. I bet somewhere in my annals, I have the voice of the Devil himself on tape. I wouldn't be surprised. I've evidence that can sink Hector into a very, very deep hole. Oh yes, evidence that'll put him away for the rest of his life. Conspiracy to pervert the course of justice, actual perversion of the course of justice, blackmail, racketeering, tampering with a will, directing murder and then some. Your tapes and mine, we'll both get our lives back." He winked and leant over and put his hand of my right shoulder. "You'll see."

"But you'll be incriminating yourself, you're in those tapes too."

"I can prove I was blackmailed, acting under duress. I can plea-bargain to spend a few years in a low security playpen, playing table tennis with investment bankers, letting my investments get fatter without being able to spend them. Then I get out and chase the sun and live out my days in peace"

"You've got it worked out"

Greyling grinned. "It's good to have your parachute ready but it's better to make sure the ground beneath you is nice and soft". He stood up and wiped his mouth. "You don't mind waiting at reception while I make a couple of calls here? It won't take a minute."

I finished my drink and left the room, closing the door behind me. A few minutes later, Greyling appeared with a thin, brown, Italian leather briefcase. He held the briefcase under my nose and opened it.

"Put your tapes and documents in here, they'll be perfectly safe. Trust me"

I was reticent about letting them out of my sight but I acceded. I opened my rucksack and tipped the contents into the briefcase. When done, he put his hand in and tidied things up a bit. He locked it shut, held it up and rattled it.

"Hear that, McCambridge? That's what freedom sounds like. Come on, let's go."

CHAPTER 37

"I used to work here, in Homicide, years ago but I guess you that"

I was back in the station where I worked all those years ago. The Mother Ship. Greyling and I stood in the foyer, waiting our turn to speak to the desk cop. In front of us, a queue. A young white guy signed papers, his mother by his side. Her face was drawn, wondering what she did wrong for her son to end up where he did, signing his daily check-in sheets pending trial. I saw it a million times before. Different clothes, different faces but the same old situation. It didn't take long for Greyling and I to pop up to the top of the queue.

"How can I help you gentlemen" the desk cop asked. Greyling turned to me.

"You don't need to stand here, take a seat and let me handle this bit"

I wasn't happy about it but this wasn't the time to pick a fight so I found a chair by the back wall, just under a portmanteau of the faces of cops who fell in the line of duty. All those moustaches, bad hair cuts, brylcream and smiles. I knew a few of them.. We all knew death was a real possibility but only for others. Never for ourselves.

It felt like returning to a familiar but damaged womb but it's the only the womb we know. It felt safe, familiar but cramped. The decor was different. A new coat of paint lay like grafted skin over the dead layers of the decades beneath. There was art work too, kids paintings and reproductions and panoramic shots of the city at night. User-friendly I think the term is. There were more women around than in my time, both in uniform and civilian clothing. The force had washed its face and had its teeth fixed but still the same old grin.

I hoped that any second, I would see my younger self turn a corner and stand in front of me. I would grab his lapels and shake all the arrogance and fuck-wittedness out of him, so that he wouldn't make all those mistakes I did. I looked over at the counter and saw Greyling hand papers over to the desk sergeant. Next thing, two uniforms stepped out of the office behind the desk and bee-lined their way to me. I stood up and we all went through the motions of arrest.

I now wore bracelets.

I bit my tongue.

***

Interview room.

Greyling sat with his arms folded, chin on chest. I sat to his right. The two uniformed officers flanked the door. A minute later a middle-aged detective blew in like debris in a storm. I didn't recognise him even though he looked at haggard as I did. His face was cragged with years of cynicism, tobacco and booze. He looked like a walking coronary. His tie hung around his off-white collar like the ragged remains of a weather-beaten flag of a cause that lost its war. I couldn't tell if he was drunk or just on his twenty-fourth straight hour of duty without sleep – or both

"I'm Detective Vince Wilson. Firstly, do you understand the charges, Mr McCambridge?" I nodded.

"My attorney, Charles Greyling here, has incontrovertible evidence of my innocence and I'm here to present it with a view to standing trial to clear my name for good. I'm come in from the cold"

"Really" Wilson cut in. "Show me it"

Greyling remained impassive, silent. He stared blankly at the table. I thought he would have piped up by now. I took a drink of water and continued:

"Mr Greyling has the tapes and documents, conversations between the late Thomas Lockie and his handler, Tammy Southworth also known as Veronica Gore who worked for Johnny Friends. You should be familiar with the name Johnny Friends. The tapes make it clear that Lockie was the gunman who murdered Mark Madigan. not me."

Wilson leant forward with hands clasped together.

298

"Is this true, Mr Greyling?"

Greyling coughed and put his briefcase on the table and shoved it over to the detective.

"It's all here but will you please excuse me for a minute? Bathroom break. I drank too much coffee this morning but please don't open the case until I return"

Greyling rose from his seat and left the room. My eyes burned a hole in the back of his perfectly combed grey head.

Wilson threw a bemused look while chewing gum down to cud, making loud slurping noises. I couldn't help thinking about Hubert's apartments and the vice-ring that put his king-size mattresses through their paces. I looked at Wilson and his piggy eyes, a prism of failure through which all light passes through to his brain.

"While we wait for the talkative Mr Greyling, let me ask you a question. If I open this briefcase, what will I find?" asked Wilson.

"Like I told you, tapes and documents but not just for my case but evidence of corruption, drug trafficking, conspiracy, fraud, racketeering, and yes, I almost forgot, the murder of Jimmy Hoffa."

The detective stopped chewing. His piggy eyes widened before he swallowed his gum.

"What the fuck do you know about Jimmy Hoffa?" he asked, his voice dropping an octave.

I told him the story about my involvement in the end of Hoffa. Warts and warts and all.

Wilson leant further forward. I caught a draft of his day-old dime-store cologne and the stale dead odour of French fries on his breath.

"And you have evidence of this, here, in the briefcase?"

"It's all there" I said

The detective put his hand on the briefcase and picked it up. He stood up and lifted it up.

"And what else do your tapes tell us?"

"Hector blackmailed Greyling into changing the will of Hubert Lonsdale. He disowned his son Hector a long time ago. Shortly after, Hector was killed in a car accident in Bermuda. But the thing was, he faked his death. He faked it because he found out that Hubert had put a contract out on his life. He then went on to set up a shell off-shore company called DD Holdings. The copy of Hubert Lonsdale's will clearly show that the beneficiary of his estate was the very same DD Holdings. Hector Lonsdale changed his name to David Lorimar and guess who the CEO of DD Holdings is? David Lorimar, aka Hector Lonsdale. I have photographic evidence too and a very reliable upstanding witness who is willing to testify"

"All that, in here, really" he asked. He started to sound like a stuck needle and my vinyl was wearing thin. Greyling was gone longer than I thought, probably pissing like his whisky like a race-horse down the corridor. I wished the fuck he'd hurry up and get his ass back in.

"Well, that's one mighty atom bomb you have in there but it don't feel that heavy." Wilson said before breaking into a phlegm coated chuckles

"Why don't you open it and see?" I said.

"I have to wait for your attorney to come back, talking of which, hey Officer Kendall, can you check to see if Mr Grayling's superglued his ass to the john. He's taking his time and the clock's ticking"

The officer left the room and shut the door behind him.

Wilson picked the briefcase up and shook it. He then shook it for a second time, this time with vigour. He raised his eyebrows and set the case back down on the table. He turned around to the other uniformed officers who stood behind me.

"Fellas, tell me, in all honesty, what did that sound like to you?"

"Sir, in my humble opinion and based upon my experience, it sounds, well, like an empty briefcase."

The other cop sniggered. Wilson coughed into his fist, trying to hide a snort of laughter.

"That's right, Officer Benson. It sounds like a fucking empty briefcase, but that's just our opinion. Say, Mr McCambridge, did you perhaps hear a rattle there at all, a slight muffled shuffle of anything that sounded like tapes or paper?"

I leant over the desk and grabbed the briefcase from Wilson's hand. I snapped the catches open it and held it upside down over the desk.

It was empty.

"There's some mistake, Greyling has them, I took them to him. He must have brought the wrong case. Where the fuck is he? I want him here, in this room now."

Wilson shook his head.

"Sir," piped up one of the uniforms.

"Go ahead, Benson," said the detective.

"I forgot to say, I just got a text message from Officer Kendal. He's checked all the johns in the building. No sign of Mr Greyling. The front desk saw him leave"

Wilson turned to face me again.

"It looks like Mr Greyling has stood you up. And as for you, Mr McCambridge..."

I don't remember much in the seconds and minutes after that but anything that was said to me was just the dismal sound of echoes as I vanished down a vortex of fate. That was the point I when I wondered if rock bottom really was as low as it got.

It wasn't.

CHAPTER 38

Dear Mr McCambridge,

> *As you are aware, after having contested and lost your third and final appeal (McCambridge vs. The People of Illinois), there cannot be further trial or appeal unless fresh evidence is presented. We are still trying to trace the whereabouts of Mr Charles Greyling but all attempts to date have unfortunately proven to be fruitless...*

I'm not sure if anyone calls me Callum or Cal anymore. McCambridge is what my latest lawyer calls me but in here, I'm Prisoner D34294923. That's who I am now. Someday, I will start not to give a fuck. There comes a time when all the ships you've ever known, slowly vanish to distant specks on the horizon and start becoming just another what-might-have-been. I hope they turn around but they never do.

I am prisoner D34294923.

Over the years, these walls of eight feet by five have been the horizons of my world. The floor is my lake, my bed is my hammock and my desk is my ship. My books, pens and writing paper are the winds that fatten my thinning sails. It's been a long time since I've tasted a decent omelette, smelt a flower, felt the sound and rush of a river flow past me, nearly being knocked down by a speeding car, kissed a woman. I've tried hard to hold onto the memories of all the sensations that I took for granted and indulged in. I relive them and experience them in my mind as often as I can.

I feel my grip of those memories grow ever weaker by the day, by the week, by the month, by the year. The taste of coffee becomes just an image of a cup of dark brown, hot liquid. The women I loved, the softness of their skin, the flagrance of their scent, their smiles that warmed my heart, well, they may as well be the hollow re-enactments of a cheap, daytime drama. I've forgotten what they are really like.

I once read that knowing how to make love to a woman is nothing like making love to a woman, any more than chewing the page of a recipe book tastes like the dish it describes. But it's all I have.

It's all I'll ever have.

I fold the letter and file it in my cardboard box. Letters from my lawyers mostly, but I get letters from women on the outside. They're strangers though, they're that strange type of woman for whom the convict is the perfect man. They always know where he is, he won't stray and will never cheat. Well, if he does cheat, sucking another man's dick or being someone's bitch-boy isn't just quite as bad as porking some bottle-blonde in a night-club toilet or a rent-by-the-hour motel room.

I write to them of course, just to pass the time. I make a point of apologizing for the delay as I didn't have the time. I'm not sure if they all get the joke but what the hell. I hope one of them is a comedy writer. Feel free to use it and make 'em laugh honey. Don't worry, I won't ask for a credit.

Looking back, it was a relief. I got tired of the hide and seek routine. All that's over. There's a comfort in defeat. I don't have to fight no more. It sucks that I used to be a cop though. That's why they lock me up for twenty-three hours a day. It's for my own protection. You see, I booked a few of my fellow guests into his hotel and they don't much like this kinda enforced gardening-leave. People forget nothing in here. There's nothing new to push old memories back. Old memories are recent memories. Time in here is a different kinda time from outside. On the outside, time may heal but time has nothing to do with it. Hurt is like a black carpet of pain. It slowly gets covered with the dust and shit of daily life until only patches of that original hot, black pain remain in view.

In here, it's different.

Nothing ever really happens.
Your last day of freedom is always yesterday. Old wrongs, old hurts just dig deeper into the skin. They stop being tattoos and become part and parcel of your bone and marrow. Those I had a hand in putting away, they never forget a cop.

They never forget a wrong turn.

This is grudge-central.

I follow a strict routine. I get up at six and do meditation for an hour. I then do a hundred or so sit-ups, run on the spot and work up a sweat before I am allowed out for my four-minute shower before the general population get a chance to get their soap and razor-blades to give me a rub-down I'll never forget .

I hear them, their voices slither down the hall outside like a mob of angry, jeering burning souls. The clang of the steel doors, the never ending ebbs and tides of a million echoes add to the sense of entombment. I've heard many nasty sounds in my life, the sound of crying, the sound of blood bubbling in slit and shot neck but there is no sound that makes one feel so forgotten by God as the sound of the hollow, cold, metallic Thor-moan of steel doors being clanged shut at night.

It's at night when the souls of the living dead start to come out and tell something of the truth of themselves. Lost voices, tearful moans, the shrieks of lunacy, laughter of minds long lost. Snarling threats are made, words curling up in the middle of the air like snakes, writhing their way back and forth in an evil dialectic. The night-time is not a time of peace. It's a time when the lid of the day is taken off and the hot soup of fear, frustration, anger and hate bubbles and brews.

I still think of my old life. I can't help thinking of what might have been. I never did find out why Hector did what he did. Jealousy is the only thing I can think of but why after all this time? He must have really hated me though otherwise he would have had me dead. I've been given the life penalty. Make no bones about it, this is a more cruel and unusual punishment than the rope, Old Sparky or sucking in gas on a gurney. A million suns may set and a million more may rise in the sky that I'll never see again but today is never today. There is never a tomorrow, only a million yesterdays.

I meet the other segregated prisoners for an hour each day for association. The ex-cop convicts I've met are the lowest of the low. One's inside for framing a black guy for the murder of a twenty-year-old marine and planting evidence on him so that he and his buddies

305

could clock up and earn overtime. That black dude was on Death Row but had his sentence commuted to life without parole. The cop got twenty years.

The others are rapists, child molesters and all the other weird cadres of sex crime. For the sake of human contact, you do pass the time of day with these sorts but you can never be buddies with them unless you know in your heart that they are innocent.

You can tell the innocent ones.

They're the ones who look frightened, dejected. The guilty ones get off on telling each other sick stories of past exploits. One of them has a friend in the court somewhere and posts copies of trial transcripts where carnal details of trial testimony are written. One of them sits by himself every day in the same spot. Always has a hand deep inside his pocket. He moves it up and down for a minute then he shivers and stops. That's when the dirty fucker has shot his load. He then smiles. I found out he killed five teenage girls in the 1960s but escaped the chair several times thanks to liberal governors in Springfield.

Ever hear a ghost story? You don't have to believe them but what they all have in common is the ghost that walks up and down the same road, at the same time of day, doing and saying exactly the same fucking thing, night in, night out. They're like faulty record player needle, stuck in a groove, playing and pausing, playing and pausing until, over time, the tape fades. I know a lot of ghosts in here and their hearts are still beating but they stopped being alive a long time ago. That's when a man truly dies, the day he stops picking fruits from the tree of life. I'm not saying that I'm above becoming a ghost myself. In fact, it's probably inevitable. I've faded like old newsprint.

It's evening time now, and I'm reading *Travels with Charley* by Steinbeck. I should read it in a day. I've read *Lord of the Rings* in three days when I thought it would take a month. Does the world have enough books? I'm testing that thesis big time.

Good night.

CHAPTER 39

One morning, some weeks later, I received a visitor.

"McCambridge." An unfamiliar voice. I looked up at the visor. I saw a pair of eyes. I didn't recognise the voice. At first, I thought it was a new guard but there was something hesitant in his voice that somehow didn't seem right.

"McCambridge, you don't know me but, look, can I come in?"

The strange sliver of politeness on the side of the daily dish of shit caught my attention.

"What do you want?" I asked.

"I need to talk with you, just for a minute, don't worry, there's no trouble, just for a minute"

"Be my guest"

The eyes vanished from the visor. The door opened and the man came in, a prison guard but no one I had met before. He was considerably younger than the others.

"You're new here, huh?" I said.

"Been here four months, they transferred me from D wing last week."

I nodded, waiting for him to cut to the chase. His eyes darted around the room as though he was viewing a room to rent. I could almost feel the words percolating in his stomach, waiting for the right moment to rise up and burp. I glanced at his name badge, *W. Gatlin*.

"Say, I notice your name, Gatlin, sounds kinda familiar."

He nodded. He took out a packet of Marlboro Lights and offered me one. I took it and leant forward to reach the shivering flame of his Zippo. He then lit his and we exhaled plumes of rich smoke. I allowed myself to relax.

"It's probably about right you remember it," he said. I let him talk more. I nodded slowly, wracking my brain. Where the fuck did I come across a Gatlin? The answer lurked like a hooker in the street corners of my mind but I was damned if I could place him. A collage of faces and situations shimmered in my memory zone. The more I tried to remember, the more I shuffled the pictures.

"My daddy, Elmore Gatlin, he was a client of yours fourteen years ago. You helped him. We found our mom, bleedin' to death. She couldn't talk. She died. They said my Daddy had killed her but we knew he hadn't. You helped find the gun. If you hadn't, my Daddy would have fried. Shit, man, I don't understand how you can't remember something like that."

It all came back to me, kind of.

1993 was the year. I remember getting a call from an out-of towner asking for help. I asked how he heard of me. *Reputation* he said. That's how the game works if you're good. Word gets around and into some peculiar places too. Gibson City, a rundown, seen-better-days-gasping-for-survival kinda township some ninety miles south of Chicago.

Gibson City, a place that puts the 'down' in down-state.

Elmore Gatlin was a farmer and, like most farmers, clinging by his fingernails to a world hell-bent on spinning him into a modernity he knew nothing about. His wife was shot and took over a day to die. He was arrested for her murder. I even started to believe he snuffed her. When that happens, you might as well quit but a job was a job. Money was tight. I was paying for Lorna's shrink at prices high enough to drive a sane man crazy.

The police searches found a whole load of nothing, but one day, I got a tip off in the mail. It was in the form of a map with a note at the back. The note told me to go and look for a bag by the sycamore tree two fields west of the Gatlin farmhouse. I went there. Found a black garbage bag, tightly wrapped in brown duct tape. I nudged it with my shoe. It felt heavy. I ripped it open. Found a black rifle and took it out and gave it careful examination, taking care not to fuck the forensics. I could tell it had been recently used. The acrid smell of gun smoke lingered, trapped in the bag. The gun was bagged and disposed pretty quick after Old Ma Gatlin cobbed it in the cornfields. Dark patches were around the barrel. I held it close to my nose.

Dried blood.

The blood turned out to belong to Heidi Gatlin. The prints on the gun were identified as those off Jared Drew. Elmore Gatlin suspected Drew. In fact he suspected them of having an affair. Homicide were pissed at him. They asked him why he kept quiet about his suspicions. They asked him why he risked going to the chair for something he didn't do if he had information as important as that. Gatlin just told them he wanted to spare his children finding out about that their mom was a whore who fucked the man next door.

His words.

Jared Drew protested his innocence. Claimed he was framed. The forensics were dynamite though. You can't cry and wail that you ain't you until they hold that mirror up and stick your face in it. Then you just sound stupid. Then again, shit happens.

Jared Drew went to the chair in 2001. From all accounts, his last day was far from dignified. You always hear about the condemned walking to their doom with head up high and accepting their fate with stoic, quiet dignity like good little Morgan Freemans. That's for the movies. The reality is they're dragged kicking, crying, screaming, pissing and shitting their bags. It's true there is a Green Mile but it's painted with many brown road markings and scorched with a thousand dug-in heels that just get dragged along. When the condemned proves to be too much of a handful, they close his cell door. He thinks he's beaten them. A minute later, the hatch opens. The prison orderly pokes in a blowpipe. That's right. A blowpipe, just like in Animal Planet when they shoot a tranquilizer dart into the ass of a monkey and then catch it in a bag when it falls from the tree.

Same principle.

The prisoner doesn't know the fuck what's going on. It's painted pink to make it look friendly but the prisoner knows it's not a gun. The orderly takes aim at the prisoner's neck or leg and blows. Dart in neck. Dart in thigh. Dart in wherever. It takes effect quickly. Prisoner slumps over. Cell door opens. He's dragged unconscious from the cell and next thing he knows he is sat upright on a chair. Then they strap him in. Legs, arms, chest, all clamped tight. Finally, the dead man's hat, a steel skullcap with a damp sponge on his scalp.

They wait.

The prisoner comes around. He's sleepy at first. The guards and medics stand around, watching him. One of them slaps him in the face. The prisoner is now awake. The prisoner gets his bearings. He's not in his cell. He's in a room. He sees rows of seats in front of him. Some are strangers, some look familiar. At closer quarters, he sees the guards. He sees a priest or a reverend or some other peddler of God and the promise of a better life. He tries to get up. He tries to move but he can't. The enormity of it dawns on him like a black sun over a nuclear landscape.

They ask him for his final words. The movies have us believe that we're in for a soliloquy of an eloquence that is not in keeping with the character of the condemned, who we all know, has led a life of wordless, inarticulate brutality.

Then the guards have their little joke. They always do this and if you ask me, it's sick as fuck. A guard rushes in, waiving a white envelope in the air.

"It's from the Governor, it's from the Governor" he cries.

The prisoner thinks it's a last minute reprieve.

The guard opens the envelope and reads the letter. He says "Please proceed. Have a nice day."

They laugh. The prisoner goes white.

A guard pushes the lever down at full throttle. Sparks do fly as the cliché says. The prisoner's muscles tighten and spasm, tighten and spasm. The look on his face is one of silent agony. The lever's released. The prisoner slumps.

Show over. Move along, nothing to see here.

That's how it was done to Jared Drew.

"When my Daddy found out you were put down for life, he went quiet for a week. He wouldn't say a word to no one. When he did come around to speakin', he told us that he's like something to be done for that boy. We didn't know what to do really, we just thought we'd send you parcels, books, magazines, rations and stuff, you know?"

"So now I know," I said. "Well, that's real kind of you all. Pass on my thanks to Elmore."

"I sure will, I sure will but that's not all. I had just started as a prison guard and well, Daddy asked if you could be sprung. I laughed at him and said 'Daddy, it ain't that easy to spring a prisoner, there's lots of other guards watching not just the prisoners but each other too'. But we both pondered and thought about it, working out all kinds of ways and means but nothin' worked. Then one day, one of my prisoners took ill, Mike Liggit, old guy, about seventy I think. I found him in his cell, he tried to hang himself but he was too heavy for the shoelaces he tied together. They must have snapped and he fell and banged his head against the side of the his concrete table.

He was taken to the prison hospital. I went with him. He's doing OK but getting some shrink treatment. That's not the whole story. What made the light go on in my head was when I went back a month later to check in with him, the staff were running around like headless chickens. I wondered what was wrong. The ward clerk told me that Liggit escaped. 'That can't be,' I said, 'not with those turrets and wires and stuff'. The clerk leant over his desk and told me 'Sir, this is a hospital, not the prison' and winked at me. They found him though, wandering around in the gardens outside. He was barefoot. He had no intention of jumping jail for where could he go? There was nothing for him outside nut I learned this, there's only one guard outside patrolling the grounds. I saw doctors and nurses and other staff come and go as you damn well please but only one guard. I tell you, McCambridge, that's the weak spot. Get yourself into the loony-bin. Then we can do business."

I stubbed out my smoke on the floor and kicked the butt towards the opposite wall. Gatlin fished another smoke from his breast pocket and gave me it.

"Take as many as you want," he said.

He got up and put his hand on my right shoulder.

"You're a smart fella. You know what I'm suggestin'" he said. He checked his watch. "If I don't go on my way, they'll think you're holding me hostage"

I nodded. "Don't mind me asking but what the fuck would I do once I am outside? It's not as if I've anywhere to go myself, ever thought of that?"

Gatlin smiled.

"How does farm work hit you?"

"Come again?"

"I mean, we would spirit you away to our homestead. You lay low for a month or two, grow a beard and start living and working with me and my sister, on the farm. We could tell folk you're our cousin from Wisconsin or some such story. They won't put two and two together. They'll try but they always come up with five"

"I've been here before Mr Gatlin. Promises of getting me outta dodge all came to nothing. I'll tell you what I told an old dead friend of mine, I told her she'd get into a bundle of trouble if anyone found out. Am I worth that? Your daddy's an old man. He don't need any more trouble, not at his time of life. Thanks for the thought though but I'm pretty much resigned. Anyone, like I also told my friend, your daddy paid me in full. He owes me nothing"

Gatlin lit another cigarette.

"McCambridge, a life is a gift that can never be fully paid for" He said. He took another drag and lifted his hand and pointed his finger at me. "I'll be around"

Gatlin turned and left my cell and locked it behind him. I got up from my seat and lay on my bed, staring at the ceiling, wondering if my heaven was up there.

CHAPTER 40

Over the coming days, Gatlin visited me with gifts of cigarettes and instant coffee, the good stuff. He kept suggesting I think about what he said. At first, I was sceptical. He seemed like a nice kid, perhaps a little green behind the gills but his country boy persona was his front. People probably under-estimated him with his slow way of talking and over politeness but I bet no one saw him coming. The idea began to germinate in my mind. I started to think it through and the more I thought about it, the less stupid it became. In fact, it seemed like a breeze.

I knew that security was pretty high in the normal prison hospital but was a bit surprised to hear it was lax on the psychiatric. I wasn't sure how much hype there was around Gatlin's story but what did I have to lose? I was here for the rest of my natural life so I figured what more could they throw at me. A month in the cooler? Big burgers.

I decided to go for it.

Gatlin looked in on me that day and I rushed over to the door. I whispered "Tonight, 1am." He nodded. I had to stick to it and prepare myself for the roller coaster that lay ahead. For the first time in years, I felt a fresh flood of living blood rushing through the dried-up veins in my soul. People wonder why lifers don't commit suicide. The thing is, after a while the cell stops being a cell and becomes your house and your workplace. After a while, the prison stops being a prison and becomes a self-contained world. A kind of medieval spaceship that just forgot to take-off at the count of zero.

There comes a point when you stop thinking about the outside. You know it's there but in the same way you know space is there, above the clouds, a distant and impossible destination, a place inhabited by strange beings in strange clothes in strange cars who are free to go where they like. Whatever possibilities you entertained that you had on the outside, all die a death inside. You just stop thinking about it. I guess it's like shutting part of yourself down to keep your other engines going, like a seed buried a mile deep in the Arctic. It only takes a certain sun to melt away the ice and then the seed starts to sprout.

7pm

The hours crawled that day and that's saying something. I slept for several hours in the afternoon and early evening in an attempt at poor man's time travel, hoping to wake up later, nearer the appointed time.

10pm

I regretted leaving it so late. Why did I say one o'clock? It just sounded marginally more dramatic than say midnight. I waited.

11pm

Gatlin shunted the hatch down. I looked at him. I mouthed the words "1am" to him and gave the thumbs up. He nodded and shut the hatch. I sat back on the bed and opened a book, *Leaves of Grass* by Whitman. I forget the poem I was reading, the words skimmed off the top of my attention like skimmed pebbles off a lake but I remembered one line above all others.

"Oh savage world of life."

12pm

I lay back on the bed, books strewn around me and on the floor. It was time to make preparations. Make it look for real. I opened a book within which I had hidden bottles of contraband aspirins inside a hole I had hollowed out. I got up and went over to my desk. I opened the bottles and poured them out. I had an idea of crushing them with a hardback book but the noise would echo and might raise attention from the other guards. That was always a risk but fuck it, I took a risk when I was born and look where it got me.

I cupped my left hand under the edge of the desk to catch the pills as I them palmed them over. I kept five and put them in my mouth and washed them down with a glass of water. I chose the quantity deliberately. Five pills aren't not enough to cause any real harm but it's enough to make it look like a serious attempt. I crushed the other pills inside my sock using my feet until they were ground small enough to be washed down the wash-hand basin without leaving any bits behind.

The bottles were empty. I put one on its side on the floor to affect a sense of distress. One empty bottle would make it look like I downed all inside it. They'll find the other empty bottles in the end when they search my cell but by that time, I'll be in the loony camp..

So far so good. It was the dead of night. The nocturnal noise of madness was starting up from the cells down the corridor. I was worried that even the gentlest trickle of water in the stainless steel hand basin would be heard at unusual distances. The night is the greatest gossip of them all. The smallest of sounds is carried like a carnival on the back of a cockroach. It doesn't make sense but it happens.

The next part was the daddy-o of the plan. I had to gather all the bed sheets and fashion a noose and find a suitable place to tie the end to. I looked around the cell. The walls were no good, no hooks. The concrete desk and bed were fixed to the floor. I needed something solid that would take my weight. I was at a loss and my heart started to drop.

Then the obvious hit me.

The door.

When you are in a room so long, you no longer see the door as a door but as just another wall that is sometimes opened by a uniform.

The door handle.

It looked solid enough. At the right angle, it would do. I went over to it to make sure that it had no give. A handle that shook, rattled and rolled would be as good as a snitch with a sneeze.

I carefully put my hand on the handle and tried to move it up and down. Rock solid. I took the long string of tied together sheets and tied one end to the handle. I tugged as hard as I could to test it. It was perfect.

The din of the other cells masked the noise I made but I heard the unmistakeable sound of heavy brogues stealthily making their way up the corridor. I looked at my watch. 12:30 Am. I bunched up the sheets and put them on the floor against the door. Prying eyes through the hatch wouldn't see them at first glance, not at that angle. I lay on top of my bed and feigned sleep, keeping one eye half open.

The plod of the sensible shoes stopped intermittently, followed by the thin metallic ring of hatches being shut on cell doors. Someone was doing the rounds. I hoped it was Gatlin. I lay still, waiting for my turn, hoping he would come along. The footsteps grew closer. I heard the hatch of the cell next door. I didn't hold my breath but I was breathing as economically as I could.

Thud.

My hatch. I glanced up. It was too dark to see if it was Gatlin but if it was him, he was too early. I let whoever it was make the opening verbal gambit. He cleared his throat. It didn't sound like Gatlin. It sounded like an older man, more gravelled.

"McCambridge, where are your bed sheets?"

Fuck.

It wasn't Gatlin. Time to think fast. I couldn't ignore him.

"Sorry, sir, is there a problem?" I asked. My heart pounded. I felt cold beads of sweat seep from under my skin. I felt wet.

"What did you do with your bed linen, McCambridge?"

I heard him put a key in the door. Fuck, fuck, fuck. I quickly remembered that I didn't use all my sheets for the noose. A dirty sheet was stuffed between the bed and the wall. I reached down as quick as I could and hoped to hell I could grasp it. I grasped it. I yanked it up as fast as I could. I am sure I ripped it but it sounded like a fart.

"I'm too warm, coming down with something, I just stuffed it down the side, see?"

Now I held my breath. A torch shone around the cell. My eyes followed the beam, praying for it to land on some unremarkable corner of the room or piece of the floor. It darted furiously around without any method. It was Ridley, a real stickler for rules and procedure.

Ridley grunted and the switched off the torch. The hatch went up. I let go of my breath. I checked my watch. 12:45Am. Tick-tock, tick-tock. I lay back, sweating cold.

I worked out that fifteen minutes times sixty seconds is nine hundred. Lying down with my mind playing host to a million squalls of worry and thought wasn't doing me any good. I decided to squeeze them all out by counting down from nine hundred, like a mantra.

1:00am.
Zero hour. I got up and tied the noose around my neck. I had to make this look good. Noose victims have welts and burn marks on their necks. I had to make it look as good as I could. I had to throw myself down fast enough to get a mark. If I do it too well, I just might break my neck. If I don't do it, my neck will look as smooth as a lap dancer's ass. I tightened the noose as fast as I could. I rubbed it against my skin half a dozen times until it felt like a Chinese burn. It hurt like hell but I had to keep going. All around my neck. I was silently screaming with pain. My skin felt it was on fire but I had to keep going, even to the point of rubbing my skin raw and drawing blood.

I stopped and felt my neck with my fingers. My fingers were sweating and it stung my neck like crazy but the hurt felt good. It was the pain of a plan coming together. I tightened the noose around my neck a little more, closed my eyes and flung myself forward hard enough to cause bruises. It was hard to do. It was counter-intuitive. I've been through a lot but I never entertained suicide. Dunno why but I never did. For some reason, I always had a goofy sense of some better tomorrow.

The rope tightened above my Adam's apple and I choked. I think I rasped rather loudly. The hatch came down just at that moment. I heard the piercing banshee cry of a guard's whistle. A cacophony of shouting filled every crevice of peace that the night harbored. I remember lots of voices, each one pouring over the last one like an ever hotter flow of urgency. Some sounded like concern, some carried blame. I remember the noose being cut from my neck and falling on the cold, hard floor. The floor felt soothing. I pretended to be limp while I was the eye of my very own storm.

I was put on a stretcher and wheeled out down the corridor. I remember the screams and the shouting, the cold, black thread of venom tying all the noise together.. I remember the flashing blue lights of ambulance and the hit of the night air. I drank that fresh cool night air as hard as I could into my lungs. It tasted sweet, almost like chewing angel wings. In that short time between prison and ambulance, I felt the cold finger of heaven on my burning tongue.

I fell asleep in the back of the ambulance, lulled deeper into slumber by the emergency around me. I was the only one there who knew I was going to be alright.

The whole thing must have been too much for me for I passed out for real. That was the best past.

So far.

CHAPTER 41

The sound of cattle, the glint of sunlight, browned in the filter of the thin lilac curtains that hung over the bedroom window. The gentle lilt of lavender caressed my nostrils, the freshness of the bed linen. I was someplace else. I opened my eyes. I was in bed. A strange bed but a plump, comfortable one. I was even dressed in fresh, cotton-blue silk pyjamas. People sat around me, smiling. One of them was an old man dressed in rumpled working denims. The other two were a young man and a young woman. I recognised the young man. He wore some kind of uniform. He looked like a cop but there was something about him that made me feel he was a make-believe cop. I couldn't quite put my finger on it. It was his face. He looked kind.

The young woman was dressed in blue jeans and a green top. She had a magnificent head of black, curly hair that fell over her shoulders and tumbled down over her breasts. It had been a long time since I saw a woman with hair like that. Hell, it had been a long time since I'd seen a woman apart from the frumps from the Quaker house who used to talk to us about our friend Jesus every Sunday. Her ringlets tumbled free and easy like the dark waters of the Niagara. There was another man present, standing behind the girl, his hand on her shoulder. He looked a tough nut. Blue denim shirt buttoned up to his neck, hangdog skin hung like stalactites from what was once a formidable jaw line. His mouth was a stern slit in a tough hide of face.

"What day is it?" I asked.

The old man stood up and lit his pipe. The aroma of Golden Virginia felt like a time machine. It took me back. My old man smoked a pipe. Same brand of tobacco too. I hadn't tasted that aroma for over forty years. I took deep breaths through my nose, holding onto the taste of tobacco as though it were a fine wine.

"Well, if you must know, today is Wednesday."

I realized the banality of my question. Did it really matter if it were a Wednesday or a Monday?

"Where am I, who are you?" I asked.

"That's more like it," said the young man. He smiled and exchanged happy glances with the girl.

"You're in your new home, Callum," said the old man. "This is the Gatlin farm, four miles outside Gibson City, Illinois. I'm Elmore Gatlin, this is my son Wilson. I think you've met him. This is my daughter Ruth and my half-brother, Alvin Truesdale. He's a Sheriff"

I looked at them again. They still had big old grins on their farm-fresh faces. Even the sheriff managed to raise a corner of unwilling skin at the edge of his mouth but his attempt at looking happy lasted as long as a blonde on the arm of a loser at a blackjack table. I locked my gaze on Ruth, her eyes, losing myself in those pools of burning cobalt blue. She blushed slightly and glanced away.

"She's a beautiful girl, isn't she?" said the Sheriff. "Shame she's your cousin though." Now he smiled with a mouth that spelt 'gotcha'.

"I don't understand"

"The cops are looking for you, even the FBI are sniffin' around. You've been seen in Indiana, St Louis, Gary, all around. They'll even start seeing you in the Big Apple itself," said the Sheriff. "But don't' worry, after a month or so, the fuss will fizzle out and they'll move on. They always do"

"You heard the man" said Elmore. "That's why you must rest up and lie low for a while and no getting up and wanderin' around neither"

"There's always a new killer on the loose. I should know. said the Sheriff. There was something about him I didn't like. He was one of those people who couldn't tell you the time of day without making you want to take a shower. My mind was a snowstorm of ripped up memories.

"Your new name is Phillip Gatlin, from Saxeville, Wisconsin," said Elmore

I sat up on my elbows.

"You saved my soul some years ago," said Elmore. The sheriff walked over to the foot of the bed and stared right at me.

"My half-brother Elmore here was accused of killing his wife Heidi four years ago. Elmore here would have fried on the chair if it wasn't for you."

"Well..."

"Hell no, you helped find the weapon that killed her and it was traced to that snake in the grass, Jared Drew."

"I'm glad I played a part in that, if you say so."

"Damn right I say so, Callum," said Elmore. He stood and stooped over the bed and stared at me as if I was for sale.

"We figured it would be better for you to start a fresh life, with us. If you want to get back to the city, then, we can't stop you but they'll just scoop you up like dog shit. Here, you'll have a life, a new life, a different life but a life. When you're ready, you'll work on the farm and learn our ways," Elmore said.

I saw a glass of water on the bedside locker and took a sip. I wasn't convinced that I wasn't dreaming but I hoped I wasn't.

"All this is a too much, I don't know, I need to rest up some more."

Elmore put his hand on my shoulder. "Take all the time you need, Callum, we're sitting down for supper at seven but we'll save you some if you sleep through it. All in your own good time"

One by one they left the room. The Sheriff was the last to leave. He stood at the doorway whilst the others clattered down the wooden staircase outside on the landing. The room was dimly lit by the breathless rays of sunshine that were still swimming through the curtains but the Sheriff formed a silhouette like he was made of black matter. I was too tired to enter into conversation with him. I gave him my best crocodile smile and closed my eyes and drifted into the void, blue, balmy tides of sleep.

CHAPTER 42

I didn't know how much time had passed but when I woke up the room was as black as Dick Nixon's heart. I felt fresher and my mind was clear. I remembered the squall of the prison corridor, my time in the hospital and climbing through a ground floor hospital window in the middle of the night and being ferried away in the back of a pickup truck, hiding under logs.

I rubbed my eyes and got up and opened the curtains. It was night-time and I was deep in the country.. A half moon hung in the sky like a silver earring. I pulled the curtains open as wide as I could and looked further out. I could hardly make out any shape in the distance, near or far. I used the meagre light of the moon to find my way around the room. I felt the walls for a light switch and when I found it, I switched it on. The light hurt my eyes.. I squinted at first but as I got used to the brightness, I saw my bed, a double bed. A large white quilt with roughly sewn green and yellow rectangular patches lay on top of it.

To the left was a closet. Opposite the bed was a desk and a chest of drawers. The walls were papered with woodchip. Pictures of people hung in little black frames on every wall. Some were photos of smiling, modern faces. Some were of more austere, grim faces of times before smiling was invented after the Second World War.

Some were paintings of women with shawls on their heads and of men with fine sideburns, great beards and pocket watches tied to their waistcoats with chain. I went over to the closet and opened it. A set of clothes hung inside and I rummaged through them. They all seemed to be my size, the shirts, the sweaters, the pants, the shoes, the underwear. I got dressed in a brown pair of cords and a white linen shirt and brown loafers, combed my hair and opened the door of my bedroom. I had no sense of time. No clock hung on the wall nor did one grace the bedside cabinet. I stood in the quietness of the landing but the quiet didn't last for long. The smell of baked ham and roast potatoes came up the stairs like the scent of a siren. The cling and clang of kitchen utensils, the dull thuds of crockery on wood.
I went downstairs, following the smell of food. My belly rumbled at the thought of a huge dinner. I couldn't remember the last time I ate.

"You're up," said Ruth. She was standing beside me on the landing. I could make out her silhouette but just about.

"I didn't see you there," I said. "It smells really good."

"Yes, come down. Let's eat."

***

I took my place at the family table. I still felt like a hostage in the hands of a benign gang. A homely spread of ham, potatoes, carrots, sweet corn, gravy and cornbread lay on thick no-nonsense plates and bowls but no one spoke. Elmore sat at the top of the table, next to an empty chair. To his right, sat Ruth. To his left, Wilson and Sheriff Truesdale. Elmore sat with head bowed. The food was passed around in silence. After we filled our plates, Elmore put a bible in front of the empty chair beside him and opened it and patted the open pages down.

He put his hands together and said, "Lord, grace will be said by my beloved wife Heidi, the mother of Ruth and Wilson." A shiver trammelled through me. I looked over at Ruth. She was staring at Elmore real hard, avoiding my gaze. She seemed like a smart woman, smart enough to know how strange this scene looked to a stranger. I looked at the sheriff. His head was bowed, eyes shut but his lips were moving, mouthing something silently to himself. I looked at Wilson but he too sat as cold as stone.

"Amen," said Elmore, bookending the silence. No prayer or any other spoken word was uttered. No one else seemed to find it strange. Perhaps this was how it was done, grace said in the silent words of his dead wife. They say the past is a different country but so too are other people's homes. They do things differently there. Elmore lifted his knife and fork and started eating. The sheriff shortly followed, then Wilson and finally Ruth. I took this as the cue for starting my meal. I dug into the ham and felt it melt in my mouth.

"Say, this is the best meal I've had in a long, long time."

The sheriff took a long drink of milk and wiped his mouth clean on his napkin. "Son, we should have told you this, it's not your fault but no one talks at mealtimes in this house."

"Words are the flies that lay eggs in the wounds of Jesus," Elmore said.

I stared at the sheriff. He lifted a hill of creamed mashed potato and stuck it into his mouth and chewed it with a relish and a violence that I thought wasn't entirely necessary. I looked at Ruth. A brief smile danced upon her mouth before she looked away again. She seemed like a girl not used to the hungry eyes of men. I bowed my head down like the others and started eating again. A little later towards the end of my meal, when I had picked up a hunk of cornbread to soak up the gravy, I raised my head a little to look at the others. Elmore was staring at me.

When we had all finished eating, Ruth got up and lifted all the plates and cutlery and went into the kitchen. The men folk remained at the table. Elmore lit his pipe.

"We can talk now, son, but never during mealtimes. That's how things are."

"I'm sorry, I didn't know. I'm sure there will be lots of rules I'll break over the next while but they're not intentional"

"That's OK, we don't have many rules around here. You've learned the most important one though" said Elmore. "Heidi didn't like idle chit-chat, that's where we got the flies in the wounds of Jesus line from. Her daddy was a travelin' preacher, it's a mighty good line and I use it myself all the time"

"I see," I said, lifting a glass of water to hide whatever bemused facial expression I may have been about to make.

The sheriff reached into his shirt pocket and took out a packet of cigarillos and lit one. He let himself relax and he sat back.

"Callum, let me tell you a little story, it's a true one. It might clarify a few things. Think of it also as an allegory if you don't take it literally. We used to have a neighbour in these parts who went by the name of Dick Krell. He was a very old man but worked his land till he fell down and died in it. He lived alone with his daughter Beth. She was said to be the most beautiful woman in south Illinois and broke many a heart, mine too but as the song says, her heart belonged to daddy. A long time ago, there was a terrible hurricane and we don't get no hurricanes much in these parts, just once in every fifty years or so. It tore up houses, tore up fences, outhouses, it even sucked up cars and tractors and livestock and people like itty-bitty bits of breadcrumbs up the mouth of a Hoover. Some of us farmers were lucky not to have suffered that much mayhem and loss. Dick Krell wasn't one of them, his house stayed his ground but his livestock was sucked up and scattered. He didn't know what to do. Around that time, a stranger was in town by the name of Gary Benson. He was a New Yorker who worked in Wall Street but had made his money and decided to spend the rest of his life working and living off the land, wandering from farm to farm, from state to state like a some kind of latter day St Francis.

He came to Krell's house and almost singlehandedly, rounded up all but three of old Krell's cattle and brought them back and rebuilt all Krell's fences. Krell was very grateful and offered Krell a quarter of his farmland in gratitude. Benson turned it down. All he wanted was a meal and a room for the night before moving on. Krell tried to persuade him to take the land but nothing gave. Krell took Benson in, made up a room for him and prepared a fine meal and threw in a few bottles of moonshine too.

Krell eventually persuaded Benson to stay a few more days as more work was needed. Benson was non-committal at first but Krell promised to pay him in advance. Benson thought it over and accepted. They worked the farm for the rest of that week. Krell noticed his daughter taking a bit of a shine to Benson though. He didn't think much of it as Beth never did seem to have a lot of truck with men but this time she seemed to be very taken with Benson.

Seven days came and gone and Benson told Krell that he would like to stay a little longer as more work was needed to get the outhouses and barns and milking equipment back in action again. Krell agreed. One night, old Krell came back to his house. There was a note on the floor. Benson had left. No word of goodbye, no nothing.

A week later, he caught wind of Benson helping out on some farm near Mazon City. Krell jumped in his jeep and drove all the way up and found the farm. A farm called Ganfry's I recall. Old Krell spotted Benson lifting bales of hay onto a truck. He walked up to Benson, pointed a gun at his head and emptied the magazine.

327

And that was the end of Benson.

Old Krell was tried and he was asked why he killed the man who saved his farm, he just shook his head and said 'Because he left and I needed him'. He never spoke another word after that. Spent the next twenty years of his life in a sanatorium until they released him back into the wild. He was found dead in the field behind his house four days later."

"What happened to Beth?" I asked.

Sheriff Truesdale didn't answer my question.

"Because he left and I needed him," he just repeated.

He got up and stubbed out his cigarillo on the earthen ashtray on the table and left the dining room. Wilson and Elmore looked at me. They didn't utter a word but I knew what they were thinking.

CHAPTER 43

One evening, a number of days later, I made off towards the Elburn River a mile or so behind the farm. I cut through some fields where the iron carcasses of long dead tractors lay in rusted splendour. Their shapes remained intact, silhouettes of death casting shadows on the whitewashed wall opposite. I went over to one and touched the side. A sliver of rust flaked and crumbled in silence. I left the metal tombstones to their silence and walked on towards the river. Once I reached the bank, I sat down and closed my eyes, trying to fill my head with the sound of the waters rushing over the stones and rocks. I wasn't in the mood for choosing my own mantra. Whatever word I chose, it was just a someone's else's word.

I lay down on my back by the side of the river, drifting in and out of consciousness, gently sensing the sunlight grow gently dimmer with the passing of a time that I no longer measured.

"May I join you?"

I opened my eyes and saw a dark haired woman standing only a couple of feet away. She was dressed in tight, blue, worn Levi's, boots and a white blouse that fluttered in the evening breeze like a pennant.

"It's a free country, or so they say."

She smiled.

"I've seen you come here a lot"

I didn't reply. It was my first time here but I didn't want to jar the small talk.

"I'm Jemima Drew, I'm sure that rings a bell or a dozen. Aren't you Philip, cousin of Elmore?"

I nodded my head.

Jemima plucked the bulb of a wildflower off its stalk and took aim at the waters and threw it in. The bulb bobbed about between three rocks by the shore before being whisked off downstream by the currents.

"My father Henry, when he was courting my mother, cut their names into an elm tree. It's still there, the elm tree, at the bottom of the field behind my house. I go there sometimes to look at it. I still make out the names, Henry and Mathilda but I doubt anyone would know who they are anymore except myself. My parents showed me when I was a little girl. I thought someday my future sweetheart would carve my name and his beneath my mom and pop's but it never happened like that. Years passed and the bark thickened and the names faded. All that's there now are gentle scars. Only I know the scars aren't just scars. Time is like that, it doesn't heal but just buries the wounds"

We sat in silence, listening to the quiet purrs of the rolling waters, watching the setting sun burnish the skies in shades of burnt orange as parting gift to the day.

"You said you see me most days but I've never seen you," I said

"Elmore told me that you wanted a new life. I thought it funny but there you go, it's a funny old world, isn't it, Phillip...or should I say, Callum?"

I sat up. "Either you're smarter than you look or someone's been spilling beans they shouldn't have had in the first place."

Jemima threw her head back and laughed.

"There's no need to be like that, Callum dear, Elmore and I, well, we go back a long way. We're practically family. No secrets in families, huh?"

"That's funny, I thought that's all families had to keep them together."

"Quite the cynic, aren't you? Ever heard of love?"

"Sure, I've heard of it, read about it even. I think I saw it on TV once"

Jemima smiled and looked away.

"I'm just wondering how many other people in this town Elmore considers to be family. The boys down the barbershop, the mailman, who else?"

"No one else knows. That's the truth. Elmore is grateful to have you around and whatever makes Elmore happy, well, it makes me happy too. I hope we can be friends. Do you think we can be friends?"

"Well, I don't want to be your enemy. You seem OK, if you're a friend of Elmore. I'm still gettin' used to things around here, that's all."

She lay back on the ground, lifting herself with her elbows.

"Jemima, since we're friends now, there's something I'd like to ask you, about Heidi."

"Go on."

"Heidi was heavily pregnant when she was murdered yet the headstone on her grave doesn't mention the baby. I took a walk to the graveyard today, just to see if anyone moved in or out since the last time I was there"

"The baby didn't die," she said, "It was plucked alive from her belly and given to a local family to raise. Only Elmore and I know who they are and where she is. It's a secret we'll take to the grave"

Oh those secrets again.

"But the autopsy report, it said the baby was dead, there was a baby in her womb, one of the bullets went straight through it."

Jemima sat upright, clutching her knees.

"There were two babies, Callum. One of them was dead, the other one was alive. We just thought it best not to mention it. What would have been the point?"

"Why didn't Elmore keep it? I mean Ruth would have helped out."

"The babies weren't his. The one that survived, we had to give it away. It would only have meant Jared knowing he was a father and what would that have done to a child, knowing that its father killed its mother and its unborn sister? No kid deserves that. We thought it best to give it to a Christian childless couple for a chance of a normal life. Who knows, but does the world need another messed up kid?"

"I'm not sure, I've never met a kid that wasn't" I said. Jemima looked away, shaking her head. " Don't mind my asking but how did Elmore know the babies weren't his?"

I knew they weren't his but I wanted to hear someone else say it.

"Heidi told him. She wrote him a note that he found after she died. They were Jared's. That's why Jared killed her. The deal was that she would leave Elmore for Jared but she changed her mind. Jared couldn't take it so he shot her"

"Why would she have written a note like that?"

Jemima shrugged her shoulders. "I don't know but people do shit like that, don't they?"

"Why didn't she just tell Elmore, why a note? I can't help wondering why the note was found after she was killed and not before. Some would say that was, well, convenient"

"I don't like what I think you're angling at but that's what happened and that's that. People do things others think strange all the time. I mean, today I went to the general store to pick up some groceries but did I drive straight back home? No, I went for a long drive through Hartson and Whittaker before deciding it was time to go home. Just a random meaningless drive, no reason for it. I just wanted a change of scene, that's all. What if someone was found murdered today in Whittaker or Hartson? What if my car was seen driving slowly past where the body was found? I'd tell you, I'd be taken in. That's what would happen. I'd be asked why I didn't drive straight home. I'd be asked why I drove to those two towns in particular. I wouldn't be able to give an answer. I'd be charged and who knows what happen me. So you see, people do things all the time and the rest of us think 'why did he go there and why did he do that?'"

She shook her head and looked away from me.

"Savage world of life," she said.

"That sounds familiar," I said.

We sat in silence, staring at the ever darkening skies that ushered in the twilight. Sometime later, I got up.

"It's getting dark. I should be getting back home. So should you."

"I like the darkness and the stars and planets way out there," she said. "In the daytime, we feel that we're the universe itself, full of our own importance but when the roof slides back on that big convertible up there, we see all the other things God made apart from us. It puts us in our place."

"Hmm, I never thought about it like that before" I said. "but I take your point."

Jemima raised a silent hand, bidding me goodbye. She looked away and I made my way back to the Gatlin's, through the fields where the dead tractors slept.

CHAPTER 44

I spent the following weeks keeping my head down on the Gatlin farm, helping Elmore rebuild the barn and milking machinery and gathering the dried grasses that were to be bundled up for beast feed for the winter. It was hard work and the squalls of intrigue that my appearance in town caused at first , had settled down now that I was part of the scene. No one asked questions. I even started to get a sense of permanence. I noticed some things though. The Gatlins kept themselves to themselves. Apart from the Sheriff, no one came to visit. Even Ruth didn't seem to have any friends nor did she visit friends or go out on the town. I thought this odd for a young pretty girl. The Gatlins were a self-contained unit. I kept myself to myself and only ventured into town on Wednesdays and Fridays. It wasn't difficult to restrict myself as the decision was made for me. The stores in town only opened two days a week. Gibson City was just a twitch away from giving up the ghost. There wasn't a lot to see or do there.

My first visit to town was to a white goods store that was stuck in a 1970s time warp. The place smelled like there was a tax on ventilation. They had bathtubs and Frigidaire units that wouldn't be out of place in scenes from *Happy Days*. The owner had greeted me with a weak smile and a high pitched 'Hi there' before scurrying back to his office. I got the impression he had long given up on selling anything and was now presiding over a mausoleum and not a store. When I told Ruth about him, she told me Mr King (that was his name) was taken aback at seeing a man come into his store without his wife with him.

It was that kind of town.

Once small convenient store and a Laundromat remained open all week though but they didn't evoke the dignified and defiant air of economic survival against the odds. Instead they gave off the scent of torpor and decay like a sick dog that someone forgot to put down. At first I avoided the bars. Too many questions at first but eventually I started going to them for the occasional beer. They asked me where I was from. I told them Saxeville, Wisconsin. It made me wonder just how many other townships like this existed in the country. I felt I had stumbled into a secret room that America told us never existed and now I knew why. The people who smile the most are probably the most likely to be the ones who hide the family cripple in the basement.

I remember that particular Friday afternoon in Gibson City. I walked down the main drag where there was only myself and a local by the name off Daniel Floyd in town. Daniel was a white guy with a big afro. He was also mute. He always stood by the crossing point with his rusted bicycle that he wheeled along but never rode. He kept pressing the buttons and looked excited at watching the WALK signs change to DONT WALK and back and forth like it was a lo-fi video game.

I tried talking to him once but it didn't go very far. He didn't seem to hear me either. Wilson told me later that he wasn't always like that. Floyd was the same age at Wilson and went to the same elementary school and he was quite normal and bright. All that changed when he was ten. They say he came home from school one day and found his Labrador dog. Someone had cut off his mother's head, hollowed it out and stuck it on the dog like a space helmet. Daniel ran upstairs where he found his daddy, hanging from a light fitting. Floyd never spoke again after that. In these parts, minors can be emancipated and the judge did just that. He got to live in the house by himself.

Some say he kept the rope and the dog head in a freezer unit.

On the first Sunday of the month, the Gatlins would go to the Gibson City Church of Jesus Christ the Lord, where they worshipped Jesus Christ the Lord, and then come home. They never asked me to join them. I guess that they wanted to limit their exposure too even though we had an agreed script. The trouble with agreed scripts is that lies scrape at the story, wearing it threadbare, showing the truth beneath.

I walked past the Nissan hut that served as the church and I spotted a graveyard beside it. Then it clicked with me that perhaps this was the place Marion Skilbeck was buried. I thought about her sometimes. Now I was in town, I felt a need to pay my respects.

I opened the gates and kept an eye out for modern looking headstones. Many had been weathered with age, names of the dead worn flat on dark stone.

Pastor Dennis Talbot stood in the far corner, dressed in his Sunday best for these parts. A cheap black suit and white shirt and blue tie knotted fat beneath his double chin. I knew him from afar but we never met. I thought I'd introduce myself.

"Welcome to our community, Phillip, Elmore tells me what a great help you are to him in the farm."

"Well, I'm glad he thinks that" I said

"I can think of happier places to spend a Friday afternoon, Philip, instead of this morbid little field of bones. So what brings you here?"

"Someone told me about a local girl, Marion Skilbeck who took her life some years back. I didn't know her but the story struck a chord"

"I remember Marion Skilbeck" Talbot said. His voice cut through my sentence like the blade of a blunt axe. "Why on earth are you interested in Marion Skilbeck?"

"I dunno" I said, scraping my feet on the ground. "I knew she lived and it just stuck with me, you know, a young girl like that, cut down in her prime. I just meant to come over here and pay my respects."

The Pastor looked at me and shook his head.

"It was a tragic story alright. A tragic story. Marion Skilbeck shot her baby twin sisters dead before turning the gun on her mother. Her father came home just in time and shot Marion before she had a chance shoot her mother and goodness knows the whole damned town down after that. We could have had another Columbine on our hands. Was that the story you heard Philip?"

"I heard it was suicide in a diner"

"Hmm. Her daddy put her in the trunk and dumped her body where he worked, stuck a gun in her hand to make it look so"

This was a land where the law is loose and things are easily veiled. This was the old way, but here it was always the way.

"This is Marion's grave right over there. The rest of her family are in the consecrated cemetery three miles from here."

"So this is unconsecrated ground?"

"Suicides, murderers and Catholics"

"There's quite a few" I said.

"Yes, for a town this size we should be ashamed of ourselves. Ashamed of ourselves"

The Pastor looking at the grave with an expression of with disdain laced with pity.

"Are you OK, Phillip?" he asked.

I cleared my throat and told him I was alright.

"Well, I'll be on my way. I hope you'll grace our church with your presence soon, perhaps next month?"

I muttered something that sounded like a halfway house between 'yes' and 'I'll think about it' but I think we both knew what my answer really was. The Pastor lifted his hand to bid me farewell and he walked slowly with a slight limp out of the graveyard.. I looked at Marion's grave. It was simple, tidy and maintained. A little glass vestibule with a fresh red rose inside it lay on top of the grave. I reread the inscription.

"Marion Skilbeck: December 3rd 1982 - June 7th 1995. Rest in Peace."

CHAPTER 45

Not a day went past without thinking of my old life and wanting it back. Chicago lay only seventy miles away but it might as well have been on a different planet. I dared never to return. In years to come, when I was in the deepest winter of my life, my name would just be a footnote on some criminology textbook, long forgotten by the cops who would have by then have moved on to the four-thousandth new murder victim. That's the thing in towns like Chicago; every dead body is just another dead tree in the forest. As soon as one falls, another dozen or so get planted around it, shading it to obscurity.

The killers all know this.

The killers use this.

At night, when all was still and the only sounds were the crickets outside in the cornfields and the tick of the pendulum clock in the landing, my mind came alive with re-enactments from my past. I convinced myself that someday my reliving past events would be so vivid, so strong that I would break open that tungsten membrane of time and go back and get another chance to do things differently.

There I will not drive Jimmy Hoffa to his death. There I will not cheat on Lorna. There I will do things by the book and keep my head down and live a life of blameless quietude and live happily without drama or rancour. This is what I dreamt of so hard, so hard every night but every night I was still there, in that bedroom in that house in that farm in that God-forgotten town. The here and now can be the biggest open prison there is. Time, the highest god damn fence of them all.

I would never have gone to that motel. I would have done background checks on Mrs Garantovich to make sure she was who she said she was. Every night I died a death and every morning I woke up to a new one.

CHAPTER 46

I remember one hot summer's day in May of that year. I was out in the field mending a fence that was flattened by a horny bull. It was all I could do to fight off the flies and mosquitoes that developed a palate for my exotic city sweat. The heat beat down on me, each sunbeam an oppression. I downed a can of water straight down my gullet. As I wiped the water off my face and licked the moisture off my hands, tasting the oil and iron of my handiwork too, a black Mitsubishi Shogun pulled up beside me and screeched to a halt, conjuring a coven of squalid little dust devils in its wake. Some of the acrid dust caught the back of my throat that cut it dry as grated bone. The window rolled down.

It was Jemima Drew.

"Wanna go for a drive?"

I didn't even think about it. I just jumped into her jeep and we sped off into the open country.

"I should have had a shower or something, I'm sure I'm stinking the wagon up on you" I said.

"Nonsense, I love the smell of a working man."

We drove further, mile after desolate mile. Not another town or soul to be seen. The cornfields waved back and forth in the wind as far as the thin line of the horizon beneath the big bare blue sky, naked off clouds.

"Where are we going, Jemma?"

"Jemma?" she said.

"I just felt Jemma seemed more natural to say. It's too hot to say Jemima"

Jemima smiled

"I haven't been called 'Jemma' since Jared's time. It just feels a little funny, that's all"

She turned the radio on and flicked to AM. An old-time country station played bluegrass and banjo music. I felt a sense of dislocation. We seemed to have driven for hours. Sometimes you forget just how empty and desolate America actually is. Our cities are massive but they are planets with miles of empty space between, apart from the wandering sporadic souls of the lost that glide between them like asteroids with bad dress sense.

"We're going to have a picnic."

"It's one hell of a long way to go for a picnic."

"But it's in my favourite spot."

After another hour, we stopped outside the little town of Pulaski.

"Even been here before?" Jemima asked.

"I think I would have forgotten"

"Hey! It's not that dull you know" She thumped me playfully in the arm "Follow me, I've something to show you."

We got out walked down the road and up a lane that led to an abandoned farmhouse. The house was wooden and half its roof had blown off. The windows were boarded up and the garden was a shamble of weeds.

"What is this place?" I asked.

"This is where Jared is."

"What do you mean 'this is where Jared is'?"

"Well, I had him cremated and scattered him inside that house. It's his mom and pop's house. I thought it was the right thing to do"

"Morbid spot for a picnic"

Jemima turned to me but had a pained look in her face.

"Callum, the Sheriff asked me to get rid of you."

I kinda knew he never liked me.

"So will you do as your told?"

"No, don't worry, I'm not going to do anything."

"Has he asked you to disappear people before?"

"Just once. But he had it coming. He raped me."

"I see."

 Small town bible justice.

"The Sheriff's scared, real scared of what you might bring to the town, if anyone finds out you're in Gibson City I mean. He ain't so hot on Elmore no more either."

"But I've kept my mouth shut. No one knows about me unless someone has a loose tongue"

"Callum, the truth is like a dead body. No matter how deep you got it buried, it finds a way to stink the whole joint up. The Sheriff doesn't want you dead though, he just wants you to leave town."

"Leave town huh? That simple. Where would I go?"

Jemima shrugged her shoulders. "I don't know. He just wants you gone"

I turned away from Jemima. I couldn't look at her. Part of me knew I was on borrowed time and perhaps I shouldn't have let myself get so comfortable, so settled. Time just passed over me like warm bath water. I didn't want to get out into the freezing cold bathroom air.

"Listen Callum, we're here now. Let's just eat, what do you say?"

I wasn't that hungry no more but Jemima did make an effort and was at least honest but part of me felt she planned to shoot me in a barn where no one would ever look. Did she have a change of heart?

She opened the picnic rug and we hunkered down. We dined on cold meats, crusty white bread and a homemade dip of crushed garlic and olive oil washed down with iced lemon-tea from a flask.

"So tell me. why is the Sheriff spooking out now, why not at the start?"

Jemima wiped her mouth.

"I told him that I told you about the twin baby. That freaked him out. You weren't supposed to know."

"Why did you tell him?"

"I'm sorry, it just came out. You weren't supposed to know. I realised the mistake as soon as I told you. I told the Sheriff about it just in case some damage limitation had to be done but I didn't think it would be like this"

"Sheriff Truesdale, he seems to be more than just a Sheriff. He seems to be in everyone's business"

"You got to understand, a sheriff in a small community like ours, well he's like a priest. He tends to the souls of people who don't think they have souls. He takes an interest. Not much happens in these parts and when that happens, people busy themselves that oughtn't be their business in the first place" She picked up her beaker and drank some ice tea. "We're country folk, it shouldn't surprise you"

"He's just a fucking sheriff, if you need people to talk to you, just pick up a phone and phone a friend."

"He's the most useful friend a woman can have round here. I live on my own, remember?"

"You have Elmore though."

"He doesn't have an army behind him the same way Sheriff Truesdale has. Sheriff can summons his people with a click of a finger. He can be your best friend too but he can be your worst enemy if you don't do right by him"

"I think I'll have to clear the air with him" I said. "There's no other way. Damage limitation and all that"

"What do you have in mind?"

"Well, I'll go to his house and pay him a visit and we'll talk it out. I knew from the get-go he didn't like me. I've been spending my time doing what I am told and keeping my profile low but he still gives me that fucking look."

"I wouldn't go anywhere near his house. If you have any visiting to be done, go to his office downtown."

"No, in his office, he's in character, dressed in his costume, acting out his part. No, it's better to go to his house when he isn't a Sheriff but just plain old Alvin Truesdale."

Jemima grabbed my elbow and shifted herself so that she sat right in front of me.

"Listen to what I'm sayin' here. There is no such thing as Alvin Truesdale. He stopped being Alvin Truesdale when he got his badge. Then he became deputy. Then he became Sheriff.

There's no Alvin Truesdale under that uniform anymore. That uniform isn't even a uniform, it's the animal hide and the animal itself. That's all there is to him now"

Jemima then grabbed my hand and pulled me close to her.

"He'll only shoot you if you go anywhere near his house. He's done it before and he gets away with it. No charges, no trial. I'm only warning you for your own good. You must understand and accept how things are done here. You gotta lose your city mentality. It will be your undoing if you don't"

"You've taken me a long way from home just to tell me all that."

Jemima lifted a packet of menthols from her purse and lit a cigarette.

"I've never known him to change his mind on anyone or anything. You'll never make him like you but you can make him leave you alone. If you try to be his friend, he'll hate you more for it. He's like that"

I picked up the last slice of bread and ate it. The picnic blanket was covered in crumbs and cigarette ash that the breeze blew back at us.

"I think we're done here Jemma. I need to get back"

"Promise me you won't go near him, for your own sake."

"OK, I promise"

I watched her lips, her mouth seemed to grow bigger, more wet. I let instinct take over and I grabbed the back of her neck and pulled her towards me and I kissed her like I hadn't kissed a woman for a million years. We fell back onto the rug and onto the grasses where we indulged in the joys and juices that our bodies had to offer.

We lay a while as the sun cooled. I felt the cold as the dew drops of sweat evaporated from my skin. I looked over at Jemma. She lay dozing beside me, her perfect breasts glistened in the dying sunlight. I didn't want to wake her and I lay back down and watched the sky turn darker and darker until it was a black velvet quilt over the sleeping heaven's above.

CHAPTER 47

Night unlike death does not last forever. The sun beckoned another day, its bony fingers of light pulled back the dark chiffon skirts of the night. I awoke and turned around to Jemma but she was gone. Her jeep was gone too. Under a rock by my shoes, there was a note. I yanked it out and read it.

> *Sorry, Callum, but I remembered I have a farm to run and had to*
> *drive off. I didn't wake you. You looked peaceful. You looked like you*
> *belonged to the night so that's where I left you. Just hitch a ride back,*
> *there's always a truck or car going north.*
>
> *Jemma*
>
> *X*

I'd no cell phone and panicked about Elmore, Wilson and Ruth. They'd be worried sick about me being gone overnight without telling them. I quickly clambered into my dirty clothes and walked up the dusty road. Trucks sped past me but I chose to walk as much as I could before deciding to hitch a ride. I walked for about another four miles until my feet hurt and I stopped. It wasn't long after that a truck pulled up beside me.

"Where you headed to, mister?" asked the driver, a man in black with long gray hair and a salt and pepper handlebar moustache.

"In the direction of Gibson City, you know it?"

"Hop in"

I got it in. We drove on. He was a man of few words and that's how I liked it. He dropped me off outside Gibson City. I thanked him, threw a five spot on the dash for his trouble and jumped out.

I returned to the Gatlin house. As I approached, I saw a gloomy figure of a man sitting on the porch.

I knew who it was. He was waiting.

CHAPTER 48

Elmore sat in his rocking chair, holding a mug of coffee. He stared at me as I walked up the lane.

"Forgotten you have a job of work to do round here?" he said, chewing his Amber-Leaf tobacco.

"I'm sorry, Elmore, I had to go out of town. Had to stay over."

"No phones in Out of Town?"

"Nope."

He spat out a wet brown pellet of tobacco that went thwack against the decking. The blob looked like a dead mouse baby.

"You want to go back, to Chicago?"

"I wasn't there, Elmore, it was outside Pulaski if you want to know."

"I see" he said. He rolled another ball of tobacco from his pouch and stuck it in his mouth. "I believe you but the Sheriff got a little jumpy. He wants a word with you"

"Why don't you call him Alvin? He's your brother in law"

"To you, son he's the Sheriff. He's Sheriff even to me. You better not go forgettin' that"

I started to think the fucker was baptised 'The Sheriff'. I've met my share of twisted-sisters like Sheriff Truesdale. People like him were never babies with proper names but conjured into existence by teenagers working their way through Alastair Crowley magic book and getting the recipe a little wrong.

"What did he want?"

"He wondered where you got to. I don't have to remind you what risk you take if you return to the city, do I?"

"I'm telling you, I wasn't in Chicago last night."

I couldn't tell him I was with Jemima. He had to take my word.

Elmore grinned and coughed.

"You go and see the Sheriff once you get washed and changed in something clean. Your clothes are all laid out on your bed"

Elmore may have been as crazy as a squirrel in a tree of wasabi pellets but he was a good soul. I patted him on the shoulder and before going inside.

In the kitchen I fixed myself a cheese and pickled cucumber sandwich and downed a jug of water. I got washed, shaved and dressed in the light brown linen summer suit that lay on top of my bed. I grabbed my car keys on the way out, walked past Elmore without saying a word and drove off.

*

It was around five in the evening and there was just another hour or two of sunlight left. I knew the Sheriff would be in his office or cruising around, calling in favours and making his puppets jump at end of rotten strings.

I drove out of town and parked in a grove, far from view and turned the engine off and waited for darkness. I reclined my seat, locked the doors and snatched a couple of hours sleep. When I awoke, the world had turned pitch black. I started my engine and turned on my lights and drove back the way I came.

It was time to visit the Sheriff.

CHAPTER 49

I phoned the Sheriff's office. Truesdale picked up. I put the phone down. Now I knew he wasn't at home, in his forbidden lair. It was time to pay him a home-visit even though I knew he was out for it wasn't him I wanted to see but to find what he was hiding. People who don't entertain visitors have something to hide. They always do.

I drove the few miles towards Truesdale's and parked my car about half a mile from his house in a field, out of sight from the main road. The moon had broken through the thicket of clouds that had started to cataract the night sky. I got out and made my way towards his driveway. Tall sycamores lined the route, bending towards one another in whispering conspiracy. I trod as quietly as I could but my feet crunched the gravel louder than I wanted.

It made one helluva noise. Funny how little things like footsteps can sound like the creak of the Devil's door when you're trying to be as quiet as the dead. I stopped every so often and stood still for a few seconds. I guessed someone like Truesdale would be the kind of man to keep a hungry dog or four on grounds like this. I took my pistol from my belt and cocked the safety catch. Any mutt that made a play for me would end up as breakfast for the buzzards. The driveway was an S shape and after I got past the second bend, the house came into view. The downstairs lights were on. I didn't think much of that. Many folks leave lights on when they're out. I concentrated on the windows, trying to detect signs of movement but nothing.

Nothing stirred.

I sidestepped through the sycamore trees and onto the lawn to be out of direct sight of the house. I snaked my way up and through the lawn to get closer. The house went in and out of view until I was spitting distance of its left gable wall. I stood still again and concentrated real hard. No sounds, nothing unusual but the chirps of crickets and distant clangs from grain mills. I slowly stepped back onto the driveway, taking long, slow strides to avoid making the gravel scrape. Seconds later, I was at the downstairs window, next to the gable. The inside lamp gave a strong light.

No curtains.

I crouched and peered in. My eyes darted left and right and up and down trying to see something strange but it was just a living room.

Then I heard a noise.

It came from around the back. A cracking sound, followed by a thud, then a grunt. It was a human, more like a child or a woman than a grown man. Then it happened again, Crack, Thud, Grunt, then a few seconds of silence. It sounded like somebody chopping wood but at this time of night?. I waited for the noise of axe hitting dead-trunk so that I could to move quickly around the side of the house, masking the noise of the gravel under my boots. I stopped when the noise stopped and started when it started. It didn't take me long to reach the back but it was surrounded by a high wall, too tall to see over.

I looked around to see if I could find anything to step on or look over, an old ladder or something but there was nothing like that lying around. The wall seemed to be around eight feet tall, just two feet or so taller than me. I thought that a good running jump at it could do the trick but it took careful timing. It would be noisy though. I walked about twenty feet away from the wall, a small journey that took me back into the lawn. The noise of chopping continued. Crack, thud, grunt, four or five seconds of silence. I took aim at the wall, I locked my sight on one particular stone, that was to be the first stone I'd step on before hoisting myself up to look over the top. I waited for the final second of silence from inside the yard. I'd use the next few seconds to make my run for it.

I counted to three and ran at the wall, put my foot to the stone and lifted my body up. I nearly didn't make it. My fingers reached the top of the wall but I didn't have enough steam to lift myself up onto the top with my arms. I held on as good as I could and my feet fished around the wall to find a decent grip. I found one and tested it so that it wouldn't crumble off. It seemed solid enough so I counted to three again and heaved myself up. This time I got lucky and lifted myself up and sat on the ledge.

I saw piled up logs stripped of bark along the sides and in the middle were neat little stacks of firewood. An axe was firmly anchored into the ground itself, the handle sticking up towards the back of the house. I saw through the windows.

Inside, in the kitchen, was a girl.

A teenager.

She was very pretty with shoulder-length auburn hair. She was washing her hands under the faucet. I wondered who she was. No one ever mentioned her. The Sheriff never even mentioned having a maid or any kind of domestic help or visitor even. He never spoke about his home life at all. I suspected he didn't have one. He was just a Sheriff, nothing more, nothing less. I watched her as she washed her hands then dried them on a hand towel. She wore workman's clothes, tee shirt and blue dungarees. She went out of view for few seconds before reappearing, this time at the backdoor before going outside again.

"Hey, hey there, lady," I called out.

She either ignored me or didn't hear me. Either way it boiled down to a big old helping of a whole heap of nothing. She walked slowly to the middle of the yard, plucked the axe from where it stood, kicked a log from one of the piles and with the axe, in one swoop, split the log in two along its length.

I called out again. "Hey, hey, do you hear me?"

She didn't even look up.

There was no other noise and I was only a matter of feet away. I removed a couple of coins from my pocket. Pennies, a nickel and a couple of times. I flung them at her feet to catch her attention. One of the coins hit her left foot.

She looked up.

She saw me.

I waved at her. I told her there was nothing to be afraid off. I told her I was Alvin's cousin but it made no difference. She just stared at me. She didn't say a word. Her face looked as vacant as department store in Pyongyang.

"Can we talk?" I called out. She looked away from me, lifted her axe and wielded it a second time on another log. When she was done, she threw the axe blade-first back into the ground and went back into the house. She closed the door behind her and switched off the lights. I turned around on the wall and jumped off, landing on all fours, slightly spraining my ankles. I shook my legs until the pain disappeared.

I dusted myself down and walked back down the driveway, past the sycamores. Their branches swayed like the arms of burnt people, the leaves like fingers, flailing in the wind that croaked and whined like cries for help. I turned up my collar, lit a cigarette and ran the rest of the way, out of the grounds and back to my car.

CHAPTER 50

I got back to the Gatlins' well after midnight. Everything was still. The aroma of the evening dinner hung in the air like a ghost that had outstayed its welcome. I opened the Frigidaire and saw a six pack of Sam Adams. I unhitched a bottle from its brown cardboard boxcar and went outside. There I saw Ruth sitting on Elmore's rocking chair, dressed in her night robe, rocking back and forth, staring into the night like a lone star in an empty universe.

I sat next to her and took a sip of my beer and lit a cigarette.

"I didn't have you down as a night owl, Ruth," I said. Ruth smiled.

"There's a lot of iceberg beneath what you see. You should take a dive sometime," she said.

"It's not the depth, it's the shipwrecks on the seabed, that's what makes diving interesting."

"Or dangerous" she said. "There's a difference between treasure trove and shipwreck. I'd say both our sea beds would make rich pickings for bounty hunters."

"That makes us almost sound like we have something to plunder"

Ruth took a drag on her cigarette. "Well, one of us has".

I smiled and let the silence throw water on the unexpected quick flame of the conversation.

"Do you like it out here?" I asked.

"Sure I like it, it's my home. Why do you ask?"

"You don't seem all that much of a corn-dolly to me, that's all. You know, I can see you perched on a stool sipping spritzers in a cocktail bar, counting how many men you've wrapped around your little finger that day."

She shook her head and smiled as she put her drink down on the ground beside her. "My, Callum, how little you really know me, how little you really know me but, say, that's something of a compliment though."

"Think nothing of it"

Ruth lifted her drink and brushed ash from her right leg. She reached into her bra and removed an outsized homemade cigarette and lit it. I recognised the aroma from my vacation to Vancouver. BC Bud they call there. Here, weed.

"I never had you down as a pot-head. Does your Daddy know?"

She exhaled with her head back with the grace and panache of Gene Tierney.

"Sure, he's my dealer"

I didn't know whether to believe her or not.

"And I bet you never guessed that I'm a dyke. A dyke in the countryside. Can you imagine?" she said, forcing a laugh. "Last place anyone expects to find one. That's why I laughed so much when you said you could see me counting the men I've wrapped around my pinky."

I shook my head.

"You're shitting me, you don't look like a dyke. Are you sure you're a dyke?"

"What do you mean 'am I sure'? I sure know who I'm sleeping with, mister."

I sat up on my seat. I had never spoken with a dyke before. At least, not knowingly.

"What, in these parts?"

"Yeah, in these parts. What we lack in gay bars we make up for in walks in the cornfields. You wouldn't believe what goes on in these parts. We just don't make a big deal of it. We bake cakes, make iced tea, fuck someone we shouldn't, straighten our clothes out, go to church and make dinner in the evening and say grace. You city people wear your hearts like a badge. You people need to be known in an instant. Out here, we're more of a slow burner kinda tribe. You will get to know us over time because we're the only people you'll ever meet day in day out, week in week out, year in, so there's not so much of a hurry to make an impression"

"Any chance of a toke?" I asked, holding my arm out.

She stretched over and handed me the joint. I took a long, deep pull on it and held it in. I could almost hear the sigh of relief from every cell in my body and mind.

"You know my secrets, Ruth, and it's only fair that you shared some of yours with me but I can't help asking, who on earth are you sleeping with in a town like Gibson City?"

She smiled like an imp.

"Right now you mean? Well if you must know, try this, Margo Talbot. The pastor's wife."

"There's no response to that" I said. "Does your Daddy know?"

I handed the joint back.

"That seems to be your favourite question this evening. Sure Daddy knows, he introduced us. Wanna ask him?" she said, jagging the air with up and down strokes of the reefer in the direction of Elmore's bedroom.

"Ha, I've never told him and he never bothered asking. Old men in these parts don't ask their children if they're gay. This ain't the Cosby Show. Like I said, we ain't as stuck in our ways as you city folk would have us. We keep it all beneath the surface, that's all."

She handed me back the joint. I took a very long draw, holding its cool smoke deep in the wells of my lungs for several seconds.

"Well, I won't tell anyone" I said, my words cloaked in gray plumes as I exhaled. I passed her back the joint. I had smoked my fill.

We sat in silence again, seeping in the night.

"Say, Cal, I ain't being heavy or nothin' but you've missed dinner three nights in a row and no one knows where you've gone or who you're with, but Alvin's going nuts about it."

"Alvin this, Sheriff that. He doesn't own me."

"Really?" she said, a finger of smoke bled from her lips. "He owns everyone"

"I'm sorry, I know he's your uncle there's something not right"

Ruth looked up at me but she couldn't look me in the eye. She tilted her head down and stared at some indefinite spot on the deck.

"He keeps the peace. How he keeps the peace is by starting little wars, making sure each side cancels the other out"

"Well, who's that girl in his house then?"

"What did you just say, Callum?"

"You heard me, who's that girl he keeps in his house? Everyone keeps telling me to not go near his house. Jemima warned me and I got tired of being warned off so I thought I'd pay the Sheriff a home visit. He wasn't there but I saw a girl, in his backyard, chopping firewood. No more than fifteen or sixteen. She saw me but she never said a word. None of it seems right. Who is she and what's she doing there?"

"Callum, you shouldn't have done what you did." I could tell Ruth was serious. She delivered each word like a telegram from a war-front.

"I don't give a damn what you think, Ruth, tell me, who is she?"

Ruth's face was a canvas splashed with deep hues of concern and anger. She sucked that joint till her cheeks nearly met in the middle of her mouth. She held it for a few seconds and lay back as she exhaled.

"Callum, I can't tell you and you can put a gun to my head but it still won't tell you. That's how it is. You shouldn't have gone there. Man, you're so lucky you're.."

"Lucky I'm what?"

Ruth looked away, shaking her head. I knew what the unspoken word was. She looked back at me from under her half-lit eyelids.

"Luckily for you, he'll never know you were there."

"I told the girl who I was."

Ruth lifted her glass, shaking the ice a few times before draining it. "Still no matter, Callum, he would never know."

We spent the next while passing the joint back and forth in the dry cool silence of the night.

Ruth rose from her seat and staggered a little before finding her feet. She went indoors without saying 'goodnight'. I lingered on the porch for a while longer, feeling the weight of the night bear ever heavier on my eyelids until I fell asleep.

It wasn't long after that, I was woken by a scream.

CHAPTER 51

I ran into the house and found Ruth kneeling over Elmore. He was flat on the floor.

"Jesus, what happened?"

Elmore groaned and looked up straight at me. I got down on the floor beside him. I held my hand an inch above his mouth. I felt the faintest hint of breath.

"He's still breathing. Call the doctor"

"No doctors" groaned Elmore, his words slurred like sleepy miners from the dark pits of his chest.

"Daddy, we need to get you to hospital as soon as we can."

"No, Doctor Mulry, I want Doctor Mulry."

"Doctor Mulry?" I asked. "Who's he ? Do we have his number?" I asked.

"They fought in Korea together," Ruth said. "His number's in the black book next to the phone."

I found the book and flicked each page until I found the name 'Mulry' circled in red ink. I picked up the phone and punched in the numbers.

*

Ruth and I waited, kneeling by Elmore's side, talking to him and keeping him breathing. We heard a car pull up just minutes later. I got up and opened the front door and let the doctor in. He ran over to Elmore and went to work fast.

"Nothing broken thank goodness," said the doctor. He was in his sixties, balding with a thick moustache and old-fashioned jam-jar spectacles. His voice was a voice you never hear anymore, it was as if Walter Cronkite had just come back from the grave. It was one of those reassuring and authoritative voices you only get to hear from 1950s newsreels and movies telling us that everything will be ok.

"Phillip, you're a big fella, help me carry Elmore upstairs to his bed."

We carried Elmore to his bed.

"Let me have a moment alone with the doctor," Elmore said, his words clearer this time but laboured. Ruth and I made our exit and went downstairs and sat on the steps like a couple kids, trying to eavesdrop on the grown-ups. We held hands. We waited for some time, listening to the muffled whispers from Elmore's room, waiting for the white smoke.

"Philip!"

It was the Doctor. "Your uncle would like to talk to you but before you come up, there's something I need to tell the two of you."

Ruth shivered and I helped her off the staircase and onto a chair in the hallway. The doctor addled his way down the stairs in a bandy-legged gait.

"Philip and Ruth, Elmore was diagnosed with pancreatic cancer eight months ago. We could have treated it but there was no guarantee of success but Elmore being the stubborn soul he is, decided to resist all treatment and just accept what God had in store for him. His words, his wishes. Tonight he lost control of his legs and took a tumble down the staircase. It's a miracle he survived the fall but I have to tell you that he hasn't got long. I could call an ambulance but all the hospital would have to offer Elmore would be morphine and a night in a strange bed in a cold room in a big white building. He wants to be with his family but, Philip, Elmore would like to speak with you, alone. Ruth, can you ring Wilson and ask him to come home?"

I put a hand on Ruth's shoulder and made my way upstairs

CHAPTER 52

Elmore's bedroom door lay wide open. I knocked on his door and went inside. A Tiffany lamp stood on bedside locker, dimly lit. Elmore was sitting upright, resting against propped-up pillows. He gently turned his head to face me.

"You wanted to see me?"

Elmore coughed and wiped his mouth clean with a corner of the bed linen. He lifted his left hand, beckoning me to sit down beside him.

I sat down beside the edge of the bed. I clenched my hands together till they went white.

"Callum, I don't have long left."

I looked at him and I held his hand.

"Elmore, the doc told us what happened. Why didn't you tell us? You had a chance, Elmore, the doc said so, you're not that old, not these days. You could have had years, even decades left."

Elmore smiled. "I know I've danced my last waltz, son, but it's good to know that there's still time for a darn good telling off, ha." His laugh faltered into a cough. I reached over to help him, patting him gently on the back. I found a cloth beside the Tiffany lamp and wiped his face clean.

"I don't deserve anymore road that the Lord laid down for me. Callum, I've a terrible blackness in my soul. I've done something so terrible that I doubt God could forgive me. The people I wronged are not around to forgive me."

I held his hand and it frightened me how such a big working man like Elmore could end up with mitts that felt like brittle bone wrapped in aging parchment. Flesh was in decline.

"Elmore, what are you talking about? Is it Korea, is that what's bothering you?"

"No, it's not just Korea, that was war. It's OK to kill fifty men you never met before when the President tells you to do it. Fifty dead slopes. I didn't even hate them, I didn't even know what the war was about but that's not what I wanted to talk to you about."

I moved my chair an inch or so closer to his bed. I leaned over and furrowed my face to listen.

"You can tell me anything, Elmore. You know that. I don't judge. We've been through our own wars together."

"Callum, Jared Drew did not kill my wife." I felt his fingers tighten on mine.

"Come on, Elmore, you're not making sense"

"Callum, can you reach over and hand me a glass of water? I feel so thirsty."

I got a glass from the dressing table at the far corner of the room and filled it with water from a pitcher. I brought the water over to Elmore and held the glass to his lips, gently helping him take a few sips. He nodded his head to indicate he had enough.

"One day I came from the corn-fields and I found Heidi sobbing her heart out, face down on our bed. Such bitter tears I never heard before. I sat beside her and comforted her. I asked what the matter was. I thought one of the kids had an accident, or worse. I braced myself for the worst but, my, I soon found that there was something even worse beyond even that. She told me she'd been sleeping with Jared Drew but that it was all over between them. I sat there numb. I didn't feel angry. Is that strange, Callum? I didn't feel one bit angry but I felt that I should be angry. I then felt angry at not being angry. That wasn't the end of it. Heidi told me she was pregnant but the baby wasn't mine but Jared's. You see, Callum, I had a vasectomy, the snip some years earlier. She told me Jared didn't know about the baby. No one but Heidi and Doctor Mulry knew about my operation. As far as the world would be concerned, I had sired a third child. At first, I forgave Heidi. She told me why she did what she did. We were going through a rough patch and I was out of the house a lot too which didn't help. At the time I thought I could handle bringing up another man's child, especially when Jared didn't know Heidi was pregnant. But when she grew bigger and the bump started to show, my well of forgiveness dried up and dried up till there was nothing at the bottom of the well but stones and bones and bitterness. Sweet Jesus, I tried to fight it but I couldn't. That night I came home, I had driven past Jared's house. I knew Jared was out, his car wasn't at home but his wife was. Jemima. I saw her at the window. I drove to a phone booth in town and I phoned her, I phoned Jemima."

The story hit me like a tsunami on a coastal ridge of shanty towns. I just sat quietly, listening, squeezing Elmore's hand but for some reason, I couldn't look at him. I wasn't disgusted or anything, I just couldn't handle the intensity of looking at his face. I waited several seconds for the shock waters to recede.

"Why did you phone Jared's wife of all people?" I asked.

"She knew about Jared and Heidi."

"So Jemima knew about Jared and she still stood by her man, huh?"

"People don't get divorced in these parts, Callum, we just don't do that kinda thing. She knew about it. I knew about it. That's not the whole the deal though. Look at me."

I looked at him. Beads of sweat formed a line on his forehead. For the very first time, I saw fear in Elmore's face.

"Jemima and I were sweet on each other too."

"Jesus, Elmore, are you for real?"

Elmore nodded and coughed.

"Callum, what I'm about to tell you, well, it's the crux of the whole thing. Jemima never wanted children, but Jared did. When I told her about Heidi having his child, she went ape.

To cut the story short, we agreed that Heidi had to be got rid of but that Jared must be made out to be the one who did it.

Jemima lent me Jared's gun. I made sure to wear a pair of cotton gloves to avoid my prints getting on it and hid the gun in the attic for four days. Four days, Lord, for four long sleepless nights and four peaceless days, the Devil and Jesus battled over my soul but Jesus's grip wasn't what it was. Jemima kept bugging and bugging me until I could take no more.

I went home that night. It was late. I had whipped myself into ball of anger. I forced myself to think of what Jared and Heidi did together and what kind of things they said about me. I went upstairs and woke Heidi up. She thought I was foolin' around at first but when she saw the hatred in my face, I frogmarched her downstairs to the kitchen where I made her write the letter. Then I shot her in the belly with my own gun and then in the head.

I thought the child was dead but it wasn't. I didn't know till later. I gave the guns, both mine and Jared's to Jemima. She put Jared's back in the closet and mine under the sycamore tree behind her house. I made sure I dipped the end of Jared's barrel in Heidi's blood before I gave it back. And that's how I sent Jared Drew to hell. I bet he's waiting at the gates, itchin' to meet me. Him and Heidi both. What a reunion that'll be. Beat that Jerry Springer"

Elmore coughed violently and took a deep breath inwards. I released my hand from Elmore's grip. His fingers retained the shape of holding a hand that wasn't there. I felt Elmore had stuck his hand down my throat and ripped my insides straight out of my mouth. I felt empty. I should have been used to it by now. I opened and closed my mouth like a dying fish, trying to say something.

"Elmore," I whispered to him. "Do you know what you've done? Do you?"

Elmore looked at me and closed his eyes.

"I'm so sorry, Callum."

I didn't know what to feel but I felt no hatred. How could I? He never did me any bad turns. Hell, it was Elmore and Wilson who masterminded my jailbreak. I owed him everything for that but he used me. He used me to frame an innocent man who went to the chair. I tried to feel indignant but for the life of me, I couldn't. I felt nothing towards Jared. Sure, it's a sad, sad situation as the song said but, to me, it might as well have been the lead story in the National Enquirer. I felt nothing. I felt detached from it all, looking down at from some place outside it all. I let go off Elmore's hand but his fingers still stretched out. I didn't know who's hand he thought he was holding. Perhaps someone's only Elmore could see.

"It's too late for bad feeling now, Elmore," I said."You're sorry for what happened and that's all that matters."

"Callum, the child Heidi was carrying. It didn't die. It lived. The bullet missed it by a whisker"

"But you shot Heidi in the stomach, how could it have lived?"

"It lived, Callum. The medics delivered it. The girl, we couldn't raise it here. We couldn't really give it to a childless couple of the town neither. Too many questions. They would think it was Ruth's. No, the child was conceived in deceit, murder was its wet nurse. We had to give it to the only person fit."

"Who ?"

Elmore coughed. "Alvin. Alvin raised her. Alvin Truesdale. The Sheriff. The girl, she's a mute by all accounts. The trauma affects her still. She's the girl you saw at his house". He coughed some more "Yeah, I know you better than you know yourself. You're like a dog with a bone. I figured you went to his house and saw something you shouldn't have. You must leave all alone, Callum, I know what you're like but believe me, some sleeping dogs are better left alone. Or shot."

I heard the front door downstairs open and Wilson's panicked voice.

"I'll let your God judge you, Elmore, that's not for me. I think Wilson and Ruth should be here right now but I need to know one thing, where's the gun?"

Elmore took a breath or two before answering.

"It's buried in a box beneath the sycamore tree in Jemima's back lawn. That's where it is. You must go and get it, Callum" he said. "For now, though, tell Ruth and Wilson I want to see them."

"See you around sometime, Elmore." He gently nodded his head and closed his eyes. I got up and left the room. Wilson and Ruth were outside.

I made my way downstairs and sat on the steps somewhere in the middle. Minutes later I heard loud sobs. I remained downstairs, staring at the shape of my shadow as it darkened a patch of carpet in the hall.

CHAPTER 53

"Callum, can I ask you something?" asked Ruth.

I nodded. We stood outside the graveyard. Everyone had gone home but Ruth and I lingered on.

"Daddy's last words to me and Wilson. They weren't 'I love you' or anything like that."

"Go ahead"

"'Something like 'Jared, Jared, no, no, please no, I'm sorry', then he slipped away. Do you think he saw Jared coming for him? Daddy looked in mortal terror. I think he saw something, Callum. Why wouldn't God protect him from Jared?"

"I really don't know, Ruth. Elmore's in heaven now, with Heidi. People hallucinate in their final moments."

I put my hands on Ruth's shoulders and looked into her eyes and tried so hard to fake enough sincerity to reassure her. Inside, I was cold for I knew Jared was waiting for him. If I were Jared, I would have come for Elmore too. God only knows what Elmore is going through right now but he was beyond any of our help.

Forever.

We linked arms and went back to the house. Elmore lay cold in his grave. After the neighbours had paid their respects and eaten the last of the sandwiches and drank the last the liquor, we had our house all to ourselves. Ruth and Wilson and I sat around the table.

"Strange Alvin isn't here, trying to take us over or something," Ruth said.

"I think we're a little old for adoption, sissy sis," Wilson replied.

"He will, you know. Watch, you'll see."

"Over my dead body," Wilson said. He got up and went upstairs to his room. Ruth and I looked at one another over plates of crumbs and chicken bones.

"I think I better find someplace else to live, everything has changed," I said.

We smoked our cigarettes and poured bourbon into paper cups. After the strike of ten, Ruth put her head on the table and went to sleep. I got up and went outside. I walked to the outhouse and found some shovels that hung on long bent nails on the wall opposite the door.

I took one of them down.

I had some digging to do.

CHAPTER 54

I snuck in around the back of Jemima's house. The house seemed empty, the windows dark, curtains drawn shut. I knew Jemima was out as her jeep wasn't parked in the drive. I found the sycamore tree, the one Elmore told me before he died. It wasn't hard to find. It was the only tree in her garden.

I started to dig.

The earth was a tough clay which made for tough digging but I had to keep going. Elmore was gone. I didn't care that much about Jemima but her secret was safe with me. I'd no one to blab to and blabbing was never a pastime I like. Alvin may have known the truth but it was just his word against Jemima's if push came to shove. What I knew about Alvin, any witnesses he would call would swear on their grandmother's graves that Alvin shits gold bars and sells them for cancer research.

The night wore on. I kept digging. I dug a trench around the tree and worked my way inwards, digging towards and under the roots. It was there that Elmore said I'd find the gun. I worked my way towards the middle. Hours of sweaty toil but my skin was kept cool by the breath of the night.

Then the blade of my spade hit something solid. I thrust the spade again at the same spot.

Thud.

I fell to my knees and starting digging out the soil with my hands like a dog looking for bones. My hands were sticky with clay, a thick paste of sweat and soil formed a gloupy paste that fused my fingers together like web. I felt tired, drained. It was harder than I thought. I wanted to melt like wax and ooze into the ground, into the earth itself and find peace beneath the craziness of it all. Then my fingers felt something, it was plastic and smooth with a hard object inside. I tried to pull it out but it was too packed into the earth to budge so I dug more and more with my bare hands, pulling at the canvas every so often until finally it gave way in such a stubborn suddenness that I fell back into the trench that I had dug hours earlier. I got up and opened the bag.

"Miaow," said something, but it sounded like the strangest cat that I'd ever heard. The same sound again but it sounded human. I didn't want to cry out 'who's there' or anything like that. I kept still.

"Well, Callum, I mistook you for a cat. You're curious alright. A curious cat if I ever met one. You know what happens to curious cats, if you read your nursery rhymes. Your mama did read nursery rhymes to you when you were a little boy or did she just fuck servicemen and mainline your diaper money"

Alvin.

"What the fuck do you want Alvin?" I couldn't see him. There was little light. The meek moon hid behind heavy clouds. I focussed and saw a faint man-shaped stain of black against the deep navy of the night, close to the back door of the house.

"Jemima asked me to keep an eye on her house while she was out of town and it was just as well I did. She didn't mention that you'd be doing a spot of gardening. What are you planting, Callum? Nothing grows in that soil"

"I dropped my watch and I was trying to find it," I said with a smirk.

"We both know why you're here" he said

"Do we?"

"The Indians have a saying, if you sit long enough by the river, you will see the body of your enemy float by. Family secrets are like that as well. Time gives them up in the end but Elmore kept nothing from me. Absolutely nothing. I make sure I control what goes on upstream and I just sit downstream with my big wide net open. Nothings gets past Sheriff Truesdale"

"If you know what's here, then why didn't you dig it up yourself?" I asked.

"Dig what up, Callum? Your watch? I have a nice Rolex of my own or hadn't you noticed? Too busy eyeing up Ruth from what I see at the dinner table"

"Let me ask you something. Why are you here? Don't give me with that keeping an eye on the house bullshit"

"It's the truth, Callum. Folks around here, you know, they mightn't look smart but we're smarter than you think. Jemima did a college course about computers. She lapped it all up. Her webcam is right upstairs, pointing out her bedroom window. She showed me how I could look at her garden from my iPad. It's easier than you think. I was drinking my coffee and powered up my tablet and took a look to see what was going on and guess what I saw? You sneaking around her house with a shovel in your hand. Being the Sheriff, I had to see what was going on"

"Talking off seeing strange people in the backyard, just who is that girl in your house? I saw her with my eyes, Truesdale" I said

"Girl? In my house? I wish it were true Callum. I wish it were true" he said.

"Come on, Truesdale, I know you live in a big house but surely you'd notice a pretty teenage brunette hanging around, just once in a while, now and then, yeah? I sure know I would"

"You're starting to see ghosts Callum. It must be difficult for you, being stuck out here, far from the bars and the good life. It's like being in a prison all over again. Just put the shovel down and I'll take you downtown"

"I don't think so. I ain't done here"

Then a gunshot smashed the stillness of the night. Alvin tried to shoot me but he missed. I ducked and ran a few feet down to the back of the garden.

I crouched.

"Don't be stupid Callum, come out from where you are. You know even you can't hide forever. You know I'll get you in the end"

I crawled on all fours, feeling for a rock or a stick I could use to surprise. I could tell Alvin was too close to where I dropped my shovel for me to try to get it back. Then I found a long rod of wood. I rolled my hands up the shaft until I felt cold metal at the end. It was a shovel. I must have dropped it further from the tree than I thought when I ran at the sound of gunfire. I waited and kept my senses on full alert. I heard his soft footfalls. I switched my eyes to where I thought they came from and I saw his figure moving closer. If I moved too quick, I was dead. If I stayed, I was dead. I figured if I was going to roll around the ground like a drunken bum pretending to be a marine commando or even play statues, death was a certainty.

I'd only a narrow window for any chance of making it

I picked up the shovel and lunged at the figure. He fired another shot and missed.. I plunged the blade at Alvin and it struck him hard. It winded him, I heard him gasp so much that I thought I might I have sliced his windpipe but I heard no gargling of blood. He slumped to the ground and groaned. I felt him grab at my lower legs like a ghoul in a rug. I lifted the shovel and with the flat metal, whacked him right on the head. The groaning had stopped. He hand fell from my trouser leg. I bent down and felt his pulse. He was still alive. I rolled him over into the trench I had dug and ran back home and got some rope and rags and returned to Jemima's. I trussed Truesdale up and stuffed rags in his mouth. I propped him up so he could breathe a little. I didn't want to kill him. I wanted him to suffer. Then it hit me that Hector wanted me to suffer too. How he must have hated me. I rifled through Alvin's pockets and found keys and a gun.

That's all I wanted and that's all I needed.

I ran around the front of the house where his car was parked. I jumped in. He was that cocksure of himself that he left the car keys in the ignition. I figured that the key I had taken from him were his house keys. I turned the key and the engine revved up and stuck the gearstick into reverse and drove out. As I looked in the rear mirror, a figure of a woman came into sight. She was running towards the car. I braked as hard as I could. She ran around to the driver's side and I rolled down the window.

"Just what the hell's going on?" she asked.

CHAPTER 55

"Ruth, it's a long story, jump in."

"Callum, I heard gunshots and I ran over. Look at you, you're covered in mud.. and is that blood?" she reached over to my ear.

"Is it wet?"

"Half you ear's gone. Urgh, you look gross."

"I'll find a plastic surgeon after breakfast. Now we go to Alvin's. He tried to kill me. He's out of action but he'll be ok but we have to go his house. He's hiding more than a mute orphan. I feel it. I just fucking feel it"

"What the fuck you talking about Callum?"

"Ruth, there's no time to waste. Just come with me"

Ruth ran out the other side and jumped in. I revved up the engine and we sped deep into the night.

CHAPTER 56

I drove like a demon. The roads were clear and it took less than ten minutes until we got to Truesdale's house.

"So you're telling me that you've never visited your uncle's house, not even once?"

Ruth shook her head.

"Why?"

"I used to all the time as a kid, but not since Mama died. Daddy told us not to. We asked him why but he wouldn't say. I figured he had his reasons but I never knew what they were."

I listened and lit a cigarette while she spoke.

"As a rule of mine, people are entitled to their secrets," I said, "entitled to their mistakes, and I'd have left it at that, but not after what I found at Alvin's house. I'll cut to the chase, Ruth, the baby your Mama was carrying when she died, well, it didn't die. It lived."

"Pardon me?"

"Autopsies in this state aren't what we see on Quincy. When someone comes in with an axe sticking out of their skulls, that's what they confirm. They don't go looking for lung tumours or shrapnel in the butt. The more obvious, the better."

"What the hell are you trying to say?"

"Elmore told me before he died. He knew."

Ruth looked at me, her eyes were a cocktail of rage. She froze in the stunned silence, choking on the fumes and dangerous vapours of revelation.

"The baby wasn't Elmore's, it was Jared's," I continued. "It was near term and the womb was ripped open and the baby fell out, alive. It missed the fucking bullet"

"Bullshit"

"Ruth, your daddy asked to talk to me alone before he died. He wanted to get a few things off his chest. I'm sorry but you're going to have hear the truth. He told me to tell you"

I knew I was lying but I was sick and tired of the secrets that everyone worshipped like gods that they pretended not to see.

I continued: "Heidi and Jared were having an affair. She fell pregnant. Elmore forgave her and was willing to bring the child up as his own but the nearer the time came the less he could stomach it. It was Elmore who shot your mother stone dead. The baby fell out, alive, and it was only a week from being born. The bullet missed her. Elmore might have been many things but a baby killer wasn't one of them. When he saw it squirming on the ground, he called Truesdale. It was agreed that Truesdale bring the child up in secret. Jemima and Elmore conspired to frame Jared for the murder. Elmore told me he dipped Jared's gun in Heidi's blood, fired a shot at her and left it at the scene. Elmore buried the gun under the tree in Jemima's yard. That's why I was there, digging like a crazy man. I'm sorry I'm telling you all this but that's why we need to go to Truesdale's house and see what the fuck is going on."

Ruth buried her face in her hands.

"You know I saw a teenage girl up there. Do the math. I think that girl was the baby, your half sister"

Ruth let her hands fall to her lap. He mouth was open, her eyes stared like the stone eyes of a ruin. She was shivering. I reached over and held her hand. Her hand was like ice and the shivering worsened. I took off my jacket and wrapped it around her and switched on the in-car heating. It wasn't that cold that night. It was just that Ruth's sky had suddenly lost its sun.

"You stay here, Ruth. You have to trust me."

Ruth was in a daze. She slowly nodded. Her cheeks were silver with tears.

I got out and walked to the front door of Truesdale's house. I stuck the key in the lock. It opened first time. I slowly turned it. The door opened and I went inside. The lights were out and all was quiet. Nothing stirred except for the low hum of the refrigerator from the kitchen.

I walked around the living room. It was very well furnished with a huge bookcase with leather-bound volumes covering two walls from floor to ceiling. In the middle of the floor was a black leather sofa with a coffee table just in front of it. A sturdy wooden bureau stood beside the window and a tall lamp broke one of the corners of the room. I walked over to his desk. It was tidily kept except for a few papers that lay higgledy-piggledy across the top. I picked them up and held them under the moonlight.

Nothing of consequence. I crumpled them up into little balls and flung them across the room. I tried to open the drawers of the bureau but they were locked. I left the room and returned to the hall. The kitchen was to my right. I looked inside but all seemed normal so I decided to go upstairs.

It was a good job Truesdale loved carpet, the deepest kind. No creaking floorboards to worry about nor the sudden shriek of dropped objects. I grabbed the banister and stretched my right leg so I could take three steps at a time. Seconds later, I was on the landing and I stood still to take in the layout. Directly ahead of me was the bathroom and along the corridor were four bedrooms in total, two on either side. Three of bedroom doors were open. One was shut. I walked up the landing and peered in the first room on the left.

A girl lay fast asleep in bed. The only thing that struck me was how unlike a teenage girl's room this was. No Hello Kitty or posters of pop stars on the wall, no TV, no computer. I walked down the landing to check out the other rooms. One was a library, every wall a battalion of books. The other room was a bedroom, empty. The final room was locked, unlike the others. I went up to it and pressed my right ear against it and gently tried the handle but no cigar. I took out two nails from my trouser pocket, left over ones from fixing the fence and stuck them inside the lock, making a pincer. I got the ends to grip on the metal snib inside. I turned the nails slowly as I could, making sure the other ends kept grip. Slowly I turned the nails until I heard a click.

I tried the handle. It turned and the door opened.

Even to this day, my soul still screams in silent agony when I try to forget what I saw.

CHAPTER 57

I turned on the light only to see how dark things could get.

The first thing I saw was a pentagram drawn in white paint in the middle of the black floor. A human skull lay at each point and there were two more in the middle. Then I heard a murmur, almost a whimper. I turned towards where the sound was coming from in the far corner of the room. There I saw a young woman in the corner, naked, hands and legs bound. She was blindfolded and gagged. Her neck was chained to the wall. To her left, a new horror, the likes only cops on the Ed Gein case would have seen. Inside their own wall mounted glass cases, the heads of two women, Their eyes open, bulging and their mouths wide open as if they were about to speak. I got the impression they never got to say the final words they dreamed off.

I scanned the room, turning slowly around. Every part of every wall was covered in glass cases with a human head inside. I counted over twenty heads, all preserved. I thought about untying the girl and removing her gag and blindfold but I thought not yet. She's OK now. She's going to be OK. The ordeal is over for her. She didn't know that but that didn't matter. As long as I did, that was all that mattered. Had I removed her blindfolds and gags, God knows how she would have reacted. Best left to the professionals. I walked over to her and bent down and patted her head, telling her everything was going to be OK. She moved her head slightly and moaned a couple of times. For all she knew, I was just a new voice in the torture chamber. I left the room and went downstairs. I picked up the phone and dialled 911

***

I left the house and returned to the car. Ruth had fallen asleep. I turned the key and drove, leaving the house behind. Forever.

I drove Ruth home and carried her to bed. Her sleep didn't seem natural. It was more like narcolepsy, a voluntary little death in the face of a life one wants nothing to do with. I covered her in sheets and put a pillow under her head. Then I went to my room, filled a navy bag with as many clothes as I could, went downstairs and left. left.

I had made up my mind. This was my last night in that house, in that town, in that strange chapter of my life. It was still night and the sun was still many hours from rising.

I still wait for sunrise.

CHAPTER 58

I drove endless miles in the direction of nowhere until I found a roadside diner and motel beside it. To a tired hungry man on the road, that's like rolling two sixes at craps. Several trucks were parked in the forecourt. I pulled up and went inside the diner. Along the counter, a row of unshaven, hunched up truckers sat on tall stools, guzzling black coffee, staring wordlessly at the rack of ketchups and condiments that hung from the wall above the coffee machine. A radio station played from speakers at low volume but loud enough to keep a lonely man company. Jingles, rock music, weather and traffic reports, familiar and soothing as the sound of a mother's voice to a boy hunted by the world.

A waitress stood behind the counter, drying plates, swaying from side to side in time to Whitesnake track. She was pretty but she had one of those 'I've seen it all' faces - old before her time.

I stood at the counter and she looked up from her dishcloth and she said she'd be with me in a minute. I thanked her and walked up the aisle of Formica tables and red plastic seats and sat down at the far end of the diner beside the window that looked out onto the forecourt. I looked out but all I saw was my perfect reflection on a dark mirror. I just sat and stared at myself, not even caring if the waitress came to take my order.

Second later, the waitress asked me if I wanted to see the menu. I told her all I wanted was a pot of black coffee and a plate of chicken nuggets and a chilli and tomato dip. She said that was quite a breakfast. I said something like 'I guess so' and smiled like a goof. She ignored the smile. She asked me why I was sitting where I was, so far from the others. I told her I was too tired for conversation. She said she was sorry and would leave me alone. I realised my mistake and told that wasn't what I meant. I don't think she understood. I felt like a shit for offending her. It wasn't what I meant. She told me my meal would be ready real soon. I nodded and lit a Lucky Strike.

She brought me my coffee and skipped back towards the kitchen. I laced the coffee with milk and sugar until it was cool and sweet enough to sink. I drained my mug and it was then I heard sirens in the distance. Like thunder, the lightning off flashing blue lamps came seconds later. The men at the counter snapped out of their slumber, sitting upright, swivelling around on their perches. From behind the counter, a phone rang and the waitress came out of the kitchen and picked it up. I couldn't eavesdrop for shit from that distance but her face was a register of shock and stun.

She came over to my table with my food and set it down. I asked her if everything was OK. She said no. She said law-men were crawling over town. She said they rescued a girl from Sheriff Truesdale's house. She told me they found a hundred severed heads in one of his rooms. I said 'oh my'. I asked if they found Truesdale himself. She said they did. He was tied up in a pit behind Jemima's house. I said that he'll fry for that. She said maybe. She told me that two years ago, the eighteen-year-old daughter of one of the cops in Truesdale's office had gone missing. Melody Grantham and she was very smart and pretty.

I asked her if she was busy. She turned around to look at the counter and looked back at me and said 'hmm so so'. I asked her to sit down and talk to me, just for a minute. She said ok and sat down.

She told me that her Melody's daddy, a local cop, had found his daughter's head in one of those glass cases. It was all they could do to stop him from murdering Truesdale. I told her if he shot Truesdale with the marksman skill a cop has, Truesdale would just die in a blink of an eye and that wouldn't be justice. I said Truesdale needed to suffer. Sometimes they make the chair last a little longer than necessary for the sicker fuckers. That's what Truesdale deserved. She nodded. I asked her how Truesdale was found. She didn't know. I told her that surprised me. She didn't seem like the kind of girl who didn't know things. She giggled and told me she could find out.

I asked her if she was for real.

She said she was for real.

I asked her how.

She told me her husband was also cop and was one of the men who had to hold Deputy Lee Grantham down until the doctor had bunged a sedative in his arm to knock him out to deliver the only peace he will never know this side of the grave. I asked about the mother. She told me she was in an asylum. She said she could yak all night but had a diner to run and that coffee doesn't pour itself. I told her I saw machines in a Target store that did just that. She smiled and told me to keep that to myself otherwise it would put all the waitresses in America out of a job. She said, what machine could smile and make a man feel special. I told her I didn't know but it's probably in Target too. She shook her head at me and smiled and walked back towards the counter.

The first glimmer of the sun eased over the horizon. My reflection on the window faded enough to let me see a small truck pull up outside. Boredom made me pay it more attention than necessary but boredom makes you look for details. The truck parked just outside the window. I looked at the man behind the wheel. Pastor Talbot. I recognised that weak, chinless fuck face anywhere. He looked nervous, shaky. He got out and made his way to the payphone a few feet outside the diner door. I got up and went to the counter. I told the waitress I'd be back in a minute. I went outside towards the payphone.

"Good morning, Pastor, hotline to Jesus?"

He jumped like an anxious rat. In fact, he looked like a rat. He was one of those guys. Call me a throwback but I do hold some stock in the Victorian science of phrenology. Never met a rat faced man that I trusted. He tried to put the mouthpiece back onto the cradle without looking at what he was doing but he dropped it. It dangled like a hanging man from the black coin box.

"Only truckers and sinners are up at a time of night like this," I said.

"God doesn't wear a watch," Talbot said.

"He certainly wouldn't wear the cheap shit you'd buy him. Who are you calling?"

"What's it to you?"

"Well, your house is only a mile from here"

"If you must know, I was coming back from the city, I had to make an urgent call if it's any of your god-damn business"

"But I saw you drive that way" I pointed towards the direction of his house "That's from your house. That other way's from the city but that's not where I saw you drive from."

His mouth opened and closed like a fish on a sandpit.

"So what. I went home to use the bathroom first. I like a clean bathroom" he said.

"So you went home, took a leak and then left to come here to make a phone call? What happened? Did AT&T cut your line?"

"What's your problem Gatlin? So what. I came here for breakfast and realised I had to make a phone call. I left my cell phone back at the house"

"Hmm, ok, that makes sense but you're a little jumpy"

"What's with the twenty questions Gatlin? Bored are you?"

I smiled at him and lit a cigarette and went back inside, leaving Talbot at the phone booth. I felt like a cat that let a mouse go only because I wanted to play with it again. Dead mice ain't much fun. I looked back at the phone booth. The mouthpiece still dangled. Talbot was back in the truck. He started it up and with screech of rubber on tarmac, vanished up the road, towards the city. I took note of the license plate. I realised it wasn't his own shiny yellow Hummer he was driving, just a shitty, beaten up, two-seater truck. I never saw him drive it before.

I returned to the counter and I asked the waitress if I could borrow her pen. She sighed and told me she didn't want my phone number as she was a married woman. I told her it wasn't giving her my phone number but that I needed to write something down. A lie wrapped in the truth. She looked a little embarrassed. She said 'oh'. I told her it was ok. She told me men were always hitting on her. I told her I could understand why. She smiled at that. I wrote the licence number of the truck on the paper and gave the note to the waitress. I asked if she could do me a special and urgent favour, one that meant life or death. She asked me what was going on. I told I was an undercover cop. I told her to phone her husband and to run a license check on a strange truck I saw on the computer. I told her the licence number was written on the piece of paper. She looked up at me. She said sure. I thanked her and gave her a twenty spot for her trouble. She coughed and tucked it into her breast pocket.

She said she saw me talk to a man outside. I said she was right. She asked me if he was the man who owned the strange truck. I said I did. I told her I never saw that jeep anywhere near his house before. She said it could've been a rental. I told her that Avis and Hertz don't rent out shit like that. She said 'I suppose not'. I handed the note to her and she took it.

"I'll see what I can do."

I thanked her a final time and left. I got in the car and drove down the road for a mile before doubling back, returning to the diner motel complex. I didn't know what I was thinking or why I did that. My mind was all over the place. I got out and checked into a bare room and flopped out on the bed and slept.

CHAPTER 59

At 10am, I checked out and returned to my car and got in.

"Hey, you not stopping by?"

It was the waitress from the diner. She was off duty. She wore tight lycra jogging bottoms and a pink singlet. I could tell from her sweaty face that she out for a run. She stood there, panting, bending over, clutching her knees. She looked so hot. My eyes oozed like invisible hands, pouring themselves over her every curve. She got her breath back and stood upright, now hands on hips. I opened the window and she lent in. I could smell her sweat. Sweet woman's sweat.

"My husband found out who owned that jeep but it wasn't owned by anyone from around these parts"

"Who owns it?"

"Some dude from California. San Francisco it was. The jeep was bought and paid for three years ago. My husband told me the garaging address is local though but in the name of a dead woman. My husband says it was found abandoned twenty miles from here this morning. My husband says forensics are taking prints and stuff"

I wondered how often she can throw the word 'husband' into a sentence. If she thought she was putting me off the scent, she was wrong, especially dressed in gym-bait.

"Did your husband get a name?"

"Hmm, let me see. I remember now, some man called Grey, no wait a minute, it was longer than that. Greyling. That's it. Greyling."

"Greyling?"

"That's the name that came up on my husband's computer. Do you know him?"

I had to rein myself in and contain my surprise. Time for my poker face.

"It just rings a bell, that's all. It's probably a common enough name. It's a big country."

She nodded. I couldn't really figure a way of getting the address. I had a plan though.

"I never got your name, honey."

"My name? Why do you want my name for?"

"Well, you know mine and if our paths ever cross, I'd like to know who I'm saying hello to."

"Rhea Freeman."

"So long, Rhea Freeman." I gave her a little salute and closed the window. I sped off west. I knew I'd never see her again. She served a purpose. You can't serve the same meal twice they say.

Mile after mile after mile, the landscape changed. The colours of the grasses changed from brown here to green there and all shades in between. Country gave way to suburb, suburb to town and town to country but one thought was hogging the highways of my head: it couldn't be the same fucking Charles Greyling. In the middle of another nowhere, I spied a roadside general store that advertised cell phones, sim-cards and a buy-one-get-one-freer on Cheerios. I stopped and bought a cheap cell-phone. I declined the offer of Cheerios. I got back in my car and I dialled a number.

"Gibson City Police, how may I help you?"

"I would like to speak to Sergeant Freeman." I bluffed on the rank, I didn't ask Rhea his rank, I didn't think it mattered.

"Putting Sergeant Freeman on the line"

"Hello, Sergeant Freeman speaking, how may I help you?"

I got the rank right.

"Hi, I'm Detective Harris from San Francisco Police Department and we've just come into information that you're interested in a Charles Greyling. It's in connection with a homicide inquiry you're conducting."

"How did you know that? We haven't even wired that to your people yet."

"Well, you know how it is, the bush telegraph got in there first but let's take our dresses off over who told who what when. I need to know where to find him. We think he's living here under a false name. Any help would be appreciated."

"Ok, I'll fax it."

Shit. I had to think fast.

"That would be awesome but could you give me his address over the phone, now, so I can hop to this right away. You can fax it for the record if you like."

"Give me a second."

While I hung on the phone, I heard a clatter of keyboard strokes, muffled voices and the shrill of telephones in Freeman's office. He came back on the line.

"Yes, he's a retired hotshot lawyer, his driving licence ID is A4399232 and his other cars are registered to 9 Fortuna Heights, Potrero Hill, San Francisco. Not sure if that's his address or his garaging address but it's what we have."

"You've been most helpful, thank you."

"You didn't give me your fax number..."

I cut the call. I got what I wanted to know. I had to get Greyling before the Feds got him otherwise I'd lose my chance.

Forever.

CHAPTER 60

Daybreak was shattered by the shrill tring-tring of the art deco telephone that hung from a marble wall. A man shuffled into the hallway, his silk dressing gown swishing with every step, dropping crumbs of his croissant onto the floor.

"Good morning, Greyling residence."

"And good morning to you too. Well, I think there is unfinished business to attend to, can we meet sometime today? Sorry for being so curt. It's rather a matter of urgent importance."

"Who is this, what are you talking about?"

"I'm talking about the protection of our mutual ways of life, the expensive manners that we have become accustomed to, surely you would be interested in keeping yourself in fine wines and cigars for a few more years at least, wouldn't you?"

Greyling recognised the voice. There was only one person spoke like that, like a snake, each word a silken rasp.

"Is this who I think it is?"

"No one seems to recognize my voice anymore, have I really been away that long? Dear me, I don't think I've changed all that much, have I? Or is it a case of some flawed psychology on your part that believes if you pretend not to know an inconvenient person that they disappear into a cloud of David Copperfield disco smoke?"

"Hector? Is that you?"

"Yes, Charles, Hector here."

"Hector, I didn't think we had any unfinished business to attend to. What do you want?"

"A fly called McCambridge has landed in our precious ointment. Meet me at 10am, Room 302, Hilton."

Tone.

CHAPTER 61

"Well, well, you haven't changed a bit. Retirement's been good to you, Greyling. Ever the silver fox."

"You don't look too bad either, despite whatever it is you've been doing with yourself all these years."

"Business is what I've been doing with myself. Business as ever it is."

Greyling swirled his mineral water around the tumbler, wishing it was a cool sharp gin and tonic. He'd given up the booze a couple of years earlier after the liver transplant which left him with a permanent look of drawn jaundice.

"Well in that case, Hector, let's get down to business. You mentioned a fly in the ointment." Greyling said.

Hector threw a newspaper down on the coffee table and turned it upside down so that Greyling could read it. Hector reached over and stabbed at a section of newsprint on the bottom left with his finger.

Greyling put his tumbler down, put on his reading glasses and bent over to read it.

"Hmm. I do read and watch the news, Hector. So McCambridge is still on the run. You scared he'll find us?" said Greyling

"McCambridge will never find me but you're the a weak link in the chain. I move around a lot but you stay put here, rooted to your ugly marble palace like a vegetable. It's only a matter of time"

"I live how I want to live, Hector. If he wants to find me and cut my throat in the middle of night, let him, but I know he won't."

"I don't think Callum McCambridge could cut anyone's throat, but he could land us, you even, for a long stint in the pen. That's worse than death and that's what he was good at"

"I live one day at a time. *Que sera sera* and all that."

Hector sat back on his chair. He crossed his legs and tapped his lips with the finger tips of his right hand. He cocked his head and narrowed his eyes on Greyling.

"You don't know, do you?"

"Know what?"

"They don't have young boys in prison anymore, you'd be serving your time with grown men, we all know that's not quite to your taste, is it?"

"That was a long time ago and you know it. After everything I've done for you and keeping my mouth shut all this time" Greyling said. His hands gripped the armrests until his knuckles turned white.

Hector smirked and rubbed his hands together.

Greyling continued "I won his trust, enough for him to give me the tapes he had. No one else could have done that but me. He knew me as Hubert's attorney and lifelong friend. God forgive me for what I did to McCambridge but I did it for the sake of the memory of Laura. I didn't do it for you Hector, I wouldn't piss on you if you were on fire"

Hector laughed.

"I have my sister and you have your young men. I guess we've always have our nukes pointing at each other, keeping the peace in a manner of speaking."

"We both want the good life. That's what keeps our fingers off the red buttons. I'd done my side of the bargain and kept it. So what? McCambridge jumped a prison van and lives somewhere out there. He could be dead for all we known. It's old news. You're acting like this is news, don't tell me you only found out," Charles said.

"He'll come after us but I think he'd like to get to you first" Hector said. "He's still alive. I've my feelers out. I don't know where he is as he's gone all hobo on us but it's only a matter of time before he makes his presence felt. Guys like McCambridge don't like hiding for too long"

"We don't know where he is" said Greyling, entwining his fingers, playing with his rings. "What can we do about it?"

"Damage limitation's the name of the game. I know you have the tapes and the transcripts but the thing is, you don't have them all."

"Of course I have them all," Charles said. "You know I do. Callum gave me everything he had. I took them away. You did read about the trial and the phantom evidence he talked about, only it wasn't phantom evidence but real evidence."

"And Callum never had the wit to copy it"

"Bullshit, he didn't think he had to copy them. So what about the tapes? Why's it such a big deal all of a sudden? Having trouble sleeping lately?"

"I sleep like a baby, Charles, but I see you have troubles in that department." Hector got up and walked over to the coffee table and picked up a medicine bottle. "Tylenol indeed."

Greyling got up and snatched the bottle from his hands.

"Mind your own business. These aren't mine anyway."

Hector smirked. "Keep your wig on, Charles."

Hector crouched down next to Greying, touching his arm. Greyling recoiled a little, crossing his arm across his chest which didn't look too comfortable.

"Charles, look me and tell me the truth, just this one time. Are you sure those are all the tapes that were ever made?"

Greyling nodded. "Of course they are."

"So what's this one then?"

Hector stood up and slid a tape from his left trouser pocket. He bent over and placed it on top of the newspaper on the coffee table. Greyling stared at it.

"What's on it?"

"You" Hector said. "That's who is on it as well as a young friend of yours. A young man, everyone having a good time. Lots of tapes were made in those days by everyone. What a crazy thing that was."

"You're bluffing, Hector, there's no such tape."

"But there is, there it is there, see? Shall I play it for you? It's really no trouble; I've had my secretaries scour the retro stores of the city to find a machine that can play tapes like this. It's a make that hasn't been made since the late 1960s. They found one eventually, a Magnavox 1v9019. The playback quality is simply stunning if not a little hissy here and there."

"What do you want from me, Hector?"

Hector clinched his jaws, his face became cold as stone. He widened his eyes and gave Greyling a stare made of bullets.

"I want you and the tapes to vanish. Properly vanish without trace. You don't come back here or America ever again. Should Callum find your house, he'll just roll back the stone and find an empty tomb. But if you stay, well, who knows how you will handle a police interview room. I don't think you'd survive the stress"

"I can hold my own with anyone."

"I can't trust you on that," said Hector.

"If I was such a time bomb, why didn't you have me killed all those years ago Hector, tell me?

"Because I never knew when you could be of use to me again but now, if they get to you, you might plea-bargain, get a gentle sentence, throwing me to the dogs to get them off your ass"

"I said I'll take my chance. You don't scare me like you used to"

Hector breathed in hard through his nose and sat down again.

"What are we going to do with you, Greyling? You seem not to care anymore and that's rather dangerous. Always give a man a reason to live and you have a well-trained animal who'll do what he's told but a man who has nothing to lose or doesn't care about losing what he has, well, what leverage is there? He's a dangerous quantity. I dislike danger, especially in quantities."

At that moment, a door to the adjoining room opened. Two well-dressed men with expressionless faces walked in. In each of their left hands, a gun.

Greyling opened his mouth to speak. He turned to Hector.

"Do you think I came here naked like Daniel into the lion's den? You think I'm stupid, don't you? You can't kill me, even if you wanted to. You see, I've just taken delivery of a brand new missile and guess what, I'm pointing it straight at you."

"What do you mean, Greyling?"

Greyling unbuttoned his shirt to his navel and stood up. He open his shirt to reveal a hollow chest with a smattering of hairs sticking out. Above his right nipple, a white plastic rectangular plaster. Beneath the plaster, a small matchstick-length microphone.

"You weren't the only folks to check in to this nice hotel today. You're done. They've got the whole conversations on tape. I've made several copies of all the tapes in my possession and each set is deposited with attorneys all over town. If I die or fail to contact them for three days in a row, they post the tapes to the FBI. An old friend tipped me about that insurance policy. You take me down, I'll see you in Hell."

"You're bluffing" whispered Hector.

"Am I? Well, if you want to find out..."

Hector turned to the men who stood at the door and beckoned them to go.

"It seems the only thing we've achieved today was the escalation our arms-race and yet we're no closer to getting McCambridge. You always fought the wrong wars Greyling. You're man who prefers a draw to winning"

"Hector, as far as I'm concerned, you and me, we're done. As the police are concerned, you're a dead man. No one looks for the dead, do they? Just get back to whatever beach you live on these days and spend the rest of your life cracking coconuts or whatever. We're done"

Hector got up from his chair, in elegant impotence like a king in checkmate. He held his hand out to Greyling.

"Old time's sake?"

Greyling stood up and shook his head at Hector.

"Go fuck yourself" Greyling said. Hector turned his outstretched palm into a fist and put it into his pocket. Greyling turned his back to Hector, lifted his raincoat and folded it carefully over his left arm and left the room.

CHAPTER 62

"Bryant and Finch, Attorneys at Law, how can we help you?"

"It's Charles Greyling here. May I speak to Mr Lloyd Bryant, please?...Mr Bryant, good morning, I am keeping very well...glad to hear it...yes...you know the special instructions that I have given you...well, can you assume at this moment that you haven't heard from me for three days?...yes...that's right...immediately please if you would be so kind...I'll be in touch to settle payment...I'd like to but I have an urgent call to make before I go...yes a vacation...a long one...a safari perhaps...let's hope I don't get eaten but you never know...very well...thank you...I'll be in touch."

Dead tone.

Greyling took a cab back to his apartment. He walked from room to room, saying a long, slow goodbye to the life he had built. He wiped a tear from his eye and fixed himself a stiff gin and tonic, reached into a bucket of ice and snatched three large cubes and dropped them in. After the fizz and fuss of bubbles had died down, he lifted the glass and downed the drink in one. His brain felt like it was on helium fire. It was years since he touched a drop. He walked into his office and picked up the lamp that sat on his desk. Under it was a secret compartment that contained a key. He took the key and opened the safe and removed a small black box the size of a shoebox and set it down on the table and opened it. Inside were several passports, savings bonds and credit cards, under different names and dates of birth. Names of children who died in infancy around the time he was born. Another old trick

"Eeny meeny miney mo..."

He fixed another drink, packed a suitcase and put the passports into his knapsack. He went into the hall and made a phone call.

"I'd like to report a crime, well, a lot of crimes actually. Hector Lonsdale, died in a car crash in 1982. Well, he's not dead. If you go to Room 304 at the Hilton you will find him or at least his fresh prints. Also, your department will soon be in receipt of tapes and documents....I can't go into details right now but when you get them, you will have everything you need......my name, I don't have a name anymore"

That was the last day Charles Greyling was Charles Greyling.

CHAPTER 63

I was on the road in the middle of the Mojave Desert when I heard the newsflash. FBI received tapes and dossiers from an anonymous source about corruption in the Chicago Police Department, the death of Jimmy Hoffa and the framing of Callum McCambridge who was still at large. I laughed at that bit. I wished they presumed me dead but you can't have it all. I pulled over and waited till the next news report at the top of the hour. I turned the volume up.

"A number of retired officers from the Chicago Police Department have been taken in for questioning about the kidnap and murder of ex-Teamsters supremo, Jimmy Hoffa. Many others are implicated, including some household names that will cause embarrassment to Washington. some of those implicated are still active and some are household names. Other evidence indicates the framing of ex-police officer, Callum McCambridge, who was sentenced to life imprisonment for the first-degree murder of Mark Madigan, who was found shot to death in a Chicago motel in 2008. McCambridge was serving his sentence in the Illinois State Correctional Institute but escaped several years later from a psychiatric unit and continues to evade capture. The public are warned not to approach him as he is considered to be highly dangerous..."

I switched the radio off and drove on.

CHAPTER 64

It was Norman Mailer who said something like there being no town in America as American as Chicago. That's true. America is everything you think it is...and the opposite too. I've tasted all the sweet fruit and lemons this town has dished up for me.

I gave myself up, this time with a new lawyer. I was dutifully re-arrested and retried and acquitted of all charges. I recall the moment the prosecution offered no case to answer. The judge ordered my release. The baritone of 'All Rise' was drowned by a frenzy of phones and cameras snapping me as I walked down the aisle of the courtroom and onto the courthouse steps outside. Microphones where stuck in my face, journalists shouting the same questions over each other like they were taking part in an auction for their lives. A limo eased up behind the throng and my lawyer whisked away real quick, down the steps and into the car. The throng surrounded the car. It looked like the world was taken over by aliens with small black furry heads, banging on the windows, trying to break inside to eat me. The driver asked me where I wanted to go.

There was only one answer. The Lonesome Cove Motel.

"Returning to the scene of the crime?" my lawyer said, smiling at me, her lipstick perfect on her cupid bow lips.

"Yeah, something like that" I said

We drove through town and stopped.

"This is it Callum. Lonesome Cover Motel" my lawyer said. I looked over at the little mountain of bricks and debris that lay at the bottom of the former car lot.

"It was demolished for redevelopment" she said "It's going to be a new office block"

"Perhaps I should reopen my Private Investigator practice in an office directly over Room 12"

"Now that would be poetic justice" she said.

I nodded and said nothing. I wondered which of those broken bricks, floorboards and rain-sodden bits of carpet once formed the space off Room 12.

I asked to be driven back to where I last plied my trade as a private dick. We whizzed around there in less than half an hour and I asked them to drop me off. I wasn't far from my hotel on West Division. My lawyer got out of the car and embraced. She asked me to drop by the next day to sign some papers and asked me if I wanted company later on. I thanked her for everything she had done but I wanted to be alone that night. She understood. We bid goodnight and they drove on.

I now stood for the first time in years as a free man alone in the streets of Chicago. I was outside my old building. It's derelict now, marked for demolition. Even innocent buildings get condemned in this town. I ventured in past the hoardings which weren't hard to negotiate. The main door was gone, leaving a gaping hole, reminding me of a face with a missing nose. The building was barricaded off but it was a half-hearted attempt. There were bits of metal fencing that lay torn all around the concrete bases. Access was easy and I could tell the building was totally empty. I walked closer to what was the main entrance and shook the fence grille. It came off the hinges with little effort.

I looked around but nobody was there.

I clambered over the metal and went inside and I stood in the foyer. I heard nothing but the distant echoes of water drops falling into puddles from holes in the roof. The smell of damp and abandonment hit me all at once. It made me feel sad, lost.

I tried the elevator but it no longer worked. The walls were thicker with graffiti paint. I took the stairwell and was hit with the familiar smell of piss and spilt liquor. It smelt stronger than I remembered. Old documents and papers from bygone businesses floated past my feet. For all I knew, some of them could have been mine. I picked one floater up and read it. It was a print out of an old email from 2002 from an Emma Dunton to an Ed Klinsman. I never knew them. There were lots of other offices in here, each in a world of its own. I read it. Emma asked Ed if he was OK.

That's it.

Nothing else. I thought it odd for someone to print such an unimportant email but sometimes there are no answers to the whys of life. I started to wonder if Ed was OK. Is he still OK? Was he ever OK? Are they having that drink somewhere? Are they together or with different people? Once upon a time, it was the most important email in the world but now it floats like flotsam being read by a forgotten man about long forgotten people who worked in a forgotten building. I crumpled it up into a ball but I thought better of it and opened it again. I carefully folded it and put it into my inside jacket pocket. I thought it would be fun to trace these people and see if they're OK. Who knows if I would or not? I might make it my comeback job. Pro bono of course.

I snapped out of my daydream and continued upstairs until I arrived at my old landing. There I found my old office. The door was just the same. My name was still on the door. I tried the handle.

It gave.

I took a deep breath and walked in. It was like a time capsule or one of those bedrooms of dead kids that parents never touch for decades. Except that it was an office, a basic one at that. My desk was still there, the filing cabinet, the chairs too. Even the ashtray was full. I walked up to my desk and saw something lying on it, something I couldn't remember. It was in a long, rectangular black box, tied with red ribbon. I picked it up.

"Welcome back, honey."

I froze. I recognised the voice. I turned around.

What the hell?

CHAPTER 65

"Gina?"

I recognised the mad, crazy red head who I loved all those years ago.

"Open it, Cal."

I opened the box. Inside, a magnum of champagne. The bottle was jet black. No label. The good stuff.

"I would have washed the glasses had I known you were coming," I said.

Gina put her hand into her handbag and took out two glasses. I shook the bottle and opened the cork and let the white foam explode all over the room. I think I roared with relief and disbelief while we both soaked ourselves with the devil's bubble bath. When the fizz settled down, I poured a glass each.

"What shall we toast to, Gina?"

"The future?"

"I don't know. I used to toast the future all the time. The future didn't like it much. I prefer to toast the here and now"

"Well I'll drink to that"

We clinked glasses and drank our champagne in one go. It's the only way to do it. Our eyes locked on one another as we tilted our heads back.

"Callum, when I left I moved to San Francisco. I moved in moneyed circles. It's how I get work. You know that, Cal. It may be a big town but those circles are small. That's where I met Greyling."

"Greyling? I don't want to know. It's history"

"No, you need to know. At first I didn't know he was Greyling. To me, his name was Henry Wallace. He gave himself a new name and a tall tale about where he came from. He claimed he was from Albuquerque but I check everyone out. I knew it was horseshit, but who cares? This is America. Everyone's allowed to reinvent themselves every now and then. Besides, he seemed like a nice guy. We dated for a while and things seemed to go well until I found a rucksack in his safe. He left the safe wide open. He was out playing golf with some of his cronies so I thought I'd have a peek. The one thing that stood out was a cruddy looking rucksack. It didn't seem to belong in there. But I knew it must be holding something worthwhile. I took it out and opened it. Tapes. Lots of tapes. I noticed him listening to those tapes all the time but with his special headphones on. He always got flustered whenever I asked about them. He told me they were just old transcripts from old times. He said it was nostalgia and it was just a weird little habit he liked. I thought it was porno at first but I left him to it. Anyway, in that rucksack was one of those old tape players. I called Greyling at the gold course to see how long he'd be. I told him to not come home for a while as I was making a surprise meal for him.

He said OK.

That gave me time. I sat down at his desk and listened to each tape one by one. Greyling was in most of them. Many of the voices I didn't recognise and names were seldom used but sometimes they were. As I made my way through the tapes, I noticed that he spoke three times after the name Greyling was used. I rewound and played it back and did it again to make sure. There was no doubt. It was Henry Wallace's voice but the same was Greyling and there was lots of talk about Hoffa being taken care off. It was dynamite."

"Was there a tape about me?"

"I did."

"Just how long ago was this?". Gina had the tape years ago. She could have sent it in and spared me the long years in prison and my time in the purgatory of Gibson City. She could have stopped it all. I started to see red. I wrapped my fingers around the stem of the glass so tight that I didn't give a shit about snapping its little neck in two.

Or Gina's.

"I know what you are thinking, 'Why didn't Gina do anything with the tapes?' Firstly, your framing was on the tape for sure, two tapes, but on the B-side of those tapes, were your conversations with Greyling and a Johnny Friends about driving Hoffa to a place where he wouldn't come back from. If I sent that tape in, you would have got off with the murder of the boy but you would have been done for Hoffa. If I destroyed the tape, you would always be on the run. It was a double bind. I thought quick and fast. What if I erased the B-sides? I would have done it had I not got a call from Greyling telling me he was outside and that he couldn't wait to see me. I thought if I took the tapes, he would notice them gone but the plan was still in my head. I put the tapes and player back in the bag and left the bag in the safe. Callum. I never had a chance to get back in the safe again and that's the God's honest truth."

I simmered down and loosened my grip.

"Gina, you could've called the police. They could have busted the safe"

"What if I did call them? That wasn't any old safe. It had a self-destruct installed that Greyling could control remotely. He told me so. Had the cops come knocking, all evidence would have gone up in smoke. Greyling was a smart guy. He covered every angle. What can I say? I'm sorry but it wasn't for those B sides"

I poured myself another drink and took a sip. It was warm by now, the bubbles tasted old already.

"So how come they didn't play the B sides in court?"

"Callum, they only played the A-sides. All the Hoffa stuff was on the A-sides. The B-sides were largely blank at the start of the tape. They would have had to play it for twenty minutes until the recordings came to life. I guess they played the first five minutes and heard nothing but white noise and figured that was all there was and stopped playback. You weren't on the A-sides, but your involvement in the Hoffa stuff was on the B-sides."

I went cold. Somewhere out there was a bomb with my name on it.

"How did you know I would come back here, to this place, at this time?" I asked her.

"I was in court when you were acquitted," Gina said. "I tried to run to you but the crowds, it was impossible. Before I knew it, you were in the car. I thought I was never going to see you again but I figured you'd like to see your old stomping grounds once more, so I came here and waited"

"I'm still predictable after all this time" I said, smiling at Gina.

Gina stepped forward and kissed me on the cheek.

"I know a Greek place we can go to in South Halstead," I said.

"Man, there's more Greek joints in South Halstead than there are in Athens, be more specific," she said with an effervescence in her voice that I hadn't heard in years.

"Well, let's go there," I said. We linked arms and left my office and walked down the stairs. A sudden chill of wind hit, it must have come from outside and I remembered I left my coat behind.

"I've forgotten my coat, Gina, wait here, I won't be a moment."

"No, let me go and get it"

"Ok"

Gina ran inside and up the stairs, the echo of her high heels zig-zagging from wall to wall throughout the dank interior. I could almost hear the walls creak with horniness. I know I did.

I stood there in the cold, waiting for Gina to come back any moment. I lit a cigarette and got lost in my thoughts, recollections of my life and wondering how I'd get back on my feet. My lawyer spoke about a hefty compensation package from the State Justice Dept. That would do nicely. I felt the nip of heat on my finger tips. My cigarette was burning down to the butt. I dropped it and squashed it under my shoe. Gina should have been back by now and I got a little worried. The building had seen better days and I wondered if she'd fallen through a floor but I heard so screams.

I went inside, calling out Gina's name and ran up the staircase and back to my office and went inside. When I looked up, I saw Gina standing by the filing cabinet, filling a glass.

"What took you so long? I got worried" I said

"Oh, nothing. I guess I just wanted to take one last look around the place" She sat on the table and crossed her legs, hitching up her skirt. "This was where we first fucked. Remember?"

"Gina, it was all I thought about. I filled many a sock with that memory, believe me"

"Callum, that's disgusting" she said, covering her giggles. She got up from the table and dusted herself down and poured a second glass and handed to me.

"Shame to let a bottle go to waste. There's plenty of time to eat" she said.

There I was again with a glass of champagne in my hand. This time it tasted colder, almost like the first glass did. It was the sweetest I ever tasted. I put the glass down and lifted my coat but it slipped from my hands.

"Come on, I'm hungry. Let's go" I said but the words themselves left me short of breathe.

I knelt down to pick the coat up but I couldn't. My fingers had no grip. I flexed them but they had no feeling. I looked at them as though they belonged to someone else. I couldn't move a single finger. I felt faint. I called out to Gina as loud as I could. I felt weak, very weak. I lay down on the floor and looking up at Gina.

"Gina, I don't feel well. I'm not used to the drink but I never felt like this before. Call an ambulance, will you?"

"Sure will."

Gina took out her cell-phone and dialled 911.

"Ambulance for 20 Creswell Street please, a man's collapsed... It's a derelict building but I'll be outside... No, we're not bums... We broke in here for old time's sake."

I would have smiled if I was able to but I felt weary.

"Also, bring the police too. The man in question has important information for them regarding a murder that took place a long time ago. You can tell them there's a black leather bag behind the door marked 'McCambridge' on the eleventh floor. It contains all they need...Tell them to play the B side in full and I mean in full...My name, my name is not important."

My eyesight was fading in and out of focus. I looked up at Gina, her face was out of focus. Her eyes were dark pits, her smile a cracked slit of a grin.

"Why, Gina?" I wanted to say more but words were defeated.

She walked to the desk, picked up the bottle of champagne and the glasses and put them into a waste basket and stood over me.

"Goodbye, Callum. Oh I almost forgot, perhaps you'd like to congratulate me".
She held out her left hand. In the middle finger, a golden ring.

"Charles made a decent woman of me in the end. We're going on a second honeymoon shortly. I'll send you a postcard"

She blew me a kiss and turned and left.

The last things I heard were the demon's wail of sirens, coming to claim me, one last time. I closed my eyes, wondering where I'd wake up.

I hoped that I wouldn't.

But I did.

THE END

About The Author

Martin J Frankson lives in the United Kingdom. He has written a number of short stories some of which have been published in *Beyond Imagination* and *The Rusty Nail*.

Further information on the author can be found within his website:
http://www.martinjfrankson.com

@martinfrankson

You can find the author on Facebook

Thank you for reading.

Credits

*This book was edited by **Emma Warnock** who not just edited it, but provided guidance and advice in the early stages of this novel's development*

(http://www.editingworks.co.uk)

*Original cover art by **Roberta Martucci**, Napoli, Italy. It was a pleasure watching the visual sobriquet to the story evolve and take shape. A wonderful artist and an honour to have worked with her.*

And many thanks to those who read work in progress drafts and who gave honest-a-god feedback especially Brenda Hutchinson, Dietrich Kalteis and Samantha J Wright.